MURDER IN HAWAII

Through the dimness, Louise could see what looked like a form on the stone shelf at the base of the cliff. Her heartbeat sped up until she realized that she must have come upon another monk seal.

But something wasn't quite as it seemed. A few steps more and she realized her mistake. This was not a monk seal, for the silhouette was irregular, not smooth and humplike. Though her heart was speeding again, she tried to stay calm as she plodded onward across the sand. Soon she could see that it was a person crumpled on the shelf.

She pulled in a terrified gasp as she recognized Matthew Flynn's distinctive new explorer's hat lying a few feet from the prostrate form. Her mind began to race. All she could think of was that Flynn had tumbled off the top of the cliff and needed CPR. She made a shortcut through the shallow water and nearly fell down in the strong surf. Regaining her balance, she determinedly slogged through the waves until she reached the shelf and clambered up it.

She ran to where the scientist lay faceup on the protruding rim of the stone ledge, his eyes open. Some blood appeared to be trickling from the back of his head. Kneeling down, she gently pressed his wrist and felt no pulse. Hurriedly, she pulled her cell phone from her purse and dialed 911 . . .

Books by Ann Ripley

HARVEST OF MURDER

THE CHRISTMAS GARDEN AFFAIR

DEATH AT THE SPRING PLANT SALE

SUMMER GARDEN MURDER

DEATH IN THE ORCHID GARDEN

Published by Kensington Publishing Corporation

A Gardening Mystery

DEATH IN THE ORCHID GARDEN

Ann Ripley

KENSINGTON BOOKS
KENSINGTON PUBLISHING CORP.
http://www.kensingtonbooks.com

KENSINGTON BOOKS are published by

Kensington Publishing Corp.
850 Third Avenue
New York, NY 10022

All Kensington titles, imprints and distributed lines are
available at special quantity discounts for bulk purchases for sales promotion, premiums, fund-raising, ed-
ucational or institutional use.

Special book excerpts or customized printings can also
be created to fit specific needs. For details, write or phone
the office of the Kensington Special Sales Manager: Kensington Publishing Corp., 850 Third Avenue, New York,
NY, 10022. Attn. Special Sales Department. Phone: 1-800-
221-2647.

ISBN-13: 978-0-7582-0820-0
ISBN-10: 0-7582-0820-0

First Hardcover Printing: November 2006
First Mass Market Paperback Printing: September 2007
10 9 8 7 6 5 4 3 2 1

Printed in the United States of America

To Eloise, the inspiration of countless writers

ACKNOWLEDGMENTS

A trip with friends to Kauai inspired me to write this book, and for this I thank Bev Carrigan, who prodded me to go there. Once on the island, I was aided tremendously by Dr. Warren L. Wagner, Rick Hanna, and Tim Flynn of the National Tropical Botanical Garden. Dr. Harrison Hughes of Colorado State University; Tim Hogan, assistant curator of University of Colorado's Herbarium; Dr. Mancourt Downing, biologist; Jim Hau of Ball Horticulture; Trux Simmons, producer-director at KRMA-TV, Denver; Erwin Moosher of Smith-Barney; and Doug Sorrell provided other valuable input. The following people read and commented on the manuscript: Irene Sinclair, Sybil Downing, Bev Carrigan, Karen Gilleland, and Jane Ripley. Special thanks to my editor, John Scognamiglio of Kensington Publishing, and my agent, Danielle Egan-Miller, of Browne-Miller Literary Associates.

So readers are not confused, most plant names are genuine, but a few are not. The possibly valuable subspecies of *Uncaria quianensis*, as well as *Echinacea purpurea "Bailey's Double Crown,"* and *Cattleya brassavola "Flynnia,"* are not available in the trade as yet and exist only in my mind. Likewise, Kauai's hotels and terrain have been slightly altered for purposes of the story.

But *Kanaloa* is a new plant species recently discovered on an islet off the island of Maui; it is a topic of great interest at the National Tropical Botanical Garden, a place all Kauai tourists should visit.

1

Late Wednesday afternoon

Louise Eldridge floated on her back and gazed up at the rustling dead fronds of the palms overhead. In this state of casual dishabille, the trees looked like ladies who'd failed to comb their long, tan hair. She smiled contentedly, for her favorite daydream had always been floating in a lagoon in a tropical jungle. Now here she was, the daydream a reality. Except *this* lagoon was put together like a Hollywood movie set, one of the amenities of Kauai's premier luxury hotel, Kauai-by-the-Sea, where she'd checked in a scant hour ago.

The heart of the lagoon was a big, shallow pond with a man-made sand beach designed for families with small children. From it branched out several isolated channels and deep pools. She'd sought out and found the most remote one for her solitary swim. Around her arose an imported jungle of palms and lacy casuarina trees, Norfolk pines as tall as a five-story building, giant-armed monkeypods, blazing philosophy trees, and snakelike cactus growing on random walls. Ringing the lagoon itself were splotches of croton, ginger, plumeria, guava, ficus, and hibiscus.

She knew all the plant names, because she'd studied them before she left home. It was her business, since she was host of the PBS garden show, *Gardening with Nature*, in Washington, D.C.

Louise turned over and dove far down into the water's green depths, emerging in the middle of the pool. In her high-cut navy blue speed suit, she easily crossed the pool in six strokes, then headed down a connecting stream into still another breathtakingly beautiful tropical scene. From the promotional literature at the check-in desk, she knew that she could swim two miles in this serpentine waterway that lay between the Art Deco–style hotel on the one side and the Pacific Ocean on the other. In all, she traversed three serene, flower-bedecked ponds without meeting another swimmer. She swam back to the first pool, then flipped over on her back again. Floating as if dead, she closed her eyes in total relaxation and nearly drifted off to sleep.

Suddenly something slammed hard into her shoulder. The impact threw her underwater and for a moment she was filled with terror. Had she run across some large sea monster that she hadn't been warned about when preparing for her trip to Hawaii?

She reemerged sputtering and flapping her arms to regain her balance. "Augh!" she yelled and looked into the amused blue eyes of a big, barrel-chested man. Masses of white hair stuck to his head like bits of plaster. Even his massive white eyebrows were in disarray, looking like dollops of meringue. He reached out his huge arms to help support her and they trolled together in the middle of the lagoon like two bobbing tops.

"My dear, I'm so terribly sorry," he boomed. "Are you hurt?"

She was still gasping for breath. "No, I don't think so."

"I wasn't paying the least attention to where I was going," he said. Despite the water cascading off his well-formed face, she recognized him from the photos sent to her with his vitae. The sea monster was Dr. Bruce Bouting. He was a plant explorer and owner of Bouting Horticulture, the biggest company of its kind in North America. His presence here at this elite botanical conference was one of the reasons she'd come to Kauai.

"Dr. Bouting?"

"Yes, my dear. And you are . . ."

"I'm Louise Eldridge," she said and noticed that he still held her with his ham hands. "You can let me go. I'm all right."

Bobbing on his own now, he pointed a finger at her and gave her a slightly puzzled look. "Louise Eldridge? I'm beginning to recognize you, too. You're the TV garden show lady."

"Yes. My producer and his wife and my cohost are already at the conference cocktail party on the terrace. But I needed a swim more than a drink after flying five thousand miles."

"*Aloha*, my dear," and he reached out a big hand and shook hers, formally, as if they were at the party going on a few hundred feet and a few artificial waterfalls away. "I'm so looking forward to being on your show . . . uh, what's it called?"

"*Gardening with Nature*. It originates from WTBA-TV, in Washington, D.C. But it's aired on most PBS stations every Saturday morning."

"Yes, yes," he said, nodding his head vigorously as he treaded water, then broke into laughter. "I was told all that but forgot for a moment. And you have some other botanist wonder boys from our conference appearing on your show. Matthew Flynn. Isn't he one of 'em?" Again, a big laugh, but a barely masked undertone of disrespect.

"Yes." They swam slowly, side by side, in the warm, salty water.

"Huh," he said. A polite but noncommittal "huh." Bruce Bouting, she knew from his bio, was famous for making plant discoveries in the farthest reaches of the globe. The story on him was that he co-opted foreigners easily with that charm and coaxed them for plant samples and seeds. She was curious to know what he thought about the flamboyant Eastern University professor, Dr. Flynn. Flynn couldn't be more different from Bouting: He spent months at a time in the Amazon, looking for plants that promised a cure for mankind's diseases. Flynn tested the plants and pitched them to American drug companies.

"I do not wish to be unkind, my dear Louise," said Bouting, "but I was told this conference was to talk about ways to promote and preserve tropical plants. Dr. Flynn's set the conference on its ear with his outrageous claims and we've been arguing about that instead of what we came for." His quiet voice turned into a bark. "Shaman, indeed—the man's a *sham*. Why, he gives a bad name to ethnobotany."

Louise must have looked dismayed, for he quickly added, "Don't worry. I'm just fed up with the fellow after a whole day of his bragging. That's why I'm being frank with you. Whatever else I am, I am a consummate professional. I can get along with him through a four-day botany conference and the filming of your show. Who else is on the roster for this program? I believe I heard it was going to be Reuter from UC Berkeley."

"Yes, Dr. Charles Reuter."

Another skeptical "huh!" straight from Bouting's barrel chest. "So I guess Reuter represents your environmentalist view."

"He's an outspoken environmentalist and I admire him. I'm sure you've heard him speak, or read what he's written on preserving native species. He's a tiger on that topic." She took several strong strokes and opened the distance between them.

"A purist, my dear," Bouting bellowed, splashing in an awkward Australian crawl until he caught up with her. She gave him a break and turned on her side and did the sidestroke.

Once he'd caught his breath, Bouting said, "Reuter's one of those priggish, angry pedants who wants non-native plants relegated to the scrap heap! Rotten point of view. The man's on the wrong track entirely. I told the conference that today and I intend to reiterate it over the next couple of days. We ought to amend the conference's mission statement to read, 'to promote and preserve tropical plants and to make some of them into market winners.' You see, dear, I'm all for market winners: That's what makes me the biggest frog in the North American pond."

Louise paused to be sure she chose the right words, for she realized she was dealing with a giant ego. She flipped over onto her back, drifted slowly backward, giving him a confident smile. "We know with all your strong and sometimes divergent views, the three of you will make a great program."

A grin spread over Dr. Bouting's face. "You're a little politician, aren't you? As long as you understand you've got yourself three divas. Sparks are bound to fly." Just for fun, apparently, he flapped an arm as if it were a flipper and sent a crest of warm saltwater into the air. "But what the heck, you people are masters in the editing room. You can cut out the rough stuff."

"Yes, thank heavens for that," she replied with the same casual air. She looked at the sun, which seemed to be hurrying toward the horizon. "Now I see I'd better go and get changed to meet my friends. People at the hotel say it's de rigueur to watch the sun set when in Hawaii."

"Indeed it is. Now, you hurry off. It was a pleasure, Louise, to swim a few strokes with you. See you at tonight's session?"

"I'd like to, but I'm not sure. I'm a little weary." She swam quickly to the edge of the pool. Pulling down the sides of her bathing suit, she climbed up the underwater stone steps to the short-clipped emerald grass. As she turned to bid another good-bye to her pool mate, she saw he was still treading water in the middle of the lagoon, staring at her figure as if he'd never seen a half-clad woman before.

"Good-bye, Dr. Bouting," she said, in a firm voice.

The man snapped out of his trance and moved his gaze from her buttocks to her breasts. "*Aloha*, Louise. See you soon, I hope."

2

Wednesday evening

Once in her hotel room, Louise realized that if she were going to see the sun set, she had time for only one of what her husband Bill called her "lightning transformations." But first, she noticed that the French doors opened onto a lanai. They provided a panoramic view of the hotel grounds and the ocean. She went out but dared not linger for more than a few moments, for dusk was descending on the colorful world outside—and on the mass of flowers that sent their perfume up to her on the second floor.

Reluctantly, she came in and locked the door and went into her routine.

Thirty seconds in the shower, thirty seconds to dry. Five minutes to blow dry and brush her shoulder-length brown hair with its alarming occurrences of gray strands. Then only two minutes to jump into a brief beige linen dress and beige sandals and dab lipstick on her otherwise makeup-free face. As a final fillip, she slipped her flat gold necklace around her throat.

She knew she'd pass in this fancy hotel, even though it was like a movie set, with its grand entrance, million-dollar view of the sea, swaying palms, beloved talking parrots in cages, lily-motif chandeliers and other 1920's architectural touches, waterfalls and lush gardens and lagoons and streams. But its cast did not live up to it. Quite unlike a scene in *The Great Gatsby*, quite the opposite, in fact. The guests she'd seen so far were laid-back to the point of drabness. Sunburnt men in short sleeves and shorts strolling along with women in T-shirts and pedal pushers. She'd seen only one woman so far who was like a throwback to fussier days—or Washington, D.C.—garbed in a sheath, jewelry, and, heaven forbid, stiletto heels. This was Hawaii, where casualness ruled. Louise was going to like it here.

Strolling through the lobby and the terrace, she failed to find her producer, Marty Corbin, and his wife. He'd brought Steffi along on this trip so that they could have a little rest and recreation in the islands and recover from some health scare that Steffi had recently overcome. Louise's good-looking cohost, John Batchelder, also was nowhere in sight.

In the meantime, the sun threatened to set without any of them viewing it—a virtual crime, she'd been told. She hurried out of the hotel and strolled down what looked like the most direct path to the ocean. Once in sight of the beach, she saw a small crowd gathering and hurried to join them, ignoring the sand in her sandals.

Stepping closer to the water, she felt a tinge of discomfort as she spied what looked like yellow police tape attached to poles. Had a body washed up on shore? Louise had barely recovered from the shock of two violent deaths in her northern Virginia neighborhood of Sylvan Valley. Surely, it would be an unkind trick of fate for death to follow her here to this tropical beauty spot.

Within this demarked space lay a form resembling a small hill. It was dark brown, with a smooth skin. She asked one of the gawkers, a white-haired man in a windbreaker, "What is it?"

"A monk seal," he said. "They're endangered, you know. We can't disturb it. Apparently they come in to shore because they need the rest."

Louise chuckled. "At least it doesn't have to pay hotel prices."

He grinned. "He's luckier than we are. It costs a lot of money to take a vacation in paradise." Putting his digital camera to his eye, he said, "I'm sure this guy won't mind if I snap his picture."

She watched the little crowd respectfully ring the yellow tape barrier and bestow proprietary looks on the exhausted sea creature. They delighted in its continued existence, despite the adversities it faced. She guessed that they'd have this same ownership feeling when they took boat or car trips to view the whales, currently in the neighborhood, mating; or the other fish and mammals that played and regenerated their kind near this lovely island.

But the big moment was here—sunset. While she could have watched it from the hotel terrace, here she was, alone with a bunch of strangers on the beach. They were all of one mind, worshipping the sun god as if they were ancient Egyptians.

A bronzed man with curly brown hair and a sleepy grin stood near her, balancing a surfboard. He was in shorts, sleeveless shirt, and bare feet. "At the very moment the sun hits the Pacific," he told the little crowd, "you're gonna see a green flash. It only lasts an instant, so don't take your eyes away." Silence fell and so did the sun.

"See, there it is," cried the surfer. As the crowd "oohed," Louise was amazed to see the green flash, like a bar of green. She had never heard of this phenomenon, but it made her feel a sense of unity with those early Hawaiians who must have thought this streak of color part of the gods' magic. Looking around at her awestruck companions, she thought, *Not much has changed.* As if his job were done, the barefoot man wandered off and the others slowly dispersed.

As she turned to head back to the hotel, her gaze lit upon a large rock cliff hanging about forty feet over the water. Though Kauai was a sea of lush green grass, vines, plants, and towering trees, this seaside promontory, like many other unusual rock formations, was a reminder of the island's volcanic origins. It was a basalt shelf, she realized, built five million years ago when the island was formed, an earlier version of the new land being built at this very moment with the fresh lava flows from Kilauea on the youngest island, the Big Island, one hundred miles southeast of here.

The rocky cliff beckoned to her. She hoped that she and John could climb up there tomorrow, though her cohost was scared of heights. This was made clear by his nervousness during the long flight over here.

She would have taken another final look at the monk seal, but decided not to. The yellow tape and the recumbent body reminded her too much of a crime scene.

3

Louise returned to the hotel in the gathering darkness and found her party already seated on the terrace. John Batchelder held the center of attention at the circular dinner table. He was tan and handsome in chinos and a glistening white shirt rolled up at the sleeves. She'd noticed his pale golden look on the plane trip here, realizing that he'd frequented a Washington, D.C., tanning salon before reaching Kauai. In the candlelight, the tan was even more enhanced. But what was even more compelling were his satyrlike, amber-colored eyes, which danced with excitement as he talked. He was so caught up in telling them about his hike up Shipwreck Rock that he could hardly eat, contented instead to sip his mai tai during pauses to catch his breath. Apparently, he'd gone up the rock while Louise was in the lagoon meeting her "sea monster." She was bemused by the thought of someone who was afraid of heights arriving in Hawaii and immediately ascending a cliff.

She and John and the Corbins had been placed

at a prime table under the stars. Lighted torches helped them see their dinners. Marty and Steffi were shiny faced and dressed in bright resort clothes. Big people already, the clothes made them look even bigger. Marty was in a shirt embossed with palm trees and Steffi in a sleeveless gown festooned with cockatoos, bamboo stalks, and hibiscus. Louise, feeling almost dowdy in her beige outfit, realized that the first thing the Corbins had done on arrival was to hit the trendy shops in the vast marble-and-carpet halls of Kauai-by-the-Sea. The clothes were quite in character, thought Louise, for Marty was talented, flamboyant, and sometimes over-the-top. His wife was just as colorful. Equally in character was the drink they'd both ordered, called a "Lava Flow," a creamy pina colada with a dramatic swirl of red crushed strawberries running through it.

"So that's the skinny on that big old cliff out there," said her producer.

"Yep, Shipwreck Rock. I wouldn't have done it, but the concierge told me it's a pussy-cat of a climb and it was," enthused John. "There are a few volcanic rocks to clamber over midway up the trail—you're on all fours then. But *man*, what a view when you reach the top—you can see for miles. And it gives you this feeling—"

Marty waggled his brown-haired head and laughed. "—that it might all collapse and you'd fall into the ocean?"

Faintly rebuked, Louise's enthusiastic cohost turned his amber eyes to her. "Louise, you'll love it. We'll go up there tomorrow, okay?"

"I'd love to." She thought about telling them about the monk seal on the beach, but decided not to take attention from John's story.

Marty said, "Glad you enjoyed your climb, John.

That's what we're here for—relaxation—part of it, anyway. Maybe we'll listen in on this botany conference—anyway, you can, Lou, you plant maven, you." He grinned at her. "We'll just swim and relax . . ."

"And shop," added Steffi, turning her big, dark eyes Louise's way. "Louise, when will you be free tomorrow to shop? We need to go to Koloa, and we'll stop at the Poi Pu Shopping Center on the way."

Unlike some women, Louise thought of shopping as a punishment, not a pleasure. But she said, "I'll be free in the afternoon." Steffi was a good-hearted woman whom Louise didn't know that well, but enjoyed on those occasions when they did get together. She didn't envy Steffi for having to live with Marty, for not only was her producer temperamental, but he hadn't always been true to his marriage vows.

"You ladies go off any time you get a chance," said Marty, "but first, let's get down 'n dirty and review what we came here for. So we're going to the National Garden."

"National Tropical Botanical Garden, it's called," Louise said. "Or you could shorten it to NTBG."

Marty waved a big hand. "Yeah, whatever." They'd already been given a heads-up about the shoot from the PBS associate producer from KHET-TV in Honolulu; he'd scouted the site for them. But Marty always liked to review preparations.

"Joel Greene is our so-called 'associate producer,'" grumbled Marty. "I don't know how he's gonna work out. He's a film major from the University of Hawaii and probably gets paid squat. He doesn't sound like he's more than twenty years old, though he does come highly recommended by Bob Squires, the guy who runs the Honolulu station. Heaven only knows who they'll send as shooter and audio engineer. Well, it seems first Joel had this great guy to interview, but he's much in demand and something came up and then he *didn't* have him. But now Joel has him again."

"Has what great guy?" asked John, his brow furrowed in confusion.

"You must mean Dr. Tom Schoonover," said Louise, "another of our reasons for coming to Hawaii. He's the foremost expert on Pacific Island plants. So Schoonover's back in the picture?"

"That's what Joel says," said the producer.

"We'll get him walking through the garden, showing us all the endangered species," said Louise. "Nobody could know their way around there better than he does."

"Yeah," affirmed Marty. "It seems Schoonover just got back from one of his plant explorer trips to the southern Pacific. Apparently the guy's pretty famous."

John raised an officious finger. "I've only heard this mentioned as a possibility. But since he wasn't in the plans initially, we need a separate program segment—or maybe he could be our lead-in to the program. Show him taking a solitary walk down the botanic garden trails as he describes the fate of all those, uh, species."

Marty, who'd almost demolished his mahi mahi main course, sat back, his large brown eyes twinkling at John. "Just what Lou said. Have her walking with this guy through the gardens and descending cliffs to capture orchids or somethin'. Then you and Lou together will be handling the 'Three Tenors' and their conflicting agendas."

The Three Tenors. That was Marty's cynical moniker for the trio of Doctors Bruce Bouting, Matthew Flynn, and Charles Reuter, the stars of their upcoming shoot. They were not expected to be easy to deal with; Louise had already confirmed that in her conversation with Bouting while swimming in the lagoon.

"Now here's what else I would propose . . ." continued John.

Louise took a bit of square-cut seared ahi, dipped it into a delicate sauce, put it in her mouth, and let her mind wander. Later, she learned it was a mistake to daydream when John Batchelder was talking.

When Marty had called two months ago with the long-awaited confirmation of the trip to Kauai to produce two *Gardening with Nature* shows, Louise had been busy. She'd been peering into a mirror in the harsh light of a January afternoon. To her surprise and horror she had discovered a change in her face.

"So the trip's set," she'd said to Marty, while still examining this unsettling change.

"Yeah. "You, me, Steffi, John Batchelder—we'll all go together."

So Marty's phone call had been a double whammy. At the same moment that she'd found that down line—that *wrinkle*—on the left side of her mouth, she'd heard that her younger cohost was coming on this location trip, the most important one in her four-year career as a TV garden show hostess.

Louise was forty-seven—almost forty-eight—and married with children. She wouldn't have cared about the wrinkle if she weren't a TV personality with a video camera trained on her face. Not that she was a sex goddess by any means, but even garden show hostesses were supposed to uphold some standard of good looks, except for the occasional British crone who made it big on TV on the basis of outrageous quips and a deep knowledge of horticulture.

Leaning into the mirror, she had taken three fingers and shoved the down line upward in hopes of banishing it forever. Then she'd remembered she was talking on the phone with her producer.

"Marty, sorry," she'd said. "I got distracted."

"Hey," Marty had said in an injured tone, "wassamatta wid you?" Marty was born and raised in Philadelphia and hadn't bothered to change his way of talking just because he'd moved to Washington, D.C. "I was gonna hang up on ya. Where ya been anyway?"

"I'm right here, thinking. I thought you said John Batchelder *wasn't* coming. Why does shooting two shows on Kauai require his presence?"

"We don't use him that much and I thought it only fair to give him a perk. God knows, as a part-time employee, he gets few enough perks. And he's newly engaged to some dame named Linda. That makes him anxious to get ahead."

Suddenly, Louise had known the truth. "He threatened to quit on you, didn't he?"

"As a matter of fact, he did," said Marty, "and I didn't find it handy for him to do that right now. But Lou, dear, don't get your nose out of joint because he's honed in on this trip. We're gonna have fun. We can even take a little side trip to the Big Island—I hear there's lots of lava action developing over there. And the programs are all about your favorite kind of people, plant explorers."

"Yeah," she muttered. "The last time I met one, he was murdered immediately afterward."

Marty had given forth a big, uncertain laugh. "That can't happen this time, can it?"

"How do you know that? We're featuring three prima donna botanists."

"Tough," said Marty. "Bouting, Flynn, and Reuter

will just have to learn how to get along. The ones I'm worried about are you and John."

She had given a last glance at her face in the mirror and turned determinedly away. "Don't worry. I'll get along fine with John. Heaven knows I try to like him. It's just that he sets up this phony competition with me. I wish he'd get over it."

"He will in time," Marty had assured her. "He needs to grow."

"The other thing about him is—well, never mind." The other thing that rankled Louise about John Batchelder, something she needn't share with her producer . . . his extreme good looks. Sometimes she wondered if it didn't unbalance the show. Here she was, a mature, only nominally pretty woman— and with a down line that some day would help form a jowl! And there was John, ten years younger and too darned beautiful for words.

The only hope for her was that she'd heard Hawaii, with its moist island air, was beneficial for the skin. That would remain to be seen. But for insurance, she'd brought with her on this trip a little jar of cream in a mauve-colored glass jar with a gold lid. She'd purchased the anti-aging cream a couple of years ago for an outrageous price. It had languished, unused, in her and Bill's medicine cabinet, but its time was now at hand.

Hawaiian music, courtesy of three ukulele players, started in the background. Louise blinked and quit woolgathering. She looked over at John, sitting across from her at the table. Bits of golden light from the bold torches flickered on his wavy brown hair. His dark-lashed eyes flashed with sincerity. Although the light was dim, Louise was sure that John had no lines in *his* face.

John was leaning into Marty Corbin's space, selling him an idea, while for some reason slanting the occasional stealthy glance her way. Had Louise been on her normal stomping ground, the competitive atmosphere of greater Washington, D.C., she would have been wary of her younger cohost's overt attempts to impress and co-opt her producer. But something strange was happening to Louise; she felt it. The air around her was pure and balmy, the fragrant flowering shrubs that crowded the edges of the terrace perfuming the air. It was all a sheer joy to the senses. She sat erect but at ease, feeling for the first time in a long time like a whole, integrated person who was completely relaxed and content with life. Even her skin felt moist and young, almost dewy. . . .

Surely, there was no dark side in this sunny land and not even the ambitious John could make her uneasy. The greatest danger was hurricanes, which had been known to ravage Kauai's hotels and beach properties, the last one, Hurricane Iniki, more than a decade ago. But this was not hurricane season, so why worry? The island was well protected against tsunamis, such as the horrible one experienced on the rim of the Indian Ocean. Here, sirens housed in yellow or green boxes perched high on steel poles squealed out warnings to islanders who were familiar with their killing power.

John was now opining on how to handle the segment with the three difficult scientists. He said, "What we might do is keep them separate, maybe 'til the very end."

Marty, sitting across from Louise, looked properly impressed. Even the dark-haired Steffi, not normally interested in the production details of her husband's WTBA-TV shows, was paying close attention to the vivacious John.

Why should Louise care? Why feel insecure about

her own career when it appeared to be going fine? And then a great guilt settled on her: perhaps her own ambition was too strong and she ought to yield to her husband. Bill, who'd relinquished his undercover work for the CIA in favor of working at the Department of State as a consultant to the International Atomic Energy Agency, had been hinting that they should move to Europe for his job's sake.

She bent her head and put down her fork. A woman of forty-seven ought to be able to sacrifice her own career plans for the sake of a hardworking husband. Yet the thought of leaving the States again, as she'd done at least five times before while raising their family of two daughters, was not that appealing. Yet the girls didn't need her—daughter Martha was married and Janie was ready to go off to college.

It was time, perhaps, for Louise to quit this TV career and go with Bill.

Having decided this, she shed her moment of guilt. For some reason, she found herself feeling almost warm and fuzzy toward John Batchelder. He was not her bête noire, she realized now, but more of a friend than she'd realized.

It was almost as if she'd become intoxicated after landing on this beauteous island only five hours ago. She was overcome with its beauty, its moist and welcoming atmosphere, altogether coopted by the sense of well-being around her.

Marty Corbin reached a big hand over and grabbed her forearm. "Lou, what's *with* you? Here we got John throwing all these ideas at me and you're sittin' there daydreaming."

Steffi bent toward her, the cockatoos, bamboo, and hibiscus on her ample bosom bending with her. "Honey, are you feeling all right?"

Louise smiled back at her. "I feel wonderful. I've never felt better in my life."

Her producer said, "Then you don't mind the fact that tomorrow you and John will go to the National Tropical Botanical Garden and meet Joel. And John will take charge of laying out the scenario for the segment we'll do with this Schoonover fellow."

"Oh?" Her good feelings toward her coanchor dissipated like one of the zephyrs that danced across the terrace. She looked at Marty in surprise. While she'd been dreaming, John had been working.

Marty leaned in toward her. "He'll be calling the shots on this one. Wants the experience, he says. And he might know more than this whippersnapper Joel."

She straightened and felt a little twinge in her back. "That's fine, Marty, just fine." She looked at John across the table. He had the expression of the cat that ate the canary. "I'll be happy to help you, John, in any way I can."

Sure, help you. Maybe help you fall off one of those steep cliffs at the garden . . . or maybe shove you into that fast-moving river that runs through it . . .

Louise forced her mind off these silly, murderous thoughts. "So, anyone going to the Main Ballroom to hear Dr. Schoonover speak?" Her companions shook their heads. She clutched her purse and rose from her chair. "Me neither, since we're talking to him tomorrow. Now please excuse me, I need my beauty sleep."

She could have kicked herself. The remark instantly revealed her fear of aging.

4

Thursday morning

Louise put on sturdy denim pedal pushers and a
sleeveless khaki-colored shirt for what would
probably be a vigorous day in the tropical gardens.
On her feet she wore her waterproof sandals.
Meeting John in the lobby, they agreed she'd drive
the rental car, since she had studied the road
maps. Their first stop was the Kilohana Golf Club
down the road from their hotel. They'd heard
breakfast at the club restaurant, Joe's on the
Green, was not only fabulous, but a bargain, especially when compared with the $22 tab for the
morning buffet at their own hotel.

Sipping her first cup of coffee, Louise began to
forgive John for being John. After all, being in
Kauai was, as the man on the beach had said, like
being in paradise. Weather perfect after a spate of
torrential rains, surroundings gorgeous, people
friendly, and driving manageable, a world away
from the paralysis of cars in metropolitan Washington. She didn't want to ruin the trip by scrapping

with her colleague as if she were still on a grade school playground.

"Man-oh-man!" exclaimed John, sounding like a little boy. "Look at that! For $6.95 you get the whole works—sausage, eggs—or how about 'Josephine's Ultimate Banana Macadamia Nut pancakes'? They're only nine dollars." He slapped the menu shut. "And they have coconut juice to run over the pancakes."

Her stomach contracted in protest. She was a purist who would never under any circumstances run coconut juice over her pancakes. Maple syrup and only maple syrup for her.

Louise took another sip of coffee and looked out on the emerald green fairway backing the restaurant. "You're going to have fun today working with Joel and blocking out this interview with Schoonover."

John looked acclimated to the Hawaiian environment in a turquoise knit shirt and tan slacks. He reached a hand up and smoothed his healthy head of wavy brown hair. Louise realized that if he were a bird, one would have called this preening. "You know, I'm ambitious, Louise, probably a little more so than you in your particular . . . situation. I want to be a producer one of these days, a Marty Corbin, if you will." Her cohost fastened his amber-eyed gaze on her and held it unflinchingly.

They both knew Marty had a solid if not brilliant reputation in the Public Broadcasting System world. Her show, *Gardening with Nature*, was his most widely syndicated product.

"I guess I sensed your ambition. It sounds like a logical move for you. Keep all your options open—you can be an on-air personality and a production expert as well." She couldn't help inserting a little jab. "Then, if you should lose your looks, you can always go behind the camera."

"Hey!" cried John in mock protest.

"But all kidding aside, John, what you're saying makes sense. I'll help you in any way I can."

Her cohost looked surprised, but instantly covered up this emotion with his broad, perfect smile. Reaching over a hand and squeezing hers, he said, "You're a honey, Louise."

Unfortunately, their compatibility lasted only about ten minutes. As she drove them to the National Tropical Botanical Garden, John let her know how he intended to run the Schoonover interview. Her heart sank, for she knew the producer had everything to do with the success of such a solo interview.

"The idea," said John, "is to keep it simple. We don't want to bore our viewers with too much science."

The oversimplified statement made her pull in a sharp breath. "John, this man is the world's expert on the geographic distribution of plants. They call it biogeography."

"No way, Louise," said her cohost, waving both hands for emphasis. "You're on the wrong track. *I* know what the writers say about you when you offer your two cents on a script. They say you get way too technical." He smiled dismissively. "You realize that even though we have an intelligent viewership, half our viewers don't even understand the concept of evolution? Think of the trouble they'd have with biogeography."

Oh my God, she thought to herself, *how can I ever get along with this superficial human being?* All she knew was that the fight had gone out of her. The weather was too fine, the breeze too balmy. She was too laid-back and in tune with Hawaii to gripe at her colleague.

"Whatever you say, John," she said.

Once at the garden gate, they drove in a back entrance for employees that anywhere else would be considered a grand entrance: gigantic banana and taro trees, beds filled with orchids, bromeliads, and ti shrubs. They arrived at a series of low-slung buildings and parked. An old jalopy had preceded them into the parking lot. Out of it jumped a tall, long-faced young man wearing a Chicago Bulls cap, threadbare jeans, and a short-sleeved white T-shirt advertising "Franz Ferdinand." Sprinting up to them on coltlike legs, he whipped off his cap, revealing a head full of dark curls. He introduced himself as Joel Greene. Here was their associate producer. A cameraman and a sound guy also would be provided from the same PBS station, which used film students from the University of Hawaii to fill many jobs.

Louise and John exchanged a quick glance. Joel looked no more than eighteen. The young man's equinelike face broke into a captivating grin. "I bet ya think I'm too young. But believe me, folks, I've been around these islands for years producing films—I won't let ya down."

She was immediately reassured, possibly by that grin, possibly by the Midwest accent. She said, "We know you won't."

As they spoke, a tall man in tan shorts, gray-checked shirt, and heavy boots emerged from a nearby doorway and strolled toward them. His face was lined and browned from the sun; his hazel eyes twinkled below his high, wrinkle-filled forehead and curly graying hair in need of a haircut. He extended a hand and said, "*Aloha*, Louise. *Aloha*,

John. I'm Tom Schoonover. You folks are right on time."

Turning to the young man he said, "And good to see you again, Joel." To Louise and John he said, "Joel's filmed the gardens before for KHET-TV. He knows us plant explorers; all we need is a hand lens, garden clippers, vasculum for carrying the specimens, a pair of tabis, some rope, and a harness and we're all set. We'll tour the place as if through the eyes of a plant explorer, then come back here and visit the herbarium."

He intoned "herbarium," the storing place for dried plant specimens, as if talking about a holy place. For this man, probably fifty-five, who'd devoted much of his life to identifying plants for the good of science, it probably was.

Another man trailed out of the building. He was swarthy-skinned, of medium height and stocky, part native Hawaiian, Louise was sure. Tom Schoonover introduced him. "And this is Henry Hilaeo, who works here at the Gardens as a botanist." He laughed. "Henry'll do some climbing while we watch." Henry was equipped, just as Schoonover had described, with a heavy web belt to which were attached several tools, including clippers and a khaki-colored carrying case.

Henry Hilaeo gave Louise and John a direct look and a hearty handshake. His broad, browned face seemed carved in stone, his brown eyes expressionless.

His stony expression surprised Louise, but she realized it shouldn't. Since she'd arrived in Kauai, she'd bought the glib line that this island was a paradise—but a paradise for whom, tourists and landowners? Was it paradise enough for a man with Hawaiian roots like Henry Hilaeo? Natives made up only 10 percent of Kauai's population and had been dealt out of a good share of their land over the past couple of hundred years. No wonder there was resentment toward white persons, or *haole*, and efforts to gain rights similar to American Indians and native Alaskans through the Native Hawaiian Government Reorganization Act. As her gaze took in the idyllic surroundings, Louise realized Hilaeo was in a particularly ironic position: He worked for an Anglo scientist in a Garden of Eden that was the vacation home of Kauai's beloved Queen Emma until bought by Anglos in the 1880s.

Schoonover clamped an arm over Hilaeo's shoulders. "Henry and I just came from a trip to the Marquesas. We've been hunting plants in some of the roughest mountains you'll ever see. The rains drove us home a little earlier than we planned." To Louise's relief, Henry's face broke into a semblance of a smile.

Hilaeo had ropes and climbing equipment clutched in one hand and was wearing strange shoes. They were blue canvas with red trim, the big toe separated from the other four, with bottoms made out of rough nubs of rubber. Apparently noticing her quizzical look, Hilaeo explained. "These fellas, they're called tabis, or surf waders. They're Japanese-made and sometimes the only thing keeping us from landing on our butts."

They all laughed. Schoonover said, "Plant explorers face very primitive conditions, that's for sure."

"Not the least of which is scraping gecko poop off your bed before you go to sleep at night," added Hilaeo. "But we came up with a bonanza of new plant species." His eyes shone with excitement.

"Yeah," said Schoonover, "and one's going to be named after you, Henry. You well deserve it." He turned to Louise and John. "Henry can climb places that a mountain goat couldn't reach. Well, enough of that. Off we go." He struck off at a fast pace to the end of the parking lot where a large, dented gray vehicle sat. "We're driving around in a staff car—it's four-wheel drive. It'll take us everywhere."

Climbing up into the front passenger seat, Louise read a warning sign in big letters on the dashboard:

Please be aware the engine cooling system is not functioning properly.

"Oh boy," she muttered to herself.

While Henry Hilaeo and Joel Greene got in the backseat, Schoonover slipped behind the wheel. He looked over at Louise, who was staring at the warning sign. He said, "Don't worry about that. The mechanic's trying to cover his, um, options. It's most likely been fixed." He grinned. "At least I know he fixed the brakes and that's the real important thing. We have lots of cliffs and rough roads in the gardens."

John, who'd been delayed, was the last to climb into the van. Once he'd slammed the door shut, Schoonover ground the starter engine a few times without success, then said to Louise, "The starter engine's another issue, y'know. Maybe that sign should read, 'Cooling system SNAFU, starter engine questionable.'" He grinned at her; she could imagine what perilous fun it would be climbing mountains with him in some rough spot like the Marquesas Islands. Then he ground the ignition again until it finally caught and they roared off.

"Look at this, Dr. Schoonover," shouted John

from the backseat, shoving a small, leafy branch at him. "I picked it off that great bush back there."

Schoonover took the sprig John had handed him. Attached to it was a pale lavender flower. The scientist carefully handed it over to Louise, then violently turned the wheel to master a tight curve, and scooted up a steep hill. Louise grabbed for the overhead handhold for support.

Only when they'd reached the flattened-out area on top did the botanist speak, his voice devoid of the warmth he'd been exuding until this moment. "You shouldn't do that, John. Think how the visitors would denude this place if everyone picked a sprig of some plant, half of which"—he nodded to the specimen now residing in Louise's lap—"are on the National Endangered Plant list. Picking plant specimens in the gardens is not allowed and could even be dangerous." Darting a glance at John over his shoulder, he said, "Or perhaps you've studied about poisonous plants? Kauai's native plants are not poisonous, but some of the imports to the gardens *are*—the mere touch of a few of 'em and you're, you know, *phttt!*"

"God, I'm sorry," moaned John. "Was that one, uh, poisonous?"

Henry Hilaeo, sitting next to him, smiled and said, "I don't think so."

John's penitential statement was unfinished. "I should have known better, Dr. Schoonover, I really should have."

Schoonover said, "Needless to say, I don't think you'll do it again." Louise thought he sounded like a priest absolving someone's sins: *Go now and sin no more.*

But her cohost's remorse was short-lived. She realized John was preoccupied with the responsibility of setting up the TV interview. "I hope this doesn't interfere with my main objective of planning the shoot for tomorrow."

"Talk to Joel back there," said the scientist. "He knows what we ought to do, because we've done it before."

He turned to Louise. "It's a piece of cake—your colleague needn't worry. Joel's very talented. I'm sure he'll set John's mind at rest." Louise glanced back and sure enough, Joel and John had their heads together and John was even taking notes. Henry Hilaeo ignored the two and turned his brown face toward the window, seemingly content to let the gentle breezes waft in and soothe his private reverie.

Schoonover drove them down a hill and into the area where visitors were shown a special garden full of endemic Hawaiian plants, that is, the ones that were there when people sailed in and began inhabiting the Hawaiian islands. They drove past several garden "rooms" developed by the Chicago millionaire and patron of the arts Robert Allerton, and his adopted architect son, John, after Robert bought the property in 1937. Each featured a fountain and statuary, or a gazebo, pool, or waterfall. They passed lush trees, many supporting orchids or philodendrons in the small crevasses where branches divided, palms of many varieties, handsome blooming pandanus, mango, banyans, monkeypods, and a vast grove of Golden Jade bamboo. They fell silent as they came upon a magnificent Morton Bay fig, its gray roots as tall as a man. The roots reminded Louise of the buttresses on the Washington Cathedral.

Schoonover said, "Now we'll get off the beaten path. I want to show you some sights that aren't on the public tour." He scooted the car up a steep hill past a secluded waterfall, near which stood another huge Morton Bay fig. They descended into the Lawai Kai valley, from which they could see the ocean. The scientist stopped the Jeep. Getting out and walking around a lava cliff and over a footbridge, they reached the sprawling white frame Allerton house. Next to it stood the simple cottage of Queen Emma, wife of King Kamehameha IV. The front yard spanning these two buildings was dotted with tall, waving date palms planted in a checkerboard pattern.

Louise looked at Queen Emma's charming little white abode and felt a wave of sadness overcome her. "She was forced to leave here, wasn't she? How heartbreaking."

Tom Schoonover said, "She was obliged to leave. Noblesse oblige, don't they call it? After some idyllic stays here, the Hawaiian king, her brother, an autocratic sort of a fellow, summoned her to Honolulu to get back to her royal work."

"It must have been like leaving paradise," she murmured to herself.

Schoonover smiled. "Robert Allerton never left at all, in a manner of speaking." He pointed out to sea. "When he died forty years ago, his ashes were scattered on the outgoing tide of that bay."

While Schoonover and Louise were pondering history, John apparently was thinking logistics. "Let's be sure to include this as part of the shoot, Dr. Schoonover."

"Indeed we will," said Schoonover, giving Joel Greene a big wink. "Joel usually does something dramatic with those fig roots—we'll let Louise pose for us amidst them—and then wind up with a flourish here in the valley overlooking the sea." He turned to Louise. "But it's the cliff you must see next. Tomorrow, you can film Henry suspended off ropes from the top, checking the cliff wall for anything new that may be growing there. It's a wonderful spot. More endemic species are concentrated on that cliff than anywhere else on this entire island."

When Schoonover said this, he displayed a zeal that Louise seldom if ever saw in a person. This scientist positively loved plant specimens. She wondered if he had a wife or family, or if botany was his whole life. Here was a man, she was certain, who would do anything for the sake of his beloved Hawaiian species.

5

Thursday afternoon

Louise picked up a smooth, round bowl made of a coconut shell and examined the price. "Huh, six dollars. A bargain. It would be nice for nuts."

"I *love* these sarongs," said Steffi Corbin, who was as tall as Louise, five foot ten inches, but sixty pounds heavier. In fact, the two of them took up most of the space at the front of the little shop in old Koloa.

When they'd driven the few miles from their hotel to this historic sugarcane town, Steffi could hardly drag Louise away from filming the town's signature monkeypod tree. Its sprawling branches spanned the roadway and reached a block in each direction and because of that she'd found it hard to photograph. Now they'd discovered a store that even Louise liked. It was old and funky, like an antique out of the nineteenth century, but it contained a wild array of trendy clothing, pricey jewelry and junk jewelry, wood sculptures, glitzy mirrors, and small chandeliers. Even the name, Jungle Girl, was perfect, thought Louise.

Steffi riffled through the pile of folded cloths until she came upon a bright blue one that she held up to her majestic bosom. "What do you think? Dare I wear this to the beach?"

"Definitely," said Louise. "I checked out the beach crowd yesterday when I went swimming. They wear anything and everything. You'll look quite in the Hawaiian tradition." But her thoughts were not on shopping but rather on the Tropical Botanical Garden, which had captivated her.

She leaned against the jewelry counter and remarked, "Y'know, that garden was out of this world, Steffi. You should have come with us this morning. You have to come tomorrow when the whole crew goes. The scientists were great. Even the herbarium was fascinating."

"Herbarium?" said Steffi, suspicion in her eyes as she stared in a mirror and held the blue cloth up to her.

"Yes. Plural, herbaria. Lots of universities and botanical gardens have herbaria. They're like international lending libraries, constantly lending or borrowing plant specimens for scientific use. Right now, this herbarium's not that user-friendly, just a big room with black metal cases holding lots of sheets of paper with plants glued to them."

Even as she spoke, she could see Steffi Corbin's eyes glaze over.

Searching for something to enliven her description, she said, "You should have seen the darling orchids preserved in bottles in formaldehyde!"

"What color?" asked Steffi, guardedly.

"Actually, they've lost their color—they're kind of gray. Tim Raddant—he runs the place—has preserved them three-dimensionally so scientists can look at their form. They want to build a new herbarium. They just need to get the funds together. It will be interesting for kids as well as adults. In the meantime, Tim treats those plant specimens as if they were his babies."

Steffi said mockingly, "Well, bless Tim's little heart. Look, I may go with you on Friday, Louise. But don't try to interest me in a herbarium. I just went through a lower GI exam. It reminds me too much of that, even though I did dodge the bullet."

Louise was confused. *Herbarium? Enema?* And then she got it and laughed. *Barium enema.* "I should have known I couldn't interest you. It isn't the first time I've grown excited about something horticultural and found it impossible to share my enthusiasm with you lay people."

"You 'lay people'?" Coyly, Steffi asked, "Why do I sense I'm being insulted? What in the heck are 'lay people'? We Catholics think that means everyone except priests."

"Oh, I think of them as folks who don't know or care anything about gardening, who don't know a delphinium from a daffodil."

Steffi laughed. "Or a hellebore from the Hellespont?"

Louise grinned. "Or an aquilegia from an aqueduct."

Her companion turned a sly glance her way. "Actually, Louise, I know more than you think. I even know some of the Latin names, as I have demonstrated. I know about *hellebore*, for instance. I happen to *have* hellebore in my shade garden." She batted her big brown eyes humorously at Louise. "But my interest does not extend quite as far as herbaria."

"Okay, Steffi. I underestimated you and I'm sorry. And now I'll concentrate on shopping.

Hand me that red piece, will you? I wouldn't mind making the beach scene in a sarong myself."

Once she'd decided on the red cloth, her eye went quickly around the store as she looked for gifts to take home. She quickly selected four chunky necklaces from a jewelry case, two for her daughters, Martha and Janie, and the other two for her and Bill's mothers. Flashy key chains were the perfect gifts for her and Bill's fathers and Martha's husband, Jim Daley.

A turquoise cap for Bill, the red sarong for her, and the perfunctory shopping was done in record time. Whether she found anything else to buy didn't matter one way or the other.

Steffi shopped slowly. She had gone to the dressing room to partially disrobe. Louise could see the saleswoman-owner of the store, a sober beauty with long, dark hair, showing her how to tie the sarong just above the breasts in order to cleverly disguise the figure flaws that waited below.

"That looks nice on you, Steffi," called Louise. Then, bored, she began investigating a dark corner. Crowded at the rear of a shelf of wood sculptures was one of the strangest objects she'd ever seen.

It was the stylized figure of a horse, about four feet long, woven of straw, but with real horse hair on the mane and tail and decorated with white and red paint. Louise squatted down and peered closely at it.

"You're not buying that, are you?" asked Steffi, suddenly appearing next to her like a large, electric blue pillar in her nicely arranged sarong.

Louise shrugged. "What can I say? This thing is so odd that I can hardly resist it. Besides, I bet Bill will love it."

Steffi shook her head. "I hate to say it, but it's weird." The Corbins' home, Louise knew, was done in Danish modern. To Steffi, buying such an odd object would be out of the question. Louise returned to the front counter. To the proprietor, who in Louise's eyes had *become* Jungle Girl, she said, in a quiet voice, "Tell me about the horse," and cocked her head at the corner shelf, although that was unnecessary since there was no other horse in the store.

It was from Thailand, said Jungle Girl. Possibly used for a religious ceremony, though she wasn't positive about that.

"Hmm. Could we come to a better deal on this?"

Jungle Girl could. Louise ended up paying $70 for it, or $15 under list price, and arranged to have it shipped home so that she didn't have to wrestle it onto the plane. While she was occupied with artifacts, Steffi fell for an expensive pearl ring. After laboriously discussing its merits with Louise and other Jungle Girl shoppers and flashing it back and forth on her finger in the subdued light of the shop, she bought it, moaning about how Marty would complain about its cost. They left the shop happily with their purchases in shiny bags. If the horse arrived home before she did, it would provide Bill with a nice surprise.

Next, because they needed to replenish the energy spent while shopping, they stopped at an ice cream shop and bought mango shaved ice cones. As they strolled down the sidewalk toward the rental car, Steffi frowned. "Louise, you and Bill have such a nice house. Why would you ever put that horse in it? I don't understand. Where will you put it? You don't even have a basement to relegate it to."

Louise took a bite out of her mango ice. "I used to be the kind of person who would never buy a thing like that. But something's changed in me, Steffi, since the murders last summer." How well she remembered that month of terror and tragedy and the culminating moments when she realized someone was trying to kill her.

She sighed and took another lick of her cone. "It's fairly easy to talk about it, now that six months have passed. But at the time, I was so scared that my hands wouldn't quit trembling for days at a time."

Steffi put a gentle hand on Louise's forearm. "Oh, my dear, it must have been awful. I wish I'd been able to help you more during that period."

Steffi Corbin had been of no help, because she lived twenty-five miles away from Louise around the crowded Washington, D.C., beltway and because they only realized what good friends they were on those rare occasions when they were thrown into each other's company. Or perhaps Marty had discouraged Steffi from phoning; her producer had been embarrassed with Louise's involvement in another murder scandal that could affect the ratings of her TV show.

"I learned something last summer," she continued. "I learned that living is dangerous and that life is precious. The experience has made me feel like living more freely and enjoying every moment. Part of it is buying something fun like that horse, which I will never in my whole life come across again. Unless I go to Thailand, which I probably won't."

Steffi said, "You mean it came from Thailand?"

"Yes, Jungle Girl told me that it may have been part of a religious ceremony there."

"Hah," hooted Steffi, "you'll believe anything."

Louise grinned. "You're probably right and I've been sold a bill of goods. But it sure was fun. We'll have to go back. I really like that candle chandelier."

"The one hanging in back of the counter, in front of that red dress with the uneven hem?"

"Yes." In her mind, Louise measured it. It hadn't been that big, possibly fourteen inches wide and dripping with fake crystals and metal curlicues in the shape of vines.

"Now, Louise," said Steffi, in her most grounded voice, "where are you going to put that thing?"

"Not in the house. Maybe out on our patio, on calm summer nights when we're entertaining friends."

"Suspended from what, the moon?" Steffi laughed robustly, one of her most endearing qualities, and tongued a dab of ice from the side of her cone. She seemed to be finishing hers more quickly than Louise. "I must say it's interesting shopping with you. You're so quick—you're like lightning! But you can be a real spendthrift. Why, that chandelier was marked eighty dollars." She fluttered her well-manicured fingers in the soft, balmy air. "On the other hand, I saw one in the Neiman Marcus sales catalog for fifteen hundred. So who knows? Maybe that one's a bargain."

Louise rolled her eyes knowledgeably at her companion. "It will be. Jungle Girl will give me a deal."

6

It was four o'clock and they'd all ordered drinks. But Louise knew right away it wasn't going to be anyone's idea of a fun cocktail hour.

Marty had wanted a brief run-through of Thursday's production schedule, so he'd asked the Three Tenors to meet "for cocktails" with the WTBA-TV crew in the hotel's orchid garden lanai. Around them were masses of fragrant orchids of transcendent beauty. This setting, thought Louise, ought to put anyone in a euphoric mood, especially a clutch of botanists. But not Bouting, Flynn, and Reuter, who'd reputedly spent all day battling over ideas during the conference sessions and looked as if secretly they'd like to kill each other. Adding insult to injury, they'd been forced to sit side by side at the round table, since they'd arrived later than the TV people.

Dr. Bouting, she noticed, was creating even more trouble at this cocktail-party-gone-wrong as he clumsily extracted his minicomputer from a black leather carryall. This was the computer he reputedly took with him on exploring trips to record horticultural notes. With his jousting elbows he managed to intrude into the space of both Charles Reuter and Matthew Flynn. They stared at him in silent irritation as they inched their bodies away.

Seeing the three men gave Louise a moment of guilt. She had not gotten acquainted with them, since she hadn't attended one moment of the conference. She hoped at least to attend the final wrap-up session on Saturday. Then, she figured, everything the botanists had been snarling about for three days would be reduced to a couple of hours of hard-fought pronouncements.

Representing WTBA-TV at the table, besides Louise and Marty, were John Batchelder and Joel Greene, the young associate producer on whom the success of this shoot might hinge. John, she noted, had lost some of his élan, his handsome hair disheveled, his shoulders sagging. Was it because Joel took over the planning of the last-minute shoot featuring Tom Schoonover? Louise felt a rush of sympathy for her colleague, but couldn't think of any right way to express it.

Dr. Bouting finally settled down, his computer at the ready. Louise hadn't seen him since she had met him swimming in the lagoon yesterday. The man looked entirely different when dry. His clothes were an expensive flowered shirt and tan pants with a razor crease; his white hair was handsomely combed. The knee in the tan pants told of his inner mood: it jerked nervously up and down without stopping.

The much younger Dr. Matthew Flynn was the picture of relaxation. He sprawled back in his chair and sipped his drink, the boredom on his well-tanned face masked with a vacant half-smile.

With his light brown hair pulled back in a ponytail, he was the handsomest of the three scientists but also the most rumpled looking. Not more than forty-five, guessed Louise, and in his wrinkled short-sleeved shirt, old shorts, and battered boots, he could have been a derelict who'd pulled up on the beach in a boat. Probably his years of working in the Amazon had left their mark on him and it was not the mark of a fancy traveler.

In contrast to Flynn, Dr. Charles Reuter, a thin-faced man in his fifties, sat ramrod straight in his chair. He was of medium height and with sparse brown hair. Like Flynn, he wore an old cotton shirt and shorts that revealed the most muscular part of him, his legs. Around his waist was a belt with a couple of hanging tools in cases. Louise noted that his heavy shoes were clogged with the familiar red alkali dirt of Kauai, which told her that this University of California professor must have gone hiking once the afternoon conference session was done. She could imagine him frowning with alarm at the non-native plant species crowding this lush island, for he was the foremost champion of controlling and eliminating the so-called exotic, or foreign, interlopers in order to restore native habitats.

In a surly tone, Reuter led off the discussion. He said, "So what's the deal tomorrow—we stand in the botanic garden and fight? That's okay, I suppose. No different from the last two days."

Marty Corbin was at his most accommodating. Spreading his big arms wide, he said, "Dr. Reuter, we intend to have more action than that. As per the letter I sent you, our cameraman will tape you as you walk through the grounds where the native Hawaiian plants are clustered . . . the, ah"—Marty consulted his notes—"the *endemic* species, I guess y'call 'em." Marty might be the producer of the very successful *Gardening with Nature*. But what he told Louise more than once was, "Just because I produce a good TV garden show doesn't mean I know diddly about gardening." Obviously, *endemic* did not come trippingly off his tongue.

Bruce Bouting, exuding largeness with his tall, solid frame, stared at the diminutive Reuter through narrowed eyes. "The guy you want to fight with is me, Charles, why don't you admit it? You don't exactly deal fair and square. You take businessmen like me to task publicly in your writings in *Nature Magazine* and other venues, simply because we seek out new species and we never get a chance to rebut your arguments. You'll never understand that plant *diversity* is where it's at—there's no way you're going to turn back the clock and restore the land to the way it was one hundred, or two hundred years ago. Look at these very islands we're visiting—why, there are thousands of introduced species in Hawaii and some are darned good market winners."

"You and your 'market winners,'" said Reuter. "The imports to these islands have not done the place an iota of good, just the reverse. So don't use Hawaii to try and prove your point—there is a higher percentage of endangered species here than any other place in the world. In your ignorance, you keep traveling the world and co-opting naive, third world officials . . ."

"Not always," grumbled Bouting. "China's no longer a third world country."

"—co-opting officials of third world and other countries into letting you take home *their* prized native species." Reuter's eyes blazed with dislike.

"Then you introduce them here under totally different climatic conditions, where they take their nod from kudzu and spread like wildfire."

"Wait a damned minute!" cried Bouting, so loudly that people at neighboring tables turned and stared, including an amused couple within easy earshot. Louise realized how out-of-place a frenzied cry was in the midst of this relaxed paradise, with its burbling waterfalls and orchid-perfumed air. "We test every plant in our research labs and fields—for months, sometimes years, to assure that they'll not become invasives. Furthermore . . ."

"Months, maybe," countered Reuter, "not years. You couldn't afford to test them for years. It wouldn't be economically feasible. No, you hurry them onto the market and into gardens all over North America."

Marty laughed and put his arms out again, as if he were trying to stop a runaway train. Sweat beads appeared on his forehead. "Gentlemen, gentlemen, please . . ."

Bouting slapped a hand onto the table top, but then gazed up in confusion, his eyes with a faraway look. "Damn it. I had a rejoinder, Charles, but it's temporarily slid out of my mind. So I have nothing further to say at the moment, but don't think I forgive you for those ridiculous attacks."

If Bruce Bouting had nothing more to say at the moment, Matthew Flynn did. He plopped his muddy boots off the chair onto the floor and sat forward, stretching out his browned bare arms on the table. "Hold on, everybody, I want to throw in my two cents. Not to *dis* you, Bruce," he said, turning to Bouting, "but I'm in Charles's camp on this." He nodded at the University of California professor.

Charles Reuter sat forward. Louise saw on his thin face a look of pure hatred. She couldn't decide who Reuter despised the most: Bouting or Flynn. "Dr. Flynn," he snapped, "you may be in my camp, but I'm not in yours and don't think I am. I have utter disrespect for the way you trammel those Indians there in Brazil and Peru. You treat their plants, their national treasures, as if they're yours and yours alone. Who do you think you are? You're no better than Bouting. You only pretend to be!"

Flynn arched back in his chair, caught off guard by this attack. Bending his head, as if he were enduring a great wrong, he slowly turned to his critic and said, "Charles, I think you're ignorant of the way I work. Whenever I retrieve a valuable plant species from a tribe, there's always a payback. I make it a policy to educate the indigenous people as to the plant's capabilities, so that they, too, can benefit from its widest use." His steady gaze then returned to Marty Corbin. "What Charles already knows, and what the world needs to know, is that we have to preserve species. And that's what I'm doing. Every chance I get, I'm out there looking for more specimens. And it's not easy working in the jungle—I've even picked up malaria, which I can't shake and which sometimes lays me low. I'm collecting plants, I'm talking to the tribal shamans who know how the plants are used, then I'm bringing them back to my lab for thorough scientific analysis."

Flynn's pale blue eyes fastened on one, then another, until he'd made contact with the six other people at the table. Even Charles Reuter was now listening. "My dear people, we cannot let deforestation and civilization and roads and gold mines destroy the thousands of plant species that remain to be identified. Why, they've existed for hundreds of thousands of years on this planet."

"Hear, hear," exclaimed Marty Corbin. "Dr. Flynn, you're great." He quickly turned to the other two scientists. "And, Dr. Bouting, Dr. Reuter, you two are wonderful. Do just what you're doing right now— uh, you can leave out the pejorative comments, or else we'll have to remove them in the editing room— but you're on the right track. Lou here—Louise, I mean—will be with you every minute. She'll feed you a few questions."

"And me," said a small voice. It was John Batchelder.

"Oh, yeah. And John Batchelder, *Gardening with Nature*'s cohost. John also will fire a few questions at you." Marty gave John a little smile. "Sorry. I forgot you for a minute."

Bruce Bouting was leaning forward, his arms balanced on the table. He turned to Marty Corbin. "Mr. Corbin, you may think this presumptuous, but I seldom give interviews. Our company, privately held, flies under the radar, you might say. That's why I want to make this interview as complete as possible. So I want you to include two of my aides in the—what do you call it—*program*."

"The shoot?" said Marty. "You don't mean add people to the shoot?" He wiped his forehead with his handkerchief and looked at Louise imploringly, as if she might help him out of this problem.

Bouting sat back and beckoned to the couple sitting nearby. They'd obviously been poised for this moment of introduction. "Come on over, you two. The worst thing that can happen is that you'll end up on the cutting room floor, as Cecil B. De-Mille used to say."

With two strides, they arrived. Bouting introduced the woman as Anne Lansing. Louise sat forward, for she knew the name; Lansing was one of the most important new garden writers in the country. About forty, Louise guessed, and tall, with a leggy look, carrying a big, stylish carry-all. It didn't hurt to wear such a short jean skirt when one's legs were that muscular and shapely, nor a blouse knotted at the waistline when one's waist was that slim. Her dark brown hair was cut in a retro bob. And she hadn't forgotten to add bright red lipstick, which went well with the flapper look of the hair. Beyond all this she had striking, large yellow-green eyes.

"I hope this isn't too nervy of Bruce," Anne Lansing said in a low, euphonious voice. She gazed at Marty with an angelic look that begged his forgiveness.

Marty stared back raptly. "Uh, probably not, my dear." Louise knew Marty was susceptible to pretty women; this had led to occasional rough patches in his and Steffi's marriage. Secretly, Louise believed a marriage "patch-up" was another reason why he brought his wife on this business trip to Hawaii.

"Anne's in charge of my new plant research," Bruce Bouting went on, "and knows almost as much as I know about our new plants." He patted the top of his black computer. "Though I do hold lots of secrets close to my vest." Anne Lansing rewarded her boss with a look of filial devotion. This woman, thought Louise, knew how to manipulate men with a look and a smile.

"But she's also known for her horticultural books," continued Bouting, "which our company, of course, publishes. I bet you've all read them.

The Secret Life of Gardens was a huge seller. *Passion in Planting* is her latest."

"Indeed we have read your books," said Louise, sending her an admiring glance. "They are very good."

"Thank you," said Anne, flashing a radiant smile.

Bouting's male assistant was younger, a large, slightly overweight blond man who stared out at the world through thick glasses. Whether justified or not, it lent him an aura of quiet intelligence, in no way diminished by his turquoise ball cap and loud Hawaiian shirt in orange with big blue flowers on it. For some reason, he reminded Louise of a wise, giant baby.

Dr. Bouting's praise of Christopher Bailey almost exceeded his praise for Anne Lansing. "Chris not only runs our research gardens, he's a wizard at crossing plants—I even named one after him. And he does a million things—I can't remember them all at the moment. He works closely with Anne, of course."

"Hi, folks, nice to meet you," Bailey said in a shy voice, his magnified eyes carefully moving from person to person. Good thing Dr. Bouting built him up, thought Louise, or it would have been hard to get any attention at all with the dramatic but dignified Anne Lansing nearby. Right now, Marty hardly seemed to have heard the introduction to the male assistant, since he was still checking out the female assistant.

At last Marty turned his gaze on Bouting. Louise knew he was irritated, for he disliked it when people came along at the last minute and tried to change a planned shoot.

"You want these two to stroll along—is that what you're saying?" asked Marty. He shook his head.

"Naw, that would be too many people strolling along."

"You probably are right about that," said Bouting. "How about interviewing Anne and Chris and me after we get through with our three-way philosophical fisticuffs?" That engaging grin overcame his face again. Louise looked at her producer and saw him again covertly looking at the garden writer. She could see he was weighing the options; after all, the elusive Dr. Bouting had done Marty a favor by just agreeing to be interviewed. And here was this attractive horticulturalist who was being offered up to him as fodder for the videocam. Even though he should, how could a man refuse this bait?

Matthew Flynn, along with everyone else, had been taking in this exchange without comment. Now he sat back and his mouth twisted in a wry smile. "Hey," he said, "I have a dandy assistant, too. This particular man cuts through a jungle with his strong, straight machete as if he's running a knife through warm butter—the clever George Wyant. He even brought it on this trip, in case he encounters an impenetrable section of jungle when we hike the Kalalau Trail up in the Na Pali. George can also treat someone who's fallen ill with malaria like a nurse at Mass General." He grinned at Bouting. "But no, you don't like either one of us, do you, Bruce? I won't insist we include my good man George in the show, any more than Charles, here, would insist on dragging in his man, Nate Bernstein. Pretty soon we'd have the whole world in it, right, Bruce?"

Bruce Bouting hadn't cracked a smile. He said, "Matthew, you have to understand that I'm a little different from you and Charles; I'm an international businessman and these are my right-hand people. Why, you know Anne and how good she is."

Flynn flashed a mischievous smile at the woman. "Yeah. Of course. We all know Anne and how good she is. *Aloha*, Anne," he said, though he must have left her no more than an hour ago at the conference session. He reached a hand out to clasp hers and succeeded in grabbing her whole forearm, as if his hand were the mouth of a boa constrictor.

A very physical man, this Matthew Flynn, thought Louise. "And Christopher is good, too," said Flynn. "Hi, again, Chris. And by the way, friend, I need to get you alone one of these moments and talk about some technical plant lab stuff."

Christopher Bailey gave Flynn a sincere nod. "Any time, Matt." Anne smiled icily at Flynn. Perhaps she knew that more important things were at hand than palavering with colleagues.

Bouting said, "You may not have heard of Chris Bailey yet, but you will. They're both rising stars in this field, topnotch botanists. Did I remember to tell you that Chris has crossed more successful new plant varieties than any scientist in the whole darned nation?"

"Yes, you did, in fact," said Marty.

Bouting went on, undaunted, "You're familiar with the two-crowned fuchsia coneflower, of course—*Echinacea purpurea 'Bailey's Double Crown'*? It's a real market winner. That's Chris's flower." He gave his assistant a fatherly smile. "Both he and Anne deserve a little time in front of the camera."

For Marty Corbin, this Linnaean lingo of genus, species, and cultivar was the last straw. He looked in despair at Joel Greene. The young associate producer nonchalantly murmured to the producer, "*No problema*." Her producer was going to give in.

"Sure," said Marty, "we can tape a scene with the three of you. You can talk over your business and how you do it." A tight little grin and he continued, "God knows it's a big enough business to be worth talkin' about." The producer looked at Anne Lansing standing there, ignoring Christopher Bailey. "But don't forget what your boss said—you might end up on the cutting room floor."

Anne Lansing smiled demurely and said, "I'm sure your cutting room floor is an interesting place to be."

7

Thursday evening

Marty Corbin looked like a big, angry bear as he sat on the hotel terrace and drank his Lava Flow. Though bears, Louise realized, did not perspire like Marty did. He was muttering something to Steffi and Louise was just as glad that she couldn't quite hear it.

Steffi reached over and grabbed her husband's hand in hers. "Now, dear," she advised him quietly, "don't be profane. You're just making it worse." She turned to Louise and smiled indulgently. "He goes to St. Thomas's almost every Sunday with me, you know. But he *does* lapse into profanity. I don't know *why* he puts a middle initial in Jesus's name."

Louise sipped her tonic water. "Maybe he has a right to be upset." She looked around the dimly lit terrace and noted the dress code hadn't changed from last night. It was a little bit of everything: a woman or two in coif, jewels, and stylish gown; most people in laid-back sports outfits; and quite a number of couples in ponchos and rough shorts. These last had probably blown in from all-day boat and snorkling trips to the rugged northwest Na Pali coast. Louise felt she was dressed up just the right amount in a sleeveless navy blue pantsuit trimmed in white, worn with a bulky white necklace.

As if he were talking to himself, Marty growled, "That man Bouting, who does he think he is?"

"Millionaires think differently," calmly retorted Louise.

"And how would you know that?" grumped Marty.

"From reading the business section of *The Times*." She added, "And certain books. *The Smartest Guys in the Room. Confederacy of Fools*. It's in their genetic code to think they can get away with things. That's why so many of them are being prosecuted."

"All I know is that now I got three goddamn segments to tape tomorrow and a whole flock of last-minute logistics. Where the hell's Joel when I need him?" He frowned out at the world, as if the young man were lurking about. "No, he had to go home. Probably having his mother change his diapers, he's so young."

"Marty," she cautioned him, "Joel's twenty-three; he told me. And he's acting like a real pro and you know it." She didn't know why her producer was still upset about having his shoot disrupted. The cutting room floor seemed a fine solution to her; it wouldn't be the first time the crew had deliberately taped demanding people who were summarily cut from the tape during editing. Instead of talking about this ad infinitum, she looked at her producer and ran a hand across her throat and made a gutteral noise.

"Huh?" he said and then smiled. "Okay, Lou. So I just cut 'em out."

"Whatever. Let's order. I'm hungry."

It wasn't the way Louise had pictured a luau,

complete with roasted pig in a pit. This one was in hotel style. It commenced immediately after the holy moment of sunset, with the trio of ukuleles, a singer, and two hula dancers performing as the torches were lit on the hotel terrace. The hula dancers were not especially beautiful except for their long brown hair and dazzling smiles, yet their rhythmic movements mesmerized the crowd. Their hips seemed to have a locomotive power totally separate from the rest of their bodies. They were big women, even bigger than Steffi, who was sitting there in her new muumuu from Hilo Hattie, another shop she and Louise had visited this afternoon. Louise had bought a muumuu too, but hadn't felt comfortable enough to wear it. The dancers, like Steffi, had plenty of bust volume but little uplift. At Hilo Hattie, when Steffi bemoaned the difficulty of finding a proper bra to wear with her dress, the saleswoman had said, "This is Hawaii, hon; you just let 'em hang."

Marty, Steffi, and John were all drinking mai tais. So that she wouldn't feel left out of things, Louise had whispered to the waiter and he obligingly placed an umbrella atop her tonic water. As they drank and waited for their dinners to arrive, a lithe Hawaiian man in feathery headdress, G-string, and little else, came out on the terrace and appeared to swallow a fiery stick, bringing applause from the audience for both his feat and his remarkable brown body.

As soon as the women stopped doing the hula, Louise's table was invaded. First to appear was Bruce Bouting, dapper as ever in a sports jacket and linen trousers. On either side of him were Anne Lansing and Christopher Bailey. Anne looked luminous in a green linen dress that matched her extraordinary eyes. Louise was familiar with this trick, since she had a lot of green in her own eyes. A green outfit brought the color out to its best advantage. Bouting was whispering in Anne's ear. Christopher Bailey had dressed up a bit, but still fit the image of an intellectual nerd with faulty vision.

"Louise, Marty, John!" cried the white-haired scientist.

Uh oh, thought Louise, *what does he want now?*

Bouting spied Steffi Corbin, whom he apparently hadn't met. He stepped close to her, bowed down and took her hand in his, and pressed it gently to his lips. "And I believe I can guess who this lovely lady is."

As Marty introduced his wife, Louise could see her producer's facial expression soften. Steffi positively melted as the scientist continued to hold onto her hand. Bouting certainly knew how to charm people, she thought.

The horticulturalist said, "I just stopped for a moment to say *mahalo* to you, Marty, for accommodating me."

Marty waved a casual hand, his gaze flicking over to the beautiful Anne. "Don't mention it."

"Well, then," said the scientist, as he bowed again and relinquished Steffi's hand, "it's been so good to meet you, dear lady. Now, we'd better be off to get our dinner. We'll see you bright and early tomorrow at the Botanical Garden."

After they'd left, Steffi cocked her head back, as if pretending to swoon. "What a charmer he is!" She looked at her hand. "I've *never* had my hand kissed before."

Her husband laughed. "Tell her the real story, Lou—about how that thin layer of refinement covers an egocentric SOB who's makin' my job into a *nightmare.*"

"He is a bit difficult," said Louise. "But as I said, it's that millionaire mentality. Bruce Bouting doesn't think like most people—"

"No," interrupted Marty, "he thinks like an over-sized baby."

8

Not long after Bouting and his aides left to find seats in the dining room, two men strolled onto the terrace. One was Dr. Matthew Flynn. The other intrigued Louise. With their complexions like finely tanned leather and their campy shorts and boots, they looked like they had just stepped out of a jungle. Singly, each was handsome. Together, they made a striking pair that attracted every eye. Dr. Matthew Flynn's white smile flashed a greeting as he strode toward their table. With him was a younger man, in his midthirties, Louise guessed, with hair bleached blond either from the sun or peroxide. He was as tall, well over six feet, and as fit looking as Flynn himself. A battered leather carry-all hung jauntily from his shoulder.

Flynn beamed down at Louise and her companions. "Since none of you have made any of the conference sessions yet," he said, "you've not had the pleasure of meeting George Wyant, my assistant in the jungles. The one I bragged about this afternoon."

Keeping his sun-bleached head low in an almost deferential way, Wyant shoved the carry-all out of the way and shook hands all around. At first, Louise could not understand why he looked a bit otherworldly. Then she realized it was because the pupils of his eyes were so large. He said, "I also help Matt, uh, Dr. Flynn, send herbarium sheets to various institutes for analysis. When we think we have something, I help pitch the products to worthy pharmaceutical outlets." He gazed warily at first one, then another, at the table. Probably he was more comfortable in an Indian village in the Amazon than a luxury hotel.

"How versatile you are," said Louise. "Have the two of you worked together for long?"

"It's been five years now that I've accompanied Matt down to the Amazon basin—thanks mainly to National Scientific Foundation funding. On a few occasions I've come with him to the islands here to work with Tom Schoonover and Tim Raddant and Henry Hilaeo and the historian, Sam Folsom. You know, contributing chapters to books they're writing. I've been with Dr. Flynn ever since I entered the doctoral program at Eastern." He finally smiled and it took years off his golden face, which would probably still look youthful when he was fifty.

"My dissertation's all about a great plant from the Amazon, one from the uncaria genus, a subspecies of *Uncaria quianensis*." He glanced nervously at Matthew Flynn, as if for approval. Flynn quietly nodded. The older scientist was slouched back on his heels with his hands resting on his hips, like a runner at the conclusion of a race. He was as relaxed as his companion was nervous.

Having been given the go-ahead, Wyant continued, "The plant has dynamite possibilities, for instance, as an anti-inflammatory. But this sub-species seems especially promising in restoring cells after chemotherapy. That, of course, would be a fantastic breakthrough. I've written a little preview of its wonders for *Science* magazine."

"Great," said Louise. "*Uncaria quianensis.* I better write that one down; I don't think I've heard of it." She took the pad and pen from her purse and jotted the name down as Wyant hovered over her shoulder to help her with the spelling.

Matthew Flynn laid a light hand on George Wyant's bare forearm. "Now to change the subject." He slid his other hand onto Marty Corbin's shoulder, massaged the spot a little as if to take the knots out, and looked down at him sympathetically. Louise noted how freely this man liked to touch people. "I wanted to tell you, my man," he said to her startled producer, who wasn't used to being manipulated this way by another man, "that you handled all that second-guessing about the location shoot very graciously."

"I hope so," grumbled Marty.

Flynn laughed and said, "I had a wild idea I was gonna throw into the hopper, just as a joke."

"What was that?" asked the producer.

"That we move all of us, the whole shoot, to the top of Tom Schoonover's favorite cliff there."

Louise said, "The one with all the native species? Actually, tomorrow, Henry Hilaeo—"

Flynn rushed on with his flippant idea. "There's a little landing flat spot on top of it. We could all go up there and argue about the future of tropical plants."

George Wyant shook his blond head. "Hey, I don't *think* so," he said slowly, enunciating each word. That was when Louise was convinced Wyant was high, even though she had scant experience in this realm. "I can just see you and Bouting and Reuter having it out up there amidst the native plants." He laughed. "One of you'd probably get pitched off the cliff."

Now Louise could guess at least part of the contents of Wyant's carry-on.

"I suppose that's a distinct possibility," said Dr. Flynn, not missing a beat. "Probably as dangerous as the Kalalau Trail."

Louise had been attracted by this most dramatic of all trails in Kauai, but there was not enough time to do that difficult hike. "I hear that trail's steep and muddy, but is it that dangerous?"

"Only if you don't pay attention on those twelve-inch-wide paths along knife-edged slopes," said Flynn. "More danger comes from the fact that the valleys are perfect places to raise *pakalolo*." A euphoric look passed over his face, which gave his audience the clue that this was the Hawaiian word for marijuana.

"I've tried it, of course," said Flynn. "Very high quality, very nice. But maybe you don't want the short course in native cannabis cultivation."

John Batchelder, looking straight as an arrow, said, "I think it's interesting."

"All right," said Flynn, in a voice that warned, *you asked for it.* "The problem up in the Na Pali is that the farmers who're growing it don't want tourists near their operations. That's the way they make their nut, because the job market here, just like on the mainland, is not that great." He shrugged gracefully. "Tourists are fine if they stay on the trails. But if they stray off the path and start to nose around, the growers are obliged to hassle 'em."

The four at the table sat in silence. "Huh," John

Batchelder finally said, "it must be pretty strong, that marijuana."

At this moment, the waiter arrived with the appetizers. He gave a sideways glance at their two table visitors, who'd become such a fixture that Louise wondered whether she shouldn't invite them to pull up chairs and join them.

Flynn continued unabated. "As you know, there are various types of cannabis—you've heard of 'Maui Wowie' and 'Kona Gold,' haven't you, John?"

"I . . . I guess so," said John.

"Two hundred an ounce and worth every cent." Another enigmatic smile, as his gaze slid from John to the dark ocean beyond the terrace. "It's definitely the best for sex." Then, as if remembering where he was, Flynn pulled in a deep breath and turned to Louise and Steffi. "Sorry, ladies," he said, "I didn't mean to get graphic."

Louise's mouth was agape, but Steffi was unfazed. Comfortable and mother-of-the-world-looking in her braless Hawaiian dress, she slanted a look up at Matthew Flynn. "I bet the ganja on this island is not as strong as some of the hallucinogenics you two run into in the Amazonian forests, right? I've read about you people in books—what do you call yourselves?"

"Ethnobotanists, though some people call us jungle cowboys or worse." Flynn's face broke in a devilish smile. "'Weird units' is how they describe us when they're *really* pissed off. We *are* weird, I'll admit that much—that's why our hotel room here is so chaotic. Clothes on the floor, room service trays stashed in corners, door left open . . . we're used to living in the wild, our whole focus analyzing how indigenous people interact with plants. And you're right, George and I have both been offered a variety of hallucinogenic drugs. Of course we take some on occasion; it wouldn't be polite not to. We ethnobotanists have been trying hallucinogens for years in the name of science. That's why, Mrs. Corbin, you are anesthetized so that some surgeon can operate on you—"

"I *narrowly* avoided that recently," explained Steffi.

Matthew Flynn bowed. "I'm so sorry. I hope everything's all right."

Steffi made a wide circular movement with her hand around her lower stomach. "Colon problems, you know. They removed polyps and told me to improve my diet." She raised a hand and crossed her middle finger with her index finger. "With a little luck I won't have any more trouble."

"Ah, good," said Flynn. "But if in the future you do face an operation, you should know that the anesthetic was probably derived, or at least chemically copied, from a hallucinogenic plant rich in alkaloids that one of us rakish scientists brought back from the Amazon."

"Yes, I'd heard about that," said Steffi.

George Wyant, who had seemed uneasy with the turn of the conversation, happily added, "There are 121 prescription drugs derived from plants." He enfolded them in a boyish grin. "And we've hardly tapped the possibilities—only one percent of tropical forest plants has even been analyzed." Louise thought with his rakish good looks and his continued ability to think, stand, and talk—even if not to talk rapidly—George Wyant would make a good advertisement for a functioning pothead.

It was not too surprising to learn that the adventuresome Dr. Matthew Flynn and his assistant weren't averse to trying the drugs and judging their quality, nor talking about it after the fact.

Nor that Flynn seemed to have sympathy for, or at least an understanding of, the illegal "farmers" who raised the crop. For now she remembered reading a critical article about Matthew Flynn, part of a mass of background material gathered by the associate producer back in Washington, D.C. It mentioned how other scientists criticized his bold plant explorations and that drugs were just "part of the scene" when botanists hit the jungle.

In another vein, the article also gossiped about how well Flynn did with the ladies in New York when he returned to civilization. This did not surprise her, either.

"'Course, it isn't always cool to take what's offered in the way of narcotics," Wyant slowly continued. "You have to remember that you've got to make it back down the river to your camp."

It was ironic, Louise thought, that only limited native crops, such as breadfruit and taro, were raised on these islands for hundreds of years after the early settlers came. Two hundred years ago, sugar cane and rice and pineapples were introduced, providing jobs for immigrants and fortunes for the land owners. Now, illegal marijuana was one of Kauai's cash crops, making this place no different from California and Florida. *Tropical plants for tropical lands*, she thought dourly, *part of the dark side of paradise*. She sat quietly back in her chair.

Seeming to read Louise's mood, Flynn said offhandedly, "Guess I said more than enough on that subject." He turned to George Wyant. "We'd better shove off, George."

Steffi asked, "Are you going somewhere for dinner?"

George Wyant, feeling more confident now that

he'd contributed adequately to the conversation, had a pleased look on his face. "We sure are. We'd tell you where we're going, but then we'd have to kill you." He guffawed, as a shocked look overcame their faces.

The younger man turned to Flynn and muttered, "Aw, me and my big mouth!"

The scientist put an arm around his assistant, as if to protect him from criticism. "That's just an old joke George has reeled off," he explained. "Haven't you heard it? He's trying to be funny but it doesn't always come off when George tries to be funny. Actually, we're going to Aroma in Lihue. You'll have to try it before you leave."

Flynn cocked his head toward a table near the center of the terrace. "I've noticed, though, that most people from the conference like to eat here. There's the good Dr. Charles Reuter and *his* right-hand man Nate. They're honored to have sitting with them the great Ralph Pinsky." He might claim the man was great, but Louise noted that his tone of voice said otherwise.

She turned her head to look. One of the two sitting with Charles Reuter was a muscular, attractive young man with lively dark brown eyes. This apparently was his aide, Nate. The other was a man who looked as if he'd never ventured out in the sun and wouldn't dare to. He had curly dark-red hair and a pale-as-milk complexion. What interested Louise most was the way he held his table mates transfixed as he leaned forward and talked, emphasizing his words with rapid gestures of his long-fingered hands.

She said, "So that's Ralph Pinsky. I read about him in the conference brochure. He's an impressive man."

Matthew Flynn grinned broadly: "Everybody thinks that Ralph Pinsky's the botanical garden director nonpareil. Interestingly enough, he ranks right up there with Bruce Bouting in terms of the volume of his plant discoveries. But Pinsky's discoveries take about four times as long to get to market, if they ever do. Not quite as nimble as he used to be in the field—*something's* gotten to him— but he's a clever guy. He's made the Greater Missouri Botanic Garden outside St. Louis into probably the second best botanic garden in the country. A real knee-jerk true believer, just like Reuter and his crowd."

As if conscious they were being discussed, the three men turned and looked over at Matthew Flynn. "Hi," said Flynn and waved. Reuter and the young, dark-eyed Nate reluctantly waved back, while the man named Pinsky gave Flynn a dismissive glance with his gray eyes and turned back to his companions.

Marty Corbin stared in the direction of the Reuter table, his eyes narrowing ominously. "So there's another Man Friday lurking around here. Lou, do you think Dr. Reuter will want *his* Man Friday on the program tomorrow, too?"

Dr. Flynn laughed and shook his head. "No way. Nate Bernstein's a behind-the-scenes type guy. He does a lot of research for Reuter, as well as some of his boss's best writing, it's said. But neither Charles Reuter nor Nate Bernstein craves publicity. You'll have enough of a challenge giving Charles face time tomorrow morning. He's what you'd call 'diffident.'"

"Shy?" cried Marty. "You've gotta be kidding, Dr. Flynn. I didn't think there was a shy person among you. I just thought Reuter was an unpleasant SOB."

Steffi and Louise exchanged alarmed glances. Marty was crabby and tired. It was time to change the subject. She looked up at Matthew Flynn and smiled. "So, Aroma is a good place to eat; we'll remember that. I bet you two know lots of good places."

John Batchelder piped up, "Louise will wangle it out of you—she always does. She's solved a few crimes, you know." He smiled smugly, as if he'd announced a secret that was only his. "She's a real snoop."

Matthew Flynn looked down at Louise with mock amazement. She felt her face coloring. "My God, an amateur gumshoe in our midst! I knew there was some reason I liked you from the moment I first met you."

"John's just kidding," Louise demurred.

"I bet he isn't," said Flynn. "I'll have to remember that and seek out your help if I need it. But seriously, dear Louise, we know lots of good places. I'll jot down a list of them for you."

"Thanks," she said. She was grateful when she saw a waiter heading their way with a huge tray bearing four large plates with covered lids. As he turned to leave, Flynn cast a haughty glance around the terrace with its torches and palms, while the waiter looked relieved that the two interlopers were getting out of his way so he could serve the food.

Whether they were a little weird or not, Louise envied the two ethnobotanists. At least they had the good sense to strike out from this luxury hotel. She wouldn't mind getting away from it one of these nights.

9

Soon after dinner, the four of them seemed ready to retire to their rooms for a good night's sleep before the busy Friday. But first, Louise went to the hotel's sundries store to buy a few items. The shop was called Island Rest, possibly because it had a large stock of medicines, including over-the-counter sleeping pills. Surprisingly, it was crowded with other guests doing the same thing.

Quickly snatching up her intended purchases, a hat emblazoned with "Kauai-by-the-Sea," a tube of 45 SPF sunblock, and a couple of pricey rolls of film, she got in line behind three others. A quibble was taking place at the front of the line, something about the fact that the shop didn't carry the man's favorite headache pain relief. Since she was tired, Louise wished he'd get on with it, grab a bottle of Advil, and let her have a turn at the counter.

The dark-haired young man standing in front of her finally swung around in disgust. It was as if he had to find something in the rear of the shop to interest him and help relieve his impatience. This gave him the opportunity to stare at a whole wall full of hats of various styles, all of which carried the logo, "Kauai-by-the-Sea."

That was how she got acquainted with Nate Bernstein.

"Kind of late, isn't it," she said, "to get in a tizzy over pain pills."

"Insane," muttered the young man, without even looking at Louise. "He should have brought his OxyContin from home." He had an intelligent face. Any mother would love those liquid brown eyes.

"You're Nate Bernstein, aren't you? I'm Louise Eldridge. I'm the, uh . . ."

"I know who you are," said Bernstein, finally deigning to look at her. They were the same height. "You're part of that TV shoot tomorrow at the National Tropical Botanical Garden. I had to sit and wait while you all met this afternoon to talk over things."

"Yes," she said. "I host the program. Are you coming to the shoot?"

His lip curled, as if this were a foolish question. "Of course. Dr. Reuter will want me there." He gave her a suspicious look. "Quite frankly, he thinks he's being set up."

"Oh, no, I mean . . . why would he think that?"

Bernstein's glance slid over to another part of the store, where scores of postcards were on sale. A pause, during which Louise wasn't even sure the young man would resume talking. "Well, at heart, Ms. Eldridge . . ."

"Mrs. Eldridge," she corrected.

"At heart, there's no difference between those two characters."

"You mean Dr. Bouting and Dr. Flynn."

"Yes. Bouting Horticulture constantly needs new products to market." He waved his strong-looking arms in a surprising gesture. "How else would they continue to make their millions and keep a throttle-hold on the wholesale plant market of North America? You got to have your bright new orange-with-yellow-tipped echinacea from New Mexico, or your hot new purple-with-green-spots species tulip from the mountain slopes of Turkey." Those brown eyes widened. "That Bouting fellow is a sleight-of-hand artist; he goes to those places, swaps a few non-important Bouting brands that he doesn't care about for priceless finds."

"Is there something inherently wrong with doing that?"

A shrug. "It's what he does and doesn't do next. Doesn't test 'em long enough to determine whether they're invasives. Doesn't remunerate some poor, benighted country that he's filched them from after he makes a ton of money off them." Nate Bernstein smiled, but cynically. "Otherwise, there's nothing wrong with that."

She said, "But Matthew Flynn has a different slant. He's only interested in plants with medicinal value."

The young man pointed an accusing finger at Louise. "That's not the whole story. He's got two games going. He also goes out and plunders the wilds for ornamentals for fun and profit, don't think he doesn't. As for the 'valuable' medicinal plants he's always touting, you have to ask, plants with value to whom? To Matthew Flynn first and foremost." He shook his head. "No, if you knew the whole story, you'd see he's a phony. Nothing, or almost nothing, has panned out—no medical miracles or breakthroughs—despite all the money he's taken up front from the NSF and from pharmaceutical companies."

"Huh," said Louise. "Then why does he have such a great reputation in the scientific community?"

Bernstein, after his animated disclosures, seemed to have wound down. There was a long pause before he continued. "I predict he'll be passé before the year's over and that golden boy image will begin to fade. Pretty soon, the funding won't be renewed." Another dry and humorless laugh. "Without NSF and pharmaceutical company money behind them, who'll pay for Flynn and Wyant's druggy little trips to the middle of no-where?" He caught Louise's eye again. "Those trips cost big money, you know, the boats, the special equipment, the professional crews from Manaus . . ."

"I heard Dr. Flynn and Wyant discovered a promising new species. Something in the *uncaria* genus."

Bernstein nodded. "A subspecies of *Uncaria quianensis;* I've read all about it. Maybe it's a breakthrough, but I don't think so, despite all the hoopla in the scientific press about it. If it did become a bona fide cancer cure the way they've been touting it, it will be an all-out steal from those poor Peruvian Indians who live where they found the plant. But watch and see. I bet their promises come to nothing. Time will tell if I'm right."

Louise thought for a moment, but a moment was all she had, for Nate Bernstein had reached the front of the line. She noticed he was purchasing a pocket knife with an attractive palm tree motif. Her newly aroused shopping "self" decided she'd buy one for her husband as a fitting gift from Kauai. She touched his arm. "Nate, we'll give

Dr. Reuter plenty of opportunity to state his positions tomorrow on endangered and invasive plants."

Bernstein turned and threw the words over his shoulder. "I trust you on that, Mrs. Eldridge."

Then, not caring that he was holding up a line of people, he turned all the way around and fixed Louise with his intense gaze. In a quiet voice that couldn't be overheard, he said, "I don't trust the others not to skewer the deal and dominate your whole program."

"Oh, no, they—" she started to say, but he raised a warning hand that was as good as if he'd told her to be quiet and listen.

"Let's look at the facts as they exist, Mrs. Eldridge. When it comes to botanists, Matthew Flynn is the young, womanizing glamour-puss with the compelling scientific spiel. And that old goat Bouting doesn't do so badly for himself . . . either with the ladies or at conning the scientific community into thinking that he's their great white hope. Charles Reuter and I consider those two are formidable opponents—and don't think they're not opponents. We're on two different sides in the struggle to save this planet of ours."

10

On the downside, it was an extraordinarily
warm day in Kauai, with no prevailing breezes
blowing for a change. Louise could feel the sweat
forming in her armpits, probably because she was
costumed specially for the shoot in a Calvin Klein
blue denim dress with a big red kerchief at the
neck for accent.

On the upside, the shoot was working like a
charm. Marty Corbin, acting as producer-director,
stayed just out of range, mopping his brow and
waving instructions to their young associate producer, Joel, and to the audio engineer, a film
major like Joel from the University of Hawaii. The
grip guided the perspiring cameraman as he walked
backward down the road, the big videocam on his
shoulder aimed at the Three Tenors. He was on
the staff of KHET-TV in Honolulu.

On the scientists' left flank was John Batchelder
and on their right, Louise. The cohosts took turns
questioning the three.

Louise was exhilarated, for Bruce Bouting,

Matthew Flynn, and Charles Reuter were quibbling at every step. However, the sight of the camera must have cooled some passions within them, for it was not an angry exchange such as the one they'd had the previous afternoon. Intelligent, animated, but not angry. With a little editing, it was going to make an exciting program for *Gardening with Nature.*

What was a little unusual at this production was the cluster of spectators just outside camera range. They had congregated promptly at 8:30 to take in the action. Louise darted occasional glances at them as they walked quietly along, as instructed by Associate Producer Joel Greene, straining to hear every word the visiting scientists had to say to the camera. Some were visitors who'd arrived early and were lucky enough to get in on a video shoot. There was the Rubensesque Steffi Corbin, looking handsome today in a light blue flowing dress, laughing merrily at every break with the scientists from the Garden. Tom Schoonover strode along rather like the lord of the manor, with solid, swarthy Henry Hilaeo at his side and Tim Raddant and Sam Folsom following along.

Tim and Sam, like Schoonover, were lean, deeply tanned men, and Louise surmised it was because their jobs took them out of doors so much. Then, they most likely surfed or swam in their leisure time. *Escapees from the mainland,* thought Louise with a smile. Though they'd surely come to Kauai in the name of scholarship, they were living and working in paradise. There must be no more pleasant scientific job than one here in this island garden.

The other spectators included Bouting's people, Christopher Bailey and Anne Lansing, who'd soon be before the camera themselves. Anne guarded against the sun with both a wide-brimmed straw hat and a cream-colored umbrella that matched her cream-colored sleeveless lawn blouse and pleated linen skirt. Matthew Flynn's assistant, George Wyant, was looking as dazed as ever, and then there was Dr. Reuter's aide, Nate Bernstein. Bernstein, who was becoming browner and more handsome the longer he was exposed to the Hawaiian sun, nevertheless seemed as tormented today as when Louise ran into him last night in the hotel store.

With a commanding air only enhanced by his good-looking safari outfit, Dr. Bouting was booming out his closing argument: "Of course we must preserve our endangered plants, but that doesn't mean tropicals aren't going to be the star plant of the future in the horticultural world, tropicals that are being bred to grow even in zone five! Tropicals that will flourish in pots in northern gardens . . . tropicals that will awaken conservation feelings in home gardeners and are an avenue through which we can educate the public to . . ."

Matthew Flynn threw in with Bouting for the most part, but said Bouting's view of tropicals was too commercial and "exploitative."

Louise had a quixotic mental picture of Bouting and Flynn in some jungle environment, fighting to the death over a new plant discovery: *"For home gardeners,"* Bouting would cry. *"For the future of medicine,"* Flynn would argue. Today, Flynn's clothes represented a slight upgrade: the shirt not quite as wrinkled as the day before, though just as worn. On the back of his head he wore a jaunty cream-colored explorer's hat that looked brand new, as if bought expressly for the taping. Yet he was more subdued today than he was yesterday, seeming to search for the right words and vigilantly observing the responses of others.

"Man will always be in search of new plants in exotic places," he said, "but caution must be taken when we pluck these species from the wilds. All plants need analysis so we can tell whether or not they will have value to mankind beyond commercial values. We need to keep searching, because in the face of population pressures, many species are disappearing, along with the indigenous people who know how to use them . . ."

The audio engineer had to move up quickly with his microphone boom to catch the quiet, ascerbic remarks of Charles Reuter. "Of course man will always search out new plants on this earth. But we know things now that we didn't know even fifty years ago . . . that the introduction of exotics into helpless, foreign environments"—he dramatically waved his thin arms—"Kauai and the other beautiful islands of the Hawaiian chain could not be a more perfect example of this phenomenon—these introductions can create environmental nightmares, with native plants literally smothered, as they have been here by these intruders. Testing. Trials. These are the responsible things to do before moving any plants into a new environment."

Reuter stopped momentarily on his muscular legs, bringing the entire on-camera group to a halt. He looked dramatically up at Matthew Flynn and Bruce Bouting for another parting shot. "Needless to say, we're one world enough to know that we no longer can steal plants away from guileless countries, even under the guise of saving humanity with a new wonder drug, not unless we in the United States wish to bear the stamp of horticultural conquerors who have no consciences."

Louise was amazed to learn that this slight man had such emotion in him and could express it so well. Now they had turned into one of the botanical garden's "rooms," the finish line for the shoot. Around them were walls of pandanus trees. Above them was the garden room's roof, a huge monkey-pod tree that spread its large arms across the sky. In the center of this space, a serene fountain burbled, as it had for almost seventy years since being created by Allerton.

"We thank our guests for this lively discussion," she said. "I know it will provoke us all to think . . ." A few more closing words, with John chiming in to say, "And this has been a perfect place to have such a wonderful exchange of ideas."

"That's a wrap, then," called Marty. "Take ten, no, fifteen, so you can get up to the john. Next up are Bouting, Bailey, and Lansing, for a brief interview. Louise is doin' the interviewing." He turned to confer with Joel Greene for a minute; Louise knew her producer hadn't decided where he was going to tape this segment.

She went over to Tom Schoonover. "Sorry for the delay, Dr. Schoonover."

"For heaven's sake, call me Tom," he said, with a smile that elevated his eyebrows and put those forehead wrinkles into play.

"We'll be shooting your and Henry Hilaeo's trek through the native plants soon. The segment that Marty's doing next shouldn't take more than a few minutes." She could feel her face coloring. "It's something Dr. Bouting kind of insisted on doing, a little summary of what Bouting Horticulture is all about."

Schoonover shoved his cap back on his head and a couple of gray curls fell onto his forehead.

"Seems as if it would make more sense to do a program on Bouting Horticulture back in Philadelphia, where they have all those vast research gardens."

"I know," said Louise, as her shoulders slumped a little. Her producer had given in to pressure. They probably wouldn't be able to use the little piece. "Where do you think they should go to tape this? There are so many wonderful spots to choose from."

Schoonover casually pointed down the road. "How about the next garden room beyond this one? It has a long, serpentine pool and there's a bench where the four of you could sit. It would make a nice background."

"Thanks, Tom. And sorry you and Henry have to wait."

His hazel eyes looked down on her perspiring face. "No problem for me," said Schoonover. "But Louise, maybe you better powder your nose before they begin taping. Nobody cares here on Kauai whether you have a shiny nose, but that producer of yours might when he sees the tape."

She grinned. "Thanks for the beauty tip."

With a big smile, he said, "If you're going to keep thanking people, you'd better use the Hawaiian 'mahalo.'"

"Oh, yes, of course. *Mahalo*, Tom." She pulled her compact and lipstick from her SportSac. As she quickly dabbed makeup on her face, she said, "So what did you think of our three visiting botanists?"

Schoonover shoved out his bottom lip in an expression of bafflement. "Y'know, all of us in this business tend to know each other pretty well. Other botanists from that conference have visited the gardens in the past two days. Nice lot of people—Ralph Pinsky, people of his stature. I could see that you and your producer were pleased with the combination of Reuter, Bouting, and Flynn—one zealous ecologist and two combative jungle cowboys."

"You think of Dr. Bouting as a jungle cowboy?"

"Sure do," said Schoonover. "He's just older than Flynn, but cut from the same cloth. One, he's got that hyperbole thing going—always exaggerating his claims. And two, he's not always interested in the consequences of his actions. Putting the three of them together is truly an explosive mixture."

She snapped her compact closed, put the top back on her lipstick and returned them to her bag. "That's why we were so happy. They didn't explode, they just politely collided."

"So that's how you saw it."

"How did you see it?"

"For professional scientists, those three have a thin veneer of civilization about them. Let's put it this way—I wouldn't want to leave them in a room together without proper supervision."

11

When doing a weekly TV gardening show, it was hard for Marty Corbin or Louise or the associate producer to predict who would make a great on-camera guest. Marty, of course, wanted scintillating guests who would banish any fears that a show would bog down in too much garden minutiae.

Dr. Tom Schoonover, with his shaggy haircut, his lanky gait, and his professorial manner, had proved to have star power. Louise could tell this by watching Marty's growing enthusiasm as the shoot proceeded.

Why the scientist was so good on camera, she couldn't quite fathom, for he was a scientist through and through, given to exchanging dry jokes about "endemic subspecies" with his colleagues that one without a background in botany found hard to interpret. But he was an impressive guide, as he led Louise and the camera through a grove of native plants, explaining that the Hawaiian islands originally contained only one hundred species and that these had multiplied ten times over during centuries of isolation. Today's challenge, he said, was that the islands were crowded with hundreds of introduced plants that came by double canoe, sailboat, steamship, and airplane and tended to crowd out the natives.

As the videocam slowly circled it, he'd described a newly discovered species as if he were describing the Hope diamond. "We recently found it on an islet off Maui. This is the only plant of its kind that exists on earth. It's been named Kanaloa, after the Hawaiian god of the ocean."

Schoonover went over to an *Ohia lehua* tree and told of the latest methods scientists used to fight the extermination of this valuable native specimen. By using high-altitude planes with infrared imaging spectroscopy, they could measure the nitrogen and water in a Hawaiian forest canopy and discover where invasive plants were crowding it out.

Eyes bright with enthusiasm, he talked about revolutionary new ways of classifying plants and animals. "Where we used to do it through intuition, we now unravel their relationships with great accuracy, using DNA, cladistics, and high-speed computers. In case you're not familiar with the word cladistics, it's a logical system that allows us, in systematic steps, to classify and then put plants in their evolutionary sequence."

Smiling, he added, "Darwin would love the logical clarity of cladistics. It helps us understand the evolutionary history of these plants." His goal now, he said, "is to encourage scientists working in this field to find out how the flowers and trees of the Hawaiian islands fit into this picture of life on the planet."

After Schoonover's turn, Henry Hilaeo showed

off his prowess. With tabis on his feet and
Schoonover up top handling the ropes, Henry be-
layed down the cliff rich with native species and
plucked a few plant samples, the videocam following his every move.

A few things went awry. Hilaeo's rope got fouled
and it took a while to untangle it. The grip stum-
bled and nearly fell into one of the elegant garden
ponds. The ID flap on Schoonover's hat was hanging out during the shoot, but it added a humaniz-
ing absent-minded-professor touch, so Louise hadn't
mentioned it.

Now, the work was done and it was time for
lunch for all who took part in the program. And
not a moment too soon for Louise. Traipsing over
cliff and dale with a camera-ready smile in that last
segment had taken it out of her. She was exhausted, her on-camera denim dress sweat-soaked
and wrinkled, her hair expanded by the humidity
into an unruly swarm of curls. But still she was
happy, for they were picnicking in a historic spot,
the front yard of Emma's cottage by the sea. From
her seat at the large picnic table, she looked up
into the waving palm fronds, then lowered her
gaze and stared across the emerald lawn into the
calm Pacific. All the complicated history of these
islands seemed encapsulated in this moment.

"Let's drink to the queen," proposed Tom
Schoonover, "and to Sam Folsom, who arranged
this nice box lunch event—and to Tim Raddant,
who rustled out a few bottles of wine he'd stashed
at controlled temperatures with the plants in the
herbarium." Sam and Tim took a bow.

Marty Corbin lifted his glass and said, "I want to
make my own toast, to all of you here who took
part in a successful shoot, with three very diverse

segments." His gaze settled on the attractive Anne Lansing. "You folks from Bouting Horticulture did a good job of relating what you're doing at your giant nursery to a setting here in Hawaii. It was not an easy task." He turned his attention next to Tom Schoonover. "Then we have Tom, here, who's turned out to be a real star. He's as good as Carl Sagan at explaining the obscure—if anyone remembers Carl Sagan."

Laughter greeted this remark. "I still don't know what cladistics is—only that it's something good." He turned to Henry Hilaeo. "And thanks to you, Henry, for risking life and limb for us."

Hilaeo's browned face cracked with laughter. "Not hardly, Marty. It would take a lot more than that to kill me."

As Louise looked around the table, she saw that almost everyone was worn out and grimy from the morning's efforts. But not Anne Lansing. She held her head high and looked cool and dignified, while others seemed ready for an afternoon nap. Anne, thought Louise, had the air of a queen herself. In fact, she was a queen, in that rarified little world of garden writers in which she flourished.

The woman had chosen a place between Marty Corbin and Dr. Bouting, two men guaranteed to give her constant attention. Bouting intermittently whispered in her ear, then turned and spoke softly to Christopher Bailey; Louise decided this was the way he conveyed instructions to his aides.

While they munched their sandwiches and drank their wine, attention turned to the sun-burnished Sam Folsom. His aspect immediately changed from the bantering scientist into the dedicated professor, as he gave them a brief but poignant history of the queen and the cottage. Louise loved hearing about the cosmopolitan monarch. Here was a woman who'd traveled across the world and been received by both Queen Victoria and President Andrew Jackson. After both her husband and only child died, she visited the beautiful Lawai Kai valley, fell in love with it, and built the cottage on the seaside cliff above where they now sat; it was later reverentially moved down into the valley near the stream.

"She admitted she had a mania for planting," said Sam, eyeing them over his half-glasses, "and the evidence is all around us. Her nurseries, one here and one in Honolulu, provided the parent stock for many of the plants you see today in the islands. But she cared for the people as much as she did for the plants, establishing the first public hospital, a girls' school, and a cathedral. She was never too queenly to relate to people. When she was here in Kauai, she would go out and work with them in the taro patches."

On a historic trip to the mountains, said the historian, Queen Emma traveled a perilous, muddy trail until she reached the overlook to the rugged Waimea canyon. "She was accompanied by a retinue of one hundred people," he said, "including hula girls, retainers, and musicians. After that trip, she insisted that a proper trail be built to reach this wild spot."

What touched Louise most was Emma's love of nature. Sam read from a letter she'd sent from Kauai: "*The cattle have so often played music to my ears. The lowing comes so sweetly on the air when the calf is called back to its supper of sweet milk at twilight.*"

When he recounted another note that the queen wrote to a friend in Kauai after her links with the island were severed, it brought tears to Louise's eyes. "*Tell me the old and new things of*

Koloa," wrote the queen, "*from natives, haoles, wild plants, animals, your flowers, and all. I do not hear of our place these days.*"

In her enthusiasm for plants, it sounded to Louise as if Emma had an innocent role in imperiling the species of her precious island retreat. She had brought in bougainvillea, as well as many other eager, exotic plants. Some grew lavishly and overwhelmed the native species.

While the rest of the people at the table paid rapt attention, Anne couldn't seem to stay focused. She began talking to Marty Corbin in a low voice— probably thanking the producer for the interview. Louise shot her boss a shocked look and he didn't continue the disruptive conversation.

But Sam Folsom kept his history lesson brief. He ended with a joke about how if people actually understood history, they wouldn't keep repeating the bad parts.

As she looked down the table, Louise noticed a couple of interesting things: Bruce Bouting behaved like Anne Lansing's doting father, laying an occasional hand on her bare shoulder, almost as if he were protecting her. And perhaps this was warranted—the woman emanated a sexual aura only partially masked by her businesslike "scientist" repartee. Louise wondered if it was that bright red retro lipstick that did it. Many men responded to her, John Batchelder among them—and Matthew Flynn and his assistant, George Wyant, but in quite a different way. The Amazonian specialists observed her warily, like animals either on the hunt or being hunted. They no doubt lumped her with their professional enemy, Bruce Bouting. On the other hand, they seemed to be old friends with Bouting's other assistant, Christopher Bailey.

Louise turned her attention to Tom Schoonover and the other resident scientists, as well as the able young crew members from the university. They were busy talking of other things and laughing it up with Marty's jovial wife, Steffi. For a moment, Louise felt a pang of loneliness, wishing that her husband had come on the trip.

Tom blessedly leaned over and said, "C'mon, Louise, stop being shy and join our conversation. We want to know the inside skinny on this. Do cameramen *never* trip up when they're walking backward for miles during these shoots, or is it only grips?" He laughed. "We've decided that if so, they must constitute a different subspecies."

12

Louise, Marty, and Steffi were conducting their postmortem in the orchid garden over drinks. After forty-eight hours on Kauai, Louise decided that half of the island's income from tourism came from drinks with umbrellas in them.

"Don't worry, Marty," she told her producer, "we have plenty of B roll, with fabulous vistas—giant banyans, huge, wormlike cacti crawling up walls, plenty of shots of blooming plumeria and pandanus . . ."

"How is B roll gonna help us integrate those three segments?" grumped her producer and took a big gulp of his mai tai.

"It probably isn't," Louise admitted. "I think we should take the Bouting Horticulture people's interview tape and shelve it. Then we schedule an early summer trip to Pennsylvania and do it right. Maybe the Kauai interview can be used, but I doubt it. We'll start afresh and do a whole program there, including all those great research gardens Bruce Bouting likes to talk about. That business is well worth a special trip. We both know we'd have done it before, except that Bouting has been so publicity shy."

"You're probably right," said Marty. "Then his insisting on us taping that interview with Anne and Christopher was just an exercise in willpower; me against that big prick who thinks he can con everybody." His face was red with anger.

Steffi reached out her hand and grabbed Marty's. "Honey, blood pressure. Don't ruin our trip tomorrow by getting all upset."

Louise looked inquiringly at Steffi. "To the Big Island, as we'd planned?"

"No," said Steffi, shifting a little in her chair. "Louise, we decided to go off by ourselves to Princeville Resort. It's supposed to have a great beach, where we can just cuddle, and if we feel really ambitious, go into the surf at Hanalei. I'm sorry if I didn't warn you we were changing our plans."

"That's no problem, Steffi. I think it's great you're going off by yourselves." And great, thought Louise, that Steffi was looking lovelier each day she was in Kauai.

She pushed back in her chair. "Speaking of swimming, I need to take a dip in the lagoon before sunset." She grinned at the pair—Marty had calmed down as soon as Steffi took his hand and they were still holding hands. "Will I see you there on the edge of the terrace, when the big orb meets the horizon in a blaze of bright green?"

Marty gave his wife a meaningful look. "At six-thirty or so? Maybe not. Give us another half-hour. We'll be down by seven and then we can skip out for a change and have dinner away from this hotel."

Louise sauntered off, happy that things were working out for the couple on this trip. The shoot today with the three prima donnas had been almost everything they wanted. And the Corbins' marriage, it seemed, might be getting back on an even keel.

Amidst a cluster of other guests, she strode down the hall and made a quick calculation as she went. It was five here and ten o'clock in Washington, D.C. She should have called her husband before this, but she'd been too preoccupied. Bill would be happy to hear that all was well on the visit to Kauai, especially since she'd expressed misgivings about having to spend five days with John Batchelder. She pulled out her cell phone and speed dialed her home number.

Bill didn't answer; a cavernous voice gave her her options. Louise was disappointed not to be able to talk to him, but he'd warned her he would be busy at work. She sat down on a large stone bench near the elevators and listened for the beep. She said, "Bill, I'm sorry I missed you. I just wanted you to know everything is great here. The shoot went better than we ever thought it would. Oh, granted that there were a couple of glitches that raised Marty's blood pressure a few points, but nothing serious. John and I are getting along just fine. After all, how can you wrangle with your colleague when you're in a place like this? As for Marty and Steffi, they're having a great time, if you know what I mean . . ."

She looked up and her face reddened as she saw a couple smiling down on her. They were waiting for the elevator and drinking in every word, though she wasn't talking in a loud voice. She gave them a frosty look and raised her chin a little. Into the phone she whispered, "Talk to you soon, dear," then snapped it shut.

13

Louise dressed casually for dinner in a light blue cotton blouse and tan skirt and her waterproof sandals. They were suitable for a predinner walk she intended to take on the beach. If she followed the path toward Shipwreck Rock, she'd get a better view of the setting sun. In fact, she would've liked to climb the rock, as John had done, but not today. The light was fading fast and though not particularly afraid of heights, she'd prefer not to be up there after sunset.

As she approached the rock, she saw a small sign attached to a bush. It read, SHIPWRECK ROCK PATH TEMPORARILY CLOSED. She changed directions and walked straight out onto the beach and waited with a few others for the fiery planet's moment of glory.

A few minutes later, the golden globe had disappeared. Like spectators at the conclusion of an Oberammergau passion play, people stood in a group and respectfully critiqued the performance:

"Couldn't see the green streak," said one. "I was hoping there'd be a green streak."

"It's because of that mist on the horizon," said the same bronzed surfer who had been there two nights ago. To Louise, the man seemed like an oracle, a rather chatty oracle at that, who made predictions on weather and anything else that might be going on in Kauai. "Mist and clouds ruin the effect. I'm sure we'll have better luck tomorrow night—I've scoped out the weather pattern and it's good. So, same time, same place." He cheerfully bade them good-bye and disappeared down the beach. Before the others walked off into the gloom, they said good night to Louise, who was beginning to feel a camaraderie with them.

To kill a few minutes before meeting the Corbins and John, Louise found a small rock outcropping and sat on it. She stared aimlessly out to sea and watched the light fade. Her gaze was drawn upward to the top of Shipwreck Rock. If she had binoculars, she might have been able to figure out why the path was closed.

Her interest piqued, she walked closer to the base of the rock. Erosion had cut into the bottom portion, but the base shelf still extended out a short distance beyond the top of the rock. This meant that the young swimmers who used the precipice like a high diving board must have to leap out in an arc to avoid this shelf and land safely in deep seawater. Dangerous, she thought.

Following the curve of the beach, Louise walked toward the rock face, not bothered when an occasional wave washed over her feet, but vigilant lest a bigger wave come in and knock her down. Distracted in this way, she didn't realize how close she was to the big rock until she looked up and there it was, immediately in front of her.

Through the dimness, she could see what looked like a form on the stone shelf at the base of the cliff. Her heartbeat sped up until she realized that she must have come upon another monk seal. Sighing with relief, she realized she'd have to report its presence to hotel security so they could set up a privacy area for the animal while it took its nap.

But something wasn't quite as it seemed. A few steps more and she realized her mistake. This was not a monk seal, for the silhouette was irregular, not smooth and humplike. Though her heart was speeding again, she tried to stay calm as she plodded onward across the sand. Soon she could see that it was a person crumpled on the shelf.

She pulled in a terrified gasp as she recognized Matthew Flynn's distinctive new explorer's hat lying a few feet from the prostrate form. Her mind began to race. All she could think of was that Flynn had tumbled off the top of the cliff and needed CPR. She made a shortcut through the shallow water and nearly fell down in the strong surf. Regaining her balance, she determinedly slogged through the waves until she reached the shelf and clambered up it.

She ran to where the scientist lay faceup on the protruding rim of the stone ledge, his eyes open. Some blood appeared to be trickling from the back of his head. Kneeling down, she gently pressed his wrist and felt no pulse. Hurriedly, she pulled her cell phone from her purse and dialed 911.

"Hurry," she muttered, until seconds later a voice came on the line and she reported the incident. "I'm going to try to help him," she told the operator.

"Do you know CPR?"

"I know the basics. I'll do what I can."

Louise looked down and realized how close he lay to the edge of the rock. Beyond the edge was deep ocean water. A sense of vertigo overcame her, but she steeled herself. There was no time for panic: she had work to do.

Grabbing at Flynn's shirt and arm, she pulled him a little farther from the dangerous edge, then straddled him. His blank eyes stared up at her. *The man is gone*, said a voice in her head. Stifling this thought, she began her work, using a method she'd recently heard about that called for pressing the center of the chest one hundred times per minute. "Help me," she whispered, as she rocked back and forth and counted. It didn't take long for fatigue to overcome her; there was nothing she would have liked to do better than to lie down beside the prostrate man and rest. But she could hear people in the distance. They would have machinery to bring back a pulse. She didn't dare stop.

". . . fifteen, sixteen, seventeen, eighteen, nineteen . . ." She avoided looking at Flynn or the roiling ocean below her and concentrated on her counting, hoping her timing was correct so that she could save the man's life.

So intent was she on her task that when the rock dropped from above, it took her a moment to comprehend its meaning. It struck the scientist's shoulder and ricocheted onto her right hand. "Ow!" she cried, holding her stinging hand with the left one. "What's happening?"

The slab of rock, a foot long and only a few inches thick, would have struck her head, she realized, had she not at that moment been squatting back before leaning forward to apply pressure to the victim's chest. She carefully lifted it off the prostrate scientist and set it aside.

With an arm out to shield her face, Louise looked up, but could see nothing but navy blue sky. Had the rock just tumbled down, or had someone thrown it?

Now rescuers were near and lights began to play around her on the rock. A whining siren sounded close, so an ambulance would soon be at hand. Though her hand was badly scraped, she continued her CPR efforts. But in her heart she knew that Flynn was dead.

She continued pumping Matthew Flynn's chest until one of the EMTs said, "It's all right now, ma'am—you can stop," and gently helped her stand up. She watched as two men lifted Flynn off the ground to put him onto a stretcher. To her horror, his unsupported head lolled unnaturally to one side. She could see the deep, gouged-out wound at the base of his skull.

"Oh my God," she whispered, and put a hand over her mouth. She didn't believe a fall from a cliff could nearly tear a man's head off. After reaching this certainty, her mind went numb. An emergency worker quietly led her off the rock and to safety.

14

The acting coroner, Dr. Henry Bartky, looked soberly over the dead body at Kauai County Police Chief Randy Hau. Hau was dark haired and muscular, with a broad, impassive face that showed no fatigue. This was a good thing, since it was two in the morning and the young chief, only forty to Bartky's sixty-five, had spent hours that evening questioning witnesses.

"Look, friend," said the coroner, "as you might already have guessed, your Dr. Flynn's injuries are not consistent with a fall from that cliff. Sure, you'd think his skull fracture could be due to the fall, but no, I say it was from a deliberate blow."

"Are you sure?"

"I'm pretty sure," said Dr. Bartky. "Someone may have wanted it to look like an accident, but made a couple of errors. I surmise that after the victim was knocked unconscious, the killer bent his head forward, which gave the person access to the foramen magnum . . . right there." Bartky pointed to the base of the corpse's skull.

"And the foramen magnum is what?" asked the police chief.

"It's the large opening at the base of the skull through which the spinal cord passes to the cranial cavity." He shot a canny look at the policeman. "Actually, our opening is farther underneath the head than in the great apes"—he cupped his hand near the very base of the corpse's skull—"which means to hold our heads up we don't need the huge neck muscles that they do."

"So, what about this opening?"

"The murderer was not ignorant of anatomy—he reached in with some sharp tool and gouged out the brain stem. It probably caused a quick death if the blow hadn't already killed him."

"So the perp wanted to be darned sure he didn't survive."

"No question of it," said Dr. Bartky. "Probably the killer intended the body to land in the deep water with all those sharp, submerged rocks, thus providing an explanation for the neck wound. But instead it landed on the very edge of that shelf. In a sense, I'd say what you have here is a murder three times over. When it's daylight, I'll venture you find the man's blood at the top of the cliff. He was bashed, gouged, then shoved off into space."

Hau silently mouthed a word, which the coroner thought was probably "darn," for the police chief was a mild-mannered man. Bartky knew Hau must be frustrated—he was scheduled to go on a vacation during his children's spring break from school. A murder was not on his schedule.

"This might turn out to be simple to solve," said the policeman.

"How so?"

"Flynn's sidekick, a Mr. George Wyant, could

have done it. We couldn't locate him last night; he's temporarily disappeared. That's a little suspicious, you have to admit." He heaved a big sigh. "Then there's always my erstwhile buddy, Bobby Rankin—maybe you know him. He teaches surfing and lives on the beach or in his car. He showed up right after we got out there last night. Bobby's expert at gutting fish, turtles, frogs—ever seen him do it? Destroying a human being's brain stem would pose no problem for him. But I've grilled him. He didn't know the man and has no motive, even if he does have the know-how."

The chief shot a gloomy look at Bartky. "So if it's not one of those two, that leaves all the people at Kauai-by-the-Sea. Do you realize how many are holed up at that hotel?"

"Whatever number it is, consider yourself lucky that the crowd's been off a little this week. Still, your crime squad's gonna have a lot of work. I hear the dead man was a scientist."

"A botanist, to be exact. Dr. Matthew P. Flynn. There was this elite conference for twelve of 'em this past Wednesday through today. Or rather, eight out-of-town scientists and four of their assistants, plus some of our local scientists. I'm told Dr. Flynn is well known for his work in the Amazon jungle."

"Is that so?" said Bartky, who was taking off his latex gloves and washing his hands.

"Why do you say that?"

"That might account for why the man appeared to be high on something."

"Drugs. Are you sure he didn't just get dizzy and fall off and hit some crazy-shaped rocks when he landed?"

The doctor peered over his half-glasses at the

young police chief, who was fairly new in Kauai. Although he was said to be bright, he was not experienced in murder, which didn't happen much on the island. "I'd be inclined to think that except for these extraordinary injuries. Also, you can't discount the woman's story. What's her name?"

"Mrs. Louise Eldridge."

"Yeah. She told you how that rock tumbled off, right on top of the prostrate Dr. Flynn's shoulder. What happened is that it smashed his rotator cuff, so the thing could have killed her if she hadn't been in the sitting-up position at that moment."

"So, bashed, gouged, and shoved into space, huh?" said the chief. "Pretty disgusting. Then the perp tried to kill Mrs. Eldridge because she might have seen them together. Also, the murderer rightly figured she saw the 'closed' sign on the path up to the cliff. The sign was nowhere in sight less than an hour later when we came on the scene. Nor was there a sign on the other path up the rock. That indicates that someone got Flynn up there and closed the entries to other visitors. This Eldridge woman would have figured that out, so she had to be taken out."

Dr. Bartky said, "News of the murder of a visitor isn't going to go over well with the locals."

Randy Hau slowly nodded. "Especially not with the folks who run this hotel. How about if we keep a lid on the fact that it's murder for a day or two, until hopefully we find the perp?"

"Fine with me," said the coroner. He thoughtfully scratched his beard. "One other thing before you go. I take it that Mrs. Eldridge knew this Dr. Flynn."

"She wasn't well acquainted," said Randy Hau.

"I guess you'd say she was *barely* acquainted with the deceased. She met him two days ago."

Dr. Bartky pointed to Matthew Flynn's effects. "Check out that note." It was a small, white sealed envelope that had been placed in a plastic bag. "It's got Louise Eldridge's name on the front of it."

"That's a good one. One of the last things Matthew Flynn does before he dies is write a stranger a note." He carefully lifted it off the pile of effects, which also included Flynn's wallet, threadbare red bandanna, pocket knife, nearly empty jar of Carmex, waterproof container with a small amount of marijuana, rolling papers, change, and a small magnifying glass. "We'll just keep this for a while, fingerprint it, and tell her later."

15

"**B**ill, it's me." She sat on the edge of the bed and pressed the cell phone to her left ear with her left hand. Her right hand, with its modest square bandage, lay unused in her lap.

"Hi, honey," said her husband in a matter-of-fact tone. She could tell instantly that she'd interrupted something. A soft tapping noise came through the phone. He said, "Great to hear from you. Uh, how's it going?"

"Bill, I wish you were here."

"So do I," said Bill. "I've really missed you. But I'll see you Tuesday morning, won't I? I'm gonna be at Dulles promptly at five-twenty. That's why I'm sitting home hurrying to get some work out of the way."

Louise could hear the continued click of computer keys. Her husband had the phone supported by his shoulder and must still be finishing an idea. She had interrupted something serious.

"The thing is, Bill, I don't think I'll be there Tuesday morning. Something's happened." She looked down at her rather insignificant bandage, as if to verify this truth. Something *had* happened and her husband wasn't going to welcome the news.

"Huh," said Bill. "What is it? Are you staying longer on the Big Island?" Click, click, click went the keys.

"Can't you stop what you're doing? Something terrible has happened. I have to make it fast; I'm already late for a meeting with the police downstairs."

The clicking noise abruptly stopped. "The police? What's happened?"

"Remember I told you about our three scientists, the ones appearing on our show?"

"I don't remember their names, but you described them well enough. The expansive millionaire nursery owner. The cute, kooky ethnobotanist. The righteous environmentalist. Has something happened to one of them?"

"Yes. To Matthew Flynn. The ethnobotanist. He's dead." Her voice broke.

"Don't tell me, let me guess. Someone threw him off a cliff up there in the Na Pali coast."

"No, it happened right here at the hotel. They have a little cliff out on the beach. It's a leftover piece of lava shelf. Kids dive off it into the ocean."

"Well, then, why didn't he think to dive, if someone shoved him? Maybe he would have lived."

She was getting angry at her beloved husband. "Because the back of his neck was gashed open by somebody up there on the cliff."

"How could you know that for sure, Louise? Let's not be overdramatic and make every accident into a crime."

Hurt by this remark, Louise felt tears coming to

her eyes. Her voice choked up. "I know because I saw it when the medics picked him up and put him on the stretcher. His head seemed barely attached to his body."

Bill slowly said, "Louise, wait a minute. What are you saying . . ."

"I tried CPR. But I couldn't save him."

Silence at her husband's end of the phone. "I am so sorry, dear. Forgive me. You poor thing. Quite frankly, I was so engrossed here writing this paper that I . . . I didn't mean to be unkind. What a terrible ordeal for you to go through. So it wasn't the fall that killed him?"

With an effort, she held back her tears and dabbed at her eyes with a tissue. "That's what I was trying to tell you. It was an awful wound. And there are other things that were odd. For one thing, there was the sign on the path."

"A sign?"

"I saw a 'path closed' sign that kept me and everyone else from going up that cliff last night. After I found Matthew Flynn, the police and I walked back and there was no sign around. So that might mean that a murderer lured him up on the cliff . . ."

"Yes?"

". . . And then put up the sign, hurried back up and killed him. Or something like that. Then there's the rock that fell down on him when I was giving him CPR."

"*Louise.*"

"It landed on him, not me," she said. Her voice choked again.

"Was this person trying to kill you, too?"

"I'm beginning to think so. I'd been working on

Flynn for about ten minutes when this rock came down. I happened to be sitting back on my haunches at that second or it would have—well, at least hurt me a lot. Bill, it must have weighed fifteen pounds."

Silence on the other end of the phone. "My God," said her husband slowly. "But why would someone want to kill *you?*"

"Police Chief Hau isn't sure. Maybe the killer thought I saw him. And it might have been treated as an accident if I hadn't come along and seen that sign, which was later removed. So if they'd found me dead, too, they might just think that Dr. Flynn and I . . . well, I don't know what people would have thought."

"Me neither, Louise. I'd better come over there."

"Why don't we wait and see if the police can find out what's behind this. The scientists and the Corbins and John and I might have to stay on an extra day or so while they investigate. Needless to say, they questioned me a lot last night. We sat there in this big, empty conference room going over the details time after time. I need to get off the phone because they want to meet with us again at ten. It's after ten already, but I couldn't seem to get going this morning."

"Louise, hold on." From the rustling sounds, she guessed Bill was looking for the hand computer he carried in his suit jacket. While he did this, she went to the closet and retrieved tan capri pants and a sleeveless white blouse to wear.

Bill came back on the phone. "I'm looking at my schedule," he said. "This comes at a hectic time, which, you know, is the reason I didn't come to Hawaii with you in the first place. I have a big strategy meeting first thing Monday morning. Maybe by Monday night you'll know if you can fly home Tuesday. If that doesn't happen, all bets are off and I'll fly over and get you."

"Another thing, Bill . . ." She was going to tell him about the injury to her hand, which had required a brief trip to the hotel's in-house medical clinic. Though located in a corner basement room of the hotel, it was well equipped with a staff nurse, an X-ray machine, and a jovial, gray-haired doctor. He had quickly slapped a bandage on her, told her to keep it dry, and sent her on her way.

As if her husband were reading her mind, he said, "Are you really all right? You didn't get hurt last night, did you?"

"I have abrasions on one hand is all. Otherwise, I'm okay."

He said, "Good. Take a sleeping pill if you're having nightmares about that scene on the beach. It isn't fun dealing with dead bodies, even if you didn't know the guy very well."

"I'll do that. I'll admit I didn't sleep well. Waking or sleeping, I still see those lifeless eyes. Bill, I didn't realize how badly he was hurt until the emergency crew turned their lights on him, or I might not have tried to save him."

"Aw, Louise," commiserated her husband, "I wish you hadn't had to go through that. Tell me, what kind of man was he, this Dr. Matthew Flynn?"

"What kind of man? I'm not sure. He was a loose cannon in the eyes of some in the scientific community. But he was likable and he believed in the work he did down there in the Amazon; in fact, he seemed to be obsessed with the desire to catalog all the plants in that region before many of them became extinct. He did discover at least one plant that turned out to be valuable to medicine, I hear, but flunked out on a lot of others. He seemed to like to shock people—he had to tell us all about his and his sidekick's use of hallucinogens in the jungle, that sort of thing."

"That's part of what they do," said Bill. "There's a book called *The River*, all about Dr. Richard Schultes, the dignified Harvard prof who was the best known of that bunch. He plunged into the study of those drugs and was one of the first to learn of the effects of the peyote mushroom, only by sampling it himself. Scientists like him have made incredibly valuable discoveries among those jungle plants."

"Yes, we heard all about that," she said wearily. "I think Flynn's assistant, George Wyant, still uses mushrooms, if you know what I mean."

"A drug user, eh? I guess I'm not surprised. But let's get back to you, Louise. You sound tired. And no wonder—trying to resuscitate that poor Flynn must have really taken it out of you. You were very brave to try to save him."

"Anyone would have done what I did."

"I wonder if that's true. But now, looking forward, Louise, the usual caveats apply."

She laughed. "They do?"

"Yes, darling."

"You sound like Soames again." When Bill fell into his bossy mode, she reminded him he was acting like the difficult husband in *The Forsyte Saga* and it usually brought him out of it. "You're telling me the conditions under which I may remain in Hawaii."

"Not exactly. What husband would dare tell his wife what to do?"

She laughed weakly.

"Look, my sweet," continued Bill, "I don't want

to sound officious. I love you and I want you to come home in one piece. You know this is for your own good. You've lived through a terrible summer; you don't need more of the same or you'll have to go somewhere for a rest cure. Ironically, I thought it would be restful for you to go to Hawaii."

"So did I. It has been relaxing, up until now."

"All I'm saying, darling, is try to let the cops there do the investigating and stay out of it."

"I'll try my best."

"Now give me the names of the other people involved. I'll do background checks on them."

With his vast network of contacts in government, especially in his role as an undercover CIA agent with State Department cover, Bill could usually pull in favors.

"But I thought you said I was to stay out of it."

"Louise, I know you. It'll be impossible for you not to do some looking around. I don't want you messing with people who might be dangerous. And obviously, at least one of them is dangerous. The least I can do is help you to know who you're up against."

She smiled, as she quickly donned her clothes. Her husband knew her better than she knew herself.

16

Louise stepped out of the elevator into the wide marble-and-carpet hall and walked in the opposite direction from the conference room where she was supposed to be twenty minutes ago. She was accustomed to being on time for appointments and it made her nervous to be late, but she desperately needed a cup of coffee from the dining room to take to the police briefing.

Immediately, she realized things had changed in the hotel. It was as if everyone knew what happened last night on Shipwreck Rock. Otherwise, why were the guests, who only yesterday smiled amiably at one another, now shooting suspicious glances at her?

A blond woman in a lime-colored suit and high-heeled lime green wedgies made her way down the hall a few paces ahead of Louise. She was schmoozing noisily with each guest she encountered, talking about the superb weather and the upcoming evening's entertainment. Apparently, thought Louise, she felt obliged to resell Kauai-by-the-Sea to visitors, wordlessly begging them not to check out and to disregard the fact that a man may have been murdered a stone's throw away.

Louise tried to avoid the woman by hurrying ahead of her to the end of the hall, then ducking quickly into the greenery that surrounded a huge brass parrot cage. The parrot, resplendently blue and yellow, with a distinguished feather tuft on his forehead, looked down at her for a long moment. Then he let her have it: "Bad baby . . . bad baby . . ."

She put her index finger to her lips. "Shhh!" she told him.

"*Bad baby!*" he screeched, even louder.

It attracted the eye of not only the woman in the lime green suit, but several guests as well. They turned and stared at her, causing her face to flame with embarrassment.

Louise rose slowly out of the plants like Venus out of the sea.

The woman came up to her and with a world-weary smile said, "That's what you get, dear, for trying to evade me. I was just trying to cover all the guests, you know, and you're one of the guests."

Distracted by the woman's enormous lime green hanging earrings, Louise said the first thing that popped into her head, "I don't need positive reinforcement, because I'd never give up the lagoon." Then she marched off with as much dignity as remained, which wasn't much.

Once out of the woman's range, Louise let out a deep, shuddering sigh and picked up speed. Bad enough to have a bird chastise her, but a bird and a bureaucrat were too much.

The reaction of the hotel guests was puzzling, she reflected. How did word get around so fast, even in this small environment? Kauai had a population of only sixty thousand and the hotel a complement of probably four or five hundred guests. Suddenly she thought of an answer. The "oracle" could have spread the news of Matthew Flynn's death. Not only his death, she realized, but his *violent* death. For though she'd barely registered it at the time, the swarthy man with the surfboard who inhabited the beach at sunset had turned up right after the police arrived.

The beach oracle naturally would have been attracted to Shipwreck Rock, what with all the commotion and sirens. The response team was bent on lifesaving at first, not securing the scene. The barefoot man would have had no trouble getting a close look at the fallen man. The floodlights had shone on the pathetic tableau, affording him a detailed view of Flynn's broken body and the blood leaking out of the back of his injured head.

It would have made complete sense for the garrulous surfer to conclude that Matthew Flynn was murdered. And if he thought this, he undoubtedly told everyone he saw and phoned the rest.

As Louise hustled down the steps toward the dining room, she realized what a shock this messy incident was for the hotel. Although Shipwreck Rock was not on Kauai-by-the-Sea's property, it was immediately adjacent; it was definitely "guilt-by-association," she thought grimly. She guessed the woman in the lime suit was in the public relations department and her one-on-ones with guests were part of damage control. In her current punchy condition, Louise wasn't sure she was guessing right about any of this, for her head felt woozy and her mind was not functioning logically. On the other hand, her visual sense seemed laser sharp. She found herself noting irrelevant details such as the parrot's yellow head tuft, the fact that the woman's wedgies had been brand new, and, from the look of them, hellishly expensive.

Of one thing she was sure: No matter how the hotel tried to soft-pedal the tragedy, it could not deny the fact that the deceased, Matthew Flynn, had been a registered guest.

Louise marched through the elegantly chandeliered room, hoping to catch the eye of a helpful waiter. She slowed up when she heard someone call to her.

"Mrs. Eldridge, hold up there." She turned. It was Police Chief Randy Hau. "G'morning," he said, in a neutral voice. "I was trying to catch up with you." He raised his wrist and looked pointedly at his watch. "We've already gathered the rest of the people together for our meeting."

"I'm so sorry I'm late," she said. "But I need—"

He interrupted, smiling. "Coffee? Food? I'm having breakfast brought in to our meeting room. Will that be good enough?"

"More than enough."

"Well," said Chief Hau as they walked back up the steps and down the long corridor to the conference room, "I heard something about you this morning."

"Oh?"

"Yes, that you're somewhat of an amateur detective back where you come from."

"You've been checking me out with the Fairfax County Sheriff's Office."

"Yes, ma'am. One of your colleagues also mentioned it. You know it's part of my job, checking everybody out. I talked to a Detective Mike Geraghty. He had good things to say about you." No smile went with this compliment. The chief was not an emotive type of man.

Louise had difficulty, after four days in the lush tropics, mentally conveying herself back to her woodsy northern Virginia home in Sylvan Valley. It was a place where she was not only known for hosting a TV garden show, but also for becoming embroiled in murder. She didn't need her lurid history known by people in this resort. But now the police chief knew.

"Detective Geraghty probably exaggerated," she said crisply.

They'd arrived at the meeting room. Hau opened one of two big double doors, which were made of koa wood carved with a flower motif. Stepping aside so she could go first, he said, "Please take a seat with the others. The food should be along any minute."

As she entered, twenty-one solemn people turned their heads and gazed at her. It was clear that they had all been affected by a colleague's violent death, but was she being paranoid in thinking they were looking at her too closely?

Seven visiting botanists from the conference were there—Matthew Flynn had made the eighth. Because Louise had not bothered to tune in on the botanic conference sessions, the only ones who were familiar were Charles Reuter and Bruce Bouting, though she recognized a third, Ralph Pinsky. Pinsky gazed at her through unblinking, large gray eyes. It was the first time she'd looked into his long, colorless face. Apparently, he was so sure of himself that he had no qualms about staring. Unsettled, she turned her attention to the others.

As usual, people sat in clusters, with the "planets" surrounded by their "moons." Christopher Bailey and Anne Lansing huddled dutifully on either side of Dr. Bouting and as usual the scientist's head was bent in busy, quiet consultation with the two of them. Nate Bernstein sat attentively on one side of his boss, Dr. Reuter. Ralph Pinsky was on the other.

Making a group all of their own were Marty, encircled by Steffi and John and the young TV crew headed by Joel Greene. Marty waved her over.

Tom Schoonover also beckoned, as if saying, "Come sit with us." Clustered around him were his NTBG colleagues, Tim, Sam, and Henry.

Unsure of where to perch, she peered into the far corner of the room and made up her mind.

The dead scientist's associate, George Wyant, blond hair disheveled, beard unshaven, and clothes rumpled and soiled looking, was holding up a back corner by himself. Slumped far down in a chair, he stared into space with eyes that seemed as dead as Matthew Flynn's. The young man wasn't high, she was relieved to see. In fact he was very low: sober, straight, and low. He saw her and tilted his head a degree or two to indicate that he'd like her to join him. She nodded back.

But first, she raised her nose and sniffed. The aroma of good coffee was filling the air and there was the rattle of dishes. Breakfast had arrived and was set on a table against the wall. Louise made a beeline to the buffet for her own drug of choice, caffeine. She noticed the enticing odors had caused Wyant to rise from his chair and shuffle over to the coffee urn like a wounded animal heading for an oasis.

17

"Hello, Mr. Wyant," she said, as she settled in a chair beside him.

"*Hey*," he replied. Louise realized *hey* was George Wyant's version of *aloha*.

"I'm so sorry about Matthew Flynn, Mr. Wyant."

He turned and looked at her. "I'm too young for 'Mr. Wyant.' Call me George and I'll call you Louise. Yeah, I'm sorry about Matt, too. We were good friends." He took a sip from the cup balanced on his lap. He had forgone food, making Louise feel a little sheepish, for in addition to coffee, she'd piled up fruits, miniature rolls, and cereal on her tray. She offered him some of the food, but he refused.

Sitting next to him gave her a close-up of his remarkably modish spike hairdo. When meeting him before, she'd thought the blond streaks might be dyed; now she could see they were the product of a bleaching tropical sun. His eyebrows, too, she noticed, were blanched almost white. With an effort she turned her eyes away, popped a small quiche into her mouth, and tried to pay attention to what he was saying.

"This is so bloody awful that I can hardly believe it," he said as he slowly and unsteadily replaced the cup on the saucer. He looked at Louise with watery eyes. "They told me you applied CPR and tried to save him. For that I have to thank you with all my heart."

"I dashed over when I saw him on that rock shelf, but I couldn't feel his pulse. He had none. I think he was dead when I got there."

Wyant stared into space. "At least you tried. Tried to save the life of a decent man."

She realized George Wyant had been nowhere around last night, not even during the couple of hours she'd spent being questioned by police after they removed the body and returned to the hotel. In fact, the authorities had mentioned his absence.

She swallowed a bite of miniature sweet roll. "Um, no one could reach you last night."

He answered unabashedly. "I told the cops where I was. I've got a girl I see when I'm here." A faint smile crossed his troubled face. "Needless to say, I don't keep my cell phone turned on when I'm at her house—she lives up in Kapaa. So I didn't get the word until I took my messages early this morning. Then I hightailed it back to the hotel. I've spent more than an hour being interviewed by Chief Hau." He nodded in the direction of the police chief, who was "doing the room," chatting briefly with a person, then moving on to the next one. He had nearly completed this task and Louise realized in another few minutes he would be over to the corner that she and George Wyant occupied.

"Matt had his own plans for the evening," continued Wyant, spreading his hands out. She saw that he wore a handsome, though worn, gold watch on his tanned wrist. "Let's face it, we didn't live in each other's pocket. He could've cared less where I went and vice versa. Only now I wish he'd told me who he had that rendezvous with."

"Rendezvous?"

"Yeah, that's what he called it, a 'little secret rendezvous.' After that, he was going to grab a bite at Brennecke's and hit the sack."

"A rendezvous on Shipwreck Rock. Was he familiar with that place? Are you?"

He smiled. "Funny. You ask the same questions the cops asked me. Am I familiar with that old lava shelf? Not really. I haven't been up there in years and I doubt Matt had gone up because there's nothing much there. It's not outstanding geologically or horticulturally. Tourists like to climb up there for the view and local kids use it as a diving board, if they're gutsy enough or stoned, that is. It makes for a kind of a high dive into the ocean."

"More coffee?" she asked him. When he nodded, she went and refilled their cups. On her return, she slid down in her chair, took up her tray again, and quietly said, "Who would kill Dr. Flynn?"

For an instant, his pale eyes blazed, but then he tried to cover up his anger. "Any number of people, Louise." He gestured with his hand toward the others in the room. "Any number of people sitting right here hated his guts. Some are jealous, some are resentful because he has a penchant for finding new plants before they catch someone else's eye. You've heard 'em ridiculing him as if he's a freak, or *was* a freak, rather. But he was no freak—he was right about what he was doing, a true believer."

The hand flapped again. "Oh, maybe we were a little wild at times, but that's part of the deal when you're spending a third of each year in a jungle with a bunch of primitives, trying to learn new languages, dealing with egocentric shamans who have all the"—he touched his temple, covered with tousled blond hair—"smarts about those tropical plants but aren't necessarily inclined to tell you their secrets. Sweating your fool head off, dirty, full of bites from bugs, some of which are hugely dangerous. Coming down for the umpteenth time with malaria—Matt, not me; I never contracted it. It isn't a life for normal people, so I guess you'd have to say that Matt and I aren't normal."

He looked down and Louise saw that his eyes were overflowing with tears. "Shit," he whispered, "I'm having a terrible time believing he's dead. I don't know what I'm going to do without him."

Her heart went out to the young man. She gently clasped his arm with her good left hand. It was the best she could do, for Police Chief Hau, noting the two of them sharing an emotional moment, stopped short on his way over to them. Instead, he gave them a wave, as if to indicate he'd talk to them later, then called the informal meeting to order.

Hau first introduced his second-in-command, Lieutenant Robert Payne, who was taller and heavier than his chief and who hovered a few feet behind him. "Ladies and gentlemen, thank you for coming," he said. "You have all heard of Dr. Matthew Flynn's death and I know you're in shock, because the violent death of a fellow human being, especially one of your colleagues, is hard to accept. I want to give you an update. As you know, his body was discovered last evening at about seven o'clock on the ledge underneath Shipwreck Rock. It was discovered by Mrs. Louise Eldridge here"—he nodded respectfully in Louise's direction and a few people turned around to look—"who, incidentally, tried to save his life by administering CPR. He was dead on arrival, however, at Wilcox Memorial Hospital in Lihue. The body is undergoing an autopsy; the exact cause of death is not yet fully determined. It's possible he received his injuries from a simple fall from Shipwreck Rock."

Charles Reuter spoke up. He said, "I think that's crap, Mister Police Chief. That isn't the word that's going around the hotel and beach. The word is that the man was murdered, the back of his head practically ripped off. That's what every guest in this hotel has heard."

A little murmur went through the small group. Hau raised his hand like a teacher wishing to restore order in gym class. "Now, folks, that much is not true. Dr. Flynn's head was *not* ripped off. However, he did suffer severe injuries to the head." Hau stood his full five feet ten inches and spoke in a quiet voice designed to encourage equanimity in his audience. "The autopsy will determine whether there was foul play involved. That's why we need your cooperation."

Nate Bernstein said, "Why are the staffers from the NTBG here and the TV crew from the shoot? You couldn't be operating on the theory that this was 'just an accident' if you've rounded up all these people to sit in on this meeting."

Chief Hau said, "We needed to include everybody who had recent contact with Matthew Flynn. It is no reflection on any one individual; it's just a matter of covering all the bases."

Tom Schoonover, angled back comfortably in

his chair, turned to Bernstein. "We at the National Tropical Botanical Garden will do everything we can to aid the investigation."

Bruce Bouting's voice boomed out, "As long as I can leave on schedule Monday afternoon with my staffers Chris and Anne, I'll be happy. In the meantime, what do you expect of us?"

The police chief said, "I'm not sure you can fulfill that schedule, Dr. Bouting. I told you last night and I repeat it—there may be a delay if we can't clear this matter up by Monday. We are asking those of you with direct contact with Dr. Flynn to be prepared to stay on an extra day or so to assist us in our investigation. Lieutenant Payne will let you know at the conclusion of this meeting who you are. We're hoping to wrap this thing up quickly, so today we will do some repeat questioning beyond what we did last night. Please be prepared for that. Do not think of it as a suspicious thing, but rather a procedural measure. You can continue with the closing session of your botanic conference as soon as I finish up my remarks, but please try to wrap it up by noon because we do have to interrogate some of you further."

The police chief looked soberly out at the little crowd. "You're not prisoners, ladies and gentlemen; you're free to go out of the hotel. You're also free to go on your planned trip to the Big Island tomorrow, though my officers, Sergeants William Yee and David Binder, will accompany you."

"I was scheduled to get out of here tomorrow night," said Dr. Charles Reuter. "I have something important coming up at the university. At the very least, I need to get out of here by Monday night."

Hau said, "We'll try our best." His gaze traveled around the other unhappy faces and he looked relieved when no one else voiced complaints. "Within twenty-four hours, or at least by tomorrow night, I'm hoping we'll have a better handle on this. You might be reassured to know that the entire special crime squad is working on Dr. Flynn's unfortunate death."

"Unfortunate?" echoed George Wyant, in a voice too faint for any but Louise to hear. "What a fuckin' euphemism *that* is."

18

Louise's WTBA-TV colleagues met her at the door as she was leaving the conference room. She hugged each one of them in turn, Marty, Steffi, John, all the while ignoring the curious glances of others leaving the room.

"How ya doin', Lou?" said Marty. "Hey, how's your hand?"

Before she could answer, he said, "In a minute we gotta talk and you can tell us then. Let's go to that orchid garden and get a drink."

Steffi Corbin slid her arm around Louise. Her brown eyes were full of concern. "We were worried about you, Louise. Could you sleep last night after that horrid experience?"

"Not very well," admitted Louise. "Maybe I'll go to the lagoon and take a nap—that is, after we go to the orchid garden."

John Batchelder had a secretive smile on his face. "Louise, people have heard how good you are at solving crimes."

She looked up at her handsome cohost. "And just how would they know? Did you tell them?"

"You don't mind, do you?" he asked eagerly. "Heck, I was kind of priming them, dropping the word here and there. I also told the police chief, just so he'd know. I thought you and I might do a little snooping."

Louise stared at him and tried to keep her temper.

"Well, couldn't we at least talk about it?"

She closed her eyes and swept her hand over her brow, as if in so doing she could wipe away her fatigue. "I'm sorry, John, I'm too tired to even think about that. Besides, Bill would hate it if I stuck my nose in this."

"Well, promise to think about it," he said, as he walked away and started talking to Christopher Bailey and Anne Lansing.

If only she could creep back to her room, put on her bathing suit, and hide on the beach in dark glasses. But Marty needed to talk. And just because they were in Hawaii, she couldn't forget that he was her producer and her boss. It wouldn't be a talk; it would be a bitch session. She supposed he had good reason to bitch—his newly taped program had been blown. Yet it seemed a petty matter to fuss about in the wake of a man's death.

"Louise, wait up." Tom Schoonover was hurrying over to intercept her before she left. The scientist's brow was furrowed with worry. "My dear lady, Chief Hau told me the whole story of last night. If Matthew Flynn had had life in him, I'm sure you would have saved it."

"Thanks, Tom. I guess we're all upset about this. I hope Chief Hau clears things up in a hurry."

Dr. Schoonover shook his gray curls. Louise noted that with each passing day that the untended hair grew, the man looked more like an out-of-work poet than a world-class botanist. "That's not necessarily going to be the case, not unless he runs into some good luck. People die all the time without someone establishing the cause. But the four of us are off now. We have a special visitor arriving at the gardens this afternoon—a professor who's doing a study of a species of Hawaiian fern."

Suddenly all was put in perspective. The visit of the Three Tenors and the other elite botanists and the *Gardening with Nature* taping were only transitory items on this man's busy calendar. The National Tropical Botanical Garden constantly hosted important visitors from all over the world; topnotch scientists must use that base as headquarters for all sorts of special research.

Tom Schoonover's hazel eyes looked straight into hers. "You take it easy, Louise. I can see you're a bit traumatized over your experience."

"It was hard to sleep. I ran everything over in my mind a thousand times."

"That's why I was surprised when John Batchelder told me that you and he might put your heads together and look into the matter of Matthew's death." He smiled and bent his head. "He told me of your pursuits in crime solving."

"John shouldn't have . . ." She looked disconsolately over at her colleague, busily conversing now with Bruce Bouting.

"I don't think you should get into this," said Schoonover. "It's a dangerous world, even in an amiable place like Kauai." He reached out and gently touched her bandage. "For instance, look at the way you've already been injured, in the name of trying to save another. You should be very careful."

Marty strolled up and hooked his arm in hers. "Excuse me, Tom. I need to whisk this lady away."

Schoonover said, "By the way, Henry Hilaeo and I are joining the group going to the Big Island tomorrow." A smile of proud ownership. "We Hawaiians like to keep track of the latest surface flow. This is the first chance I've had since I came back from the Marquesas."

"Then I'll see you tomorrow afternoon," Louise said, as Marty tugged on her arm.

The scientist put an index finger up, a teacher's habit, she suspected. "And don't forget—I've told the others—you need clothes that cover you, good walking shoes, a big bandanna or handkerchief, a generous bottle of water. Walking stick optional."

"Thanks," said Louise.

"Off we go, Lou," said Marty, hardly able to mask his restlessness. "See you later, Tom, but not tomorrow. Steffi and I are traveling to the north country."

Steffi and John fell into step with them and they walked the short distance to the orchid garden. They took what Louise had begun to think of as "their" table.

She glanced over the adjoining hall and saw her old friend, the blue-and-yellow feathered parrot. The parrot returned her gaze and she looked quickly down, afraid he'd recognize her and start to screech again.

With a gin and tonic in hand, Marty grinned evilly over at her. "You should have had a drink, too. It's eleven-thirty, not too early. Whatever you have there, we can drink a toast to the fact that we've just blown about fifty goddamned grand."

He raised his glass and she automatically raised her mineral water, although she hated specious toasts. Steffi good naturedly contributed a clink from her glass of white wine and John with his cocktail.

"Maybe Matthew Flynn could be edited out," proposed John. Louise didn't know what he'd ordered, but it was pink and reminded her of a Shirley Temple, which she and Bill used to order for their underage daughters.

She gave her cohost a quizzical look. "Mai tai?"

"Yeah," he said sheepishly. "A special one with raspberry juice. It's a little early for me, but I need it to put some steel in my spine."

Marty Corbin sat back and laughed. "Steel in your spine? Johnny boy, don't you mean 'lead in your pencil'?"

John Batchelder looked offended. "For Pete's sake, Marty, I'm talking about getting up enough nerve to do a little investigating. I'm *not* talking about getting laid—you know I'm engaged to be married."

Marty continued to chortle until Steffi reached over and gave him a companionable poke in the arm. "Cease and desist."

Louise looked at the Corbins, Steffi in bright hues, as usual, Marty looking more comfortable now in his Hawaiian shirt and shorts. The couple looked happy, though Louise always worried about the next dame that might come along and catch her producer's eye. Their bonhomie made her wish again that Bill was here.

"With all due respect to editors," she said, "I think it would take a genius to edit Matthew Flynn out of that tape. Let's consider ourselves lucky that we have some good footage of Tom Schoonover and Henry Hilaeo and the National Tropical Botanical Garden."

Marty leaned forward with his forearms resting on the glass-topped table. He nodded vigorously. "I am, I am, I am. And we now have a great connection with the formerly elusive Dr. Bruce Bouting, who in previous years wouldn't give us the time of day when we tried to get him to stand still for a program. Him and his privately held empire . . ." He looked at Louise, then at John. "You two can hustle up to Philadelphia and visit Bouting Horticulture ASAP."

"Or as soon as the flowers are in full bloom," amended Louise.

"Yeah, we'll get a great story there, get that Anne Lansing and that goofy-looking Christopher whatever-his-name-is in action." He exhaled heavily, leaned back, and swigged his drink. "That'll square it with the general manager. But I hate to think what will happen if I come home with a suntan and tell him we only got one lousy program out of this expensive trip. Yep, two programs are a much better outcome."

Louise stared at her friend the parrot again. "It seems kind of cold and heartless for us to be so worried about losing money. Haven't we talked about it enough?"

Steffi reached over and patted Louise's hand. "You're quite right. Marty's talking way too much. My dear Louise, you must be in shock. I can't imagine what it would be like, doing what you did. CPR. Why, I wouldn't even know how to do it!"

Louise said, "It didn't do him any good, unfortunately. But I did have some inkling as to how to do it—I'd just read about the recommended method in *The Times*. You locate the center of the chest and apply pressure with your palms one hundred times a minute."

Steffi said, "No breathing in the mouth?"

"No. And you're not supposed to let up on that pressure until someone comes along with mechanical equipment."

"That must have about killed you." Steffi's big eyes were wide with concern. Louise would have liked to tell her the whole story, of how the rock had fallen or been thrown and hit Matthew Flynn's shoulder. For how could she fail to notice the bandage on Louise's hand?

At that moment, Steffi asked, "And, dear, so what's up with your hand?"

"I scraped it on the rocks." It was the same slight revision of the truth that she'd told to a couple of other people who'd inquired.

"Isn't it awful to know that a man we just talked to is dead?" said Steffi. "And such an attractive man."

John Batchelder arched one of his well-shaped eyebrows. "A little on the loose side if you ask me."

"Oh, John," rebuked Steffi. "Thousands of people take drugs, if that's what you mean by loose. Anyway, it was his young pal who was high the other night, not Matthew Flynn." She sighed. "I enjoyed meeting them, because it reminded me of my carefree hippie days in the late sixties." Her languid gaze slid over to her husband, fifty-five, a bit jowly and with a decided paunch. Louise had to keep remembering this man was the object of Steffi's desire. "Remember, honey? Nobody knew or cared back then that drugs were so"—she wiggled the first two fingers of both her hands to indicate quotation marks—"'evil.' We just enjoyed them for what they were, a nice, mind-altering high."

"I think Matthew Flynn and George Wyant are— I mean, were—a product of their work environment," said Louise. "If we were down in those jungles, we might sample some drugs, too."

Steffi leaned toward her. "But Louise, having known Matthew Flynn just a little, doesn't it bother you at all that someone probably killed him? Don't you have any desire to investigate? I know you said you don't like to talk about that sort of thing, but—"

"I don't, Steffi, especially since the authorities haven't told us whether his death was an accident, or something else. The rest of you can speculate all you want, but I'm staying out of this."

John had finished his drink in record time; he beckoned the waiter to come and take his refill order. "Not me, Steffi. I intend to go out there"— he swept an arm wide, to include the acres of hotel grounds—"and put my ear to the ground to see just how well I can do at this detecting business."

His feckless grin scared Louise. But she really didn't care what her colleague was up to. "Friends, I'm going now to do a little snorkeling and then have a nap."

Marty frowned. "What about the hand?"

"I can always put a fresh bandage on. If you need me for something, you can find me in a chaise longue underneath the monkeypod tree on the east side of the lagoon."

Before she left, her acute vision picked up the fact that Marty and Steffi were holding hands under the table. What was it, Steffi's salutary poke in the arm, or maybe recollecting the old hippie days? Whatever it was, this vacation was turning out to be a real second honeymoon for the Corbins.

19

She'd navigated her way to the elevator and was ready to press the button when a strong arm reached out and restrained her. Dr. Bruce Bouting, a smile on his face, loomed just in back of her. "Louise!" It was as if they hadn't seen each other during the police briefing just a half hour ago.

"Dr. Bouting. Is the final session of the conference over?"

He flapped his big hand. "No meeting, in fact, transpired. It was impossible for us to concentrate under the circumstances. In fact, it seemed almost disrespectful to meet. We're all going to write a summary and send it to the chairman." He held his outspread fingers together like opposing claws. "The chairman gets to mesh everything," he said, as the fingers interlaced, "and come out with some kind of summary statement." His laugh boomed out. "It will thereupon be sent to various botanical journals and get lost in the annals of horticulture."

"Are you going up on the elevator?"

"Oh, no, dear. I'm in the President's Suite on the

ground floor. It's on the corner at the end of the hotel, facing the sea." He pressed a big hand on her arm. "Lest you think me extravagant, I allow Chris Bailey to occupy the other bedroom. And it's practical, since our business discussions often run late. I stopped you because I want a word with you. Can you sit for a moment?" He indicated the stone bench close to the elevator.

"For a minute, but I'm awfully tired. Last night was exhausting."

She sat on the end of the bench, leaving the white-haired scientist with lots of room. But he sat so close to her that one could barely squeeze a quarter between. Peering down in her face, he said, "You were a real heroine, but that's not what I want to talk about. I've heard all about your detecting skills, Miss Louise, from your friend John."

She laughed. "I've never been called 'Miss Louise' before. Can you drop the 'miss'? I'm Mrs. Bill Eldridge."

"All right, Mrs. Bill Eldridge. Since you have an analytical kind of mind—and even more important, because you had the misfortune to find his body—I wondered what you thought happened to our friend Flynn."

"He either fell, or someone pushed him."

"And if the latter, who do you think might have done such a thing? It really bothers me; I keep thinking about it." He angled his face closer to hers. Was he trying to intimidate her? If so, she wasn't going to let him. "Did you see something last night that would give you a clue?"

"Dr. Bouting," she said in her calmest voice, "I met Matthew Flynn only three days ago. All I knew about him was from his vitae and a couple of newspaper and magazine articles that I read. How would I possibly know, or be able to guess, who'd push him off a cliff, if it turns out someone did?"

"Fine, fine," said the scientist, bobbing his white head up and down. "That's fine. You wouldn't be able to guess, even though you were there trying to resuscitate him. And I suppose if you'd seen something additional, the police would have told you to keep it to yourself."

"Perhaps they would have."

"So I guess you have no theories at this time. Well, I do. And I wanted to share them with you." His eyes were full of excitement; she wondered what sick beast Matthew Flynn's death had awakened in him. Perhaps he was one of those voyeurs who dallied at fatal car crashes so they could see broken bodies, or who endlessly dwelled on macabre murders reported in the media.

She looked at him without speaking.

Apparently sensing she was losing patience, Dr. Bouting went on quickly, "Flynn is more than a 'medical' plantsman. He has gone, in recent years, to several continents—oh, probably more than several—but several that I know about, at least. His celebrity as a plant explorer has put him much in demand from this one and that one. On each of those trips, one in Turkey, one here in Hawaii, and one in, of all places, China, he's beaten out some other poor bloke by discovering a new and valuable species. Now, is that not a motive to kill?"

His face was within inches of hers. She noticed he'd cut himself badly on the chin while shaving and the septic stick he'd apparently used to stanch the flow of blood hadn't quite done its job. Had the man been nervous about something?

She said, "One needs a very strong motive to kill. There are always more new plants, aren't there?

People are always winning and losing, aren't they? And even you—I hear that you're probably the most renowned collector, I mean in terms of quantity, if not quality. I can see you leaving your competition behind in the dust, just like Dr. Flynn may have done."

He broke into laughter and used this as an excuse to sling an arm around her shoulder. Once there, she could feel his fingers pressing randomly into the flesh of her upper arm, as if he were fingering piano keys. "My dear, you are charmingly frank. I am tops at uncovering new varieties, especially ones I think your average backyard gardener will love. But I hasten to add that I am not among the three people that Matthew Flynn, in recent years, has beaten out with his discoveries."

"Who are you referring to?"

"Well, Tom Schoonover and Henry Hilaeo, for one—I treat them as one, for it could be one or the other, or maybe a conspiracy between the two of them. Flynn made a huge orchid find here a few years ago right under the noses of the folks at the NTBG. *Cattleya brassavola 'Flynnia,'* I think they call it."

"They named it after Matthew Flynn?"

"Yes. And in Turkey, Flynn bested Ralph Pinsky. Do you know Pinsky?"

"I know who he is. He was in the room this morning, I noticed."

"Yes, indeed," laughed Bouting. "You can't help noticing him. He's white as a ghost—looks like a new species himself. And his chest is caved in; maybe the poor guy has consumption."

The scientist paused in his account to give Louise a knowing smile. "Ralph's like me: very successful, but flies under the radar. He's not even as

public a personality as I am, but almost as successful at finding plants. Fancies himself, of course, as
a little superior to me, because he tests his imports
practically to death. He can afford to; he's publicly
funded. If I did that, I wouldn't make a dime."

"What happened in Turkey?"

"Let me tell you the story. He got dealt out of
the discovery of a fantastic new Turkish tulip. It
was rumored to be growing in the Taurus Mountains for years. Matthew Flynn found it right in
there when Pinsky also was searching. It's thought
a little spy might have tipped Flynn to the location."

"When did this happen?"

"Last fall," said the white-haired scientist. "And
when I say searching, I mean Pinsky was practically
killing himself. He's not been a well man, not up
to plant explorations any more, though he dis-
guises it well. I heard it was to be his last trip."
Bouting gave himself a demonstrative tap on his
cheek. "What a slap in the face to have someone
deal you out of your final, great discovery!"

"Hmm," said Louise. She had barely heard of
Ralph Pinsky and now Dr. Bouting was proposing
him as a murder suspect.

The arm was still around her shoulder. She said,
"Dr. Bouting, I'm not running away. It isn't necessary to put your arm around my shoulder."

"Oh, sorry," he said, taking his arm away. "I
hardly noticed."

"Now, who's the third man?"

A little laugh. "Actually, my good employee,
Christopher Bailey. This gorgeous little two-tone
mum plant in the hills of southern China—Chris
had heard about it and was planning on chasing it
down, but along came Matthew Flynn the season

before him, to take credit and promote it into production, actually, with that company, you know the name . . ." He looked blank, but then snapped his fingers and smiled. "The *Florissant* Company—there, it came back to me. I believe he has some kind of arrangement with Florissant." Louise guessed that Florissant was one of Bouting's biggest competitors.

She turned and looked straight into Bouting's shiny blue eyes. "This is all interesting, but it has nothing to do with me. Why don't you tell the police all these things?"

He waggled his head in a manner she thought frivolous for a man his age; the waggle said, *I'm smarter than you think!*

"Oh, I did, my dear," he said. "I told that police chief about Ralph Pinsky and how he has such a reputation to uphold and of course so do these guys out here on Kauai at the National Tropical Botanical Garden. I mean, not with the public, but they have to live up to their own private expectations. I believe Tom Schoonover is in that same lofty category as Ralph."

"Did you tell the police about Christopher Bailey's experience with Dr. Flynn?"

The scientist averted his gaze. "I meant to, but quite frankly, Louise, it slipped my mind. As I said, I told Chief Hau of the other two contretemps with Flynn. But I will do so, next time I see him. I'm telling you all this, Louise, because sometimes amateurs do the best job at solving crimes."

"If it was a crime."

He reached over and took her left hand. "My dear, you are so engaging. I won't trouble you further if you don't feel like putting on your investigator hat and corroborating all the beach gossip. I thoroughly enjoy talking to you, no matter what you decide to do."

She gently took her hand back and stood up. "Excuse me. I have to go now."

"As for myself, I think I'll go to the lagoon for a swim." The blue eyes gleamed again. "Maybe I'll see you there?"

It took an effort to keep the disappointment off her face. If she went to the lagoon, instead of the quiet afternoon sunbathing and swimming she'd looked forward to, she'd be stuck with this amatory old man. She knew conferences were fraught with romantic couplings and she shouldn't let Bouting's flirtatious ways bother her. For all she knew, he treated all women the same way.

She came up with a solution. She would go snorkeling first, then hide out in a woodsy alcove closer to the monkeypod tree; that was where she would drag herself, her chaise longue, and her Mike Davis book, *Ecology of Fear.* She would enjoy the solitude there.

Bouting was still waiting for an answer. With a man like him, one had to feint.

"I may just rest in my room."

20

For the past half hour, Louise had been obsessed with Kauai's beautiful assortment of multicolored fishes slowly swimming among the half-submerged rock outcroppings. But the pull of the water caused a warning bell to go off in her mind. Her fears were confirmed when she put her webbed feet down and stood in the surf. It had the strength of a giant and was attempting to shove her into the deep, or else cause her to collide with one of the volcanic rocks that peppered the ocean floor.

Hurriedly removing her snorkeling mask, she glanced ashore in alarm. She saw that rough sea warnings had been posted. A lifeguard holding a rescue raft stood on the edge of the sand and yelled a message through a bullhorn at a swimmer who'd ventured out too far.

It took her a few minutes to struggle the twenty-five feet to shore. Once there, she readjusted the top of her flowered bikini, then warily examined the beach. She'd been safe from Bruce Bouting as she'd paddled about, head-down, admiring the fish. Now there was no sign of the scientist, but she still had to get to her lagoonside hiding place without being seen.

She hadn't recognized the man standing directly in front of her on the sand. "*Aloha*," he called. "We meet again."

It was the beach oracle. His brown body, clad only in a swimsuit, was canted jauntily at an opposite angle to his worn surfboard, his hair a disheveled mop of brown curls, his eyes crinkled almost shut in a cheery smile.

"Well, hello," said Louise. "It seems you're always somewhere on these beaches. Maybe it's time we introduced ourselves. I'm Louise Eldridge."

He bowed his head. "Bobby Rankin at your service. The beach is my home. I make my living here and I sleep here."

She glanced over at the sumptuous luxury of Kauai-by-the-Sea. "You live right here?" she blurted out.

He gave her his sleepy grin. "I sure do. And I eat here—lots of breadfruit, mangos, papayas, bananas . . ." He raised a brown arm and pointed like Poseidon toward the rough Pacific. "I catch lots of fish right off those rocks. That's why I was close enough to heed the call of the sirens last night. I saw you trying to revive Matt Flynn—I don't think you noticed me."

"I must admit I was pretty out of it last night."

"There was no saving him, was there? What a mess his head was."

"It sure was," she said and knelt down to store her snorkeling equipment in her beach bag, apply a dry bandage to her hand, and put on her "Kauai-by-the-Sea" hat.

As she completed these tasks, Bobby Rankin

said, "The saltwater must have stung that wound like the devil."

"It did at first," said Louise, "but it doesn't take long to get used to." Getting back to her feet, she looked at him and said, "Have you ever seen anyone take a dive like that off the rock?"

"Sure. Lots of kids dive off Shipwreck. I've done it plenty of times myself." He loomed above her, a dark silhouette with an aura of light about him because of the sun at his back.

"You teach surfing, I guess."

He nodded. "Yeah. And deep-sea diving on occasion. Work by day, party hard by night. All the time, for the past twenty years."

Observing as closely as she could without seeming rude, Louise saw that the man's skin was leathery and lined and realized he was probably fifty or more, older than she had first thought. "What did you do before that? Did you live in Hawaii?"

"No. Twenty years ago I dropped out of real life on the mainland—Chicago, to be exact. I was with Smith-Barney. Traded options on the CBOT."

"CBOT. Uh . . ."

He translated for her. "Chicago Board of Trade." Bobby gave long, low laugh. "It was making me plain crazy."

She chuckled companionably. "You must see a lot, living on the beach."

"I do. I meet a lot of the people who come to Kauai, one time or another. I see plenty of people doing foolish things in the ocean. Once in a while, I aid in their rescue, sometimes I'm there when they drown. We have fifty to sixty drownings every year."

"On *Kauai?*"

A big shrug. "On all the islands. You know, people who unlike you don't pay any attention when they see swim warnings posted. Locals don't like to talk about the stats. I guess they figure it will hurt tourism. But back to Matt Flynn; I've got to say, I've never seen a body in worse shape than that one. Usually, they're bloated and blue."

She stood up and smoothed her bare stomach with her hand, restraining a desire to gag. "I don't need to know more."

"Sorry. Didn't mean to gross you out." He fell into stride with her as she walked back toward the hotel.

"You knew Flynn, didn't you?"

"Yeah, a little bit." He flicked a guarded glance her way. "Flynn was a great surfer, you know."

"No, I didn't know that." A stab of sadness made her heart ache for the dead man, who'd been a surfer, a jungle cowboy, an Eastern University professor, and a lover of life.

Bobby said, "I guess the police haven't said whether it was an accident, or something else. You and I know, though, that was no accident. Somebody really *split* the back of his head. I'll give you money they'll be searching for a weapon off the rock by end of the weekend."

"Why do you think that?"

"Because it's a good place to throw a weapon. The murderer probably thinks the water there descends like a mountain. I mean, folks read the guidebooks and picture a huge, twenty-five-thousand-foot tall cone that is the underwater base of this island. But I happen to know that there's a shelf down there about eighteen feet. Some big, gougy knife—I figure that's what the killer used—could have been flung down there. It wouldn't slide all the way from here to eternity, like some gullible murderer might think. It's perched right down there, ready for some diver to retrieve."

Louise was tugging to retrieve a memory of something said about a big knife . . .

They'd reached the mouth of the path leading to the hotel's lagoon. The surfer said, "You take it easy, now. Will we see you at sunset?"

She shook her head, already missing the thought of the quasi-religious sunset ceremony. "As much as I enjoy those streaks of green, my colleagues and I are going off campus tonight."

He waved. "I may be busy at sunset, too. You have a good time and stay out of trouble, now."

She glanced at his tall, muscular figure. The man who was always on the beach, at daybreak and at dusk, who'd turned up just moments after she'd discovered Matthew Flynn's body; surely he had been questioned about Flynn's fall. The police probably knew the man, for he was as much a fixture here as beach umbrellas and hotly contested beach chairs.

Approaching the lagoon, she saw that the coast was clear. No Bruce Bouting lurking about. Dropping off her beach bag in the shady alcove, she walked back to the family beach, found a big, white chaise longue, and dragged it the considerable distance to her hiding place.

She adjusted the chaise and looked up. The monkeypod tree let through only dappled patches of sunlight, but just for good luck she slapped sunblock on her face, shoulders, chest, stomach, and legs. Then, hoping to take a quick nap, she adjusted her hat over her forehead and lay back. Before she could close her eyes, however, she glimpsed a nearby Sago palm, which brought her wide awake again. She sat up straight and stared at it.

The plant was a beauty, its repetitive, curving leaves a masterpiece of order. Louise knew little about fractals, but conjectured that this palm was an example of fractal geometric design in nature.

She lay back on the chaise and quietly groaned. Would that her life had such order! A wave of depression swarmed over her, as powerful as one of the salty ocean waves she'd battled. Instead of order, she realized, her life often verged on chaos. Why was it that she was continually drawn into crime? It was never of her volition. Nonsensically, the words of the poet Emily Dickinson came to mind: *Because I could not stop for death / He kindly stopped for me . . .*

Death had *unkindly* stopped for her more than once. Last summer, she'd had no desire to find two corpses buried in her own backyard garden, nor was it her wish to stumble upon Matthew Flynn's body last night while viewing a Hawaiian sunset.

Her husband was right: At all costs, she needed to stay out of the police investigation or she'd end up needing that rest cure. With this thought, she closed her eyes and drifted off to sleep.

21

Cold drops fell on her calf and she leapt from sleep into wakefulness. "What!" she cried, sitting up suddenly so that her book fell to the grass.

"Gotcha," said John Batchelder, standing over her and grinning like a kid. His 7Up was poised over her leg.

He plunked down beside her chair. "You were dead to the world, Louise."

She gradually relaxed again and rested her head back on the chaise, her hat tilted far over her eyes. "John, I'm exhausted. You've interrupted my sleep."

Her ebullient colleague had no regrets. "You're the one who said I could find you here. So here I am, loaded with ideas."

"Ohhh," she groaned and shoved her hat back so she could get a look at him. It was shocking, for she'd never seen this young cohost of hers without his clothes on. The reverse was also true, she realized, as she reclined there in her brief, two-piece suit.

Besides his handsome face and outstandingly attractive golden eyes, John had a body with surprisingly wide shoulders and slim hips. She was relieved not to have a view of anything more—his bathing suit was an old-fashioned boxy style that might have been popular in the fifties. Since she knew he'd seen her turning her laser eye on him, Louise admitted as much. "John, you've got a very nice body. I hope your fiancée Linda appreciates that." She tried not to smile.

"She does, she does, I swear she does," said John. Louise realized he was in one of his manic moods. She'd read about hypomania in the *Times*, which had published a chart on the subject. She'd diagnosed her compatriot as being an "occasionally" manic type without the tendency to get depressed. Since she noticed the same qualities in herself, she'd concluded it was a positive and not a negative. "Louise," he said, giving her a sincere look, "let's not dwell on how beautiful my body is, though I sincerely enjoy the compliment. What I want to talk about is the murder."

"You're sure it's a murder?"

"I'm pretty sure. I could tell from that little bit you told us last night, before the cops advised you not to tell us any more."

"Well," she said, "aren't you the smart one."

"Yes, I am," he said and pulled a notepad out of his beach bag. "I've got notes, Louise, lots of notes. I've been taking them all morning." He fastened his gaze on her again. "Look, we've got to investigate."

"Why?"

"Well, we're right here. We've gotten to know all these people. It had to be one of the people we've been dealing with for three days or so. Here, let me read this." He flipped open the notepad. "Number one; George Wyant—who looks awful, I might add—has had some big fights with the dead man."

"How do you know?"

"He told me himself after that police briefing. It was like he was in a confessional. 'I feel so bad because I'd just gotten in a big battle with Matt over how to proceed next with something-or-other-research on something-or-other plant.' Didn't get the name of the plant."

"Maybe it was the plant the two of them were hoping would be a medical breakthrough."

"Yeah," said John, "that was it."

"It's the subject of George Wyant's doctoral dissertation."

"Well, there you have it—one suspect in Matthew Flynn's murder."

Louise couldn't help smiling. "I think we're getting ahead of the police."

"It isn't going to hurt. I don't think they have that many cops out here, Louise. There's not much crime in the islands, you know."

"I suppose not."

He flipped over another page. "Here's what I've got on Charles Reuter. Want to hear about that?"

"Sure," said Louise. She pulled her hat farther over her eyes and closed them.

"I heard, from Chris and Anne—you know those two—that Charles Reuter has waged a print fight in *Nature* and magazines like that with our Dr. Flynn. Reuter, and by extension, you might say, his man Bernstein, hated Flynn's guts."

"That's what Chris Bailey and Anne Lansing told you, hmm?"

"Yep. Dr. Reuter is one of those who takes seriously the fact that third world countries have been

ripped off forever by botanists coming in and steal-
ing their plants. He apparently accused Matthew
Flynn of hypocrisy in the way he operates in the
Amazon."

"So that's enough motive to kill a person?"

John shrugged his expansive, golden shoulders.
"I don't know. What do you think?"

"In the interests of full disclosure, I guess I'd
better tell you what Dr. Bouting told me this morning."

"You'd better," replied John. "He's a smart old
coot and he's sure been around."

"He told me of several instances where Dr. Flynn
beat out someone else while plant hunting in foreign lands. For instance, Flynn's discovery of a cattleya orchid right here in Hawaii. Bouting thinks
either Tom Schoonover or Henry Hilaeo would be
sore over that."

"So we have Wyant, Reuter, Bernstein, Schoonover, and Hilaeo. Of course, we can't limit the suspects to just them. There's also the Bouting
crowd—Bouting himself, or Chris, or Anne. But
what would their motive be?"

"Chris, as you call him now, was outmaneuvered
by Matthew Flynn when they were both hunting
for a species of mum in China. So, incidentally,
was Dr. Ralph Pinsky. That plant grab took place in
Turkey." She pointed to his notepad. "You'd better
jot down Pinsky on your list, if you insist on making a list. On the other hand, the Bouting Horticulture people don't seem to have a reason to kill.
Their company's making money hand over fist.
Christopher and Anne and their boss seem to get
along well. Why ruin everything by committing a
murder?"

"I see your point," conceded John.

She waved her hand in the air, warming to the topic at last. "We have to remember something about people who murder—most of them only do it once. And the person wouldn't kill lightly, just for the sake of killing. The person would have had to have a good reason. I'm not sure these motives we're talking about are strong enough. On the other hand—"

She didn't want to share this with her colleague, but her husband back in Washington, D.C., might shed light on the question of motive. She ought to hear back from Bill before the day was over.

"On the other hand what?" asked John.

"On the other hand, it's very responsible of you to be so concerned. Murder is an insult to us all. That is, if it *is* murder."

"Quit saying that, Louise," rebuked John. "You know darned well in your heart—" He had been hunched forward, his arms clasped around his bare legs, staring out into the ocean. Suddenly, he sat up straight and slapped a palm against the side of his head. "Of course," he said, "*that* could be the weapon . . ."

He leaped up and shoved his beach bag onto his shoulder. "I've just had a brainstorm: I know where the murder weapon is and I'm gonna go tell that police chief all about it." He loped off across the lawn. Louise took a deep, relieved breath and soon drifted off to sleep again.

22

Police Chief Randy Hau had been at it for hours, interviewing hotel guests in this improvised police office that looked like a peacock's den. He'd be glad to return to his dull beige-walled office in Lihue when this was over. Not only were the surroundings overdone, but his stomach was growling. All he'd had to eat this day was that puny gourmet breakfast in the conference room. With this Matthew Flynn death, not only was he overdue for lunch, he was overdue at home to start a two-week vacation with his wife and little boys. He sighed, picked up his Coke from the sandalwood desk, and gulped down the remaining contents.

Kauai-by-the-Sea's public relations manager Melanie Sando had turned her well-equipped office over to the chief for the interviews. Otherwise, he would have had a stream of protesting hotel clients traveling the twelve miles to police headquarters. Lieutenant Payne came to the office door, cocked his head back a fraction of an inch, and reported, "Got another one."

"Fine," said Hau. "Send him or her in."

"Him," said the lieutenant, looking dubious. "It's John Batchelder, one of the TV people."

He'd had a few words already with Batchelder. What else did he have to offer? Maybe he was a nut-hatch, thought Hau. Suspicious deaths brought out the nutty side of characters who had their own theory of what happened.

"*Aloha*," said the man, who wore only a bathing suit and one of the hotel's distinctive towels with green and white stripes and the hotel emblem slung around his wide shoulders. "I'm John Batchelder. We met in the police briefing this morning. I'm with WTBA-TV; I'm cohost of the gardening show."

"I remember talking to you, Mr. Batchelder. You look excited. Sit down first and relax." Hau could see the man was bursting to tell his story.

Batchelder sat forward in his seat and whipped off his sunglasses, revealing what Hau thought of as a sissy face. "Chief Hau, I heard something the other night, Thursday night, I guess. No, I take that back. It was Thursday afternoon when a group of us were talking about the Friday shoot at the tropical gardens. Now, I distinctly remember Dr. Flynn bragging about his assistant."

"George Wyant, you mean?"

"Yeah." Batchelder looked around the highly decorated office, momentarily distracted, or was he having second thoughts? "I feel a little uncomfortable about telling you about this. I mean, I have no gripe with George Wyant; I hope you understand that."

"Just go ahead, Mr. Batchelder, with your account. What did Dr. Flynn say about his assistant?"

The young man's eyes were unusual, thought Chief Hau. He couldn't decide whether it was the shape of the eyes or the character of the man that gave them that look.

Batchelder said, "Matthew Flynn bragged about how well George Wyant could cut through the Amazonian jungles with his machete. Like a 'hot knife through butter,' or some such metaphor."

"That's very interesting, Mr. Batchelder. Did Dr. Flynn mention that he had a machete?"

"Yes, he said Wyant carried it with him in case he needed it when he went to the Na Pali coast, or something."

Hau leaned back in the tall-backed leather executive chair. "Why would you think the machete was pertinent to Dr. Flynn's death?"

"Because of what Louise said when she first came back to the hotel last night. She told us Matthew Flynn had a terrible deep gash on his neck and that his head was partially crushed."

"Of course. She told you and the Corbins that, right? I don't think she mentioned it to others, because I caught up with her and told her to keep the details to herself."

Batchelder's remarkable eyes widened. "Oh, I'm sure she did. That was all she ever told us about it, except she did describe the way she hurt her hand."

"How'd she say she did that?" The thrown rock had convinced Chief Hau that it was murder, for investigation showed there were few loose rocks on the top of the Shipwreck Rock cliff.

"She said she scraped it when she was moving his body back from the ledge."

Good girl, thought Randy Hau. *Mrs. Eldridge knows how to tell a white lie.*

On the other hand, it didn't matter whether or not the Eldridge woman had gossiped to her friends.

The word was already out through Bobby Rankin that this was more than an accident. In fact, when Bobby had dropped in a few minutes ago, he cheerily admitted to the chief that he was the one who'd passed the word that Flynn's head was almost "torn off." No one but Hau and his evidence technicians knew that the pool of blood found this morning near the edge of the cliff indicated clearly that a murder was committed up there and the body then thrown over the edge.

"So, getting back to this machete, you apparently believe that it might be the murder weapon—provided that it was a murder."

"That's what I think," said Batchelder. "And what's more, I think you might find it if you sent some divers down off Shipwreck Rock."

Randy Hau, a native of Kauai, knew that water and knew there was another slab of underwater lava laid down at some earlier time, all around 5 million years back. He and Bobby Rankin had just finished talking about how it might make sense to dive down and search that shelf and how Bobby could have the job if he did it discreetly.

Hau stood up behind his desk and extended his hand. "Good thinking, John Batchelder. We'll look into this."

Batchelder smiled broadly. "I enjoy the thought of helping the police. Remember, I did tell you that Louise Eldridge has done just that on a number of occasions."

Chief Hau nodded his head. "You mentioned that this morning. She told me that she wasn't interested in pursuing this case."

Batchelder chuckled. "She may not want to, but I do. And when I learn something, I'm going to bring it right to you, Chief."

"Um, Mr. Batchelder, do all the speculating you want, but please try not to get . . . involved. After all, if you think Matthew Flynn was killed, that means there's a killer out there. Right?"

"Right," said the young man, looking uncertain.

"So you be careful. Let us do our job, okay?"

"Yes, Chief Hau, I take your point." He bounded out of the office, apparently eager to get on with things. Randy Hau rolled his eyes. It was one thing to have a local friend like Bobby Rankin helping him out, but John Batchelder was too much. Manic, Hau would say if he were to make a diagnosis. He just hoped the fellow didn't get himself in any deeper than he could handle.

The bane of the police's existence, the chief had heard, was the amateur detective butting in. He'd never had this happen before and it was dispiriting that it had to happen with his first murder case.

23

The kielbasa from the lagoon-side snack shop cost only three times what she would have paid at home, so Louise thought it a relative bargain, especially since the snack shop itself was picturesque, complete with faux thatched roof, to resemble an old Hawaiian house. Refreshed from her nap, she was at last doing the ultimate tourist thing: simultaneously eating, lounging, and reading. She could almost forget the recurring image of Matthew Flynn's eyes staring up at her.

She was well protected, shielded by a mass of shrubs and trees. She heard people chatting as they passed, but did not see them nor could they see her. Just beyond the foliage was a bench where people stopped to rest and converse in low but audible voices. One conversation was between giggling newlyweds. The bride had misplaced her birth control pills in the excess of luggage in their hotel room. The groom assured her that they probably wouldn't need them right away. Louise stared out toward the voices, knowing how wrong he was.

She felt her back muscles tensing; the do-good busybody inside her said to leap up and tell this couple that they'd better find those pills if they weren't ready for a baby next November. She thought the better of it, sat back in her lounge chair, and reminisced.

She'd gotten pregnant with daughter Martha on her and Bill's honeymoon. It was something that caused her mother-in-law, Jean Eldridge, to count carefully back over the weeks once the baby was born. Martha had not cooperated and had been born ten days early. Jean's raised eyebrows had not lowered during Louise and Bill's twenty-two years of marriage.

She smiled and went back to her book and thought about her wonderful Martha. She'd never regretted the early arrival of that baby.

After a few minutes of solitude, she heard a new voice through the bushes. It was intense, though not excessively loud. "Either one of you is capable of murdering Matt," said a man. "Chris hated it when Matt beat him out on that China trip. You disliked him on general principles, even though you pretended you were friends. What I can't figure out is why you couldn't leave the man alone, always bad-mouthing him every chance you got, trying to destroy his reputation."

The voice belonged to George Wyant.

"Killing Flynn would have been a tempting possibility," said another man. His voice was off-hand and cold. "Matt could be a nice guy, I'll admit that much, but he was a thief. He stole other people's ideas and ran with them. That's what he did to me in China, but he did it to others, too. Somebody just got ticked off enough to get rid of him, that's all."

Louise could scarcely believe it, but the person talking was the seemingly shy and mild-mannered Christopher Bailey.

A woman spoke next; it took only a few words before Louise realized it was Anne Lansing. "How clever you are, George, deflecting suspicion from yourself onto Christopher and me. Ask yourself if any of those petty issues you're talking about constitute a reason for killing Matt. Conversely, you had every reason. With him out of the way, you have your magic plant discovery all to yourself. You no longer have to share credit with Matt."

A few profanities from George Wyant, then a momentary silence. Wyant apparently walked off, while Christopher Bailey and Anne Lansing remained behind. They conversed in such low tones that she couldn't understand a word of it.

Louise had been totally relaxed in the hour between John's hurried departure and the arrival of these three bitter adversaries. Now, all was quiet beyond the green tree barrier, but she was a bundle of nerves, just the way John Batchelder would have liked it.

Though she hadn't wanted this to happen, all her detecting instincts had been activated by the conversation beyond the trees.

She closed her book. Mike Davis's account of the catastrophic ecology of California had lost its charm. It was time for a swim in the lagoon. Maybe it would get her back into the vacation mode she longed for.

She slipped her blue swimming goggles around her neck, leaving the rest of her possessions near her chaise longue, and walked out of her woodsy alcove to the edge of the water. With relief, she saw no one. She had shaken off Bruce Bouting.

Putting her goggles in place, she dove into the water, which she knew was deep in the center, and swam vigorously across it and down the waterway that led to the next pool, then across that pool and into another channel. Not wanting to run into Bouting, she returned the way she'd come. Once back in the greenery-shrouded surroundings of the first pool, she saw another swimmer preparing to come in the water. For a moment, she was dispirited, certain that Bouting had finally caught up with her. She pulled her blue goggles off her eyes to see better and was relieved to find it was someone else. Nate Bernstein.

Nate stood on the edge of the pool in a stylishly baggy swimsuit pulled dangerously low on his hips by the contents of the suit's huge cargo pockets. As he busily unloaded a water bottle, two paperback books, his cell phone, and a slim wallet, Louise thought he looked like a young, hip model out of a sports ad. But the effect was ruined when he glanced down at her and opened his mouth to speak. In a petulant voice, he said, "I don't know why you want to talk to *me*."

"I want to talk to you?" she asked, treading water in the middle of the pool. "Who told you that?"

"That guy John. He said you're some kind of detective and you'd want to talk over the, quote, 'murder' with me."

"Oh, no, I wish he hadn't said that." What could she do with her audacious colleague, John? "Uh, the talk of an alleged murder has put him in an investigative mood. I'm so sorry. It really has nothing to do with me. John's a little overeager. But he means no harm."

Bernstein gave a wry laugh. "Then you'd better tell him to shut his big mouth. He talks a big game, all about how Dr. Reuter and I had reason to hate Flynn and did we know who might have wished him harm? He's as tactful as a stone. What gets me is that Dr. Reuter and I wasted so much time with you TV people. We gave so much and are going to get so little. I bet you won't even use the segment, will you?"

"I'm afraid that's true. Surely you can understand that. And it's a shame, because Dr. Reuter did so well in that tape."

"Matt Flynn gets exactly what he deserves, but everyone else has to suffer."

She swam a few idle strokes and turned to face him. He waited patiently on the steps. "That's harsh. What do you mean, exactly what he deserves?"

"Chickens always come home to roost. Live by the sword, die by the sword."

She swam a few strokes closer to where he sat. "That is so violent."

"It's just that Flynn ravaged the environment under the guise of saving it. Now the environment's ravaged him."

"Another glib phrase, but not very accurate." Here she was, drifting in the middle of this beautiful pool and getting angrier by the moment. "The environment didn't ravage him, Nate. Some person knocked him hard in the head and threw him off that cliff."

Nate Bernstein looked triumphant. "I *knew* you knew the real truth. He didn't have an accident at all. Why, a guy I met on the beach said his head was nearly—"

"Stop," she warned, "I don't want to hear the myth of the severed head again." She ducked under the water and swam away, as if she could wash off all the idle statements.

When she came up for air, she was at the far edge of the pool and Nate Bernstein had entered the water and was swimming toward her. A little intimidated, she did a couple of backstrokes to put some distance between them.

"Hey," laughed Bernstein, "what's the matter? You're not frightened of me, are you?" Actually, his large brown eyes level with hers were a scary sight. "Look, Mrs. Eldridge," he said in a wheedling tone, "you're not a bad sort. Maybe you can understand this—did you ever think that Flynn's demise carried out a greater good? Maybe it was his bad karma that was his downfall."

"Whose greater good are you talking about?"

He swam away, but called back before turning the corner out of sight. "I didn't say, did I?"

Louise's relaxing swim had been spoiled. She got up and sat on the big gray stone steps, deciding whether to return to her private reading spot by the tree or to the hotel. She glanced at Nate's little pile of possessions. The paperback on top had an intriguing title: *The Shape of Water*. She was tempted to examine the other title and to peek inside the slim wallet, but only briefly. Then her love of nature set her straight, as her gaze was caught by a nearby hibiscus bush. It was overburdened with magenta flowers. She strolled over and surreptitiously picked one—to relieve the weight on the branches, she told herself. Stashing the flower near her towel, she looked up guiltily and saw that someone had observed the theft. Nate Bernstein had silently plied his way back through the channels and pools. He climbed up and sat beside her, glancing at his possessions to be sure they hadn't been disturbed.

"Stealing flowers, huh?" he said, smirking.

"I'm sure no one will miss it," she said.

"I really don't care," he retorted, resting his head on a hand and staring morosely out into the pool. After a long pause he said, "Louise, I'm not as bad a person as you think."

She looked at him curiously. "I'm glad to hear that."

"The fact is, I don't know quite what's going on around here and I wish I did."

At that moment, a person in swimming cap and goggles rounded the curve of the channel and swam into the pool. Charles Reuter, spying the two of them sitting on the steps, crossed the pool in three strokes and stood in the shallows, his dripping-wet goggles hiding his eyes. Although thin, he was muscular looking and fit. He pulled off his cap and goggles, revealing a tense, lined face. "Having trouble, Nate? Mrs. Eldridge, I bet you're asking too many questions. The fact is that neither one of us wants to talk to you." He climbed the stairs and Nate deferentially got out of the way, while Louise sat where she was and caught the splash. "C'mon, buddy," the professor said to his loyal assistant. "Let's get out of here."

Talk about karma, she thought, *meeting those two was the essence of bad karma.*

In fact, her afternoon had been filled with trying encounters. She stood on the edge of the lagoon and dove vigorously and deeply into the center of the cleansing water, this time just barely touching the bottom with her outstretched hands. Then she swam off down the channel again, determined to go as far and as fast as her body would take her, Bruce Bouting and everybody else be hanged.

24

Saturday night

The woman at the back of the line boldly examined Louise, taking in her swept-back hair with a hibiscus blossom tucked behind the ear, the gaily-flowered muumuu, and the silver sandals. Apparently not impressed, she said, "Do you have a reservation?"

"Yes," said Louise, adjusting her magenta flower. "I'm with them," she said, nodding to the Corbins and John Batchelder, deep in conversation ahead of her in the line. "We're a party of four. Do you have reservations?"

"Of course," said the woman, and fastened her gaze in on Louise's golden-tanned cohost. "This place always takes awhile to seat you, though."

"They do seem busy," said Louise. She looked out at the restaurant's charming garden. "A lovely garden, isn't it?"

The woman waved a hand on which reposed a large diamond ring. "It's like any garden, don't you think? But this place has excellent food; we come here several times each visit."

"So you come to Kauai often?"

"For a month every year. Have you found any new good places to eat on the island?"

"We haven't been around much. We've had to stick pretty close to our hotel."

"Kauai-by-the-Sea?"

"Yes."

"We own a house in Poi Pu."

"How nice."

"Kauai-by-the-Sea is nice. But someone fell to their death last night right on the hotel grounds."

Louise said, "I believe it happened adjacent to the hotel grounds."

"Horrible thing. Maybe the man was drunk. I heard he was drunk. But I also heard the fall ripped his head off. Did you hear that?"

Louise said, "I don't know too much about it, but I don't think his head was quite ripped off. I only know I'm glad to be eating somewhere besides the hotel for a change."

"It would be tiresome to eat there too much," said the woman.

"I couldn't agree more. Tell me where you and your husband eat."

"One of the best places is in Lihue. Aroma, it's called. We eat there at least twice while we're here, once on the way home, because we take the nine-thirty night flight."

"I've heard of Aroma."

"And of course there's the Gaylord Tavern. And a darling little Chinese place in Kapaa for lunch. It's right near the Safeway."

"Hmm," said Louise, taking the small notebook from her silver evening purse and jotting the new names down. Exchanging notes on culinary hot spots quite clearly ranked right up there with sunsets as important group activities in Kauai. "We had an excellent breakfast at Joe's on the Green," she offered.

The woman sniffed dismissively, as if Louise had failed a test. She turned her back on her and addressed a couple who'd strolled up to the rear of the line. "Have you two found any new good places to eat this year?"

"We certainly have," said the man, but just as Louise was about to get the scoop, Steffi yanked her by the arm.

"Hurry it up, Louise. Whatever are you doing? Our table's ready. Use it or lose it."

The porch on which they were seated was dark and comforting, with lots of candles flickering here and there. "Isn't it delightful to be eating dinner in a new restaurant?" said Louise to her companions. "Though I do feel bad about missing sunset on the beach."

"Hey, Louise, last time you did that you found the body," said John. "Maybe you'd better give up sunsets on the beach." Her cohost had a kind of permanent smile on his face; Louise knew he was waiting for someone to ask him why.

"Why are you smiling?"

"Because I've had a good day."

They gave their drink orders and Louise decided to try her first mai tai.

Marty congratulated her. "Good, Lou. You're really going native, dressing native for a change and drinking the native drinks." Then he turned to John. "What was so good about today?" he asked. He and wife Steffi still were holding hands, so Louise decided they'd had a good day, too. The second honeymoon was still cooking.

"I've talked to just about everybody about the murder."

Louise's heart sank.

"Oh, so it's definitely murder?" persisted Marty, running a hand through his curly dark hair.

"The cops don't say so, but Louise and I know, don't we, Louise?"

She sighed. If only they could talk of something besides what happened to poor Matthew Flynn! "What did you talk to everyone about, John?"

"I challenged them, told them you and I were doin' a little investigating. We are, aren't we, Louise?"

She shook her head. "No. John, why are you going around ruffling feathers? I ran into Nate Bernstein and Charles Reuter at the lagoon. They were very annoyed and guess who got the brunt of it? Me. What did you hope to learn by egging them on, implying they had a grudge against Flynn?"

"To get a rise, of course. I did that with everyone." He sat forward and put his elbows on the table. "But Louise, my pièce de résistance, or whatever you want to call it, was this: I told the cops about George Wyant's machete."

The machete. That was the reference to a knife that she'd tried to remember. Her colleague, she noted, was much quicker at putting these things together than she was.

"Matthew Flynn told us George Wyant cut through jungles like a knife through butter with his machete."

"And you told the police about that?" This morning, she'd felt strangely protective toward young George Wyant. Now she wondered if she'd been wrong to feel that way.

"Yep," said John. "I told them I thought he carried one with him. And that it could be the murder weapon. What else better to make a deep wound, as you described it, in the back of Flynn's sorry neck? I told Chief Hau that if they send divers out there, they might find it off the rock. He told me he was going to follow up on that."

Marty, Steffi, and Louise looked at him in silence. Steffi said, "That's not bad detecting, John, dear. I bet the chief loves you."

"He seemed really appreciative. I told him I'd keep him abreast of anything else I turned up."

Louise had her nose in the menu. "I'd like to get abreast of a good dinner," she said, smiling up weakly at her companions. "I'm overdosed on murder."

They all ordered fish. To Louise the best part was the dessert, so complicated that just reading about it took her breath away. Baked Hawaii: coconut and passion fruit sorbet on a rich, Ghirardelli dark chocolate brownie encased in a golden baked Italian meringue and flambéed with framboise liqueur served on lilikoi creme.

John, who ordered double chocolate cake with caramel sauce, begged a bite of hers. "God, I wish I'd ordered that."

Louise said, "When we come here again, you can order it."

"But we're going home," insisted Marty. "We oughta be out of here by Monday night, shouldn't we?"

Louise said, "I hope so."

John walked beside her as they left the restaurant. The woman with whom Louise had talked while waiting in the line was seated with her husband, finishing her dinner. She cast an all-knowing look at Louise. Louise could practically hear what she was thinking. *Middle-aged, sex-starved woman gloms onto younger, dashing-looking man.* Just as they passed the table, Louise tucked her arm through John's, looked up at him with a tender expression, and said, "Where're we going next, baby?"

Confused and a little annoyed, John nevertheless didn't let loose of her arm and fortunately didn't react until they passed the couple's table. Then he said, "Quit pretending that you feel for me, Louise; I know you think I'm an odd duck. But you just watch, I'm going to show you the stuff I'm made of."

When they arrived back at the hotel in their rental car, they ran into George Wyant striding through the lobby toward Options, the hotel's posh nightclub. Uncharacteristically, he had on long pants and looked like a normal tourist rather than a jungle cowboy. Louise thought he might stop for a word with her. Instead, he swung around and marched straight up to John Batchelder and practically bumped him in the chest.

Though John was tall, Wyant was a good three inches taller and more muscular as well. "You little prick," he growled, "going around all day making snide cracks about everybody. Insinuating that I killed Matt, who mentored me and stuck by me even when others thought I was a lightweight and who's good to his widowed mother and unmarried sisters. You know, a regular, good person with decent principles. You're the one, aren't you, who tattled to the cops about my machete? Well, you'll be happy, you turd, that I'm in big trouble, because someone lifted my machete from my room."

His bloodshot gaze flicked onto Marty, Steffi, then Louise. "It could have been anyone. And now they think it might be the murder weapon and that

I killed my friend." He poked John in the chest sending him stumbling backward. "And you, you creep, you're responsible for the whole thing. For all I know, it could have been you who stole it." Another sharp poke with a strong finger: "How do you like it when the tables are turned, huh? Did you do it? Did you steal the machete? Did you kill Matt?" His voice had risen and people in the lobby turned and looked.

Wyant finally noticed the ruckus he was causing. He stepped back from John Batchelder and turned to Louise. "You're a nice lady, Louise. I don't know why you're hanging around with such bad company." He spun around and resumed his way to the hotel nightclub.

Louise noticed one thing: George Wyant may have been on his way to getting drunk, but he wasn't high. It wasn't drugs doing the talking, it was right from the heart.

25

Sunday morning

The phone rang, breaking the soft peace of morning sleep.

"Wake up, sleepyhead," said Louise's husband. "It's report time."

"Hi, darling."

"I have a lot of information for you, Louise," said Bill. "But first, how are you? Did you sleep all right?"

"I slept in, with the aid of a little pink pill. And no dreams of poor Matthew Flynn. But it's hard to wake up."

"Have the police figured out what happened to that poor guy? Maybe you don't need all the petty gossip I've collected."

She sat up on the edge of the bed, pulled her white lawn nightie straight underneath her, and tried to concentrate. "The authorities haven't made much progress, or at least they haven't told us. They're diving for a weapon they think might have been thrown in the ocean."

"My God," said her husband, "talk about a needle in a haystack."

"A weapon might have landed on an underwater shelf just beyond where I found Matt's body."

"Well, that's better. So you call him 'Matt,' huh?"

"I'm getting to know him better since he's dead than when he was alive. Bill, let me get my pad and pencil. I want to take notes." She returned in a moment. "Ready."

"Louise, none of this is going to blow you away. On the other hand, it's interesting. Who knows what small fact may turn out to be of value?"

"Who knows? What do you have?"

"First, I'll tell you I don't have a take on those people at the National Tropical Botanical Garden or the people from the Honolulu PBS station."

"We can forget those young PBS freelancers; they didn't even know Matthew Flynn. But I need to know about the four from the tropical gardens. And now there's another dark horse—except he's very light-complexioned—Dr. Ralph Pinsky, p,i,n,s,k,y, director of the Greater Missouri Botanic Garden."

"I'll see what I can get on him and on Schoonover et al. tomorrow. The rest of them have been checked out pretty thoroughly. Let's talk first about Anne Lansing and Christopher Bailey, Bruce Bouting's people. Anne Lansing has an impeccable reputation. She's the daughter of the prestigious Dr. Richard Lansing, head of the biology department at Northern. She got her BA degree there, then went on to Eastern for a master's degree. She's a 'hands-on horticulturalist of note,' that's what one source told me. Along with writing she heads Bouting's new plant research. Maybe you know all of that."

"As a matter of fact, I do. What about Christopher Bailey?"

"He and Anne are both candidates to succeed Bouting. Bouting apparently doesn't care that Bailey left academia. That happened after he was charged with falsifying the research on his dissertation at Washington University, where he also earned his undergraduate degrees. This incident drove him into commercial horticulture, where he's said to have a golden touch, plus a good business head."

"Bouting claims that he's a genius at crossing plants and producing gorgeous new ones."

"Yeah, if you say so. I don't know anything about crossing plants. I only know you don't cross *wives.*"

"Very funny, Bill. Speaking of wives, what about their personal lives? Married? Divorced?"

"Bailey was married back a ways to someone he met at the university, but it didn't last long. Anne Lansing's never been married and if she gets interested in someone, it's known that the paternalistic Dr. Bouting will have to pass on the guy. He's very proprietary about her. According to one source, Anne and Christopher are both married to their careers."

Louise nodded. "That seems right."

"Anne Lansing has a penchant for publicity. If she isn't writing the article, someone else is writing about her, in *Garden Design* or *Architectural Digest,* since she designs the occasional garden for the rich and famous—that sort of thing."

"A go-getter."

"Very ambitious, it's said. However, Christopher Bailey is seen more with Bruce Bouting in the administrative offices. This is one of the largest horticultural firms in north America, did you realize that? Apparently, it's enormously profitable, privately held, and Bailey is being coached on how to keep it that way. From what I heard, Anne Lansing might be slated to take over the research and development end."

"That wouldn't represent much of a change from what she does now," said Louise.

"I guess not. Now, to move along to Nate Bernstein. *Dr.* Bernstein, rather, who did his graduate work at Berkeley in record time, with Dr. Reuter as his mentor. He's a brilliant young man, is thought to collaborate in—and I think that might mean ghost write—some of the best articles for his boss. Bernstein landed in jail once for environmental picketing in Sacramento, but not a big deal, I wouldn't think. All in all, he's respected and considered a comer in his field of environmental science."

"That takes care of three of the four assistants. I need to know everything I can about the fourth, George Wyant. Apparently the police are zeroing in on him." She told her husband about the missing machete.

Bill said, "The word I get on Wyant is that he's reasonably scholarly and promising, but that the life he and the deceased Matthew Flynn were leading was on the wild side. Though, as I intimated to you before, I think that's part of the game for your average, everyday ethnobotanist. Also, there's lots of trumpeting from Dr. Flynn and George Wyant about 'medicinally valuable plants' that don't turn out to be medicinally valuable. However, Flynn's and Wyant's university, Eastern, doesn't seem to mind as long as they keep trying. Neither do their other money sources, such as the National Scientific Foundation, because once in a while they strike pay dirt. They think they're going to again with some other discovery now being analyzed for its alkaloids, or something . . ."

"It's a subspecies of *Uncaria quianensis.*"

"Hmm," said Bill, "are you sure you don't know more than I do about these guys?"

"What else about George?"

"George, huh? Is Wyant a likeable fellow?"

"Yes, but he might have killed his mentor."

"Well he's sensitive, it turns out. He was hospitalized for a month with a mental breakdown three years ago after a trip with your Dr. Matthew Flynn to the Amazon. Both caught a vicious little virus and it's thought George's addictive personality caught up with him that time, too."

"Well. Anne Lansing must have met both Flynn and Wyant at Eastern. Or did she?"

"I didn't find that out," said Bill. "But I got the impression that those people in the Massachusetts–New York–Pennsylvania corridor all know each other. That means Flynn, Wyant, Bouting, and Bouting's two assistants, Bailey and Lansing, were pretty well acquainted. In fact, they're all up-and-coming scientists, so I'm sure they crossed paths at national and international conferences."

"Great research, Bill."

"I've friends who helped with this. Next, let's go to the scientists, starting with the deceased. Matthew Flynn, a full professor at Eastern, made a huge splash when one of the first plants he brought back from South America turned out to have value for treating Parkinson's and other nerve diseases. He was kind of a showman, so lots of people think he was a phony. Quite the bachelor-about-town, too, in both Boston and New York. You didn't fall for his good looks, did you, Louise?"

"No, darling. So if he was a man-about-town, that must mean he was unattached. No family?"

"Just a divorced wife somewhere in his past and a mother and younger siblings he helped support. And though he had that Don Juan image, it was rumored that he had been smitten lately with one true love. Name of the woman, unknown. This could be important, according to that source, because it would mean an end to his adventuresome life."

"Something George Wyant might not have liked?"

"Exactly."

"Besides, Bill, I got a few other vibes from Wyant," said Louise. "I had the feeling he was attached to Matthew Flynn as more than just a friend and assistant."

"That thickens the plot a bit," said her husband. "Now who's next? Bouting?"

"No, Charles Reuter. Dr. Reuter has a strange past. He was charged by his wife with mental cruelty during a bitter divorce action a couple of years ago. But then they reconciled and now live together again, but 'uneasily.' Hah," barked her husband, "doesn't that describe most marriages?"

"Not ours, honey," said Louise.

"I'm glad you think that. This Dr. Reuter's considered a troublemaker and excessive critic in the scientific community. He brooks no opposition, his opponents say; in other words, he *slaughters* 'em."

"Interesting, considering the way Matthew Flynn was killed."

"But on the plus side, Reuter is the ultimate do-gooder, a great advocate of third world countries.

He believes in giving back to them for snitching their plants."

"He's talked about that a lot at this conference and during our shoot."

"You're going to have trouble using that program, with one of the on-camera people dead and gone."

"It's awkward. Marty's pretty upset about it. Fortunately we have a great interview with Tom Schoonover from the gardens. Bill, the only one left to talk about is Bruce Bouting."

"I left the best for last. He's our multimillionaire headquartered there on a huge acreage in Bucks County not far from Philadelphia. You know all about how he's one of the busiest plant collectors in the country, spending lots of time abroad searching out new ones. You must know all about his research gardens and all that. After his wife of forty years died five years ago, he married another woman, but they were divorced last year. Even at that, he's rumored to be quite the womanizer. I have to salute him for that, Louise, for they say he's sixty-six."

"Since when do you salute womanizers?"

"Actually, I'm just havin' a little fun with you. To be sure you stay alert during my report, I enliven it now and again with some racy stuff. Now, here comes the most interesting thing about Dr. Bouting: He's evidencing early signs of dementia, probably Alzheimer's disease."

"That's pretty private. How did you weasel that information out?"

"The person who did probably got it from someone at the company who might be worried about its future and wants to see a change at the top. I don't believe I am unduly Machiavellian when I guess that the source is an ally of one of those two assistants out there in Kauai, Anne Lansing or Christopher Bailey. Maybe one or the other wants to hasten Dr. Bouting's leave taking."

"Bill, this is great. How can I thank you?"

"When you come home, give me a lei."

"My dear, you're funny. I'll do just that. So we agree we'll wait this out?"

"As long as you feel safe there. Do you?"

"Yes. No one's after me. Though John Batchelder has been acting a little odd . . ."

"Is that something new?"

She laughed. "He's going around playing detective."

"Good, let him, as long as you don't. The only danger I see there for you is from Bruce Bouting. He's horny as a goat, they say. You already mentioned something about him being annoying, a polite way of saying the same thing. Watch your step; you aren't in danger of being murdered, just preyed on by a man old enough to be your father."

26

Louise was to meet her friends at ten and it was already twenty after. She'd rushed into her tour clothes, a lightweight wash-and-wear white shirt with red bandanna and cargo pants that, if necessary, could be unzipped to make into shorts. She descended the elevator and tried to hurry down the big hotel hall, though it felt as if she were walking through a very thick mass of air. That was what a sleeping pill did for her and why she rarely took one.

She was approaching the end of the hall, with the orchid garden lanai on one side, the parrot's cage on the other. As she was about to pass the cage, she was horrified to see the bird glaring at her in recognition. He ruffled his feathers, as if he were winding up for a performance. That turned out to be true. Jumping up and down on its perch, he screeched the same line as when he first met her: "Bad baby . . . bad baby . . . *bad baby!*"

"Oh, just shut up!" she hissed at him. "I didn't do anything to you—I'm *not* a bad baby!"

A cluster of four passing tourists looked at her in disgust. "Can you believe anyone would talk to a dumb bird like that?" said one.

"No, only an idiot would," said another. "She must have been rude to it in the past for it to call her names like that."

Louise slunk her way down the steps and into the dining room. To her relief, she spied her colleagues, Marty, Steffi, and John, already seated at a table on the terrace. She made eye contact with a nearby waitress to signal the need for coffee, then sat down. "Hi," she cryptically greeted her companions, then put on her dark glasses, took her crushable Kauai-by-the-Sea hat from her carry-all, and pulled it down onto her head. That damned bird would never recognize her again.

"Well, *hello,* Lou," said Marty. He looked self-satisfied, easy for someone who'd already finished his princely breakfast. "Is that a disguise? What's the matter with you?"

To Louise's numbed ears it sounded like "Whassamattawidyou?"

"Give me a moment. I've been seriously harassed on the way here."

"No kiddin'," said Marty. His brown eyes snapped with anger. "Who harassed you? That Wyant fellow?"

As Louise shook her head, Steffi said, "Was it that police chief?"

"No and no," said Louise. "It's that dratted parrot."

John Batchelder, polishing off an omelet with pancakes and sausage on the side, threw back his head and laughed. "That's giving me the first laugh I've had in days. A parrot, giving Louise Eldridge a hard time!"

Louise stared at them darkly, through deep-tinted Armani lenses. "Just answer me one question: Does that bird scold any of you?"

"You mean the one across from the orchid garden?" asked Steffi. "Or do you mean the one farther down the hall?"

"The blue and yellow guy across from the orchid garden."

One by one, they shook their heads. Marty asked, "What does he say to you that's so terrible? Does he cuss you out?" He chuckled. "Or does he make dirty cracks?"

"No and no," she said again, annoyed at her companions. "It's just so demeaning. He yells 'bad baby' when he sees me."

Her colleagues laughed. John said, "You are kind of a bad baby, you know."

Marty said, "Don't be a wuss, stand up to that bird." He laughed again.

"You think it's funny," she said, flipping shut her menu with its endless choices. She already knew what she wanted, an abstemious breakfast of granola and juice. "It wouldn't be so funny if it were happening to one of you."

Steffi said, "Sweetie, you're probably still suffering post-traumatic stress from finding that dead man, Dr. Flynn. I hope you got some good sleep last night."

"I did, Steffi." She squeezed her friend's hand back; she needed someone like Steffi to be kind to her at this moment.

Marty dabbed his mouth with his napkin, leaned back, and said, "Well, Steff and I are off for a drive to the north shore. But you and John can have a nice relaxing day visiting the Big Island. Kilauea is all over the news this morning. A new vent has blown its stack. The crowds it's attracting are enormous." There was growing irony in his tone and a devilish look in his eyes. "What could be more relaxing than standing on a volcano that's spewing molten rock high into the air?" He leaned over to Louise and said, "Honey, there's worse things than a hysterical parrot. You and John just try not to get burned up, you hear?"

It wasn't until the van had taken them to Lihue Airport that Louise realized Tom Schoonover had come on this field trip to the Big Island for a reason beyond viewing the new lava flow. At the airport gate, Tom cleverly drew the other twelve in the group together to talk about lava viewing. The scientist was dressed casually, as usual, in tan shirt, shorts, and ball cap. They hovered around him like a class of schoolchildren.

At that moment, Louise knew that Chief Hau had urged Schoonover and Henry Hilaeo to come with the group as an additional element of security, an undercover element. And Tom was pulling it off: The two Kauai County policemen assigned to the group stood back politely while he outlined a plan with the know-how of a professional tour guide.

"Lava viewing, folks, and I'm sure you who have experienced it before will agree, is the most fun at dusk." An enthusiastic raising of his eyebrows created a mass of friendly forehead wrinkles. "And this is an historic moment in the current Kilauea activity event. As of the day before yesterday, not only is there an active vent directly into the sea, but a new flow has broken out of a fissure a mile from the ocean. Lava is spewing high into the air and creeping down to the water. Allegedly, these are the highest geysers seen since the Puu Oo vent broke open in 1992. This surface flow of pahoehoe makes it easy viewing for a change. We won't have to walk over acres of hardened a'a, which is often the case when you come here—it's rough and crackly and hard as heck to traverse, so thank your lucky stars you don't have to cross it. So, we'll shoot for getting there at dusk. Okay?"

There was a murmur of agreement.

Schoonover rubbed his hands, as if in anticipation. His hazel eyes crinkled with pleasure. "Let me finish quickly. Since we arrive at Volcanoes National Park around twelve thirty, that gives us three hours to see the other sights. Some may want to come with me when I hike the Kilauea Iki crater; it is adjacent to the larger crater. It takes you across an old lava field with lots of new plant growth in it and a tropical rain forest as well. I have to warn you that it's a little steep in spots."

John Batchelder gave Louise a wall-eyed look; she guessed he wouldn't choose to take the crater hike.

Schoonover continued in a reverential voice. "These craters, folks, with their steam vents and tiny new trees, are the essential story of the volcano—destruction leading to rebirth."

"I'll go down the crater with you," said Charles Reuter with a grin. "You had me with 'old crackly lava field.'" Louise was glad to see the man had a little humor in him. "Nate will come, too."

"Great," said Schoonover. Apparently sensing he'd digressed, he snapped back into a practical mode: "Some may prefer an easier trip—driving around the big Kilauea Crater, maybe visiting the museum, and walking the Thurston Lava Tube. If you do the tube, remember the best part is the second part, which is pitch dark and has stalactites.

"In other words," he continued, "we can go in

two directions. Sergeant Yee and Sergeant Binder"—
he nodded at the two uniformed policemen—"have
agreed to be our drivers. They'll pick people up at
one of two places. At four o'clock, the two carfuls
can regroup at Volcano House and we'll grab dinner. That gives us plenty of time to drive in tandem
down Chain of Craters Road and park as close as
possible to the fireworks. Once there, we employ
the buddy system; it's better to be with someone than
to be alone."

Sergeant David Binder chimed in. "A reality
check, folks: The plane back to Kauai leaves Hilo
at ten-thirty. That means we have to depart the Volcanoes National Park area promptly at eight. That
allows maybe a couple of hours to view lava. We'll
have lots of company down there at the vent because people all over the world have heard about
it. You'd never get a hotel room on the Big Island,
so good thing we're flying back tonight, where you
do have a room."

Schoonover smiled at the policeman and turned
to his little tour group. "The lava's an absolutely
captivating sight and you'll feel like staying all night.
But under the circumstances, we're lucky to be
able to make this trip at all. Two hours of viewing
ought to be fine."

27

Early Sunday afternoon

It was a windy trip and the pilot had warned there might be turbulence, but they had nearly reached the Big Island. Travel time to Hilo from Lihue was less than an hour. In that scant period, Louise, sitting in a rear seat, watched Bruce Bouting in safari hat and dashing khakis flourishing a silver-tipped cane and working the plane like a celebrity working a room. His hat shoved well back on his thatch of white hair, the plantsman was the picture of a bon vivant, she noticed. The only thing missing was a drink in his hand. And yet he was a high-strung bon vivant, talking a little too much for anyone's comfort, his blue eyes darting about as if he were concerned about a surprise attack from the rear.

He chatted about things Louise knew from reading travel books: how this hottest spot on earth with its myriad volcanic craters had attracted thousands of people over the years, including notables like Mark Twain and European royalty, who stood gaping in awe at the boiling lava in the Halemau-mau crater.

"It's a truly hypnotic experience, if you haven't been here before during an eruption." He spoke of how they would have to be careful, since the steam vents occasionally broke open and scalded a bystander or two to death. "Or, even more remotely, the earth could open up right by your feet, exposing a brand-new vent in a lava tube that has been pressured toward the sea." On a more personal note, he told them about how he'd tumbled down the steps to the hotel dining room this morning. "A depth perception thing, you know." He'd ended up with a sore knee. Thus the cane. He'd have to save the knee for walking down near the lava flow.

Injured knee or not, he hardly sat at all on the short trip, traveling from seat to seat. He started in back, chatting first with her and John, who had been busy talking about some future program ideas for *Gardening with Nature.*

Since Louise sat in the aisle seat, Bouting took that as an excuse to lean into her space; she could even smell his peppermint breath. Hadn't he understood her message that she was married and unavailable? It was a windy day today. She wondered what would happen if they ran into turbulence. Would the flirty old coot topple into her lap?

Then he'd moved over for a few polite words with Nate Bernstein and Charles Reuter. Reuter, for a change, didn't give him the cold shoulder. Maybe the prospect of a field trip had mellowed him. Next, Bouting had a conversation with Ralph Pinsky, the one he'd claimed had a possible reason to murder Matthew Flynn. It was short and apparently unproductive, with Pinsky seemingly more interested in adjusting and readjusting the cord on his wide-brimmed Trilby hat than talking.

Louise knew how hard it was to engage the soft-spoken Pinsky, for she'd tried to talk to him as they'd waited to board the plane. He'd looked down at her through those blank eyes and deflected every question. Then he turned the tables and inquired about her, her TV program, and even asking her what she raised in her northern Virginia garden. His pleasant midwestern twang barely masked his standoffishness.

Bouting stopped next to talk to Tom Schoonover and Henry Hilaeo, but that was also a no-go, since Tom was busily editing page proofs and Henry was his usual taciturn self.

Finally, the scientist approached the two sober-faced Kauai County policemen sent with them on the trip and tried to jolly them up a bit. Then, looking drained, he returned to his seat near his seatmate, Anne Lansing, who was togged out in a khaki-colored suit with a turquoise bandanna at the neck. He jumped up again when he spied Christopher Bailey leaving the minuscule restroom and limped up to his aide. This forced Ralph Pinsky to crowd around the horticulturalist to get into the restroom and John, next in line, to press against the bulkhead.

Bouting began whispering to his aide, appearing agitated. Christopher looked at him with his usual devoted and businesslike expression and tried to calm him down. Anne then got up and joined them, offering Bouting a pill and a plastic water bottle. Once he'd downed the pill, she and Chris quietly persuaded their boss to return to his seat.

Louise wondered about the exact state of Bruce

Bouting's health. Today, his infirmities were noticeable, but fortunately, Chris and Anne were there to act as nurses. She was relieved that the man had finally come to rest; he had tired her out just watching him.

Only George Wyant, huddled in a seat behind the cockpit and frowning out the plane window, had been spared Bouting's manic chatter. Wyant was a traumatized human being, she observed, only a shadow of his cocky, youthful self. Was it because he'd killed Matthew Flynn and knew the cops were closing in, or because he didn't kill him and wondered who had? One thing was sure, everyone in this group thought Flynn had been murdered. Thanks to the young man's public outburst last night, word had spread that his machete was missing and the police were suspicious of him. They also knew that divers had gone down off Shipwreck Rock to look for a discarded weapon. It would be an uncomfortable day for George Wyant.

Louise was startled out of her thoughts when the plane took a hard bounce. The pilot immediately came on the loudspeaker and warned that they'd encountered "a little rough air." This sent John Batchelder hurrying back to his seat.

As he secured his seat belt, he turned to Louise. "I have something to tell you."

"What's that?"

Just then, the plane made a convulsive sweep downward, then up again. Her colleague froze in his seat and closed his eyes. John was suspicious of the least deviance in airplanes, even the sound of landing gear descending and retracting, much less this bucking-bronco ride. "I'll tell you about it later," he said through clenched teeth.

In the hustle and bustle of leaving the plane,

she failed to ask him what he wanted to tell her, for he was still shaky from the rough landing. And she had her focus on another person, George Wyant.

She decided to take the initiative. True, the police might be checking him out as a murder suspect, but she felt sorry for the young man. It wouldn't hurt to be nice to him, especially with two uniformed police around in case she'd judged him too sympathetically.

28

At the rental car lot, those who preferred exploring the Thurston Tube and the periphery of the Kilauea caldera got in one van with Sergeant Binder. They were the gimpy Dr. Bouting, Anne Lansing, Christopher Bailey, Henry Hilaeo, and, to Louise's surprise, John Batchelder. Louise had guessed that her cohost disliked the prospect of hiking down four hundred almost-vertical feet into the Kilauea Iki caldera. Sitting happily between Bouting and the toothsome Anne in the backseat, John gaily waved good-bye to her.

Now on her own with a clutch of scientists and Sergeant William Yee, Louise approached the droopy-shouldered Wyant. He was like a tall young tree suffering from drought.

"*Aloha*, George," she said.

"Hey, " he said. She could sense that through his dark glasses he was trying to read her face.

"So you're hiking with us today. That's great."

"I had to do something besides sitting in that hotel." Apparently convinced her friendliness was genuine, he fell in step with her. She glanced at the others, Tom Schoonover, Ralph Pinsky, Charles Reuter, and Nate Bernstein, and could hardly restrain a smile. She would be hiking in one of the world's magical places with five outstanding botanists. She only hoped they'd accept Wyant into the group.

As she turned to Tom Schoonover, she said, "I see that you've wisely sent Henry Hilaeo with the others."

The scientist dropped his gaze, as if he didn't want to reveal his true feelings. "I'm not quite sure what you're getting at, Louise." He held out his hand. "Here, let me help you into the van."

It was a brief trip to the trail head in Volcanoes National Park. After that, the next three hours unfolded like a dream. From the moment they began their magical descent through a tropical thicket into the caldera, her scientist companions took on a different persona. They accepted her and the Kauai policeman, Sergeant Yee, as eager pupils. If anyone bore animosity against George Wyant, it seemed to be forgotten. What brought them together was their passion for nature. They chattered happily about each passing wonder like children at a theme park, with even George chiming in.

Once they'd descended from the lush forest to the stark lava floor, they saw a small green growth in the cracks in the barren ground. Ralph Pinsky, no longer unapproachable, caught her eye. "Mrs. Eldridge and Sergeant Yee, you newcomers to the field of botany must check out this fine new little *Ohia lehua*," he said, pulling out his hand lens and bending over the tiny tree for a better look. "It's somewhat imperiled and is making its way under difficult conditions." Politely, he handed the lens to Louise and said, "It's one of the first plants to take root after a lava flow. The honeycreepers, the iiwi, and apapane find sanctuary in this active volcanic world. They feed on these lehua blossoms." She gave it a close inspection, then passed the lens on to Sergeant Yee.

The sergeant looked, turned to her with a grin, and said, "I feel like I'm in an advanced placement science class. What about you?" She agreed, then returned the lens to the scientist.

Forgotten, seemingly, by all of them was the fact that Matthew Flynn was dead and his death a mystery yet to be solved. For here they were, in a unique place where new land was being formed by molten rock before their eyes, where volcanoes had given rise to a tumultous, otherworldly landscape of craters, forests, lava tubes, hills, and nature systems such as the lush rain forest in which they now walked. Ascending again into the rain forest, the scientists greeted each new variety of fern and plant such as a rare lobelia, as if it were an old friend, identifying and sometimes arguing about its provenance. Tom Schoonover, the taxonomist, was bowed to as the final authority. In the wonder of it all, time seemed to stand still.

But all too soon the hike was over. They finished their climb to the crater's rim and saw that the six from the other van were lounging in the shade, waiting for them. John gave her only a distant wave as he continued to converse with Anne Lansing and Christopher Bailey. In two vans they drove the short distance to the historic Volcano House, where they were to have dinner.

It took only the walk into this rustic relic of a building for her to see that John had fallen under

Anne Lansing's spell. It was obvious in the way that he ignored her and made a beeline to Anne's side and took a seat next to her at the table. Louise quickly sat in the seat on the other side of him, but then was faintly annoyed when Bruce Bouting sat on the other side of her.

Before Dr. Bouting could launch into his monologues, she turned to her cohost. "John, you were going to tell me something."

He pulled in a noisy breath between his teeth, then looked self-consciously around in case anyone had noticed. No one had. "Not now, Louise," he said, in an impatient voice and immediately turned back to Anne Lansing.

She dipped her head to get a better look at Anne. Louise saw that the woman's clothes clung to her curves in a tempting way. Her unusual yellow-green eyes, red-painted lips, and glossy bob were only accented by the bland colors that she wore.

Louise sighed. She'd have thought a newly engaged man like John would have more self-control. For some reason, she'd had a protective feeling toward John, but realized this was silly; her colleague ought to be mature enough to handle dealings with strange, beautiful women. She studied her menu, ordered the restaurant's famous duck à l'orange, then turned to Dr. Bouting, resigned to the fact that she was trapped in his conversational lair. Looking into his lively face, she searched it to find the good there, the good that her wise father said resided in every man.

"My dear," he said, a gleam in his eye as he reached over a big paw and placed it on hers. She had the clear feeling he'd temporarily forgotten her name. "We dropped into the snack bar here earlier for a soft drink and saw the most incredible films of old eruptions. Those volcanists, what plucky people they are, walking right up to the flows! How I wish I were twenty years younger."

Smiling philosophically, she withdrew her hand. "Indeed, Dr. Bouting, you seem to be doing just fine at the age you are. You are quite an unstoppable man."

29

Sunday evening

In a herd of other cars, the two vans moved slowly down toward the sea, where the action took place. Within ten miles of the new vents, they could see eruptions of lava into the sky. While their excitement grew, their pace slowed. The cars had to maneuver into a crowded parking lot. National park rangers in their muted green uniforms ringed the area, waving flashlights to direct the drivers into snug parking slots.

"My God, that's wonderful," exclaimed George Wyant.

"It truly is," echoed Charles Reuter. "I've visited this place before, but I never thought I'd be able to get as close as this."

Nor did I, thought Louise.

Along with a crowd of other wide-eyed visitors, they stepped out of the van for the hike to the edge of the flow. The first thing that struck Louise was the noise, not only of the excited crowd, but the explosive sounds from the lava vent, then the crackling sounds as the thick, viscous pahoehoe thinned out and turned into a'a. Finally, there were the huge hissing reverberations from the boiling sea as two thousand-degree molten rock hit its cool depths.

Before anyone dispersed, Tom Schoonover managed to round up the group. "This is going to be one of the exceptional experiences of your life," he told them. "I urge you to stay together, with a partner or partners. It's perfectly safe, but be wary of a change in the wind, which might blow noxious fumes your way. Watch out underfoot. If you fall, you can get cut badly by the jagged lava. Don't forget to drink water to avoid dehydration. You must, of course, stay within the boundaries set by the park rangers."

"Something we already understand full well," snapped Bruce Bouting, who seemed to soar loftily above all instructions.

Tom Schoonover continued unfazed. He looked up through a sky still rosy-colored from the sunset at a white quarter of a moon. As they watched, a cloud passed over it. "Consider the sky and the clouds and the moon, folks, and then look there." He pointed to a molten trench some thousand yards up the hill, where the earth was boiling. Orange lava spewed far up into the air, then fell into hundreds of rivulets that came streaming down toward the sea. "It's eating up more ground as we speak—and also creating more benches of land near the ocean."

Louise caught her breath, for in the dimming light Tom's face looked almost saintly. "Again," he said, "that pattern of destruction and creation which we are privileged to see. Now, go enjoy this wonderful moment on this wonderful planet. And remember to go with a buddy or two for safety."

The others hurried off, Charles Reuter and Nate Bernstein in the company of George Wyant, who'd lost his desolate manner and seemed almost a happy man. Ralph Pinsky had pulled a professional-quality face mask out of his fanny pack and adjusted it over his nose, then went off with Henry Hilaeo.

Bruce Bouting walked away with his loyal employee Christopher Bailey, but Louise noticed that when Christopher reached out and took the older man's elbow, Bouting shrugged him off and stalked forward with the help of his cane. So much for the buddy system, she thought.

To Louise's disappointment, John grabbed Anne Lansing by the hand and whisked her away as if they were young lovers. She frowned, for she had wanted to share this experience with her colleague, not some person she'd met only days ago.

Though the two Kauai police came to oversee things, Louise noted they'd already drifted off, seemingly spellbound by the shooting fountains of lava. This was a once-in-a-lifetime experience, for Hawaiian residents as well as visitors.

She looked around and through the dimness saw Tom Schoonover standing nearby. "I guess it's you and me," she said, smiling.

"My pleasure, Louise. Let's be off." They went to a line demarked by yellow electric flares placed a few feet apart in the ground. The crowd was wandering this line, but Louise could see none of the people in their party, for darkness was closing in fast.

Inside the flairs the treacherous pahoehoe slowly descended at a southeast angle and eventually would cross the Chain of Craters Road. This beleaguered road was moved once before because of lava flows. As well as houses and beaches, it was gradually being obliterated by Kilauea's eruptions.

To Louise, the lava looked like a thick, slow-moving, hydra-headed orange monster, each head with an ugly snub nose. It curved itself into sinewy patterns as it moved slowly down the slope. She gasped, to be so close to the earth in an act of creation. Then suddenly she gagged and choked, as a strong whiff of sulfur came her way. Hurriedly, she covered her nose with her bandanna.

Tom was doing the same thing. "The wind is shifting," he said, "and that's not good. Let's step back a little; I think we'll be more comfortable." She followed him and they stationed themselves farther away from the flow, halfway between the vent and the ocean. The biggest crowds were uphill and downhill from them, either watching the lava as it burst out of the vent, or as it rolled into the sea, creating hissing steam clouds five stories high. A huge spurt of liquid orange, twice as high as the fifteen- or twenty-foot spouts that had been coming out of the new vent, blew its way into the dark sky.

Louise could hear the crowd of hundreds oohing and aahing. A few even applauded, as if nature were a stage impresario trying to please his audience. But she noticed park rangers hurriedly moving uphill to warn the crowd. The surface flow appeared dangerous.

"Wow," said Tom, "Kilauea's certainly putting on a show. With fountains that high, I'd think those rangers would establish a wider perimeter. I hope those people who've climbed close to the vent are safe."

Louise worried about her colleague, John. Was he safe, from both the lava and the woman he was with?

They watched in respectful silence for a few

minutes before they were interrupted. "Excuse me, Dr. Schoonover," said a man's voice out of the darkness. It was Sergeant Yee. "I need to talk to you." He took him aside, which immediately alarmed Louise. She edged closer to the two and heard enough to scare her.

". . . and I'm afraid people are scattered all over; we can't find half of them. These fumes are a big concern."

Tom turned back to her. He gripped her arm for a moment. "Louise, you know the way to the car, right?"

"Yes."

"Then either remain here, or if the wind changes again and the fumes are getting to you, wait at the vans. Would you do that?"

"What's wrong? Can I help?"

"I have to leave," he said impatiently. "Just don't get lost, okay?"

"I won't."

The two men hurried up the hill toward the volcano vent. Louise had a sick notion in her gut. Where was John? Then she realized her protective instincts were kicking in again and that John Batchelder was perfectly capable of taking care of himself.

She patiently waited for five minutes, though it seemed like an hour. Out of the darkness a figure appeared, coughing and hacking. It was Anne Lansing. She moaned, "I have to get out of this. It's too much for my lungs."

"Anne, did you see John?" cried Louise from behind the handkerchief she held on her face. The fumes were coming their way again.

Anne pointed vaguely uphill. "He was so darned timid that I left him with some old women. Everyone's moving—it's gotten less safe, the rangers say. People in our crowd are going every which way; I just saw Henry Hilaeo wandering around alone. Ralph Pinsky is way up top, about as close as you can get to the vent." She put a hand on her chest and coughed almost convulsively. "But not me. I'm sorry—I have to get out of here. I should have stayed with John on safer ground. I'll be at the car." As she hurried off, she called back, "If I were you, I'd stand back farther from that line. Or else come back to the vans with me."

Louise hesitated, even as she suppressed a cough and realized Anne was the smart one here—Anne and Ralph Pinsky, the one with the business face mask.

Where was John? Tom Schoonover and the policeman were already looking higher up for people. On a hunch, she decided to search downhill. Coughing from the effects of another whiff of sulfur, she pulled her bandanna securely over her lower face. Then she walked along the line of electric flares, encountering few others. Warily, she eyed the tendrils of orange-red lava meandering ever closer to the flairs. Then she heard a faint cry of pain. "Awwwww!"

"John!" she yelled, "is that you?"

"Louise . . ." It was a muffled lament, followed by spasms of coughing. "Louise, help us, I beg you . . ."

30

In spite of the heat, an icy fear overcame her, but did not stop her from charging downhill toward his voice. "John, where are you?" she screamed. The heat was closing in on her, the fumes constricting her throat.

"Here!" he cried faintly.

She raced down the hill a few more yards and straight across the safety barrier, accidentally kicking some kind of stick on the ground as she went. Ahead was a dark shape dangerously close to the molten rock. "Oh, my God," she muttered, rushing toward the river of orange as she pulled her Maglite flashlight from her cargo pants. Focusing the thin beam ahead of her, she saw John lying on the ground. His left arm was extended, holding onto the hand of another man who was caught in the stream of lava.

The condition of Bruce Bouting made her cry out in horror. His prostrate body was being devoured by that many-headed orange monster; she saw that there was no saving him, as his clothes and body smoldered and seemed ready to burst into flame. She had to act quickly to save John. Shoving the flashlight back in her pocket, she reached down and twined one of his arms in hers and said, "Let go of his hand, John. Someone will come for him. I need to take both of your arms."

He let go, but howled with pain as she connected with his other arm and dragged him away from the lava. She screamed, "Help us! My God, please help us!"

As she pulled John across the ground, passersby rushed over to help her get him to a place of safety outside the perimeter of lights. She crouched down, got her flashlight out of her pocket, and shone it on him. "Oh, John, you poor thing," she groaned. The left side of his face and his left arm were burned an ugly red and black. "But you're going to be okay. I know you are. And you can see, can't you? That's the important thing."

He looked up at her and his amber-colored eyes were wide with a blank expression. "Yes, Louise, I can see you. Not well, but I can see everything . . . and you have to understand . . . it was all for love . . ."

She knelt down and kissed him on the right side of his face. "You were very brave. You tried to save Bouting's life, didn't you?"

He stared up but no longer seemed to see her. It was as if he'd moved into another world.

"Oh, my God, he's dying!" she cried.

Tom and the two Kauai policemen rushed up. Tom tried to pull her to her feet. She tensed her thigh muscles, hunched her back, and resisted. "No," she said.

"Louise," the scientist explained, "I don't think he's dead; I think he's in shock. The ambulance crew will be here in a moment. They'll take care of him. Look." He pointed to a group of uniformed EMTs approaching. "They're here now with a stretcher. You've done enough."

At last she allowed Tom to help her stand up. He put an arm around her and gently led her away. After a few feet she refused to go farther. "No. I want to stay here. I want to know what happened."

"And so do I," said Tom.

The two ambulances had arrived silently, without sirens, probably afraid that sirens would panic the sizable crowd. Quickly, they set up two small floodlights, so what occurred next seemed to Louise like a macabre play, with her as one of the players. Technicians concentrated on the first casualty at hand, moving John Batchelder onto a stretcher, slapping an oxygen mask onto his face, and rushing him to an ambulance. Two other technicians scrambled into special gear that covered their heads and faces. She was startled to see a large fire extinguisher in the hand of one.

Louise went over to the ambulance, wanting to do something. John's eyes had closed. "I can go with him," she pleaded with the muscular man who appeared to lead the rescue team. "I think it would help."

The man put his hands up to bar her way, as two EMTs unceremoniously shoved her colleague into the vehicle. He shook his head back and forth. "No, ma'am, you'll be more help letting us do our work of trying to save him."

The man slammed the ambulance doors shut and Louise turned away, her gaze drawn back to the line of flares. Beyond it the orange lava continued on its relentless path. She looked up and saw that Tom Schoonover still stood at her side. "I don't need a nursemaid," she told the scientist.

"I know that," said Tom. The two technicians, looking like two astronauts on the moon, had reached Bouting with a stretcher. There was a hiss and a plume of steam from the fire extinguisher and she realized that Bouting's clothes were no longer smoldering. They carried out his body, a mass of livid third-degree burns clad in singed tan cotton. Burned to a lesser extent was the hand that John had been clutching in his attempt to drag Bouting away from the killing lava.

Looking around, she noticed that all but two of the people in their party were now gathered around the rescue workers. There were soft exclamations from a few, but mostly awestruck silence, as they watched the man being delivered to the second ambulance. True, the body had an oxygen mask on, but the EMT wielding one end of the stretcher grimly shook his head as someone quietly inquired about the condition of the man.

A figure suddenly ran into the circle of light. "Oh, no, *Bruce!*" screamed Anne Lansing, who had just arrived from the car park and recognized the victim. She rushed to the stretcher as it was being lifted into the vehicle and tried to embrace the elderly scientist, but the muscular technician pulled her away. Then, seeing that she was about to collapse on the ground, he held her awkwardly in his arms.

Next, Christopher Bailey, the second of the missing people, appeared out of the darkness and rushed to the ambulance, where the stretcher had already been put in place. Hopping up into the vehicle, he looked down at his badly burned employer. "For Christ's sake, what happened to him!" he yelled. Technicians gently ushered him back onto the ground, where he stood looking wildly around through his thick glasses. He saw Anne Lansing standing nearby, bent over with grief; he strode over and took her in his arms. From above her head resting on his shoulder, he looked out at the spectators—Charles Reuter, George Wyant, Henry Hilaeo, Ralph Pinsky, Tom Schoonover, and Louise. It was as if he were cataloging each of their crimes.

While they stood there together, the lava, which to Louise was now like a living presence, continued its inexorable flow downhill, making loud crackling noises as if defying humans to interfere with its course toward the sea. With difficulty she switched her attention to the park rangers and the two Kauai patrolmen. They were efficiently querying people about what they had seen.

She had the ghastly feeling that this scene had been played before in Volcanoes National Park. It was simply standard operating procedure. She'd read a little about the dark side of the park, though it did not advertise its disasters. Just as the tempting waters of the Hawaiian beaches led to X number of drowning deaths per year—was it fifty to sixty a year, as the beach oracle had told her?—the tempting surface lava flows of the Big Island, the fieriest place on earth, led to a burning death every now and then, often enough that there was a standard operating procedure. Their questions were polite, but their underlying questions were, *How did the dumb jerks get so close to the lava? Didn't we warn you all?*

No one appeared to know how or why Bouting and John went over that safety line. Were they lured there, Louise wondered, by a desire to get up next to that dangerous orange river? Bruce Bouting, they all knew, was fixated on this earthly wonder; she wouldn't put it past him. Perhaps John had spied him there and tried to help him out of danger.

"I was up and down the line," said Ralph Pinsky, in a muffled voice. He still had not removed his mask, but that made sense, for they stood on the edge of the electric torch barrier and the wind sent an occasional drift of sulfur their way. "I saw Bruce doing the same thing, walking the line, then changing his mind and going the other way."

Tom Schoonover put it to Christopher Bailey, "Christopher, you and Bruce were supposed to be a pair. And there he was, with a bad knee at that. What happened and how did he get within that line of lights?"

Bailey, who still had an arm around the despairing Anne Lansing, glared at him. "First, who do you think you are, Dr. Schoonover? I'll tell the authorities, but you're not one of them." Turning to a park ranger who appeared to be in charge, he said, "I *was* paired off with Dr. Bouting, who incidentally is my employer and my mentor." Another dirty look sent Schoonover's way. "He walked with the aid of a cane, because he had a bad knee that was kicking up."

The park ranger said, "We found a cane not too far from the body."

"He was an independent kind of a man," said Bailey, "and he didn't like me holding his arm. In fact, he told me to get lost, because he wanted to plod around on his own." Bailey's eyes teared behind the thick glasses. He let go of Anne, took off the spectacles, and unashamedly let his tears flow. "I don't know *where* he went, because that big flare of lava went up and it distracted us all. When that excitement died down and you park police told us to move back from the line, he'd disappeared. I spent the rest of the time looking uphill for him, because I figured he'd go where there was the most action."

"Thanks," said the ranger. "Anyone else with a sighting of this Dr. Bouting and the younger man who was found with him?"

"Sure, I saw him," said Henry Hilaeo, who was standing on the edge of the crowd. "Bouting, that is. Ralph had disappeared, I don't know where. And then along came Bouting, hurrying uphill as fast as his bad knee would carry him. Earlier, I'd seen him crabbing at Chris Bailey there"—he nodded his head in Bailey's direction—"and saw that the two of them weren't gonna stay together."

Anne Lansing raised her head. "I was with John, uh, whatever his last name is. He was very timid about everything, not wanting to go uphill, not wanting to go closer than ten or fifteen feet outside the established boundary." She closed her eyes as if in torment. "I finally told him, unfortunately, that I wanted to go explore on my own, for I couldn't see things that well from the distance. The last I saw, he was talking happily with a group of older women."

Others chimed in, only to say that they could hardly see anyone in the darkness and had observed neither Bruce Bouting nor John Batchelder.

"Unfortunately, these accidents happen," said the park ranger. Sergeant Yee was on his phone; Louise suspected he was talking to Chief Randy Hau in Kauai. Yee pulled the ranger aside and talked to him quietly, after which the ranger announced, "We'd like to question you a little more up at park headquarters."

In the headquarters near Volcano House, it was Louise, the park ranger, and Sergeant Binder, though she would have preferred Sergeant Yee, whom she now felt she knew. But he was busy questioning others. While the park ranger already seemed to have concluded that this was another unfortunate accident, Binder saw it in a more suspicious light. He asked the questions.

"Mrs. Eldridge, Mr. Batchelder is your coworker. Then why did he hang out today with Dr. Bouting's group?"

"He preferred not to take the Kilauea Iki hike, so he went with the other group. He seemed to be enjoying the company of Bouting's assistant, Anne Lansing. They were together again tonight, but then Anne had a coughing spell and had to go to the car."

"Would Mr. Batchelder take that kind of chance, going across the line of lights, wanting to brave it and see just how close he could come to disaster?"

"He wasn't that type of person. In fact, he was just the opposite. He didn't even enjoy flying in airplanes."

"Tell us exactly what led you to walk down the hill and what happened once you heard John Batchelder cry out."

She gave him all the details she could remember, including the fact that when she was a few feet inside the safety line, she kicked a big stick that lay on the ground. "Later, I realized it probably was Dr. Bouting's silver-tipped cane."

"And how far away was this cane from Dr. Bouting's body?"

"It was a good ten feet away and I probably kicked it five or six feet closer to the two men."

She looked her interrogator in the eye and they both drew a somber conclusion. There was no earthly reason for Bouting to chuck his precious cane. Did someone separate him from it?

"Did Mr. Batchelder have any enemies in the group of thirteen that came with you from Kauai?"

"No. The only possible enemy he could have had was me. I was the only one there who knew him for more than four days."

"And what do you know of Dr. Bruce Bouting— did he have any enemies that you know about? Did you pick up any vibes today that made you suspicious in this regard?"

"As I've tried to explain, John and I have known Dr. Bouting and the other scientists and their assistants for only four days. Today, I didn't sense anything unusual in the air. In fact, everyone got along better than usual."

She wondered if her police inquisitor was getting tired of her repetitive answers. Maybe she should tell him about the scientist's squabbles with the others. "Dr. Bouting did have some arguments with his fellow scientists—I think Chief Randy Hau is already aware of this."

Sergeant Binder's eyes lit up. Louise guessed that he was doing what she was doing—trying to find a connection between the horrible events here tonight and Matthew Flynn's brutal end.

"And what, in your opinion, was at the heart of these disagreements with fellow scientists?"

"As I said, Randy Hau has heard this already. At the heart of the arguments was the feeling that Dr. Bouting's commercial motives weren't as 'pure' as some other scientists' when he hunted plants in foreign lands. There were issues such as introduc-

ing exotic plants that might become noxious pests
and overwhelm endemic plants . . . that's a situation that exists right here in the islands . . . "

Louise looked over at Sergeant Binder and realized it might have been different had Sergeant Yee
been doing the questioning. From her experience
on the hike, William Yee was fascinated with nature
and plants. But she was boring this officer almost
to tears with her horticultural ramblings. With
glazed eyes, he allowed that he was now done questioning her and quickly called in the next person.

31

Louise huddled in a window seat in the back of the charter plane, hoping no one would sit beside her and talk. It had been grueling over the past hour, telling and retelling her story to the park ranger and Sergeant Binder.

She yawned, feeling exhaustion in every pore. Yet she knew she could not fall asleep; too many images of that gruesome death scene were flashing through her mind. Even the smells clung to her, the sulfur fumes and the odor of burning flesh . . .

They'd left Kauai this morning with an unlucky thirteen people and they were coming home with only eleven.

Just ahead of her sat Anne Lansing and Christopher Bailey. As Louise took her seat two rows behind them, she noted that Bailey held the deceased Dr. Bouting's carry-all on his lap. The scientist had left it in the van when he went to observe the lava flow. Bailey held the leather case reverentially, as if it had been blessed. Within that stylish piece of luggage, she knew, was Bouting's sleek black computer with its precious store of plant information. Just what would become of it now?

"Louise!" someone hissed. She was jolted awake, not even realizing she'd been asleep. It was Anne Lansing. She stood unsteadily in the aisle and looked down at Louise. "Can I join you?"

She'd already told Tom, who'd wanted to sit with her, that she'd prefer to be by herself. He had gone back and taken a seat next to Henry Hilaeo.

Louise looked up at the woman. Her eyes were red-rimmed, her cheeks swollen from crying, her makeup half-gone, and her hair tousled and out of kilter. She nodded and Anne sat down and leaned into her. She immediately wondered if she would regret this.

"Oh, Louise, why, why?" cried Anne. "How could this have happened?" It only took that statement to release a new flood of tears, some of which landed on Louise's wash-and-wear white sleeve. Anne's big turquoise bandanna, which had become a handkerchief, already was saturated and now became super-saturated. "Why did he do such a foolish thing? He had everything to live for."

"He appeared to. Why do you think he'd go so close to the edge?"

Her hands flared open, like two graceful flower petals. "Oh, it was his nature; you should have seen him on our China trip a few months ago. He'd clamber up ridges and walk on precipices that even Chris and I were afraid to traverse." A momentary pause for a blow of the nose and wiping of more tears. Then silence.

Anne said, "I've been keeping this thought at bay, Louise, but I can't help wondering if someone did this to him."

Now it was out there, the thought in everyone's mind.

Anne leaned back in her own space, for which Louise was grateful. Louise said, "That thought crossed my mind, too. Certainly the authorities are sensitive to the fact that this is the second scientist in a group of eight who has died in the past two days."

"Twelve scientists at the conference," amended Anne, "if you count those from the NTBG."

"Yes. I guess we should count them, too." Even in her sorrow, the woman had a mind like a steel trap. Louise could not explain what happened next. Perhaps because two deaths in two days were too much for her, Louise laughed out loud. A genuine laugh, one that turned heads. "It's so ludicrous, but forgive me, I can't help thinking that this is like an Agatha Christie mystery. Could this be a case of slowly killing off all the scientists who came to the conference?"

"But Louise," said Anne, "that doesn't track."

"What do you mean?"

"Well, four of the eight visiting scientists have been permitted to go home already by Randy Hau." Anne's tear-swollen eyes were nevertheless alert, a reflection of that active brain at work. "That weakens your theory—the only visiting scientists left are Charles Reuter and Ralph Pinsky—and George Wyant. I suppose he's considered a scientist." She slumped back in her seat. "Of course, there's also Schoonover and his people."

"I was just making an inappropriate joke, Anne," said Louise. "I certainly hope that this isn't the work of a person who intends to kill even more people. I can believe that Matthew Flynn's death was deliberate, but what happened tonight is another matter. The park rangers as much as admitted it—people die once in a while at the Kilauea volcano, even though the Big Island doesn't broadcast statistics. That's because people take chances they shouldn't. Your boss was in that frame of mind. He *fantasized* that he could be one of those volcanists striding alongside the molten lava, risking life and limb for science."

"I know. I suppose I just strengthened your belief that he may have done this to himself." Anne sighed. "I must say, Louise, that your friend John is wonderful. I only hope he pulls through. I wish the best for him in that hospital."

Anne's tears resumed and now Louise was crying. She fumbled in her pocket for her own bandanna. "He is wonderful." Louise choked out the words. "And he'd better live, because I've just discovered what a truly fine person he is."

Anne turned her intense green eyes on Louise. "You've known him a long time."

"Four years."

"I've been with Bouting Horticulture for ten years now. Dr. Bouting—Bruce—has been wonderful the whole time, guiding me, giving me opportunities to explore with him, teaching me the business. Besides that, he's been like a father to me." Louise had seen the two together and felt that this was indeed a close parent-child bond. "You see, my own father's gone and it's as if Bruce were his substitute." At this, Anne broke down again and said no more.

Louise hadn't heard the detail from her husband that Anne's prestigious professor father had passed away. Bouting's death was a double loss for this woman. Her seatmate's eyes were at half-mast, she looked as if she, too, were exhausted and might fall asleep.

Before she did, Anne turned to Louise and put a soft hand on her arm. "I hear you've solved a couple of crimes in the past, Louise. If you decide to look into Bruce's death as anything other than a horrible accident, would you tell me?"

"But I don't intend . . . well, yes, I guess I could tell you if I did a thing like that."

"You want to know why?"

"Why?"

"Because I'd like to help you. If a killer did this, I want to help you catch the bastard. The Kauai police chief is a nice man—maybe too nice. I'm afraid he's inexperienced in things like murder. And the situation is only made worse because Bruce died on the Big Island." She gave an impatient shake of her bobbed hair. "Those federal rangers act as if it's just another self-inflicted accident by a careless tourist. I'm going to hire a private investigator if they don't come up with some answers."

As she drifted off to sleep, Louise thought that one could do worse than have the very smart Anne Lansing pursuing the truth about Bruce Bouting's horrible demise.

32

Monday morning

Louise reached over to stop the terrible little song in her ears. She grabbed her cell phone off the table and took a moment to pull herself awake. It was morning and she was in Hawaii. And something terrible had happened last night in this tropical paradise. Then it all came back, the spurting volcano vent, the awestruck crowds, the sulfur fumes, the two bodies lying near the streaming pahoehoe . . .

John Batchelder was terribly hurt. Dr. Bouting was dead.

She flipped the phone open and pressed it to her ear. "Hello," she said.

"Louise, darling," said her husband, "are you all right? I heard the news. My dear . . ."

Louise lay back on the pillow and cuddled the phone to her ear. "Bill, it was horrible. I don't know if John's going to make it."

"It must have been like a nightmare, from what we've heard in Washington. I got a call from Charlie Hurd, our old friend from *The Washington Post*, hours ago. He recognized John Batchelder's name and figured you were in Kauai, too. I waited as long as I could so you could get some sleep. Tell me a little of what happened."

"Dr. Bouting got too close to the lava and John tried to pull him away from it." She swallowed, trying not cry.

"And Bouting died right on the spot?"

"I think so. He looked dead when they took him away on a stretcher. John has burns on the left side of his body. I'm sure he's in terrible pain." She could almost feel those burns on his arm and the side of his face. "They wouldn't let me stay with him there."

"At least he's alive, Louise, according to the last news here. How could this have happened? Don't they have a safety fence near that stuff?"

"Not exactly, just a row of electric torches and quite a few park police monitoring people. I don't know how it happened, Bill. There were hundreds of people up and down that line. It was so exciting for everyone and the lava was literally exploding up at the new vent. We were supposed to be in pairs, but it was easy to get separated—everyone in our party seemed to get separated. One of the Kauai policemen with us was worried, so people went looking for the others. I decided to look for John . . . and I found him."

"He went to help Bouting?"

"He was trying to drag him out, but Bouting must have weighed well over two hundred pounds. His clothes were burning—*he* was burning . . ." She began to feel sick with the memory. "John tried, but the fumes were overcoming him. I pulled John out of there as best I could."

"You probably saved his life. But take it easy now. You don't have to give me more details."

She looked at the bedside clock, which read eight o'clock. "Bill, I have to go. I have to find out how he is. And the police want to talk to all of us—I'm already going to be late." She swung her legs off the side of the bed and stood unsteadily.

"Hold on a minute," said her husband. "Look, two of the three principals in your TV program are dead. I don't like it."

She went over and unlocked the French doors and stepped out on the lanai. Before her was a view of the achingly beautiful plants and trees of Kauai and beyond them, the glorious ocean. "I'm not in danger."

"It took awhile to come up with that conclusion, Louise."

"I had to think it over. Right now, I feel like one of the walking dead. But my brain is starting to function again, because things are coming back to me that I haven't told the police. Just before John lost consciousness, he said something to me."

"What was that?"

"He said that it was all for love."

"Not very definitive," said Bill.

"You don't think so?"

"Did he mean his love for mankind is why he put his life on the line and tried to save a man he hardly knew?"

"That could be it," said Louise.

"I mean, John was a sincere, kind of mawkish guy, wasn't he?"

"You mean, '*Isn't* he?' He's not dead, Bill."

"No, he's not. I'm sorry. Louise, you don't sound so good. Should I come there?"

"No, don't come. I'm coming home. I can't believe they won't let me go home tomorrow . . . and yet I hate the thought of leaving John behind in a hospital."

"You may have to. Now, Louise, it's important that you stay in touch with me. If you don't call, I'll worry about you."

"I promise to call."

Her husband's voice had taken on an air of caution. "Now, are you up to it if I give you some information on those other scientists?"

"I'm out on the lanai. Wait until I get back in the room and get organized." She stepped inside and found her pen and pad and sat down in a chair. "I'm ready," she told him.

33

"I have material on five additional people, four from the National Tropical Botanical Garden, plus that St. Louis guy, Dr. Ralph Pinsky. Now, the two most important people from the gardens there seem to be Tom Schoonover and Henry Hilaeo. The other two, Tim Raddant and Sam Folsom, are not as, shall we say, pertinent. They're said to be talented, comfortable in their own skins, and contented at what they're doing."

"Good. I'd hate to think a man who runs a herbarium or a science library is also a killer."

"Let's start with this Schoonover fellow," said Bill. "He's a little more controversial. I hope he doesn't turn out to be mixed up in a crime, Louise. I can tell by the way you talk that you like him."

"I do. But tell me what you know."

"You know his background already. Schoonover is *the* authority on Hawaiian island plants and Pacific plants in general. He's said to be a hide-bound honest man; this sort always rubs some people the wrong way. Believes peer review should mean peer review and not a glossing-over approval of a scientist's work from another busy scientist who hasn't read the work. Makes everyone who contributes to his books certify the authenticity of the material, et cetera. He's generally very collaborative and willing to give credit to others. After all, lots of scientists come to Hawaii to do research. But the fairly recent expedition of Matthew Flynn presented problems for the people at the gardens. Flynn went off on his own with his aide-de-camp . . ."

"George Wyant."

"He got lucky and quickly published his findings about a special orchid. It left a bad taste in the mouth of the staffers there who work their tails off in behalf of protecting the species they have and finding new ones."

"Are you saying Matthew Flynn didn't follow protocol?"

"I guess that summarizes it. Protocol probably would have had someone like Henry Hilaeo accompanying them during their field work."

"And what about Henry Hilaeo?" Hilaeo, with his unsmiling stare out into a world dominated by foreigners; but did his gloomy look mean anything?

"Hilaeo's a success story," said Bill. "He's mixed race, but has a lot of Hawaiian blood in him. As a teenager, he got into trouble—petty theft, that sort of thing. But an interested teacher redirected him and he earned a degree at the University of Hawaii and then a graduate degree at Berkeley. He's working on his doctorate."

"It's interesting how these scientists cross each other's paths as they go through years of education. Maybe Henry Hilaeo knew Dr. Charles Reuter."

Bill said, "He not only knew him, but he has him on his doctoral committee. If Hilaeo is the sort who holds grudges, Matthew Flynn was a logical person against whom to hold a grudge."

"But even if Hilaeo did hold a grudge against Flynn, he didn't have a reason to dislike Bruce Bouting, did he?"

There was a long silence. "Why would you say that, Louise? I thought we were talking about people who could have been mixed up in Matthew Flynn's death. Are you talking about two murders now? What are you implying?"

"Bill, I feel it in my bones, that's all. I think someone gave Bruce Bouting a shove into that lava. For one thing, the cane he was carrying was too far from his body. He wouldn't have left it behind if he'd gone poking closer to the lava flow."

Another silence. "I don't like your being there alone."

"It's all right, Marty and Steffi are here. Anyway, no one is the least bit interested in me. And maybe I'm just being paranoid and the man fell into the lava by sheer accident. Go ahead and tell me about Ralph Pinsky and then I'd better get dressed."

But her husband was off on another tack. He said, "Now that I read these notes again, I see that there's a pattern. There are at least four hard-nosed purists among your scientists—Charles Reuter, Nate Bernstein, Tom Schoonover, and Henry Hilaeo. These are people who are impassioned on the topic of endangered species—who look askance at and don't necessarily trust bold plant explorers."

"Pinsky is another of those plant explorers," said Louise, "and he's best friends with the four 'purists.' That makes five purists, as you call them."

Bill said, "Pinsky has a terrific reputation, but

he's tough. He may be the purest scientist of all, because he doesn't stand for any BS. Doesn't let charlatans in the field get away with anything, not if he has a chance to thwart them. He brings plants and seeds to his botanic garden, tests them to be sure they're safe and practical, then gets them into the commercial market."

"He's one whom Matthew Flynn outsmarted; Flynn discovered a plant that Pinsky had been coveting, right under his nose."

"It may not matter for long, Louise. Your Dr. Pinsky recently was diagnosed with lung cancer and he doesn't have a good prognosis. He's undergone chemotherapy, which means it's advanced. The man is a quiet sort, but very prestigious and proud—and, as I said, tough. He has no family; it's said that plants and his botanic garden are his life. He also writes a column for some garden magazine, *Garden Concepts*."

With the phone clasped to her ear in one hand, Louise wandered over to the dresser, opened the drawer, and removed her fresh underwear for the day, then went to the closet and took out a yellow cotton sundress and her white sandals.

"But here's a tidbit that I found interesting," continued Bill. Though she'd be tardy for the meeting with the police, she didn't want to miss out on anything her husband had worked so hard to learn. "They say Pinsky is foolhardy when it comes to his own health. He's planning one last field trip, though his field trip to Turkey last fall was supposed to be the last one."

"I can guess why he's taking another one," said Louise. "He wants one more shot at finding a new species. Matthew Flynn copped the Turkish tulip the last time."

He didn't react for a moment. Finally, he said, "What scares me about all this is how deadly serious these scientists are about their work. It blows me away to think that pinching plants could be a motive for murder."

She was just about to argue the point when Bill added, "Another thing—if Bruce Bouting was the victim of foul play, there could be two murderers out there."

34

Louise had hurried into her clothes, but still she was late. She came down the elevator and jogged down the hall to the conference room, relieved that this route through the hotel did not take her by her noisy adversary, the parrot. If it screamed at her one more time, she might be tempted to commit avian homicide.

Pulling open the carved koa wood door, she hoped to find that the police chief had ordered up rolls and coffee, as he had the last time this unlucky group had met.

No food, she saw, as she entered the room. Again, she was the last to arrive, but this time the chief was not so forgiving. "Please sit down in back, Mrs. Eldridge," he briskly informed her. "We've already started and now you've set us back a bit."

Red suffused her face as she slipped into a seat in the last row. Mercifully, Chief Hau took a moment to rustle his papers as Louise tried to regain her composure. How could she tell the chief she had the same legitimate excuse as the last time—

her clever husband was giving her information on the principals in this case, some of which might prove of value to him.

It was a smaller group this time. Nine of the eleven civilians who went to the Big Island were here, as well as Marty and Steffi Corbin. The other visiting scientists, the local TV crew, and the NTBG's Tim Raddant and Sam Folsom had apparently been dismissed from police consideration.

The Corbins turned their heads and gave her concerned looks, but the rest of the group focused on what Police Chief Randy Hau was telling them.

Casting a disapproving glance in Louise's direction, he said, "I'll repeat briefly what I just told you for the benefit of the latecomer. After last night's events, no one need plan to fly out of here today or tonight. I know you want to get home, so we'll gauge this day by day. I think it's a bit premature to reserve a day flight for tomorrow afternoon, but you can make tentative reservations, if you wish, for the nine thirty flight tomorrow night."

The murmurs began then, as people could not contain their feelings about this disruption in their busy lives. Louise closed her eyes for a moment, trying to hide her dissappointment. After the events of the past few days, she longed to go home and fall into Bill's arms. Yet the thought of leaving John behind in a hospital was uncomfortable, almost scary. There was a murderer on the loose. Her cohost could have witnessed the killing of Bruce Bouting. Would a person who'd shoved a man into two thousand-degree lava hold back from killing a witness lying helpless in a hospital?

Dr. Charles Reuter spoke up and to Louise's disappointment he had lost the bonhomie he'd exhibited yesterday when they hiked the Kilauea Iki caldera. In a voice filled with disapproval, he said to Randy Hau, "Before the latecomer arrived, you were about to tell us why we have this continued delay in our departure for home."

The police chief's impassive face showed no disapproval of the scientist; he was probably happy that people weren't yelling at him. "First of all, let me report on the two people who didn't return with you last night. I'm sorry to say that Dr. Bruce Bouting was dead on arrival at the Hilo Medical Center last night. He suffered severe burns, as well as smoke inhalation."

Louise noted that Anne Lansing's head drooped as she heard these words, as if she hadn't been there when Bouting's body was placed in the ambulance. Christopher Bailey, sitting next to her, put an ample arm around her shaking shoulders.

"John Batchelder is in the Hilo Medical Center," said the chief. The minute he mentioned John's name, Louise felt tears coming to her eyes. "He's suffering from burns he acquired when he tried to pull Dr. Bouting away from the lava. He's being transferred this morning to Wilcox Memorial in Lihue, where a doctor on staff is a burn specialist."

"John Batchelder's a real hero," commented Tom Schoonover. He turned back and smiled at Louise. "That makes two heroes from the Washington PBS station."

The dark-haired police chief looked back at Louise and then down at Schoonover, who was in the front row. "He sure is a hero. And so was Mrs. Eldridge the other night on Shipwreck Rock."

"How is he doing?" asked Marty Corbin.

"Our latest report on Mr. Batchelder is that he's

hanging in there, but naturally he's in a lot of discomfort. I want to assure his friends that he is receiving very good medical care."

Ralph Pinsky spoke in a calm voice. "Chief, I have an important medical engagement on the mainland. I realize how traumatic it was for everyone last night and I offer my condolences to Miss Lansing and Mr. Bailey, as well as my best wishes for the recovery of Mr. Batchelder. But the reason for our staying here is what?"

Chief Hau said, "It's because we've uncovered some new facts about both the death of Dr. Flynn and the death last evening of Dr. Bouting."

A hush came over the group.

"Ladies and gentlemen, this may be very disturbing to you, but both of these deaths have highly suspicious elements. At this time, we're withholding final judgment, but we're obliged to investigate each of them as if it were a murder."

Steffi Corbin gasped; others began talking excitedly to those sitting near them.

Chief Hau put up a hand, demanding silence. "Now we know you were questioned last night at Volcanoes National Park by my two men and the park rangers. But we want to question all of you again, in the hope that we can shed some light on what happened there in the park, as well as what happened Friday night on Shipwreck Rock."

He held up a lined yellow pad. "I want to schedule you for interviews before you leave this room. I hope it's clear that you must remain on the hotel grounds until you're told you may leave. And that means eating all your meals here. Kauai-by-the-Sea is being guarded by a sizeable group of my officers."

George Wyant, decked out as usual in his old

shirt and shorts and hiking boots, threw back his blond-tipped head and laughed out loud. It was a raucous sound in the quiet room. "For God's sake, we're in detention! I have an idea. Why don't you ship us to Molokai?"

Louise wished the young man didn't talk so recklessly, especially since the police might have evidence linking him to a murder or two.

The ever-serious young Nate Bernstein turned to Wyant and said, "That was completely uncalled for and utterly insulting."

"Lighten up, buddy-boy," said Wyant. "Can't you recognize a joke when you hear one?"

"Not a very funny joke, George," retorted the solemn-eyed Bernstein. "If you'd ever read the history of what happened on Molokai and the terrible lives of those poor, benighted lepers, you'd never . . ."

"Okay, that's enough now," barked Police Chief Hau. "Mr. Wyant, Dr. Bernstein, let's not quibble. We know this disruption in your plans is not welcome news. But we'd like to think that you're all cooperating with our investigation. You're free to swim, eat, drink in the bars, and even dance, if you want, on the patio tonight. We just don't want any of you to leave the hotel. Tom Schoonover and Henry Hilaeo are free to leave the hotel, but not the island. Are all these details understood?"

George Wyant stared at the police chief. "And I bet you'd like to interview me first, wouldn't you?" he asked in a quiet voice.

"You're quite right, Mr. Wyant. Why don't you sign up for the ten o'clock slot?"

At that, the meeting adjourned and the quiet group changed into a talkative crowd.

Steffi and Marty hurried over to her and Steffi

enfolded her in her ample arms. Again, Louise felt a visceral sense of comfort. She envied people with large mothers; Louise's own mother, though affectionate and given to hugging, was slim and kind of bony. With someone as ample as Steffi, it was like being embraced by a big pillow, but a pillow with feelings.

"Oh, Louise," her friend said, "you look so pretty in your yellow dress, but I know inside you must feel awful. I heard that you were the one who found John." Her big brown eyes were filled with remorse. "We feel so guilty, because we drove up north and had a glorious, peaceful day, while you all were caught in this tragedy."

As soon as Steffi released her, Marty put a big arm around her bare shoulders. "Hi there, Lou. That was one bad time you had down there on the Big Island. D'ya think John's gonna make it? How'd he look?"

"He looked—"

"How bad were the burns?" interrupted Marty. "Will they affect his looks? What will John Batchelder do if his looks are ruined?"

Steffi grasped his arm. "Marty, stop that! What a thing to talk about now! Let's just hope he lives." She turned to Louise. " How bad off was he, honey?"

Louise was recalling guiltily the way she'd teased John about losing his looks—of how he could always turn to producing if this ever happened to him. "The burns were pretty bad on his left side, especially his left arm. And, there were burns on the left side of his face. I hope those weren't too bad. The fumes probably were as hard on him as the fire. I think we should get permission to go and see him."

In an excited voice, Steffi said, "I like that. We

can find out from John what happened. I can tell they think someone shoved Bruce Bouting into that horrible lava!" With that she hurried over to talk to the chief.

Marty shook his head. "I know this murder stuff is your bread and butter, Lou, but . . ."

"Not really," she objected.

"Well, I sure would like to go home."

"There's something ironic here, Marty," she said. "I've always had this fantasy of swimming in a lagoon in a tropical paradise. Now here I am, trapped in my fantasy, condemned for the unforeseeable future to swim in the hotel lagoon, to partake of endless luaus and eat the overly rich food in the dining room, to drink interminable mai tais—"

Marty chuckled. "And only be released when and if the police solve the crimes."

Suddenly, Chief Hau called out to them. "Hold on, folks. I forgot one thing: the media. TV crews and reporters are all over the place, but are being kept off the hotel grounds so as not to disrupt the routine of Kauai-by-the-Sea. That doesn't mean they won't try to contact you one way or the other." He twisted his face in a semblance of a smile. "Maybe they'll even shout at you across the shrub barriers on the grounds, so be forewarned. We would prefer if you didn't share with them any details you have of these two tragic incidents. What you do later, once this is cleared up, is your own business, of course."

Marty poked Louise hard on the upper arm. She turned in surprise at the unexpected jolt and saw that his brown eyes were lit up like an excited child's. "The media, Lou, the media! *Inside Story*, to be exact. They'll eat it up—I should have thought of it right off the bat! That's how we're gonna re-

coup our losses on that program with the two dead
scientists. Recoup them and make a profit, besides."

"You mean you're going to sell the tape of that
program to *Inside Story*?" she asked.

"Why not?" said Marty. "You can bet every network is out there right now clumsily trying to re-
enact what happened to Matthew Flynn and Bruce
Bouting, because we all *know* human tragedy drives
the TV news. And what could be more enticing to
them than footage of a guy who gets his head
chopped and then is thrown off a cliff . . . and another guy who's shoved into a raging river of lava!"

"*Marty*," said Louise, alarmed at her producer's
unchecked emotions.

He interrupted her. "I don't even have to deal
with *Inside Story;* I could sell it to *any* of the major
outlets. I don't have a *reenactment*, I have the genuine article, the tape with the two murdered scientists alive—walkin' and talkin' and sweatin' and
arguing their fool heads off in the National Tropical Botanical Garden!"

Louise felt as if the bottom were dropping out
of the world as she knew it. She'd felt this way before when humanity proved to be too hard to take.
At the moment, it was her own producer who was
kindling in her this sense of doubt about the in-
herent goodness of man.

She looked straight into Marty's eyes. "You're
quite an operator, Marty." She looked down at her
wristwatch. "Let's see, Bruce Bouting was burned
to death twelve hours ago." With that, she turned
away and walked across the room.

By the time she'd approached Randy Hau, her
ire had cooled somewhat. The police chief smiled
at her, apparently having forgiven her for her tar-

diness. "G'morning, Mrs. Eldridge. Um, everything all right?"

"Not exactly," she said glumly, "but you don't want to hear about it. Chief, I have to tell you about something John Batchelder said last night, just before he lost consciousness."

Hau looked around and saw George Wyant across the room, waiting to go with him for a private interview. He put his finger down on the yellow-lined sheet. "How about eleven? Can we get together then?"

"Yes. And where will we meet?"

He nodded in the direction of the hotel lobby. "We've taken over the office of Melanie Sando, the public relations director. It's the second from the end in that line of offices behind the registration desk."

Melanie Sando, Louise guessed, was the woman in the lime green suit who'd had words with her the other day. "Fine. I'll see you then. I talked to my husband this morning; that's why I was late to the meeting. He told me some things that might interest you. He has quite a conduit of information back in Washington, D.C."

"He does, huh?" said the chief. "A State Department employee, isn't he? Well, I won't turn down any help I can get, Mrs. Eldridge." He shook his head. "There's a terrible dearth of physical evidence in these kinds of incidents. They're outdoors and there are no fingerprints, for one thing. I look forward to talking to you." He smiled. "And I forgive you for being tardy. Just don't let it happen again."

As she turned away, she nearly bumped into Tom Schoonover. He'd put on his cap again, as if ready to return to his workplace. "Louise, I need a word with you. Have you eaten this morning? You don't look like you have."

"No. And I'm famished."

"Good. Let's go catch a bite—which, knowing this hotel, they'll call brunch." After a momentary smile, worry lines appeared on his broad forehead. "I've got a problem, something I need to talk to you about rather urgently."

Louise glanced over at Marty and Steffi, who were talking to a desolate-looking Anne Lansing. As she watched, Steffi reached out a consoling arm and put it around the younger woman's shoulder. Anne could use Steffi's compassion right now. Over the distance, Louise exchanged a chilly glance with her producer.

"My friends might have expected me to eat with them, but just as well that I'm not. I'll tell them that I'll meet them later." She smiled at Tom. "Anyway, how could I resist such a nerve-wracking invitation?"

35

"Let's get out of the hotel to eat," said Tom.

"That would be nice," said Louise, "but I doubt the authorities will approve."

"I'm suggesting we go to the restaurant overlooking the spa pool. It will give you a little change of scene."

"Good," said Louise. "We can watch people doing their laps while we eat."

They walked outside and down the flowered walkway to the Final Redoubt Spa, a low-slung building separated from the hotel by a flower-lined walkway. Beyond the orchid-bedecked registration desk was a covered lanai. Beyond that was the spa's lap pool where two swimmers slowly plied the lanes.

When Louise and Tom were seated at one of the glass-topped tables, Tom took off his hat, revealing his lengthy curls of gray hair. He put a plastic bag he was carrying on the table. Apparently he saw her staring at his head and ran a hand through the mop. "I know. I need a haircut. Just haven't had time since coming back from the Marquesas."

To herself, she thought, *This man needs a wife. Men with wives don't get this shaggy looking.* On the other hand, she rather liked the shaggy look.

He handed her the plastic bag. "This is a gift for you. I thought you'd like it and that it might come in handy some time."

"Well, thanks," she said, pulling the contents of the bag onto the table. It was a coiled length of rope. In fact, it looked like the rope Henry Hilaeo had used to rappel down the cliff. She smiled. "Is it—"

"Yes, it's a hunk of Henry's rope, actually. Henry suggested I give it to you as a memento."

"It's a very nice reminder of you and Henry and Tim and Sam and the gardens."

He shook his head in a humorous kind of way. "And you never can tell when a girl might need a piece of rope. It's not something, like a plant, that will delay you when you leave the islands."

After she put the rope back in the bag, they both ordered a gourmet omelet called the Hawaiian Sunrise Special. She said, "What is this urgent matter, Tom?"

For a moment, he fidgeted back and forth on his filigree-backed iron chair until he hit a comfortable spot for his back. "Sore back this morning," he explained cryptically. "Louise, this is what bothers me. I think you're in a precarious spot. Randy Hau hasn't said anything about it, but don't you feel a little threatened?"

"You mean by what happened last evening?"

"Yes."

"I told my husband I was in no danger. Are you saying I am?"

"Let's think it over," said Schoonover, leaning his arms forward on the table and looking her straight in the eye. "Even if two scientists have been the victims, that doesn't mean this is some kind of deal where scientists get picked off, one by one. You know, one of those 'Murder at the Mansion' plots."

"Funny," said Louise, "but I facetiously mentioned that very thing last night to Anne Lansing on the plane. You have to admit it's less a joke now that two scientists are dead."

"You have a point there. But you also have to look at what happened to John and why he was there with Bouting last night."

She stared into the distance, not focusing on the lap swimmers in the pool nor the somnolent sunbathers lining its edges. "Tom, I think I know how John got into trouble. I bet he was snooping around. As you probably heard, he was determined to investigate Flynn's death. He told practically everybody about it."

"And since you and John were sitting and talking together all the way to the Big Island, the perpetrator might think that you know everything that your friend John knew." He gave her a somber look. "That could put you in jeopardy. I would hate to think of anything happening to you."

The memory of the plane trip clicked back into her mind. "John might have been on to something. A few minutes before we reached the Big Island, he went up front to use the restroom. He was excited when he came back, so he must have learned something up there. He said he had something he had to tell me."

"What was it?"

"He didn't tell me. Remember the turbulence when we started to land? John's nervous about flying in the first place. He just held on and could hardly talk. Then, in the Volcano House restaurant, I asked him what it was that he had to tell me."

"What'd he say then?"

"He said he couldn't discuss it then. In fact, it didn't seem important anymore by that time."

The waitress brought their brunches, but neither was that interested in eating. Tom Schoonover said, "Let's go back to the plane incident. Who was near him up in the front of the plane?"

"Unfortunately, half the people in the plane. When Christopher came out of the bathroom, Bouting hurried up to the front and was animatedly talking to him, but in his usual whispery voice. Ralph Pinsky gave Bouting a dirty look and went into the restroom. John was right there, waiting behind Pinsky in line. Bouting seemed upset and Christopher was trying to soothe him. Anne Lansing came forward with a pill and a water bottle. Bouting took the pill and then she and Christopher helped him back to his seat."

Schoonover said, "I caught some of that action out of the corner of my eye, but I was pretty engrossed in my editing."

"All the while," said Louise, "George Wyant was hunkered down in the front row seat within easy earshot. It's unclear to me what upset Dr. Bouting, or what John heard, or from whom he heard it."

She picked up her fork and tried her omelet, a mélange of eggs, mushrooms, onions, chipotle bits, and green pepper. It made her long for the simplicity of breakfast at home.

Schoonover said, "You were sitting pretty far forward, but you couldn't hear what anyone was saying?"

"No," she said. "It was all very sotto voce."

Schoonover grinned at her, his hazel eyes crinkling. "I love it when you speak Italian."

"Very funny," she said.

He dug into his own omelet with gusto, consuming half of it in a matter of minutes.

Later he said, "What you've told me doesn't allay my concerns, Louise, it only exacerbates them." The worry lines were in full force. "It tells me John could have picked up vital information. He carried that information with him and ended up nearly dead near the lava flow."

She had a heavy feeling in her stomach. Maybe it was the food, or maybe it was her companion's sober admonitions. "Heaven only knows what John found out," she said. "I hope I can visit him soon and he can tell me. In the meantime, the police must be scratching their heads trying to come up with answers. For one thing, you scientists all know each other in a number of different ways. Bill says—"

"Bill. Your husband."

"Yes, I talked to him this morning. He says there could be two killers hanging around this place." She made a face. "Isn't that cheery news?"

He nodded. "He's right. That's a definite possibility."

She looked warily at her companion, for now she was getting into personal territory. "There are a hundred little reasons for disliking someone— for instance, the issue of someone taking credit for a plant discovery when he discovered the plant by underhanded means . . ."

Schoonover gave her a sharp look and his eyebrow wrinkles deepened.

"But it probably takes a bigger reason to kill someone than that," she finished.

"Mmm."

"Then there's the hypothesis that a 'true believer' was knocking off a couple of people whom he considered unworthy to be scientists."

He broke into a hearty laugh. "I bet you number me among those true believers."

"Yes, though I don't think you'd kill anyone."

"There's another obvious theory."

"Obvious to you, maybe. What is it?"

"Suppose on Friday evening that Flynn's killer was observed by Bouting, either when gathering up a weapon—and I have no doubt that the police have now fished Wyant's machete out of the Pacific Ocean and have the weapon—or when the two went up the Shipwreck Rock path. That would be a logical reason for the assassin to shove Bruce into a handy stream of red-hot liquid rock."

"And what about John?"

"I hope John recovers so he can tell us. He could have been snooping—he probably was. He happened upon this dark deed and despite considerable personal fears did the courageous thing, plunged in there and tried to save this man's life. He'd have had a better chance, of course, had Bouting been a smaller man."

"Did you know Bruce Bouting well? I mean, well enough to know about his health?"

Tom shrugged. "I saw him intermittently over the years at conferences. I think I know what you're getting at. I'm certain the man was suffering from early Alzheimer's."

"That's what Bill discovered. Bill's with the State Department, so he's been able to do a little checking on people." Suddenly she was embarrassed. This opened up way too much of her personal life to a man she'd known for less than a week.

"Hmm. Your husband's checked people out?

Obviously he wants to protect you from harm, Louise. I also want to protect you. So let's talk about Bouting's health. Here you had an older man who was suffering from a terrible malady and had the worst of it ahead of him. But I'm sure we both agree that, whether he was sick or not, falling into molten lava is not the way he wanted to die."

She sat back, feeling full of vague regrets. Maybe she'd said too much to this man. After all, Tom Schoonover was within the umbrella of suspects. He wasn't even going to be restrained from leaving this hotel, since his home and his beloved gardens were just a few miles from here. What if she were wrong and she was talking to the killer?

He leaned forward again, forearms on table, as if he were going to pour out an intimate secret. "I have one little piece of advice for you, in case you're tempted to snoop around like your colleague did."

"Yes?"

"I'm guessing that the police have little physical evidence, since these are outdoor crimes. Now, the scientific method is a belief system that posits that you have been able to provide evidence that is physical and self-evident as far as the truth is concerned. If we rely on our senses, we're in trouble, for the senses play tricks on us all the time. We know what happens when there's an accident: Different witnesses to the event see different things. It's easy to be mistaken in things we observe and even things we hypothesize. We must test our theories."

Not an intimate secret at all, she thought, but a science lesson and an intriguing one at that. She shoved her long brown hair back from her face. "But I don't even have any theories."

"Yes, you do," he said, "you just presented some

of them to me. And if you think about it longer, you'll have more. Just be careful. And remember, we're never sure what happened in the past." He laughed. "It's much easier to predict what's going to happen in the future."

Schoonover said, "And I have a prediction, Louise. Two people have been killed right under your nose." He opened his arms wide, as if to encompass the world. "The mystery of it is as fascinating for you as finding a new species would be for me." He hunched forward again. "I predict you can't stop yourself from delving into the matter. And I'm telling you to be darned careful when you do."

36

As Louise walked into the office to meet with Chief Randy Hau, she saw that the room bore the hallmark of the publicity director. She'd only run into the woman briefly during the embarrassing parrot incident but knew she favored lime green. The two visitor chairs were done in this color, while the draperies were a lime background with wild accents of pink, yellow, and royal blue. Good thing that this was Hawaii, thought Louise, where over-the-top colors and patterns in furnishings and clothes seemed quite in harmony with the over-the-top colors and patterns in nature.

The police chief got up from his borrowed executive chair and stood behind the blond desk. "Mrs. Eldridge, please sit down." She did and was surprised at how comfortable the chair was. He picked up a white envelope off the desk and handed it across to her. "I want to give this to you before I forget. We found it in the pocket of Matthew Flynn's shorts the night he died."

"I suppose you read it."

"Yes, we had to, of course. It's perplexing. Maybe you can explain it and how you came to know this man. After this mysterious message, there's a list of island restaurants and their locations."

She slipped out the small note paper and read.

Louise—
   From one gourmet eater to another—keep your mind open and your eyes, too. And if something should happen to me, check out the equipment!
Matt

Then followed a list of seven restaurants on the island, all with Chinese, Japanese, or Hawaiian names. He'd written rough directions to each, including the homey landmarks that the islanders tended to use as guides: "*Turn left at the Exxon station and go about a half a block. Then hang a right and go 'til you see a big Sago palm in a yard on the left— that's it.*" As Louise remembered from living in London as a foreign service wife, Brits did the same thing. They started out by pointing a finger firmly in some direction: "*Go about three blocks that way, luv, to the old church. The name of the street will change, but don't get a stitch in your knickers over that. Then take a left for a ways, past the greengrocer . . .*"

Louise gazed thoughtfully over at Chief Randy Hau. "What on earth could he have meant?"

Hau said, "It's odd. In fact, it's ominous. And it indicates to me that you must have been acquainted with this Dr. Flynn, something you didn't tell me after we found him dead."

"But I wasn't acquainted. I only met him when I came to this hotel."

The chief's eyes were slightly narrowed. "You're sure of this? Your friends will say the same thing?"

"Of course. I only talked to him, let's see, four times, once on Thursday and three times on Friday. And never at length and never alone."

The chief waved his hand, as if in dismissal. "Okay. Then that's settled. You and I have other things to talk about. First of all, tell me about last night and about what John Batchelder said to you when they were putting him into the ambulance. In fact, tell me everything you can think of from last night. Then let's talk about what your husband learned about these people."

When she related John's words about "it was all for love" the policeman looked puzzled. She told him how she found the two men near the lava, being sure to describe how her foot collided with Bouting's cane, which she'd inadvertently kicked closer to the two.

Hau nodded solemnly again. "And what did you conclude from that?"

"Bouting didn't get that close to the lava all on his own. Someone persuaded him in there and shoved him the rest of the way."

"When the police heard that from you last night, they came to the same conclusion."

Soon they got around to the subject of Bill's background checks. The chief knew many of the same things Bill's efforts had uncovered through his Washington, D.C., sources, but not all. He was unaware that Matthew Flynn was going to discontinue his work in the Amazon, nor did he know that Ralph Pinsky had terminal lung cancer. He had heard that Bruce Bouting was in the early stages of Alzheimer's disease. He also had heard about the succession plans at Bouting Horticulture, where it was thought Christopher Bailey would take over the top position and Anne Lansing would share in management.

They exchanged a look. It was the first time she felt the man might actually like her. He said, "We both realize the problem. There are dozens of theories that we could develop out of all these small bits of information."

"That's true. If it was a single killer, it could be an obsessed environmentalist who thought Flynn and Bouting both were frauds. As for Matthew Flynn, it could be someone who resented him for ending his work in the Amazon, or for getting there first to discover a rare plant . . . especially someone who's dying and doesn't appreciate being cheated out of a final big discovery. Or *another* plant explorer beaten out of a discovery on his own Hawaiian turf."

"And in the case of Bruce Bouting, there's always the theory that Anne Lansing and Christopher Bailey wanted to hurry up the changes at the top. If there are two killers, it makes it doubly complicated." He scratched his head and frowned. "The trouble is that there's so little physical evidence. We have Matthew Flynn's blood up on Shipwreck Rock and nothing else. The park rangers have scoured the site of last night's incident in Volcanoes National Park and have come up with nothing except Bouting's cane. We have you to thank for telling us where it originally was lying."

"There's also the machete," she said guilelessly. "Have you found it?"

When he hesitated, she said, "You might as well tell me. If you don't, the beach oracle will."

He smiled a little. "Oh, I get it. Bobby Rankin. Is

that what you call him? He's supposed to keep anything he found to himself, but there were lots of spectators on the beach when he came up with it Sunday afternoon."

"Was that helpful, finding the machete?"

Hau fidgeted in the high-backed chair. "There are no fingerprints, of course. Unfortunately, anyone could have taken it from Wyant's room, including Wyant. The maid has told us that those two gentlemen, Flynn and Wyant, always kept their room door propped open, apparently because they were used to living in the out-of-doors and couldn't stand locks and dead bolts. Wyant solemnly denies he did it, of course."

Louise stared into the middle distance, where her eye was caught by the pink, yellow, and royal blue pattern in the drapes. So disorderly, like a conclusion reached through evidence of the senses. It reminded her of her talk with Tom Schoonover about the scientific method. "Tom Schoonover says you can make a ton of mistakes relying on your senses and even your hypotheses. He says that what you need is to test your theories." She didn't mention that Tom thought she might be in danger; she was trying to keep this thought at bay.

"I'll go along with that, but it's not that easy to test theories."

"Here's this disparate group," she said, "consigned to the hotel grounds. Why don't we use some ruse to get everyone together tonight? Could you call another meeting?"

Chief Randy Hau cleared his throat and considered her idea. "That may seem a little odd, since we just had one this morning. But there may be another way to do this. Now, as you might guess, Kauai-by-the-Sea hates having a murder investigation taking place in its midst, much less having guests held against their will. Melanie Sando, who's a very uptight lady at this point, tells me the hotel is anxious to do something to preserve its image. She's suggesting that they throw a little dinner party for you folks tonight."

"That's a perfect way to get people together."

He sat forward with a hopefulness Louise hadn't observed before. "There's a great singer, Joan Clayton, booked into Options this week. Melanie calls her a *chanteuse*."

"She's wonderful," said Louise. "She sings all those old romantic Cole Porter numbers."

The chief said, "Melanie thinks she could talk this woman into singing, what do you call it, a little group of songs . . ."

"A set?" suggested Louise.

"Yeah, a set,"said the chief. "She could sing a set . . ."

"Do a set, I think they say."

"Yeah. Do a set, a special little entertainment deal, for after the dinner. Think that's too hokey?"

"Everyone will love it."

"We'll tell them the hotel thinks of it as a farewell dinner and it is; we hope to get you folks on your way by tomorrow night—that is, if we feel we have enough information from everybody."

"Marty Corbin would help. He's a great master of ceremonies. Nobody will ever suspect you're trying to learn something. Maybe he could whip up a program with audience participation."

Randy Hau restrained a big sigh. "It's worth a try. I'm telling you, these are difficult cases. Outside of reinterviewing people, we have little else to focus on—that and John Batchelder. When Mr.

Batchelder comes out of his pain medication stupor, I'm hoping he can tell us something."

"Which brings me to the question: When can we visit him? Has he arrived yet?"

He raised his wrist and consulted a bulky wristwatch. "That's all planned. It's almost noon, so chances are that he's arrived and they're getting him settled in. I'm going to drive you and the Corbins there; it takes a half hour." He smiled briefly. "Less, if I run the siren."

His brown eyes stared at her. "Mrs. Eldridge—"

"You might as well call me Louise."

"Louise, as of early this morning, John Batchelder was still out of it. You people are John's good friends." When he said this, she felt a twinge of guilt in her chest. Had she been a good friend to John?

Hau continued: "I'm counting on you to help pull him back, so he can tell us what happened." He shook his head again. "He's one of my best hopes."

She recognized the haunted look in the policeman's eyes; she'd seen it before in the eyes of Fairfax County Sheriff's Department Detective Mike Geraghty. It was the look of a law officer who feared he was going to end up with an unsolved murder on his hands. In this case, it was two unsolved murders.

37

Monday noon

Louise wished she'd had the nerve to jump in
the front passenger seat of Police Chief Randy
Hau's car. Instead, she sat stiffly between Marty and
Steffi Corbin in the backseat. Since she still had
not forgiven her producer for being a money-
grubbing opportunist, she exchanged little conversation with him. Nevertheless, they made progress
in other ways. As they traveled to the hospital in
Lihue, Louise, the chief, and the Corbins mapped
out plans for the evening. The hotel would foot the
bill for a dinner and entertainment in the Lanai
Room, an open porch for private parties adjacent
to the hotel dining room.

Before they left to go to the hospital, the chief
had had Lieutenant Payne search out Melanie
Sando, who contacted Joan Clayton. He soon had
a call back from his assistant saying the deal had
been made. The singer, who'd been found in a
massage room in the Final Redoubt Spa, agreed to
make a brief appearance in the Lanai Room for
this special group of hotel guests under surveillance.

After a few songs from Clayton, Marty would stand up and emcee a spontaneous little program. Steffi was enthusiastic about it. "Who knows what you might learn about people?" she said. She was in charge of contacting the eight people. The list would include the whole crew: resident scientists Tom Schoonover and Henry Hilaeo, as well as the visiting scientists, Christopher Bailey, Anne Lansing, George Wyant, Charles Reuter, Nate Bernstein, and Ralph Pinsky.

"Hell," grunted Marty, "getting a free dinner from the hotel isn't going to change things. It's like George Wyant said, we're under house arrest."

Randy Hau glanced back at him for an instant. "I prefer not to think that, Mr. Corbin, but in a sense it's correct. We can't afford to endanger anyone else's life."

Marty turned to Louise and in a quiet voice said, "Lou, you and I have gotta make up, despite the fact that you disapprove of me for being crassly commercial."

"I guess we do," she agreed.

Marty sealed the reconciliation by leaning over and giving her a little peck on her cheek. "And whatever happens tonight, I gotta take care of you. I had a phone call from Bill and naturally I had to tell him the cops think both Flynn and Bouting were murdered. Understandably, your old man is worried. He's given me my marching orders— wants me to see that you stay out of trouble."

"So he called you." Louise smiled. She liked the fact that her husband wanted to protect her long distance.

At that moment, the chief smoothly turned the wheel and everyone in the car fell silent. They passed through one of Kauai's most enchanting sights, the famous Tunnel of Trees, a stand of roughbark *Eucalyptus robustus* whose branches overarched the road. Again, Louise felt the resonance of Kauai's ancient history, for these trees probably had stood here for a century or more.

Once at the hospital, a middle-aged, brown-eyed nurse with dark, wavy hair ushered them into John's room, apologizing that the doctor had been called away. Louise was not as surprised as Marty and Steffi at the voluminous dressings that swathed the left side of John's body and head.

"My God!" whispered Steffi, turning her eyes away as she sought the comfort of her husband's arms.

Marty Corbin looked over Steffi's head at John and said, "Thank heavens he didn't get it too bad in the face. But by God, he's out like a light."

John was laid out as if dead, his tanned face serene, his eyes with their long black lashes closed against whatever the world had to offer. *He looks as if he'd be willing to sleep forever*, thought Louise. And no wonder, she thought, since only the night before, he had ended up in a veritable hellhole filled with lethal fumes and flowing orange lava. She shuddered at the memory.

Chief Hau looked her in the eye. "Louise, why don't you go to his bedside—the nurse tells me it will be all right. See if you can rouse him." The policeman hauled a chair up close to the right side of the bed for her.

"Thank you," she said and sat down and took John's hand. There was no reaction. She gently squeezed it and said, "John, it's Louise. Can you wake up? Try to wake up and talk to us. Marty's here and Steffi's here. And the police chief wants to talk to you, too."

Her colleague's head moved slightly in her direction and he moaned. What she'd not been able to picture sufficiently was the pain he must be in, pain controlled with heavy doses of morphine, according to the nurse.

The woman stepped up next to Louise and bent down over the patient. "Now, John," she said, in a clear voice, "your friends are here and they want to talk to you. Can you wake up?"

His answer was another moan. The nurse looked at them and said, "I believe you'd better go. He's due for more pain medication and he's indicating pretty clearly that he needs it. So please step away from the bed while I do my job." When they did, she swept the privacy curtain around the bed. They heard her murmuring to him and he moaned back, as if in reply. Then there was silence.

Opening the curtain again, the nurse said, "This man isn't quite ready to talk to you. He's emerging from a very bad place, but he hasn't quite come up yet."

"When do you think he can talk?" asked the chief. "He has information we need badly."

The dark-haired nurse cocked her head to one side and looked at him, as if deciding what she thought of Chief Hau. They looked at each other, recognizing that both were natives, he with more Hawaiian blood, she with more European, possibly Portuguese, blood. Evidently she decided he met her standards, for she smiled and said, "I'll tell you what, Mister Police Chief, you give me your card and I'll phone you up the minute that he decides he can put two words together. How's that?"

Hau nodded gravely. "I like that. I'll be anxious to hear from you."

38

Monday afternoon

Louise and Steffi stood at the elevator, negotiating with the man. But the man wasn't giving an inch.

"Going shopping again?" growled Marty Corbin, running an exasperated hand through his dark, wavy hair. "You went shopping four days ago and wiped out a half a week's salary. How about going to our room and getting a little shut-eye instead? It's much cheaper."

Steffi gave Louise a look, shrugged her ample shoulders, and hit the elevator button. "I guess you're on your own, Louise."

Louise gave them a quick wave good-bye and turned down the hall in the direction of Kauai-by-the-Sea's cluster of upscale shops. It was amazing, she thought, the effect that violence had had on this hotel. The number of guests seemed much diminished and she realized some had checked out following Matthew Flynn's demise. She could only guess that Dr. Bouting's death, even though a hundred miles away, must have further discomfited the hotel's clientele. Right now, for instance, she walked down a huge hall totally by herself; a clever purse snatcher could take her bag and get away with no trouble. A rapist could come along and drag her into an empty conference room. Where were all those police that Chief Hau had talked about?

She walked a little more briskly. She didn't need clothes, but she did feel a need for a particular article of clothing. Maybe it was Tom Schoonover's warnings, but she was beginning to run scared. She intended to be ready for trouble.

She entered what seemed to be the larger of two clothing stores, Clothing-by-the-Sea, whose front racks were filled with skirts and slacks and dresses in the most brilliant patterns that Louise had ever seen. A tall, young saleswoman appeared. She was dressed in a black lace top with a low-cut bustier underneath that showed a good third of her breasts. Below this she wore a black silk skirt with an uneven hemline. A bit dressy for daytime sales work, but with her long, swinging brown hair and a well made-up youthful face, the saleswoman pulled it off. Louise thought of her as wearing a costume that represented the ultimate in what an unfashionable customer might attain if she listened to the counsel of this wise young woman.

"*Aloha,*" the woman said. "How can I help you?"

Louise looked around dubiously into the sea of flowers, birds, and palms that swam before her eyes. "Do you have anything plain colored? I need a top with lots of pockets in it. And it has to be something in olive or tan." Louise noticed she was veering toward neutrals these days and supposed that in a decade or two she'd be wearing no bright colors at all—only olives and tans, the color of tree bark and autumn grass.

The young woman didn't pause an instant. "I believe we have just what you need." She led Louise to the back of the store, a whole new world. One corner featured slinky cocktail clothes in the mode of the saleswoman's outfit. In another corner there were racks of designer sports clothes in solid colors. She pulled out a high-fashion pullover with lots of pocket detail and held it up for Louise to view. "What do you think of this, for instance?"

"I'm amazed," said Louise. "This is just what I want."

"We aim to please," she said, flashing a wide, perfect smile. She took several garments off the rack for Louise to try on and led her to the dressing rooms.

As Louise approached the door of one of the cubicles, the adjacent door opened and out walked a woman in black. It took a moment to recognize the striking, handsome figure.

"Anne, hello."

"Hi, Louise," said Anne Lansing. She was wearing a long-sleeved black top and matching slacks cut in fashionable ankle length.

"A lovely outfit," commented Louise.

"And it's off-season, so it's on sale," said Anne. Since she was as tall as Louise, Anne's green eyes gazed straight into hers. "I intend to wear it to Dr. Bouting's funeral back in Philadelphia. Frankly, I don't usually wear black. I can't get used to myself in black. But there'll be hundreds of people at his funeral and they'll expect the company's 'heirs'"—she put up two fingers of each hand, to indicate quotation marks—"to be in mourning. So I intend to do it right. This outfit, plus black Manolos and a veil with a black rim."

"I know how much Dr. Bouting thought of both

you and Christopher Bailey. He obviously groomed you two to take over."

Anne gave a sad little sigh. "It will be a bit of a strain, but the two of us definitely are slated to manage the company now. Though his grown children, you know, will be here tomorrow to claim his personal possessions." She shook her head and Louise noted tears forming in her eyes. "Yes, we'll manage the company. But it's such a terrible way to be promoted, you have no idea."

What could Louise say? "I know how sad it is for you and Christopher. But still, I hope the two of you come tonight to the dinner." She showed her the pile of clothes in her arms. "One of these will be my fashion statement, just a sporty thing."

Anne said, "I don't particularly want to come to a dinner with the other captives, but I will."

"It'll be very nice and low-key, I hear. Joan Clayton's going to sing. That alone should make it worthwhile."

Anne's expression brightened. "I love Clayton's music, though it will probably make me cry. Excuse me now while I talk to the salesgirl about this outfit."

Louise was about to go into her own dressing room, but paused to peek into Anne's, since the door was ajar. She had neatly folded her shorts and blouse and placed them on a chair, then hung her belt on the back of the chair. Suspended from the belt was the usual plant explorer's rig. *That's okay*, thought Louise, *these plant hunters have nothing on me. I'm doing that myself tonight, carrying around my own equipment.*

The sight of the garden clippers on the belt piqued her interest. She looked across the store, where Anne Lansing was being fussed over by the modish saleswoman. She stepped into the dressing room, took the tool from its plastic case, opened the blades, and casually put a finger against the two-inch-long rounded "business" blade.

"Ow," she moaned, as she saw blood appear on the finger. She'd cut herself on the razor-sharp edge. It was the right hand she'd scraped the night Matthew Flynn died and was still festooned with a small bandage. Cupping her left hand under her right to catch the blood, she quickly locked the blades and returned the shears to their case. She withdrew from the room and slipped into the adjoining one. In her purse, fortunately, was the red bandanna left over from the preceding day's visit to the Big Island. She twisted it around the wound, then turned her attention to the clothes she was to try on.

She was delighted to find that the first pullover she put on was lightweight and voluminous, yet good-looking. That was the thing about designer sports clothes, she reflected. They had that extra pocket or zipper or fashionable cut so that they rose far above the level of the casual clothes Louise usually wore.

When she exited the room, her newly cut hand hidden under the pile of pullovers, there was Anne, looking at herself in a mirror and holding up to herself a simple black linen dress the saleswoman had selected for her. "Are you taking these?" Louise asked her. "They're very attractive."

Anne nodded. "I think so. I need black outfits almost as soon as I get back to the East Coast."

Louise couldn't help noting the ring on her hand that stood out against the black fabric, gold set with an opal. "What a beautiful ring."

Anne slowly extended the hand toward Louise.

"It is beautiful, isn't it? It's my engagement ring, except we hadn't announced it yet. So I sometimes wear it on my right hand." Her eyes suddenly filled with tears, which overflowed down her cheeks and onto the black top.

Louise put a hand on her upper arm. "I am so sorry to bring this up."

Anne shook her head, sobbing now. "No, no, I shouldn't wear it if I don't want people to notice it. It's just that now, with Dr. Bouting's death, I don't know that I will go ahead with my engagement."

"Oh, my goodness." Louise was about to advise Anne that she had to go on with her life, but bit her tongue. This was private business. The woman would have to work things out on her own. "Again, I'm sorry."

Anne Lansing stretched a hand out and touched Louise's forearm. "Louise, if it turns out that Dr. Bouting was killed, well, will you have a chance to do anything?" There was such hurt in those yellow-green eyes that Louise felt the tears begin to rise in her own eyes. "The police seem so clueless, though I did hear a rumor that they found a machete in the water off the cliff."

"I heard that, too," said Louise. She started to tell Anne that she'd visited John Batchelder and saw signs that he might be able to talk. Then Louise remembered something her older daughter Martha had taught her: *Don't disclose anything to people who are involved in a murder inquiry.* "I don't know much about what the police are doing, except they're certainly keeping an eye on us." She smiled and bid Anne good-bye.

As she left Clothing-by-the-Sea and made her way down the hall toward Island Rest, she wondered if she should make a stop back at the public relations office. Police Chief Hau undoubtedly was still conducting interviews. As a veteran gardener and a TV garden show host, Louise was dismayed at this new way of looking at an everyday garden tool, but she now knew that each of the scientists carried a lethal weapon on his or her person—sharp-bladed garden clippers. She would not bother Police Chief Hau with this information; he had eyes to see, just as she did. They were carrying their lethal weapons in plain sight.

She went into the sundries store and purchased a package of small bandages of various sizes and a couple of other items for the evening. She opened one of the bandages and put it on her new wound. The old wound, she noted, was healing nicely enough for her to ignore doctor's orders and get it wet. Forced to stay at this posh hotel for an extra day at the very minimum, she wasn't going to be denied its finest treasure, the saltwater lagoon.

39

Louise felt a little guilty going off swimming, but she had no real obligation to return Charlie Hurd's phone calls. When she returned to her room, she'd washed the blood out of her bandanna, then listened to Charlie's messages. By the time she'd played the sixth one, she was exhausted.

"Louise, it's your old pal Charlie. Look, if you call me soon, I can still get your story in the late edition of the Post. *And I know you have a story there—I bet you're right in the middle of it. Your husband acknowledged as much. And I know your sidekick got burned last night. Now, Louise, for old time's sake and for John Batchelder's sake and because we* need *one another, you and I, you should call me back and* pronto! *Aloha, now, or whatever good-bye is in Hawaiian, and I really hope you'll call. Here's the number in case you've forgotten . . ."*

The rest of the messages had been pretty much the same, although the pleading tone increased as Charlie approached deadline. She could picture the cocky little reporter sitting by his telephone in *The Washington Post* city room, praying that she'd call with a story that would be a big scoop. He'd be dreaming of a headline that read something like, "Gardening Diva Describes Tragedy at Volcano." She reflected that such a story would be no worse than Marty's selling the tape with the dead scientists to some TV news outlet. At least she wouldn't be selling, only telling, the story.

Her bedside clock read three o'clock, eight o'clock Charlie's time. She was sure it was past deadline. She'd call him tomorrow.

She put on her yellow bathing suit, grabbed her beach bag, and left the hotel by a side door, noticing a patrolman watching her leave. She was taking the circuitous way to the lagoon. A green-and-white-striped towel was slung over her shoulder, a beach bag on her arm. The route she took went by a prized garden filled with what Kauai-by-the-Sea's literature called "a sampler of the island's most noteworthy native plants." It was a lush spread of plants and trees, many of them higher than a man's head. But among them she spied just that, a man's head in a turquoise ball cap. It was Christopher Bailey.

She sauntered over to the edge of the garden and saw that he was busily snipping samples of plants with a speed and ease that told her that his clippers were as sharp as Anne Lansing's.

When he saw Louise, he slid the gloved hand holding the shears down to his side and casually concealed them behind his hip. "Well, hello there, Mrs. Eldridge."

"Hello, Christopher. Just call me Louise. Is this a great garden, or what?"

He pulled the tool forward and snapped it back on his belt, apparently deciding to own up. "It is, um, Louise. I've been given permission by the hotel management to take a few plant samples."

"I'm curious," she said. "For what purpose?"

"Oh, just a little study," he muttered, "screening for plant diseases."

"Oh. I'm on my way to swim before the sun goes down too far. Are you joining the group tonight for the dinner?"

He looked caught off guard, as if dinner were something he rarely gave a thought to. "Oh, the dinner. I hear the hotel is footing the bill and some famous musician is playing. I guess I can stand it for a while." He smiled at her and once again it made him resemble a big, wise baby.

When she arrived at the lagoon, she went through her usual routine, finding an unoccupied chaise longue and dragging it laboriously over to her private glade under the monkeypod tree. Realizing that she'd eaten little today, she went to the snack stand and ordered a smoothie with strawberries, raspberries, and papaya. Thus equipped, she returned to her lair.

After downing the smoothie and reading a few pages of her book, she fell asleep. An hour or so later—she couldn't tell because she didn't wear a watch—the raucous cry of a big bird wakened her. Noting the position of the sun in the sky, she realized it was now or never for a swim.

Standing at the edge of the water, she thought of the people she'd met in this pool—first, Bruce Bouting, then Nate Bernstein and Charles Reuter. It was amazing that the place wasn't crowded with guests; instead, it was as isolated as the Garden of Eden must have been when Adam and Eve went out for the evening. She dove in, savoring again the natural feel of the saltwater against her skin. Angling to the surface, she began to swim her usual course: the pool, the channel, the second pool, another serpentine channel, and then the third pool, at which point she turned around and came back.

Though she would have preferred it otherwise, Louise was alone with her thoughts. It was impossible not to speculate on who murdered the two botanists. She could think of at least one motive, involving professional jealousy or a company takeover, for each of the eight scientists. But that was motive to commit one murder, not two. Besides, they seemed weak and insufficient reasons. *Would someone kill over a purloined orchid, or mum, or tulip? Would someone risk everything to climb faster to the top of Bouting Horticulture?*

Two pieces of information baffled Louise and both of them unfortunately involved her. In his note, Matthew Flynn urged Louise, whom he barely knew and yet knew to be an amateur sleuth, to "check out the equipment" if something happened to him. And after Bouting was shoved into the lava, John Batchelder told her that it was "all for love."

Because of that provocative note from Flynn, she had checked out some equipment this very afternoon—Anne Lansing's well-sharpened garden shears and, later on, Christopher Bailey's equally razorlike tool.

Her head felt dizzy when she thought about it, that ghastly moment when she'd looked upon Matthew Flynn's horrible neck wound. Didn't it make more sense to think the murderer used a machete? Maybe Flynn had sensed that his erratic assistant George harbored murderous intentions and wanted someone to know about it. As for

John's murmured words last night at the volcano, "love" was not a topic that had come up among scientists quibbling about native species, invasive plants, and "market winners." The only thing that came close was Anne Lansing's remark that because of Bouting's death she would delay the announcement of her engagement. The murder of her boss only interrupted, and did not promote, the woman's happiness.

It was peculiar, the huge influence that these scientists, Bouting, Flynn, Reuter, and even Schoonover, had on their assistants. They guided them, instructed them, and thrust them forward; they were almost like fathers to them. Louise saw this in Christopher Bailey, Anne Lansing, George Wyant, and Nate Bernstein—and in Henry Hilaeo as well. These loyal employees wrote for their bosses, slaved for them, helped think for them, but lived in their shadows until something moved in the political firmament in which they operated.

It seemed odd that the only person she hadn't thought about much was the pale, pensive Ralph Pinsky. Yet Pinsky had the least to lose of any of these scientists; he was a dying man who'd spent a whole career preserving and studying plants. Why would he hesitate to murder men whom he felt were at cross-purposes with this lifetime goal?

She had returned to the first pool now and swam slowly across it. She was sorry to have to leave this idyllic place and rejoin a group of people whose nerves were getting as frayed as the bottoms of an old pair of jeans.

By the time Louise stepped out of the lagoon, she was humbled. On previous occasions when she'd been caught up in a murder inquiry, she'd been convinced that she could discover something the police couldn't. This time, she didn't feel that way.

The person who could help was her colleague, John. But John, who'd sat with her near this woodsy spot and bragged of how he would investigate Flynn's death, was in a hospital, semiconscious, moaning instead of talking. And because she was tied closely in people's minds to her colleague, the murderer could be thinking of harming her. Tom Schoonover had tried to tell her that this morning, but it hadn't sunk in until now.

She looked around the woodsy alcove and realized how alone she was out here. Her breathing quickened and her heart threatened to start its annoying palpitations. "Darn," she muttered to herself, "where are those cops who are supposed to be patrolling this place?"

She grabbed up her beach bag, slid into her flip-flops, and hurried back toward the main building. She passed no one until she reached the family beach. There, a few fathers and mothers lay on chaise longues while their small children dumped imported sand into plastic pails with plastic shovels.

The children were the only ones unaware of the shadow of death hanging over Kauai-by-the-Sea. The parents, she guessed, had come on special family package deals. Unlike other guests who had more money to fritter away, they weren't going to let a couple of murders drive them home early.

In her hotel room, Louise found a surprise package, a long flower box. Opening it, she saw within its rustling waxy papers a lei made of white plumeria blossoms. She held it up to her face and took in its elegant perfume, then ripped open the envelope holding a card. It read, "From an admirer."

She frowned. She had enough mysteries in her life right now without adding more. Nevertheless, a lei would add a touch of class to the casual outfit she intended to wear to dinner.

Remembering her promise to stay in touch, Louise, still in her bathing suit, sat on the edge of the bed and phoned Bill. Her husband, in his later time zone, sounded exhausted and was preparing to go to bed. She told him about the day's happenings and the condition of John Batchelder.

He said, "Let's just pray for the best for John. I hope he has good doctors there."

"He does."

"And Louise, you must call Charlie Hurd at the *Post* first thing in the morning. I'm busy as all get-out at work and I'm constantly having to fend off the guy's phone calls. He's called about eight times. I feel sorry for the fellow. There's a great story dangling out there. After all, you saved John Batchelder's skin. But you won't give Charlie the time of day."

"Bill, the police chief doesn't want us talking to the press while he's still looking for the murderer. Besides, I don't exactly feel like talking to him. It's self-serving to talk about how I 'saved' John. Any passerby would have done the same thing. I don't want to be associated with the kind of outrageous thing that Marty's doing, either."

"What's Marty doing?"

"He wants to sell the tape of our program with the three scientists."

"Hah," said Bill, "and no wonder. It's a hot property, since it features two murdered guys. Who does he want to sell it to?"

"*Inside Story*," said Louise, "or someone else. He thinks lots of media outlets will want to buy it.

What bothers me, Bill, is that he decided on doing it this morning. Dr. Bouting died only last evening."

"It is macabre," admitted Bill, "but Marty's trying to recoup his investment. PBS has too much good taste to run it, but lots of other media have coarser taste. There's one glitch: He might have trouble with those on-camera releases you have people sign—they might not allow him to use the tape in another program. Whatever happens, look at it this way—your producer's doing no real harm. And it might do some good to air the tape—it will publicize the issues those three scientists were talking about to a huge audience."

"Oh," she groaned, as her shoulders drooped in defeat.

"Now, let's get back to Charlie for a minute," insisted Bill. "You and he have been through a lot over the years. In fact, he saved your skin last summer. Don't you think you owe him an interview?"

"Okay, I'll call Charlie first thing in the morning. Before I hang up, dear, I don't suppose you sent me flowers, did you?"

"No, but I wish I had, because I miss you. Did someone send you flowers?"

"It's a lei made out of white plumeria blossoms. It probably was from Marty. He's trying to make amends with me." She told her husband good-bye, but didn't tell him that she felt spooked, as if someone might be out to get her. Otherwise, he'd be conflicted, trying to balance his hectic work life and a purported threat to his wife five thousand miles away.

She showered and then dressed carefully in what she now thought of as her defensive outfit. Too many layers for the tropics, but better too many than too few. Far from a fashion statement, these clothes were pure practicality and she intended to wear them around this hotel until the murders were solved. Louise now had her own equipment, and both her cargo pants and her new pullover had lots of pockets, hidden and otherwise, in which to hide it.

40

Monday evening

As Louise walked down the big hotel hall toward the Lanai Room, she noticed the light was fading outdoors. She felt a pang of regret that she had missed the ritual of sunset and the chance to talk again with the beach oracle. Tomorrow she intended to catch up with Bobby Rankin. Who knew what crumbs of information the surfer might have picked up on the beach that might be important? She realized this criminal investigation might only be unraveled when someone like Bobby turned up an essential clue.

Down on the main floor of the hotel, she found her anxiety growing as she approached the dining room area. It took a moment to remember why: It was that parrot. She had not had to pass by her avian enemy during the entire day and he'd dropped from her consciousness, thank heavens. But now she was forced to pass his cage. She had a solution that would discourage him from screeching at her.

As she approached the bird, she hoisted the bottom of her bulky pullover over her face as if to remove it. Blinded but anonymous, she sidled by the cage. The bird, probably perplexed at the sight of someone with no visible head, remained silent; there wasn't even a cheep from him. Once she reached the dining room steps and before anyone saw her, she shoved her pullover back into place, readjusted the lei around her neck, and headed for the Lanai Room.

The small crowd had assembled and she realized she was late again. There were a couple of extra people: Tim Raddant and Sam Folsom had accompanied Tom Schoonover and Henry Hilaeo, even though they were not among the "captive" guests. She was glad, for she liked the NTBG bunch. Tom asked her to sit with him at the dinner table. Reluctantly, she told him, "I think I'd better hang loose."

He smiled and said, "I understand. By their deeds ye shall know them. " He turned away to talk to Henry Hilaeo.

At the small bar at the side of the room, she decided to break her usual abstemious rule and have a drink. Knowing vodka was less likely than other liquors to leave her with a headache, she ordered a vodka and tonic. Then she wandered the room, which was spacious and could have held sixty. Partially helping to fill the empty footage was a concert grand piano in one corner. This was for Joan Clayton's accompanist, Louise realized. She had expected the visiting scientists to be out of sorts, so it was surprising to see most were in good temper. Apparently they were resigned to the delay in their travel plans, though she overheard Charles Reuter assuring Ralph Pinsky that the police would give them the go-ahead to fly home in the morning. What made him think the police would get to the bottom of these two murders by tomorrow morning, she wondered.

Police Chief Randy Hau and Lieutenant Payne circulated among the guests, acting as informal hosts, even though the hotel was the purported sponsor of the event. Though many were in a sanguine mood, Anne Lansing was unsmiling, dressed soberly in her new black linen dress. She wore Christopher Bailey on her arm like an accessory. George Wyant stood by himself, bent over like an old man and staring out at the ocean. Louise went over to talk to him.

"Hello, George," she said. When he turned and looked down at her, she stepped back in surprise. His pupils were so large that his eyes looked completely black. His blond beard had a day's growth.

"*Hey*," he said and turned his gaze back to the sea. She stood silently, a little put off by his apathetic manner. He looked at her again and noticed she was staring at his eyes. "Don't *look* at me like that, Louise. You might get high, too, if you were on the verge of getting thrown into a Hawaiian jail." He ran a hand through his streaked blond hair and scratched at the back of his scalp, as if oblivious as to where he was. His ravaged face, his demeanor, and his untidy clothes made him look like something the ocean threw up on the beach after a storm.

"George, tell me," she said, "how can they tie that machete to you? Anyone could have taken it from your room."

"I know. Someone named *Anyone* did take it, just to pin this thing on me." He stood up a little straighter. "Chief Hau says they'll know by tomorrow if they're going to charge me. You better believe that they've been on the horn to Eastern and to

Brazil and to Peru—to any place I've had the faintest connection with—to see if they can get the goods." His head lolled sideways toward his shoulder. "It's so fuckin' tiring, Louise. I can't stand it without a little help from my friends."

"George. I'm sorry. I wish I could do something."

"Huh," he grunted, "and I thought you were some kind of detective. I don't see you *doin'* anything." He nodded toward the front of the room. "Anyway, they're signaling us that we have to sit down. Do you want to sit next to a pariah like me?" His anguished eyes searched hers.

"Of course I'll sit next to you."

What could she lose? Even men condemned to Death Row received visits from compassionate nuns. George hadn't even been arrested yet.

The table was U-shaped. She and George Wyant took seats at the end of one of the U's legs. Police Chief Randy Hau sat at the right-hand corner, Lieutenant Payne at the left hand corner, the better to eavesdrop on people, thought Louise. Marty and Steffi Corbin were given the seats of honor in the center part of the U. That was appropriate, for he would soon let them all know he was in charge of the night's activities.

Charles Reuter, Nate Bernstein, and their buddy, Ralph Pinsky, sat together on one side of the table, while the proprietor Christopher Bailey sat next to Anne Lansing on the other side. The National Tropical Botanic Garden foursome were scattered among these clusters of people.

Food arrived on huge platters, with waiters and waitresses going to each place to serve. As a young woman hoisted in a platter of fruit, she tripped, so that pineapple chunks, slices of guava and papaya, strawberries, and grapes flew far and wide. Ralph

Pinksy, sitting nearby, hurried over and crouched down and efficiently helped the red-faced waitress clean up the spill.

A short, bald-headed supervisor rushed in and tried to shoo him away with thanks. Then, in a low voice he started lighting into the young woman. To Louise's surprise, Pinsky grabbed the man's white shirt with one of his scrawny hands and quietly said something to him. The man nodded agreement while looking warily into Pinsky's pasty face. The scientist released his grip on the man's shirt and calmly resumed his seat and his conversation with Charles Reuter. An interesting man and a fair one, thought Louise.

It was a sumptuous meal, featuring lobster and broiled ono for the main course. Not until after dessert and coffee had been served did the apparition that was Joan Clayton appear. As the woman entered the room, Louise turned to George Wyant and whispered, "I can't believe that she's in her seventies."

"Yeah," he whispered back, "she sings like she's twenty. We saw her at the Café Carlyle a few months back."

Her pale blond hair was arranged like a halo around her head, her large blue eyes defined with subtle makeup. Her mature body was in a flowing blue gown that shimmered in the overhead ceiling spotlights as she moved. She turned to the crowd with a gracious smile, then sidled over to the piano as if she were a lion tamer about to win control of a savage beast.

Her balding accompanist was already seated and awaited her with the same expectant look that was on the faces of the spectators. The singer slowly leaned back against the flank of the piano, with one hip cocked forward, the classic diva's pose.

"My God, is she good," whispered George Wyant. "The picture alone is worth it, even if she couldn't sing."

The singer gestured with her chiffon scarf at the seated man and said, "This is the wonderful Richard Steele. And now we'll do a few songs by my favorite composer, Harold Arlen." They opened with the upbeat number, "I've Got the World on a String," followed with "That Old Black Magic," "The Man That Got Away," and "It's Only a Paper Moon."

When she launched into her final number, her face was tilted up and her countenance was almost beatific: "*Last night / When we were young / Love was a star / A song unsung . . .*"

Louise didn't know whether Joan Clayton was experiencing God or the heartbreak of lost love. But she did know that the artist had touched her audience. Louise saw that Steffi and Anne had tears in their eyes. The men held back, but some of them, too, looked as if they might cry.

41

The performance was over. Joan Clayton bowed low and the applause of the small crowd followed her out of the room. Marty Corbin went over to the piano and quickly picked up the gauntlet, lest the crowd slip away. He told them, "We're honored to have Mr. Steele stay with us for a while. As promised, we expect you to perform in a little amateur competition." A few murmurs of protest, though in informing people about the dinner this afternoon, Steffi had mentioned the "little amateur competition."

"Remember," said Marty, "it doesn't matter how bad you are. Just think of *American Idol,* and go for it." He chuckled, signaling another joke coming their way. "Just because you've spent twelve years or more working on your scientific degrees doesn't mean you can't get up in front and make fools of yourselves. We want to have some fun, don't we, in the midst of our captivity?"

This got him a laugh. Ralph Pinsky raised his hand slightly and Marty pointed to him. "We have a volunteer. Ralph, what do you want to sing, or play, or do?"

Without cracking a smile, Dr. Pinsky said, "I'll sing 'The Party's Over.'"

The bald accompanist nodded and smiled and the redheaded scientist walked up to the piano and struck a pose that mimicked Joan Clayton's. People burst into laughter. Then he broke the pose and he and the accompanist got their heads together to negotiate the key in which he would sing.

"Who would have thought there was humor in that man?" Louise said to George Wyant.

"There's more to Ralph than meets the eye," Wyant said in a low voice. "You know all the talk about how Matt 'stole' his Turkish tulip? Bruce Bouting passed that tale around. But Matt told me that Pinsky accepted his coup like a gentleman."

"Maybe that's just what Matt thought," said Louise.

"Yeah," admitted Wyant, "I suppose he could have been putting on that phony polite face he wears most of the time. But the fact is that both Matt and Ralph got the same tip on the plant from the same party."

"Is that right?" she whispered back.

"It's happened more than once," said her companion. His eyes shifted nervously, as if he were saying too much. "Frankly, some scientists will pay tipsters for that information. I think Matt may have done that on a few occasions."

"Did you ever suspect that Matt got to that tulip first because he paid more than Pinsky did?" she asked her companion.

A loud "Shhh" came from Steffi at the head of the table, so George Wyant answered her question

with a silent affirmative nod. Louise's lip curled in
a sardonic smile as she reflected on the skulldug-
gery that seemed to lie behind these romantic
plant explorations in foreign lands!

Ralph Pinsky was ready to sing and Marty was
about to draw him out before he started. "So, Dr.
Pinsky, we all know you, yet we don't know you.
You're the director of a prestigious botanic garden. Tell us something personal about yourself—
for instance, your early life and how you got the
nerve to get up here and sing a song."

The pale-faced scientist answered gamely. "I've
always wanted to work with plants; I've had my own
garden since the time I was a young child. Everything I grew was successful, so I had virtually no
choice but to make botany my life's work. I believe
part of man's destiny is the preservation of plant
species. This is at the very heart of my work." His
pale gaze raked the crowd, as if defying someone
to argue the point. Then he broke into a semblance of a smile. "As for the second part of your
question, my mother was a frustrated cocktail
lounge singer. She'd play and sing at the upright
piano for hours. Eventually, in self-defense, for she
wasn't that skilled a songster, we kids—there were
three of us, myself and two sisters—would join her.
I know every song from 1940 to 1960 by heart."

Marty stepped aside then and Ralph Pinsky
sang. His voice was a plaintive tenor, perfect for
the sad love song. "*Take off your makeup / The party's
over / It's all over / My friend.*"

Again the room broke into applause. Pinsky's
eyebrows arched upward, as if he were surprised at
the favorable reception. Louise leaned forward, to
see if others were ready to volunteer. Otherwise,

she would have to get up there and perform; she'd promised Marty she'd do it to keep things rolling.

As she scanned the U-shaped table, she couldn't tell who was enjoying this evening and who wasn't, for people had the kind of polite, amused expressions on their faces that one saw on the faces of nightclub crowds. A patina of nervousness on some faces, because of the request for folks to make public spectacles of themselves. Surprisingly, Anne Lansing got up from her seat and came forward. Marty put a comradely arm about her shoulder. "Ah, the lovely Anne Lansing."

Without any prompting, she gave a little autobiography. "I'm the product of my father's heritage—he's head of the biology department at Northern and is quite proud that I'm helping develop new plant varieties. My mother is a writer, so I also follow in her footsteps, since a great share of my time is given to writing garden books."

"And what do you want to do?" said Marty. "Sing? Or perhaps perform magic tricks?"

A few chuckles, which Anne ignored. She turned to Richard Steele and said, "I'll sing 'Precious Lord, Take My Hand,' in the key of D."

The accompanist nodded. She turned back to the crowd and said, "This is dedicated to those who have recently passed on. It was written by Thomas A. Dorsey, the father of gospel music, expressly for Mahalia Jackson."

Anne sang in a low, mellifluous voice, thick with emotion. The crowd gave her rapt attention. Steffi Corbin began sniffling into her handkerchief once again. Anne appeared to be expressing the grief she felt over the death of Bruce Bouting. With a quick glance at George Wyant sitting beside her,

Louise could see that his head was bent in sorrow. He heard the message of the song and applied it to the loss of *his* deceased mentor, Matthew Flynn.

"*Precious Lord, take my hand / Lead me on, let me stand / I am tired, I am weak, I am worn; Through the storm, through the night / Lead me on to the light /Take my hand, Precious Lord, lead me home . . .*" When Anne finished, the applause was almost as strong as it had been for their celebrity guest.

Louise stared at Anne Lansing as if she'd never seen her before.

Several things happened next. Marty felt the need to lighten the mood and happily someone else felt the same way. A jovial-looking Sam Folsom strode up to the microphone. The historian of the National Tropical Botanical Garden announced he would sing, "Hey, Jude." As he discussed keys with the accompanist, two people left their seats, Christopher Bailey and Charles Reuter.

Bailey had the look of someone who needed to use the men's restroom. But Dr. Charles Reuter, who whispered in Nate Bernstein's ear before he rose, wore the expression of a man bored out of his skull who just wanted to get away from this place.

Louise faced a dilemma. In the past few moments, certain truths had already clicked into place. Details she'd been absorbing but not processing for days suddenly fit together.

Neither of these men had anything to do with the hypothesis taking shape in her mind. Yet she knew she had to find out what they were up to. After all, as Tom Schoonover had said, "You must test your theories." She was glad she'd worn her defensive outfit.

Putting a look of urgency on her face, she said to

George Wyant, "Have to visit the ladies' room—back in a moment."

She slipped away barely in time to trace the actions of the two men. Reuter, fortunately, had a patterned shirt with orange in it and she caught a glimpse of him striding down the main hall. But that meant little; she waited until she saw him hurry onto one of the elevators. Now what had happened to Christopher Bailey?

Hurriedly turning into the only other nearby corridor, she was just in time to see Bailey heading for Options. Why would he want to go to the nightclub when he was already at a party? Maybe he wanted to hear Joan Clayton sing again. She slipped into the depths of the club and tried to make out his figure in the dimness. She could see his silhouette against the pale green backlights of the bar. He was ordering a drink. He paid for it and made his way to a table in the corner, then got up almost immediately, leaving the drink behind and moving quickly to the exit at the back of the room.

Louise looked to the left and right when she reached the nightclub exit and saw that to the left was a side door to the hotel. She pulled back for an instant, afraid he'd look back to see if he were being followed. Then she sprinted down the hall, peered out carefully, and pushed the door open.

Beyond a few chirping insects, it was deadly quiet out here. She followed the walkway to the right, but could not see Bailey, but she could see a plainclothes policeman pacing back and forth in front of another hotel entrance. She realized that Bailey must have gone in the other direction, toward the lagoon and the ocean.

Because of her visits to the lagoon, this was a

route she knew well. She quickly made up the distance and spied Christopher's silhouette against the occasional lights on the trail. A wave of apprehension went through her as she watched the man—he was dodging carefully from bush to bush. This was not the behavior of an innocent person.

First, it was just an instinctive reaction, to tail people who'd left the party and see where they were going. Now, she realized, it could be dangerous. But after all, wasn't that why she'd worn her defensive clothes? She pulled off a few petals from one of the plumeria blossoms and discreetly scattered them as she walked the path. Hansel and Gretel had nothing on her.

No question, Bailey was trying to elude the police. His suspicious demeanor astounded her, for she had just come to a completely different conclusion about the killer.

42

Christopher Bailey was following a wide, sweeping curve through the swimming pools and the lagoon, then past the swimmers' ocean beach where she had snorkeled. Beyond this beach the land rose gradually until it appeared to be at least twenty feet above the ocean. On the ocean side of the path were picturesque black volcanic rock outcroppings that tumbled down to the water. They were as much a subject of tourist photographs as Shipwreck Rock at the other end of the property. On the other side of this path was a sumptuous lawn and the hotel's exclusive one-story suites.

Bruce Bouting had bragged about staying in the President's suite in a corner of the hotel facing the sea. And his loyal assistant, Christopher, was his sometimes roommate. She sighed and her footsteps slowed. She was on a wild goose chase, for most likely all that Christopher Bailey wanted was to go to bed and get a good night's sleep.

But a residual curiosity remained. Why did he deliberately elude the eye of a policeman? She continued to follow him, but at a longer distance. Once he was near the ocean wing of Kauai-by-the-Sea, he did not follow the walk that led to a main entrance, but cut across the perfect lawn and headed for the corner suite. Louise fell even farther behind, for now she was on a strip of open lawn with no shrubs or trees for cover.

A lanai with a railing lined the ocean side of the suite, for what would a president be in Hawaii without a lanai on which to sit and sip drinks? With an agility that amazed her, the weighty young man mounted a few steps and unlocked the door of the suite. When he flicked on a light inside, she dashed across the remaining lawn.

Slowly she circled around the end of the property and found, just as she had suspected, that there were generous-sized windows in the side rooms of these premier suites. What was more, Christopher Bailey was clearly visible in one of them. All Louise had to do was to grapple with Kauai-by-the-Sea's million-dollar landscaping efforts. The big windows were bounded by lush gardens.

From her experience as a gardener, she knew some tropical varieties were a good deal friendlier than others. She slid through tall ginger plants, rare palms, and tree ferns, delighted that she hadn't stabbed herself as yet. Now shrouded in greenery and only a couple of feet from the window, she could see the man inside clearly in the brightly lighted room. He didn't appear to realize that anyone could look in on him from the window; it was amazing the false sense of security these thick tropical gardens gave people. He was standing by a huge bed, zipping open Dr. Bouting's sleek carrying case and withdrawing the scientist's black computer, the repository of his horticultural secrets.

She wondered about the computer. According to Anne Lansing, Bruce Bouting's relatives were flying in to gather his personal effects. Wasn't the computer a personal effect?

He sat on the bed and fired it up, then began to tap the keys in a businesslike, mundane fashion. He stopped and started more than once, pausing a few moments in between each effort. It reminded Louise of herself, when she sat at her computer jotting down notes. After a few minutes, Bailey calmly shut the computer down, and to her dismay, turned his head and stared out the window.

She froze, wondering if she in any way looked like a tropical plant. Then she remembered those thick glasses and only hoped it was hard for him to see distances. He didn't appear to see her. He took the computer and tucked it back inside its case and shoved it under the bed. His actions couldn't have appeared more normal.

Through the closed window glass, Louise could not hear a ring, but Bailey pulled out his cell phone from his pocket, apparently to answer a call. This was a little strange, she thought, but perhaps a friend was calling him from the mainland. Louise suddenly felt too warm in the balmy night and decided she'd had enough.

Slowly, she slid from the arms of the ginger, palms, and tree ferns and hurried back the way she had come. Not too fast, in case a stray policeman spied her. If stopped, she would simply say she'd gone out for a little walk. In a matter of moments, she was across the lawn and back on the path.

Now she had a chance to think about what she'd seen. Christopher may have sneaked out of the hotel, but he'd done nothing suspicious, simply gone to his own room and checked some equipment, so to speak. She recalled Matthew Flynn's mystifying admonition: *Check the equipment.* But why or how could Flynn have had anything to do with Bouting's computer-stored information?

At the very least, she would suggest to Police Chief Randy Hau that he check on, or possibly confiscate, Bruce Bouting's computer. Before she could do that, she had to go back into the hotel and rejoin the party.

On her left was the expanse of luxurious hotel lawn, while on her right, twenty feet below, was the restless ocean. Its waves lapped noisily against the rough-hewn rock debris from ancient volcanic eruptions. Since the path was only a yard from the precipice, it made her nervous to walk here in the dark. She hurried toward the lights.

Without warning, she felt a hard shove.

Suddenly she was tumbling in the air and didn't even have time to cry out. She had been pushed forward with such force that she barely escaped hitting any of the rocks, which would have meant landing in the water. But as she scraped along the rocks, one of her knees hit an outcropping and her hands grasped a rock projection and held, even as she felt the flesh of her palms scraped raw. Her body swung around and she hung suspended. Then, blessedly, her left foot found a ledge so she could support her weight and she cautiously moved the right foot onto the small outcropping.

For an instant, her mind focused on a detail of her survival. Volcanic rock was an unfriendly rock, totally opposite from smooth granite, which was eons older than these blackish clumps. With its rough, porous surface, it tore at snorkelers' legs as they innocently viewed fish. It certainly fell short of Louise's standards for decorating a garden. But now she loved each small pockmark and rupture in the rubble to which she clung like a barnacle. This imperfect rock had saved her life.

Above her was total silence. Louise realized someone up there had tried to kill her. She shrank her body close against the uneven surface and hardly dared breathe. Then she heard a low chuckle. Apparently, her fate seemed amusing to the person on the path.

She waited, hoping to hear retreating footsteps on the path but not daring to take a chance. Resting her cheek against the rough rock, she tried to relax and remain strong. For several minutes, she did. Then she knew she had to climb her way out of this before she lost her strength. Twisting her body from side to side, she found a small ledge higher up on which to put a foot. She felt secure enough to release one hand and take the flashlight from the button pocket in her pullover. The roiling waves were ten feet below her and the path about the same distance above. Shining her light, she saw a route up, if she only had the nerve to move her feet to a higher ledge.

Among Louise's fantasies was one that involved trekking in Nepal—but only up the foothills to a first base camp, certainly not up to the summit of Mount Everest.

Now, unwillingly, she was training for Everest.

Her flashlight was crucial. Since it was less than an inch in diameter, she found she could clench it between her teeth. Carefully, she moved a foot up and shifted her weight there, moved her hands and grabbed onto two insubstantial protrusions of rock. Somewhere, she'd read the "rule of three," that one should have three of the four extremities in place before ascending or descending.

Having achieved this, she made a tremendous move into midair and brought the other foot up. Now she was on firmer footing, able to lean into the rock so that she could release both hands. The problem was going to be the next leg up: It looked dangerously vertical, with no visible hand or footholds.

Shoving up her pullover, Louise grabbed at the knot in the length of rope that she'd tied there when she got dressed for dinner. *Well, Tom Schoonover,* she thought, *this is a nice reminder of my visit to Hawaii.* With a frantic hand she undid the knot. Aiming her flashlight high up, she carefully checked out a protruding rock above her head, then set the light on a ledge so she could handle the rope. Holding it in three loose loops, she flung it up and encompassed the rock. Giving it a practice tug to be sure it wouldn't move, she used it to pull herself up those last difficult few feet.

A sense of relief quickly vanished, and her breathing quickened as she realized what jeopardy she now was in. She was lying on a forty-five degree slope of damp, slippery red earth and could feel her body slowly slipping back down toward the rocks and the churning sea. Instinctively, she dug her fingers into the moist Kauai soil and slowly squirmed her way up the incline, using her fingers like pitons to save herself from falling backward.

Finally, she reached the path, which was blessedly flat. She lay her head down, exhausted, feeling like a beached monk seal, and fell asleep. After a minute or two—or was it ten?—she regained consciousness and wondered why her face felt wet.

She touched it and discovered blood flowing from her temple. It had spread down the side of her face and was dripping onto the ground. She rummaged in another buttoned pocket, brought out her red bandanna and pressed it on the wound.

Louise got unsteadily to her feet and made an assessment. Fingers raw and scratched from having been used as talons; arms and knees cut and gashed; forehead suffering a serious cut; and the right leg strained with what could be a pulled muscle. She needed first aid. Holding the bandanna to her forehead, she considered returning to the hotel. She sent a final glance back at Kauai-by-the-Sea's premier suites. The suite where she'd spied on Christopher Bailey was in darkness, but why?

The possibilities flooded over Louise. Christopher Bailey wasn't the murderer. It was the person who'd shoved her over the cliff. And that person probably was on the way to the President's suite. Louise had to go back and have a look, before Bailey became the killer's third victim. She realized she might already be too late.

43

By lying on the dirt incline above the rocks, Louise was able to reach down and unhook her rope from the promontory rock that had helped her to safety. When she got back on her feet, she realized she was not only scratched and bloody, but also stained with Kauai's famous red soil. She drew up her pullover and carefully wound the rope around her waist once more, knotting it loosely for comfort.

She walked purposefully toward the corner suite, looking about frequently to be sure no one was following. Again, she rounded the corner of the low-slung building and threaded her way through the same garden in which she had stood before. The curtains were drawn. Had she made the trip for nothing, or did she dare go up on the lanai to peer in the front windows? A flashlight would have been useful at this point, but she realized she'd left hers back on the rocky ledge.

She heard a small sound. Gasping, she turned to bump straight into Christopher Bailey. She stared up into his scary, big face. "No," she cried, just before he slapped a big gloved hand across her mouth. As she groaned loudly in protest, he forced her to walk to the stairs of the lanai. "Up we go, Louise," he told her and shoved her up the stairs and into a large room, closing the door behind him. He flipped a switch, and two huge table lamps lit up a room decorated with plush couches and chairs, a wall-sized flat-screen TV, and an antique games table with four chairs.

Looking at her in the light, he made a grimace of disgust. "Hah—what have we here? A real *mess.*" She was aware that her pullover and cargo pants were smeared with dirt and blood, as were her face and disheveled hair. "And what's here?" he said, staring at her waist. He shoved up her pullover and saw the rope, one end of which had become partially untied and hung down. "Okay, that might come in handy." He unwound it from her waist and set it aside. You've got to walk," he muttered. "Put your hands out," he ordered. When she did, he pulled out a roll of gray duct tape and bound her wrists together in front of her.

She stood uncertainly, looking at the young scientist. His cheeks were flushed and his eyes bright behind his thick glasses. "What do you think you're doing?" she asked him. "People will be looking for me. I just happened to be taking a walk when I looked in that window. I want you to let me go."

"Let you go?" said Christopher. "You gotta be kidding. You've been snooping. If you hadn't done that, no one would have bothered with you." Noting her bleeding forehead, he said, "We can't have your blood in here." He ripped off a couple more strips of tape and covered her entire forehead. "There," he said. "Now there's someone I want you to meet."

Through the door of the adjoining bedroom walked Anne Lansing, in her black linen dress accessorized with latex gloves. These two intended to leave no prints behind. Anne smiled when she saw Louise and came over and sashayed in front of her, a frivolous little twirling dance step, as if mocking her own image as a dignified botanist. "Oh, precious Lord," she cried, examining Louise from head to toe, "are you ever a mess! And your face— you're beginning to look like a mummy. *Are* you a mummy, Louise?" she teased.

Louise decided she'd get nowhere by acting like a scared rabbit. She stared back at the woman and slowly shook her head. "No, I'm not a mummy, Anne," she said in a calm voice. "And yes, I'm onto your game."

"Are you trying to tell me you knew I was in on this?" said Anne.

"From the moment you got up in the Lanai Room and revived your father from the dead."

Anne tossed her dark bobbed hair. "Oh, of course—I'd told you on the plane back from the Big Island that Daddy was dead." She smiled. "I'd forgotten that little piece of embroidery."

"You played the distressed mourner again when you got up and sang that song, 'Precious Lord.' What a piece of acting that was."

Anne laughed. "I succeeded, Louise, dear. That whole room felt sorry for me and my deceased boss. Why, your friend Steffi was crying—and she wasn't the only one. Too bad you had to pry. You sealed your own fate."

"You tried to get rid of me out on that cliff," said Louise.

"But you *do* have survival skills, don't you? We'll do better next time." Anne turned to Chris. "Didn't I tell you she was on to me?" She looked at the tape that Christopher still held in his hands. "We've talked to this woman enough; it's obvious she's alone. Let's shut her up."

With a swift move, Anne took the roll from his hands and ripped off a long strip. First, Louise trembled, as all the television images of dead bodies with taped mouths came flooding over her. A taped mouth was the beginning of the end, she knew. Then she became angry at the audacity of this woman. She could feel a welcome rush of adrenaline replacing her fear. With every part of her being she concentrated on the approaching enemy.

Anne moved quickly, the tape poised in both hands. Louise swung her body far to the left and bunted her head against her assailant, causing the tape to fly back and entangle in Anne's hair and hers.

"*Ow!*" cried her assailant. With venom in her voice, she said to Christopher, "Hold on to her." While he clasped her shoulders in his big hands, Anne roughly slapped the tape over her mouth. Her eyes stared into Louise's. "How about another strip?" she asked, as she ripped off another length and shoved it onto her face. Now Louise could hardly breathe through her nostrils.

Anne turned to her cohort. "Don't let her just stand there—*do* something. Sit her down and show her who's boss."

Christopher grabbed Louise's rope and came over to her, shoving her into one of the chairs positioned around the card table. He wound the rope around her and tied it so tightly that it hurt her arms. Leaning his face so close to hers that she could smell his sour breath, he quietly said, "Don't even *try* to move from here." Then he slapped her face with such force that her head snapped back on her neck. The pain filled her head and light rays shone all around, as if she were in the center of a star. It traveled through her body like an echo, while tears came to her eyes and rolled down her cheeks and over the duct tape. But fortunately she was not unconscious.

From now on, though, she would be acting. She closed her eyes and dropped her head down on her chest. Through her nostrils she pulled in small, short breaths, the way she suspected an unconscious person would breathe.

"Oh my God," said Anne, "you've overdone it, Chris. We still have to get her out of here. How's she going to walk?"

Chris put a hand on the pulse on her throat. "I didn't hit her that hard. Or I didn't think I did. Anyway, she'll wake up. Come on now."

Through a slit in her eyes, Louise could see him put his big arms around Anne. Anne turned her head away from his face and said, "Not here, Chris, please."

Dropping his large arms abruptly, he said, "If not here, then where? For God's sake, Anne, what *are* you?"

Anne headed for the adjoining bedroom and he followed her. As soon as they left, Louise bent her head down and reached up and with her bound hands to try and pull the strands of hair from under the duct tape, for the pressure was giving her as much pain as the slap to the head.

She was grateful they didn't bother to close the bedroom door, for she could hear them clearly.

"What am I?" said Anne. "I am just what you think I am, Chris, your devoted fan."

"My *fan?*" he said, incredulously. "After all your promises today, you're keeping me at arm's length? What do you do, tempt men and then kill them? Don't be cute. I know you slit Matthew Flynn's neck and shoved him off that cliff; I knew it from the minute I heard about it. And Bruce—there's no way that man was dumb enough to fall into a pool of lava unless he had a good shove from someone who knew he was on to them."

Anne's voice was cool and reasonable. "Chris, darling, stop and think. I would never have done these things if I hadn't had to. Matt made such a fuss. Matt was smitten with me after that conference last year, but then it all turned sour and I dropped him. Once we'd arrived here in Kauai, he threatened to tell Bruce about me. Can you believe it? He was going to say that I'd promised him I'd steal Bruce's secrets."

"Huh," grunted Christopher, "you mean Flynn thought he'd get both you and Dr. Bouting's special plant info?"

"I suggested that as a possibility. But Matt acted as if he were appalled. Who would have thought *that* man had scruples?"

Christopher said, "Be straight with me. He dropped you, not vice versa."

"Oh, no," Anne hurriedly assured him. "After the argument over whether or not I'd get into his computer secrets, I knew Matt and I weren't a good team, so I dropped him."

"Have it your way," said Christopher Bailey, his tone loaded with sarcasm. "Anne, you are a piece of work! Do you ever make promises that you keep?"

"Of course," she said, in a mollifying tone, "the ones I made to you. Now, Chris, don't get all bent out of shape."

"Oh, honey," he said, in a softening voice, "why did you have to murder him?"

"I didn't intend to. We had a plan to meet on Shipwreck Rock. And then things escalated and he told me a decent guy like Bruce deserved better than me. So I hit his head with a convenient rock."

"And then you got out your clippers and slit his neck and made sure he was dead. Or did you conceal George's machete up there and use that?"

"The clippers worked fine—the top blade, you know, very good for gouging into the foramen magnum. George Wyant seemed like the perfect fall guy. That's why I threw his machete off the cliff the night before."

"My God." Christopher Bailey made an unpleasant gargling noise, as if he were close to vomiting. There was a long moment of silence. Finally, he said, "That was premeditated."

"Well, maybe it was. But Chris, I couldn't have Matt ruining everything for me. Everything was for *us*, because you know if I went down, so would you. The old man viewed us as an unbeatable business team."

"Look, Anne," said Christopher, in a voice so soft that Louise had to strain to hear, "I guessed it was more than business with you and Bruce."

Louise leaned far out in her chair, hoping to see them. Only a small light emanated from the room. Anne Lansing and Christopher Bailey were sitting together on the edge of the bed.

She was amazed at the thought: Anne Lansing was not Bruce Bouting's daughter figure, she was his mistress. Had John Batchelder found this out? Was this what he'd meant that it was "all for love"?

"I suppose you couldn't help suspecting," Anne said, "though Bruce and I were terribly discreet. I fell out of love with Matt and fell into love with the old guy. Frankly, he was the best lover I ever had— and he was a free thinker. He didn't give a damn if I had affairs with other men. He got a kick out of me and I got a kick of out him. Chris, I'm . . . just a little bit pregnant with his child. He was going to marry me!"

"You're pregnant with his child? Then why did you shove him into that lava?"

"Because he was just too smart. He'd had a whiff of my romance with Matt, not that he cared, of course. But he became suspicious that I was the one who killed him and that bothered him. In the end he was this righteous old throwback to another age. You know good and well that it was all he could talk about on that plane, in his indirect way."

"It must have been a cinch, having a guy with a lame leg to deal with . . ."

"Going down to view the lava was my opportunity. But I swear to God, Chris, I'm really sad about it." Her voice was breaking with emotion. "You know how much I respected and cared for him— and I am carrying his baby. I didn't want to kill him."

"You could say he was dying anyway," said Christopher in a thoughtful voice. "He was losing ground, day by day. Frankly, I'd thought of it, but I didn't do anything . . ."

"I know you thought of it, because you were more impatient than I was. I could see it in your eyes. It's bittersweet, seeing a brilliant man like that and knowing what's happening to his great brain. Only you and I can understand this." The words were soft and tender.

Louise peeked in again and could no longer see them. They apparently had fallen back onto the bed and she heard rustling sounds of clothing. She realized it was a pragmatic move on Anne's part, offering her partner in crime her body—as pragmatic as it must have been becoming pregnant with the millionaire Bouting's baby. But Bouting was gone now. From now on, Anne Lansing's future was tied to Christopher Bailey's.

She dropped her head again, as if unconscious, figuring that once their tryst was done they would come hurriedly out of the bedroom.

It was a brief intimacy. To Louise's ears it was strained on one side and an explosive release of tension on the other. At last, Christopher Bailey had gotten laid; now there was a new bond between the two. They were talking quietly, as lovers did after sex.

Little patches of conversation came through.

Anne: ". . . take her as far from here as possible, so this suite has no connection to her death."

Louise wondered where they intended to take her.

Christopher: ". . . then come back here so we can chill out and you know . . ." One bite of the apple—and a little bite at that—obviously was not enough for him.

Anne: ". . . and the password . . . try again . . ."

Christopher: ". . . better to wait until we get back to the office and outsmart those dimwit IT people . . . the server room unlocked during coffee breaks . . . we'll access his stuff any time we want."

Anne: ". . . one more detail—John whatever-his-name is . . . so why don't you take her. And I'll wait . . ."

Louise could feel her muscles tighten. They wanted to dispose of her. After that, they were going after the helpless John Batchelder, lying in that Lihue Hospital.

Unexpectedly, the loud voice emerged from the bedroom, followed by the man who uttered them: "I don't want to do it!" Tugging to adjust his pants, Christopher came out of the bedroom and straight over to Louise. She had closed her eyes again.

"Look at her, she looks comatose," he said. "How are we going to get her out of here?"

Anne came up beside him. "You did that."

"No, I didn't. She was all right for a minute after I hit her."

Anne said, "Concussion, I bet."

"I don't care," said Christopher. "I don't intend to lead this lamb to slaughter—you're the expert—*you* do it."

Louise groaned, pretending that she was regaining consciousness, though her head continued to droop on her neck. Anne pointed to her and said, "Look, she's all right; she'll at least be able to walk. All right, I'll go with you and help get rid of her." She went up to Christopher, to give him what Louise saw was a little more sexual reinforcement. Caressing his cheek and then running her hand down his chest clear to his groin, she said, "Remember, we'll have some fun when this is done. Also, remember that we're in this together now, as of our conversation this afternoon."

He leaned into her, wanting more. "This afternoon, though, I wasn't one hundred percent sure you were a double murderer."

She looked up at him. "Well now you are and you're my accomplice, honey. We're what they call conspirators. And we're going to be the king and queen at Bouting Horticulture when this all settles down."

"And what about your . . . condition?"

"Don't worry about that." Then she broke away from him and said, "But enough of this, we really don't have time. We'll take the ocean path all the way up to Shipwreck Rock—that's the best place to do it."

As he loosened the rope binding Louise to the chair, he said sarcastically, "With your experience, it should be a cinch to stage an accident up there."

Anne turned on him. "Don't mock me! Things went wrong because I thought the bitch saw Matt and me up on that rock." She reached over and abruptly grabbed Louise's arm and heaved her up from the chair. Anger seemed to have given the woman extra strength. "Get up, bitch. You're going to walk. Chris, help me here; get the other side. That dinner party will be breaking up—someone could go out for a smoke and see us."

With one supporting her on either side, they ushered Louise across the room, flipped off the lights, and shoved her out the door. Now they were out in the balmy Hawaiian night and Louise was headed for death. Although she couldn't speak with the revolting tape on her mouth, she did not intend to go quietly.

44

Her hands were bound in front, as if she were in prayer. For that she gave thanks. The tape was tight, but this did not mean that Louise could not reach up a few inches to the bottom of her lei, which still hung round her neck, and grasp petals with the tips of her fingers. Scattering petals was the only hope that she had for survival and a scant one at that. Though Christopher Bailey and Anne Lansing each held an elbow, she used every bump or irregularity on the path as an opportunity to pull a petal from one of the white blossoms and let it fall to the ground.

Pretending to be injured was not difficult. Her head felt like a large, aching balloon. Every scratch and cut from her head to her shins pained her. Though her leg muscle had improved, she limped along as if she had a sprain. She went slowly, stumbling over every small obstacle.

Anne and Christopher were mostly silent, except for an occasional murmured exchange about how they needed to hurry and how they'd take to the beach if they saw policemen out on the grounds. They didn't use their flashlights, an agreement they'd talked about when they left the hotel suite. Louise's slow pace soon made Anne impatient. Occasionally Christopher lifted her along, as if she were a puppet. Soon they were past the rocky cliffs where she'd been shoved onto the rocks. Now they were in the danger zone, for they had to take her by the oceanside path that ran in front of the hotel's main building, past the lagoon in which Louise loved to swim, then on to Shipwreck Rock. Kauai-by-the-Sea landscapers kept the path by the hotel in perfect shape, so it was harder now to fake missteps and to drop the telltale plumeria petals.

"Get up!" hissed Anne Lansing, after Louise's latest stumble. Louise was sure she was on to her Hansel-and-Gretel routine. "I think you're faking this. Get going!" She gripped Louise's arm tighter and practically dragged her along the path.

"Cool it, cool it," warned Christopher, who had to crouch down to avoid anyone seeing his tall figure.

They reached the southern boundary of the hotel property, marked with a line of gracefully curving gardens. No gate here, for this was Hawaii, where beaches were for everyone and high security gates reserved only for posh neighborhoods. Hotels were known for their open, welcoming ambience. So they went unimpeded, straight to the red dirt trail that led to the forty-foot cliff.

Shipwreck Rock was classed as an interesting little side tour in the pantheon of Kauai tourist sights. Louise had wanted to climb the rock since the moment she'd seen it the afternoon she arrived on Kauai. John Batchelder had promised they'd hike it together. The irony struck her; she was finally taking the tour with two people intent on killing her.

At first, there was a crowd of shrubs at the entrance to the trail, unidentifiable in the dimness; this was the place where Anne Lansing had posted the "closed" sign the night she killed Matthew Flynn. The ground became more open, with only the occasional dwarf tree emerging here and there through the light-colored sandstone.

The trail continued up a series of steep, rugged switchbacks. Anne occasionally used her flashlight to guide the way, quick bursts of light no more than the glint of a firefly. With the rough ground, there was plenty of stumbling about and thus opportunity for Louise to drop petals on the way up. Occasionally, she glanced at the quarter moon and prayed it wouldn't reveal what she was doing. They came to a wider place in the path, where just ahead lay the pile of rocks that Louise had heard about from John. Getting over them was difficult, he'd said. For Louise to do it with her hands tied was going to be a problem for her two adversaries. But it was a good place to mark with flower petals. This time Anne noticed Louise pulling at the lei.

"What are you doing?" she hissed, pulling Louise to a stop and causing Christopher to lose his grip on her other arm. Anne pulled out her flashlight again and shone it down on the path and saw a few white petals on the red earth.

Pulling in a noisy breath, the woman grabbed the lei from around Louise's neck. "She's probably been spreading these petals along the way," she told Christopher. "More reason to hurry." She turned and slapped Louise's face. "You are too much trouble," she spat out. Louise promptly put down her head, as if hurt again.

Anne pulled Christopher a step away and made her pitch. "Look, Chris, I've helped you get her almost all the way. She's still in one piece, so it'll be clear she drowned and didn't die of some injury. I'll help shove her sorry ass over this pile of rocks. Then you can even carry her to the top from there. Don't forget to take off the rope and the duct tape. Then give her a tap on the head and pitch her out. Her body will fall in deep water."

"There's no way, Anne, that I'm going the rest of the way without you. As you told me back in the room, we're in this together. Now, let's get going."

"Chris," she demurred.

It was hard, Louise observed, for Anne to use her gentler wiles in this rough setting. She said, "A strong man like you can easily do it alone."

Ignored during this argument, Louise half-turned her body so they couldn't see what she was doing. In her right bottom zippered pocket was her last resource, a can of pepper spray. She had to pull her bound hands far to the right to reach the zipper, then laboriously shove it open to reach the spray. At any second she expected one or the other of them to see what she was doing and stop her. At last she had the small cylinder clutched in her fingers. This probably was her last chance to save herself, she well knew.

Trembling from the effort, she unbuttoned the leather flap, put her index finger on the trigger and turned around to face her antagonists. And just in time. Her disagreement with Christopher temporarily resolved, Anne approached her. Louise tilted the spray upward slightly and shot her in the face and kept shooting.

"No-o-o!" cried Anne, her hands clawing at her eyes as the burning pepper cut into them.

"Shut up, Anne!" cried Christopher, as Louise was about to redirect the spray on him. Before it reached him, he grabbed her and threw her bodily down on the ground, as easily as if she were a rag doll. Her last effort was to put her bound hands up, praying for her life.

For a moment, she was no longer the center of a star, she merely saw them. And then all went black.

45

When Louise regained consciousness, she heard a man's voice from a long distance away. He seemed to be giving people orders about where to search. Gingerly, she tried to move her aching body and found that she could. She was lying beside the pile of volcanic rubble.

It took a few moments to remember that she was up on Shipwreck Rock trail with two people who were bent on killing her. Where were they now? She lay quietly and opened her eyes. The smell of pepper spray wafted through the air, so she knew she'd been unconscious for only a few moments. She turned her head to avoid the acrid smell. As she did, she saw two silhouettes against the moonlit sky, looming almost directly above her. Louise froze in fear. Then, one figure bent down, overcome with a paroxysm of coughing—Anne was suffering the effects of the pepper spray.

"Listen," whispered Christopher, "I hear them coming. "We've got to get out of here."

In a rasping voice, Anne croaked, "We still have to get rid of *her*."

Louise closed her eyes and wished she could shrink into the ground.

"Don't be crazy," hissed Christopher. "For God's sake, you can hear their voices. Look, you can even see their lights."

Anne broke into another fit of coughing, but choked out the words, "Don't you get it, Chris? If we don't take the tape off this woman, they'll catch on to everything."

"No!" cried Chris, forgetting to keep his voice down. "I didn't want to do this in the first place. Now, goddammit, let's go!"

The figures disappeared from Louise's view. She heard their fading footsteps and realized that they'd headed for a back trail off the rock.

She smiled as she realized her emergency equipment had worked. She'd driven her enemy away.

Now, a man's voice. His words were echoing up to her from forty feet below. ". . . keep your eye out, folks," he was saying. ". . . we've found more over here . . . we've picked up her trail . . ."

Then another excited cry from below. "This way—let's get going!"

Her heart thumping with excitement, she knew she had to tell them that she was up here. She sat up and struggled dizzily to her feet. Peering over the side of the precipice, she saw lights probing the darkness almost below.

She used her fingertips and clumsily ripped the duct tape off her mouth. Hoarsely, she yelled, "I'm up here!" Balanced precariously on the edge, she waited for someone to glance up.

"Hey!" said a voice from below, "where did that voice come from?" A light played on the nearby rocks, while another beam shone into her face. She blinked her eyes and nearly fell.

"She's up on the cliff!" cried someone. "I see her." Overwhelmed with relief, Louise slumped back to solid ground.

"Louise, is that you? Hold on. They're coming!" It was Steffi's voice. Comforting, wonderful Steffi Corbin.

The first to reach her were two policemen, who immediately set up a couple of flares on the path so they could see. One was Sergeant William Yee. As he discreetly examined her with his flashlight, he murmured, "Take it easy now, Mrs. Eldridge, we're going to help you," then gently removed the duct tape from around her hands.

"Oh, thank you," she said, cautiously wriggling her arms to stretch the muscles. Next he directed the light at the tape on her forehead. "Do you want that off?"

She reached up a hand and touched it. "Maybe not; there's quite a cut under there. It might start bleeding again. But thank you," she said.

The other policeman had been on his radio, communicating with the ground. He said, "Mrs. Eldridge, we need to know who did this." But then more flashlights bobbed up the trail. Marty Corbin and Tom Schoonover appeared from around a switchback, followed by a man in ragged shorts and flip-flops—the beach oracle.

Marty, gasping for breath, rushed up to her and hugged her. "My God, Lou, we're glad to see you alive. I shoulda tailed you out of that restaurant the minute I saw you get out of your chair."

"Marty, you don't know how good it is to see you."

Tom Schoonover came over and laid a gentle hand on her arm and smiled down at her. "Good thing we had a little help from our friend here." He cocked his head at the disheveled Bobby Rankin, who hung back, a large, blank grin on his face. "Bobby was, um, having a smoke on the beach when he sighted three figures rushing in this direction along the hotel path."

Bobby, red-eyed and unsteady on his feet, tried to assemble his thoughts. "For a minute I thought it was an apparition. And that made me think maybe I ought to give up my beach life because I was goin' crazy. Thank God I finally realized it was real people I was seein'."

The policeman with the radio interrupted. "Gentlemen," he said, "step aside for a minute, please. Mrs. Eldridge, before we take you out of here, we need urgently to know who did this to you. Do you have an idea of where they might have gone? Can you confirm that your assailant was Christopher Bailey?"

"Christopher Bailey and Anne Lansing. Don't ignore Anne Lansing. She's worse than he is—she killed Matthew Flynn and Bruce Bouting."

"My God, Lou," cried Marty, "you don't mean it!"

The policemen looked at one another in wonder. Sergeant Yee said to her, "I know you wouldn't say this unless you were sure."

"I've never been more sure of anything in my life."

"When did they leave?"

She sighed. "Not more than a few minutes ago. I'd say, five to six minutes."

Yee told the other policeman, "They must have taken the back path down. Better tell them that below." The other got on his radio.

Louise continued, "I squirted Anne in the face with pepper spray and she yelled a lot. Then they probably saw lights approaching below. They ran away after that."

"Any idea of where they'd have gone?"

She focused her jumbled thoughts. "They might have gone to Bruce Bouting's suite—it's the President's suite. They want his computer, I know that much. I saw Christopher trying to work out the password. After that, I don't know what they'd do. They can't escape this island, can they?"

Sergeant Yee looked at her and shook his head. "No, ma'am, I don't think so."

Tom Schoonover quietly said to her, "Can you walk, Louise?"

"I think I can, with help."

He turned to the policemen. "Then if you don't mind, we'll escort this lady down the path," and he put an arm around her waist. "Marty, want to take the other side?"

"Yeah," said Marty. "She doesn't look good for doin' much of anything on her own."

His little attempt at humor somehow set the tears in motion. They trickled silently down her cheeks, but her snuffles gave her away. Tom handed her a handkerchief and she wiped the tears away. "Sorry. It's just that I'm so glad to be alive."

46

Monday night

"I really feel fine," lied Louise, as she sat in the small white clinic. Actually, her head ached and so did her bruises and cuts. But she feared if she told the truth, she'd end up in the hospital in Lihue. Instead, she was back in the basement medical clinic of Kauai-by-the-Sea, with the smiling, gray-haired doctor pointing a light in her eyes.

This time, she took a closer look at him. Around fifty, he was the picture of happiness and good health, with a deep suntan on his face and muscled arms. Louise decided he was another escapee from the mainland. The nurse efficiently took a few X-ray photos and within minutes the doctor reassuringly reported that she had no broken bones.

He snapped off the light and said, in a faint Southern accent, "There's no doubt, Mrs. Eldridge, that in the course of your adventures you've suffered a slight concussion. But look at it this way—you're not nearly as bad off as the man I treated this afternoon. He was swimmin' out too far and got shoved up against some lava rock; suffered both a serious concussion and a broken leg. *He* ended up in a cast and traction."

"Good heavens," murmured Louise, "that's terrible."

"Not the worst I've seen, either," said the doctor. "I'm always busy. The ocean brings me lots of business."

"There are quite a few drownings, I hear."

"You wouldn't believe how many. People who don't pay attention to those discreet warnings posted on the beach. Actually, they ought to print them in one-foot letters. This land isn't always paradise, you know."

He cocked his head and surveyed Louise's droopy eyes. "Now, my dear, I'm warnin' you: if you go to sleep right now, which I know you want to do, it could be dangerous. You might never wake up again. But if you stay up for an hour or two, you'll be just dandy. You have friends here with you, I understand."

"They're waiting for me upstairs in Options."

"Good," said the doctor. "The police chief, who insists on asking you more questions, and those friends ought to keep you up long enough. Be sure to eat somethin' and drink a lot of liquids, but lay off the mai tais. Now let's take care of your wounds."

After getting a booster tetanus shot, she was washed up and stitches and a bandage were applied to her forehead. Her lacerated hands were wrapped until they resembled white gloves. Finally, she was released. "Remember," said the doctor, "you take it easy tonight, Mrs. Eldridge. And that's no kiddin'. Tell that police chief not to be too hard on you. And check in with this office tomorrow mornin' to get new dressings."

Louise went upstairs to the police chief's borrowed office and slumped down in the nubby lime green chair. She told him everything that had happened since she left the Lanai Room party less than two hours ago.

Even to Louise, it sounded barely credible, more like the Perils of Pauline—"*I was window-peeping, then I was thrown off a cliff, taped and bound like a UPS package, slapped around a bit and dragged up to the top of a cliff where I was supposed to be thrown off into the sea . . .*"

The more she talked, the more uncomfortable Police Chief Randy Hau looked. In the next thirty minutes while answering his questions, she discovered that this terrible nightmare she'd suffered was not over.

47

Despondent and wanting nothing more than to go to sleep, Louise had gone instead to Options and found her friends sitting in a dark corner of the nightclub.

"We thought that after what you'd been through that you'd appreciate privacy," explained Steffi. Apparently noting her long face, her friend added, "Are you going to be all right?"

"I need to eat," Louise said. "Then I can talk." Marty, Steffi, and Tom Schoonover had a second nightcap, while she gobbled down snacks and hors d'oeuvres—little spare ribs, pot stickers, small wraps filled with cheese and artichoke, potato chips and nuts, all of which she could handle with her awkward bandages. Her companions occasionally reached over and shared.

Louise figured she could last another hour if she kept busy eating and talking. She had to remain awake at least that long to guard against, as the doctor said, "going to sleep and never waking up again."

After giving her a few minutes' reprieve, Marty said, "Lou, I'm sorry this happened to you. I knew you were in trouble five minutes after you left the Lanai Room. I'm only sorry the cops wasted twenty minutes scouring the hotel and checking your room to be sure you weren't there. Now tell us how this all unfolded."

She said, "I have so much to tell you that I hope I keep it straight. I'll give you the latest news first. It's hard to believe this, but Christopher Bailey denies everything. They found him in his hotel room about a half an hour ago. His 'time line,' as Randy Hau calls it, doesn't coordinate with mine. He says he left the party because he was bored. He allegedly went to the men's room, then here, into Options, and got himself a drink. That's all for sure, because I followed him here."

Tom Schoonover said, "You did? You certainly put yourself in danger."

She shrugged. She didn't want to think right now of how impetuously she had acted. "Bailey's told the police that he hung out for a half hour here and after that craved some exercise. He says he walked around for a while outside the hotel, then went back to his room about an hour ago. That accounts for all of his time, but it doesn't agree at all with what I told the chief."

"He was lying," said Marty.

She nodded. "He was in and out of this place in five minutes and went directly to Bruce Bouting's suite. But there's someone way more important than Bailey—Anne Lansing. She's missing."

"Oh, God," said Steffi, "I don't like the sound of that."

"Some policeman saw her leave the party and take the elevator up, as if she were going to her room. After you found me on Shipwreck Rock, they checked her room. There's no sign of her."

"But you said she's the killer," said Steffi, her big brown eyes wide with concern.

Louise pulled in a breath. "She is. And she's dangerous. At least the police realize that and have taken steps to protect John in that hospital. I'm betting he saw something to tie Anne to Bruce Bouting's death."

Tom said, "I gather they need proof of your story."

"Yes. And there isn't much proof at the moment. The duct tape they slapped on my face and hands won't have prints, because Bailey wore latex gloves. Bouting's suite will have Bailey's and Anne's fingerprints all over the place, but it's natural that they would be there because it was Bruce Bouting's office away from home, so to speak."

She looked at her friends self-consciously. "I told the chief to try the bed—the two of them had a sexual interlude on the bed. But he said that wouldn't prove anything, either."

"Wow," said Steffi. "They had sex while you were there?"

"Yes, but they didn't take much time with it. My presence didn't stop them, or her, from saying or doing anything. Anne told Christopher exactly why she had to kill the two men. She was romantically involved with both of them, but more recently with Bouting. But Dr. Flynn threatened to tell him just what kind of a girl she really is." Louise looked at her table mates with sorrowful eyes. "To understand what kind of a girl Anne really is, you should know that she threw George Wyant's machete off the cliff the day before she killed Matthew Flynn."

Schoonover shook his head as if in disbelief.

"That's premeditation. If not the machete, then how did she . . ."

Louise bowed her head. "This is the worst part. Once she knocked him out, she used her pruning scissors and gouged his neck with them."

"How horrible," said Steffi, putting the remains of the potato chip she was munching back on her plate.

Louise gave her companions a few moments to digest these grisly details before she continued, "There's one thing I can't understand—the note that Matthew Flynn wrote me. He had it in his pocket when he died." She told them its contents and Flynn's admonition to "check out the equipment" if something happened to him.

Steffi said, "Whose equipment were you supposed to check out?"

Suddenly, the words didn't register. A wave of fatigue coursed through Louise and her mind went blank. Vacantly, she stared out into the pale green dimness of the nightclub, where a few dark-silhouetted figures, looking like part of the hotel's art deco motif, moved stylishly about the dance floor to the music of Frank Sinatra. Through the shadows, she saw what looked like an angel in a nearby booth. With a start, she realized it was the golden-haired Joan Clayton. The singer was sitting with three others, chatting and eating like an ordinary mortal. No one seemed to care. This was private time, for she had done her gig for the night, just as Louise had done hers . . .

"Louise," said Steffi, shaking her by the shoulder. "Are you all right? Here, take a sip of water. You're not drifting off, are you?"

"I guess I was," said Louise, swallowing several big gulps. "Sorry."

"What I asked you is, what equipment was Matthew Flynn talking about?"

"I honestly don't know. Maybe Matt had a premonition that someone was out to harm him. He knew each of his fellow scientists walked around armed with a weapon in the form of a sharp pruning scissors. Then, there was George's machete, handily stored in their open hotel room for anyone to take." She heaved a deep sigh. "I could tell sometimes that he was wary of the others. When he heard I'd helped solve a few crimes, he must have had this need to tell me about his worries."

"How right he was," said Marty. "Someone *was* out to harm him."

"When are they going to arrest Anne Lansing?" Steffi asked. "I personally do not feel comfortable knowing that this vicious woman is at large somewhere on this tiny little island."

"If they could find her," said Louise, "they certainly would hold her for questioning. Like Christopher Bailey, she'll probably deny everything."

Tom Schoonover played with the swizzle stick in his bourbon and water. "I get the feeling from what you've told us, Louise, that everything hinges on you as an eyewitness." He focused his unblinking gaze on her.

She nodded. "That's true and it doesn't make me feel very good. They need evidence from that suite. The rest of it happened in the out-of-doors again."

Marty Corbin threw a couple of almonds in his mouth, chewed noisily for a minute, then said, "I never realized that crimes outdoors are not as easy to solve as ones indoors, where some dumb perp lays his hands on things and leaves fingerprints and then stashes the murder weapon in, for instance, his closet in a plastic bag." He chuckled. "And leaves his bloodied running shoes with their distinctive pattern in a trash can near his home."

Schoonover looked at the producer and absently scratched his curly gray hair. "We've all seen too many *Law and Order* episodes. I think in actuality there's a high percentage of murders that are never solved." He turned to Louise and said, "Be that as it may, let's let the authorities handle it from now on. You did a great job, Louise, of ferreting out those two."

"It wasn't very scientific, Tom. I wasn't testing a theory, as you suggested. When Christopher Bailey left the party, I'd already decided that Anne Lansing was in on these murders. So I asked myself, what was Bailey doing, running around looking guilty?"

"So, what's the answer?" said Marty, reaching over and taking a sparerib. "How'd he get in on it? He wasn't involved in murdering Flynn and Bouting. Or was he?"

"No," she said. "From their conversation, I gathered that Christopher was suspicious of Anne, but that he only came right out to talk about it with her this afternoon. As I told the chief, he was dying to get his hands on Bouting's computer program—he was searching for passwords. I saw him puttering with the computer but I didn't know what he was doing. He hadn't had the nerve, but when he discussed it with Anne, it was clear she wanted the same thing. Later, they decided to wait for an opportunity back at Bouting Horticulture— something about outwitting the 'ITs.'"

"The information technology people," translated Tom. "They're the company's computer nerds. He may have outwitted himself. In a sophisticated computer system, there'll be a record of those unsuccessful searches."

Steffi said, "You didn't really explain this to us very well. Why did she murder those two?"

"Start out with the fact that Anne and Bouting were lovers. Actually, Anne is what she calls 'a little bit pregnant,' and Bouting was going to marry her."

"Really," said Steffi widening her brown eyes. "She was sleeping with that old man? I bet she got knocked up just so he *would* marry her."

"Possibly," said Louise.

"Then where does Matthew Flynn enter the picture?" asked Tom.

"Matthew Flynn was her former lover. When they arrived here on Kauai and Flynn saw how close Anne was to Bouting, he threatened to tell him about her and how she'd intended to run off with Bouting's secrets."

"You mean," said Steffi, "she loved Flynn and then switched her affections to the old man?"

"Yes, Steffi, that's about it. The cause of her breakup with Flynn was because he didn't approve of her stealing her boss' prized plant information."

Tom said, "I for one am glad to revise my view of Matthew Flynn—the man did have a sense of honor and justice in some arenas."

Steffi shook her head in distaste. "Imagine that young woman with that old guy."

Louise wondered if Steffi knew that Bruce Bouting had been sixty-six, only seven years older than her own husband. In seven years she doubted that Steffi would look on Marty as an "old guy." She proceeded to eat more spareribs, feeling better the more she ate.

"And what did she do for him?" persisted Steffi. "Didn't you say he had early Alzheimer's? It's quite a bit for a woman of whatever age she is—thirty-five, forty, something like that—to take on that responsibility."

Louise paused to swallow a mouthful of tangy meat. She said, "I had the impression she really loved him and he loved her; she fulfilled more than one role for him, daughter figure and lover as well as smart business partner. He'd given her a ring—I saw it on her finger one day. It sounded like it would be an open marriage, but a marriage nevertheless. I don't know if she would have stuck around through all his final days, but I'd guess she would—there's a huge inheritance to be had."

"I get it," said Marty. "This wasn't really about plant secrets, was it?"

"No, dear," said Steffi, reaching a hand over and pressing her husband's hand. "It was all about love—sort of."

Marty waved his free hand in the air. "A dame who promises every guy she fell in love with something a little different—that's a very dangerous sort of dame. Good thing you left that trail of petals, Lou, and that Tom caught on to it. He was pretty systematic, the way he had us looking for you. He even had the good sense to realize that zoned-out beach bum probably saw something."

She looked at Tom. He smiled and said, "I'm glad you were able to make use of that lei."

"You sent it?" she said. "I don't know what was more useful, the lei or the rope."

"Or the pepper spray," added Steffi. "A girl can't have too much equipment," she said and held her drink up. "Marty." It was an order.

Marty beckoned the waitress at Options to come

and get some fresh drink orders. "And more nuts, please." He looked at Louise, still eating, then told the waitress, "And what else can we get more of? How about if we look at the menu again?"

He turned to Louise. "If we have to hang with you, Lou, we might as well eat. Don't you think so, Tom, Steffi?"

Tom grinned. "I do."

Steffi said, "Let's get more of those darling little artichokes and cheese numbers. Not good for the figure, but this is a special night." She gave Louise a fond look. "Our Louise is safe."

Louise glanced at Tom Schoonover. He was looking down at the table, pursing his lips, his worry wrinkles in play. She knew he didn't consider her safe—not yet.

48

The bad dreams that accompanied violence in Louise's life came to visit.

This time it was an uncomfortable feeling of suspended animation, as if she were floating along the paths of the Kauai-by-the-Sea Hotel without setting foot in the red alkali soil. People passed her going one way or another, people with a motley assortment of appearances, old people, young people, Hawaiians, Hawaiians with mixed blood . . . but the ones threatening her with their dark looks were Anglos carrying curved knives . . .

With a hot bath, fresh bandages on her cuts, and two more pills in her system, sleep had not been hard for Louise to attain. She had put on her roomy blue satin pajamas, come out of the bathroom, and slipped under the covers.

An hour later—she later learned afterward that it was midnight—Louise felt something being shoved down onto her face.

Still half-asleep, her small cry of protest was nothing but a whimper. She thought she was

Ann Ripley

dreaming. She began struggling for breath and her head began to spin from lack of oxygen. It was as if she were falling into an abyss, a dark place where she never again would see her beloved Bill and Martha and Janie . . .

Almost at the bottom of this dark pit, Louise came awake. She tried to scream, to tell the world that she was in trouble, but the sound was deadened to a muffled yelp. Then, like a gift, adrenaline rushed through her body. With her bandaged hands, she pummeled the creature who was sprawled on top of her trying to suffocate her.

"Owww!" cried the person, as Louise's blows struck home. The pressure on her face decreased, but she still was frantic for a breath of air. Though she continued to strike her unseen attacker, her weakened body felt as if it would soon close down . . .

The covering flew off her face and the lights of the room came on. Louise blinked in the brightness. The bed was still shaking from a continued struggle and she shrank under the covers, peering out at an unbelievable scene. Beside her on the bed, Anne Lansing, her green eyes now almost black because of her dilated pupils, wrestled wildly with Lieutenant Robert Payne, who was trying to get a grip on her flailing arms. He finally did, hauling the woman to her feet as uncaringly as if she were a sack of rags.

Louise sat upright in the bed, her eyes wide with concern. "Don't treat her so roughly," she cried. "She's *pregnant.*"

"Sorry, ma'am," said Lieutenant Payne, though to Louise his hard face looked unrepentant. Her gaze was drawn to the big pillow lying next to her that was to have been the instrument of her death and she wondered why she was protective of Anne.

She realized it wasn't Anne, but Anne's baby she'd worried about.

"Just put your hands up, Ms. Lansing," barked Police chief Randy Hau, who'd entered the room and was approaching with gun drawn. "You can release her, Bob, but watch her carefully."

As Lieutenant Payne let her go, Anne said, "Oh, Chief Hau, I am *so* relieved you're here." Though she wore a dark T-shirt and jeans and her web belt with equipment around her waist, she somehow gave off the aura of a lady in distress. Louise saw that now that Anne's pupils were returning to normal size, her eyes were red-rimmed and swollen from the pepper spray.

Sending a reproachful look toward the lieutenant, the woman said, "This man *attacked* me. As Louise said, I'm pregnant; who knows what harm he's done to me . . ."

"Ma'am," snapped Randy Hau, "cut the comedy. You're unharmed. Put your hands up."

She slowly raised her hands to the level of her shoulders.

"You broke in here to assault Mrs. Eldridge. Lieutenant Payne stayed with her in this room on my say-so, just so he could protect her against you."

"No, no, you have it wrong." The graceful hands opened wide, as if she were a saintly supplicant.

"Keep your hands in the air, ma'am."

Her hands went up again. "Just let me explain," she said. "I came here expressly to talk with Louise." She sent a glance Louise's way. "We're sort of friends, you know. She's been very supportive of me since Bruce died. I came to talk to her, because she's had a terrible evening—I was there—and Christopher Bailey was the cause of it. I know everything that happened now."

The bloodshot eyes had what Louise could only describe as an amazingly believable look. "Christopher killed Matthew Flynn and then he killed my wonderful boss, Bruce Bouting!"

"Oh, such rubbish!" exclaimed Louise. "I've never heard such bald-faced lying." Without warning, she began to shake as if she had a fever.

Lieutenant Payne stepped over to Randy Hau. "We're arresting this woman, right, Chief? I suggest we get her out of here." He cocked his head at Louise. "I think she's, uh, you know . . ."

Hau nodded. Payne put handcuffs on Anne Lansing and Mirandized her.

The police chief came tentatively over to the bed and said to Louise, "Thanks. I hope it wasn't too stressful on you."

"No," she said, afraid to say more for fear he noticed her tremors. When Randy Hau had proposed this plan to her, Louise had had no idea the results would be so physical. She'd thought that the lieutenant would capture Anne as she climbed up the porch of the lanai, not when the woman had half-smothered her.

They both watched as Lieutenant Payne led Anne Lansing away in handcuffs. The woman jolted to a stop at the door and looked across at Louise. Her voice was like a drop of pure poison. "They'll never prove this, Louise. It's your word against mine and I'm a very convincing wordsmith." The green eyes continued to stare at Louise, until Payne prodded her out the door.

Hau said, "Sorry about that. Um, maybe you need someone to stay with you the rest of the night. Do you want me to call your friend, Mrs. Corbin?"

Louise thought of how Steffi would be glad to help: She would come in and sit by her bed and

soothe her until she fell asleep, like a mother sooth-
ing a disturbed child. But she was not a child. "No
thanks, Randy."

"I've got to tell you, this worked out great."

"I guess so. I'm glad she didn't get out her garden clippers. In that case, your timing would have
been off."

49

Tuesday morning

Louise got up at six-thirty and put on the first clothes she could lay her hands on, navy shorts and a white T-shirt and her waterproof sandals, in case she had enough energy to walk upon the beach. Her head still felt as if it weren't part of her body. Maybe she *had* suffered a concussion.

She'd had a fitful night since Anne Lansing invaded her room. Anne's hate-filled countenance and her final words rang in her ears, "*It's your word against mine.*"

For all she knew, Anne Lansing could have been arrested and out on bail by this time.

Louise knew her choices were either to take a pill and sink back in bed, or go downstairs, get coffee, and face reality. The coffee sounded better, so she grabbed her SportSac and left the room.

Downstairs, despite the early hour, there was a bustle of police activity in the lobby area. It was as if the entire Kauai County Police Department had moved its headquarters to the Kauai-by-the-Sea Hotel. She wandered by the registration desk,

where sleepy-eyed employees looked vaguely resentful about the prospect of another dull day.
Business had fallen off sharply at Kauai-by-the-Sea
since it had become tainted with homicide.

Behind the desk was the hall leading to the public relations office where Chief Randy Hau had set
up shop. Hau was standing at the door of that office, staring into space. When he saw her, he beckoned her in. "Did you get some sleep?" he asked.

"Some. Did you?"

"Very little. I've been questioning people for the
past six hours." He beckoned her to the familiar
visitor's chair, while he settled in the executive
chair. He waved out in the general direction of the
hall. "As you can see, we have plenty of personnel
here. We've been gathering every bit of evidence
we can from the suite and when daylight broke, we
started on the cliff and on the path between the
two."

"Oh, good. Um, where is Anne Lansing?"

"She and Christopher Bailey both have been
moved up to Lihue. She's been charged with assault and he's detained for questioning. I'm going
back there as soon as I brief you to question them.
I've asked the islands' FBI agents to come in and
help with the interrogation. The two of them are
lawyering up, of course. Their attorneys will be
showing up soon."

"Anne denies everything, I'll bet," said Louise.
A despondency was settling over her again; she
thought of Tom Schoonover's remarks about the
statistics on murders that were never solved.

The chief said, "You'll be amazed at what she's
got to say. She claims that Christopher Bailey con-
fessed to her that he killed the two scientists—
Flynn because of some quibble over a plant,

Bouting so that he could take over as head of the company. She says he forced her to help him take you up Shipwreck Rock. You were to be disposed of because you got the goods on him."

"What about Christopher? Is he sticking to what he said last night?"

Police Chief Hau nodded. "His position is that he was not part of anything."

"But I'll swear he was. Maybe you can at least show he's been trying to access Bruce Bouting's computer secrets—prints on the computer keys, or evidence he was searching for that password. As for Anne Lansing, she ought to have pepper spray residue on her somewhere."

"She does," said the police chief. "And I'm sure we'll find residue up on the cliff. She doesn't deny that you sprayed her with pepper. She says it happened when she helped Bailey take you there."

Louise's head was swimming, just listening to the lies. She got up from her chair and said, "I'm sorry, but I have to go get some breakfast. Let me know if you need me for anything, Randy. I'll do anything to keep those two behind bars. If they get out on bail, I don't trust them not to come after me again."

"I need you to think back on any detail that might help us pin the murders on her—something that puts her with you in this scene."

She paused for a moment by his desk, thinking. "I am remembering more things. In the suite, look for red soil on the rug near the gaming table. I must have dragged in some of it."

He shook his head. "Red soil is fungible. I don't think that will make the case."

Then it came back to her, Anne's cry of pain when Louise hysterically bunted her in the head.

"I have something better. Look for strands of my hair in the duct tape the police removed from my mouth last night. When she started putting the tape on my mouth, I fought her. Some of my hair stuck to the tape and hurt like the very devil. Some of her hair strands probably got caught."

"Very good, " said Randy Hau.

"So I can go now?"

"Yes, but I suggest we talk again after you eat. Who knows how much more you'll be able to call up? Frankly, we're up against two smooth characters. Ms. Lansing is particularly convincing to those who haven't seen or heard of her. We want to tie both of them to the events of last night at the very least."

"But not to the murders?" She swayed slightly as she stood by the desk. "That woman is like a black widow. She might get away with the whole thing."

He looked at her strangely. "You promised the medicos here that you'd check in. I don't like the look of you. Are you feeling okay?"

"I'll go to the clinic after I eat."

Louise walked down the hall toward the hotel dining room, noting that people were up now and getting ready to face another day in paradise. She was nearing the parrot cage. Not caring any more, she started to stroll by, but then saw the bird staring at her, a mass of feathery shivers as it wound up for another temper tantrum. She stood before him and decided to stop being a wuss. She raised a bold hand in the air, as if she were a traffic cop ordering a citizen to stop. The bird looked baffled, twitched its feathers one more time, and then became as still as a statue. She nodded at the bird and marched on to the dining room.

Once seated at a table, it was decision time

again. She was ravenous. Would it be the lavish array of food laid out on the buffet table, or a custom breakfast of bacon, eggs, and toast that would take at least fifteen minutes to get to the table? She opted for the bacon and eggs.

Sipping her coffee, she stared out unseeing at the palms and causarina trees and allowed herself to wallow in depression. It felt as if the American justice system now rested on her shoulders. Two violent murders. How could she prove that Anne Lansing had committed them?

Looking up, she saw Tom Schoonover walking across the room. He sat down and joined her. "Hi, Louise."

"What are you doing here so early?"

"I was worried about you. I phoned Randy Hau to see how things were going. He told me what happened in your room last night." He shook his head. "I'm so sorry."

"Tom, all the police have is that incident in my hotel room. About everything else, Anne and Christopher are telling different stories. She's indicting him, while he's professing total ignorance of what went on."

"We can hope for the best," said Tom. "At least Anne will be brought up on charges of assault."

"And she gets away with murder."

After ordering his breakfast, Tom folded his hands in front of him and stared at her. "I have a possible solution. If the police can establish that Christopher was trying to break into Bouting's computer program, they'd have him. It certainly sounds logical that the family would bring charges against him. Then the district attorney could offer him a deal if he'd testify about what Anne Lansing told him. He might be happy to do that for a reduced charge."

Once they were eating breakfast, she said, "This is not going to be an easy day."

He smiled sympathetically. "It's as if you won the lotto and found out there's no money in the pot."

She looked up from her plate and saw the sober-faced chief hurrying toward them. "What now?"

"Maybe there *is* money in the pot," said Tom.

Randy Hau came over to their table and put a faintly trembling hand on Louise's shoulder. "Good news," he said, and couldn't help grinning.

"Sit down, Randy," urged Tom Schoonover, and pulled out a chair for the policeman.

"I couldn't wait to tell you," he said, leaning forward toward them. "A cursory examination through a magnifying glass of that duct tape is all I needed. I got quite a clump of *your* hair—uh, brown with a couple of gray strands—and a few strands of shorter, darker hair."

"That's Anne Lansing's."

"Yeah. And since it came out at the roots, there'll be no trouble doing DNA testing. That's a terrific boost to our case against her." His face slowly broke into a smile. "And we have other good news."

"John?" she asked.

"Yes," said the chief. "John Batchelder can talk. He woke up a few minutes ago and came out of his semicoma. He told the officer stationed at the hospital what happened."

She closed her eyes for a moment and a sense of peace enveloped her. "What did he say?"

"He's a witness, in a sense, to both murders. Down there at the lava flow on Chain of Craters Road, he was tailing Anne Lansing."

"Hmm," said Tom Schoonover. "I wouldn't have thought he had it in him."

The police chief waved away a waiter who wanted to serve him coffee. He continued, "John saw Anne cajole Bruce Bouting into going inside that safety line. He *witnessed* it when she shoved him into the lava. Not only that, on the trip over to the Big Island, while standing in the restroom line, he overheard Dr. Bouting hint that she'd murdered Matthew Flynn."

The chief paused and grinned, self-consciously running a hand through his dark straight hair. "I can't tell you how happy I am—my first two murder cases, solved."

"And what happens to Christopher Bailey?" asked Tom Schoonover.

For a minute, Randy Hau's face clouded. "His case is different, but with your help, Louise, I believe we can make a case for attempted murder."

She remembered Christopher's reluctance to drag Louise up that cliff. "Yes, but he's nowhere near as culpable as our deceptive friend, Anne—an unwilling participant, but she talked him into it. I realize now that John was trying to tell me about her before he lost consciousness after the accident. He wanted me to know that Anne's love life was behind Matt Flynn's death. She killed him to preserve her romantic relationship with the wealthy older man. Then she had to kill the older man when he saw right through her."

Tom said, "So, in order of ascending importance, her motives were love, money, and staying out of jail."

50

As if traveling through some secret Hawaiian grapevine, the news spread rapidly through the hotel. A crowd began to gather around the table where she sat with Tom and the police chief. George Wyant, Charles Reuter, Nate Bernstein, and Ralph Pinsky had arrived—half of the contingent of eight visiting scientists from the mainland. Of the other four, two were dead and two were jailed. On everyone's lips was talk of how Anne Lansing had now been tied to the killings.

Wyant was the first to reach their table. He was clear eyed and professional appearing, in white shirt and clean tan khaki pants, his worn leather carry-all slung over his shoulder, and hardly looked to be the same man who'd arrived stoned and unshaven last night in the Lanai Room. "I've *heard*," George cried. "You bloody did it, Louise!" The young scientist reached down to where she sat and clasped both of her hands. "I can't thank you enough. You *cared* enough when Matt and Bouting died to pay attention and do something about it.

And not only that, you treated me decently when almost everyone else thought I might be enough of a shit to murder my best friend."

She smiled up at him. "I don't know why, but I always believed you didn't do it."

"Whatever the reasons," he said, bending down now and enclosing her shoulders in a giant hug, "I won't forget you when I'm down in those jungles." As Wyant strode off, Ralph Pinsky, Charles Reuter, and Nate Bernstein, who were being filled in by the police chief, sauntered over to where Louise sat, to say good-bye and compliment her on helping to find the killer. Pinsky's and Nate Bernstein's congratulations seemed unreserved. Charles Reuter still looked at her with faint misgivings, as if no TV type could be trusted. A true believer, that one. She doubted that Marty Corbin would get *this* man to sign a release to sell that tropical garden interview tape to *Inside Story*, or any other TV venue. She couldn't say she'd blame him; Reuter was the only remaining living figure on the tape—besides Louise and John Batchelder, of course.

Finally, the group dispersed and there was only her and Tom Schoonover. As they walked outside along one of the hotel's flowery trails, he told her what bothered him. "Here you are, Louise, with all those cuts and bruises. You're lucky you're here and in one piece." He waved a hand in a general northerly direction. "And your colleague up in Wilcox Memorial Hospital—my God, Louise, he narrowly avoided being killed. Most likely he'll bear the scars of his experience for the rest of his life."

"I know where you're going with this."

"You do?"

"You think we're foolish."

He stopped her on the path. "Maybe a little foolish. And John much more so than you. At least you weren't poking around near a two thousand-degree stream of hot lava; being reckless in that environment usually means death. You thought you were safe when you went out on the hotel grounds and followed Bailey, but you weren't. Knowing as much as you did—I gather you were already suspicious of Anne Lansing—you shouldn't have gone out alone."

She exhaled a big breath. "I know. I was afraid to wait, for fear we'd never find out who killed those two people."

Tom smiled at her with those friendly hazel eyes. "Your intentions, Louise, are only too good. And so are John's, but I think he was imitating you, trying to outdo you, perhaps, and thus taking big chances." He shook his head. Louise felt sorry for him: Here was a logical scientist, trying to fathom the souls of two reckless amateur detectives. "Frankly, you both suffer from, oh, I don't know how to characterize it . . ."

She looked at him. "I believe you'd call it hubris."

"But hubris connotes arrogance and I don't believe you're arrogant. Next time, think before you act. Now, on a lighter note, I expect the rest of the visitors will be heading out on the afternoon flight. But I heard you mention to the chief that you might stay on so you could accompany John home. Promise to call me if you decide to stay over. Henry Hilaeo and I will be happy to tour you around. Maybe you'd like to check out Kauai's coffee industry, since you like coffee so much. Maybe hike some of the Kalalau Trail, if you're up to it."

"The Kalalau Trail? I will be up to it." It was a

primeval wilderness that she never thought she'd get to see on this trip.

When Louise returned to her hotel room, she lay on the bed while she phoned her husband at his office in the State Department. She did a masterful job, she thought, of downplaying her adventures and emphasizing the fact that the killer was in custody. She didn't mention her cuts and bruises; there was no need to alarm Bill, for they would be partially healed by the time she arrived home Saturday. She'd decided she would delay her departure to accompany John home when he was medically evacuated. It was the least she could do for her friend.

Again leaving out the details, Louise assured her spouse that she'd have plenty of things to do in those few days. "More sightseeing, a little more shopping, maybe." She didn't mention that she might hike the most treacherous trail in the Hawaiian chain. But after twenty-two years of marriage, her husband could read her well, even over the long distance line.

"Look, I figure you'll be hanging out with that Schoonover guy."

"How do you figure that?"

"Let's just say I feel it," said Bill. "I want you to be careful not to fall off knife-edged ridges. I also want you to be careful of something else. Remember that you're married to me and I love you and I'm waiting for you to come home to me. Don't think just because I didn't come over there to be at your side that I don't think about you, oh"—his voice was airy but with an underlying serious tone— "about once every hour."

"Bill, you're a darling." His statement was surprising. He seldom felt it necessary to proclaim his affection. But she supposed it was given in the same spirit as when she told Bill, when some attractive woman came on to him, that the interloper had better not try anything or Louise would scratch her eyes out.

After talking to Bill, she took a moment to leave a phone message for her *Post* reporter friend, Charlie Hurd. "Aloha, *Charlie. I'm busy right now, but I promise I'll phone you later this afternoon with as much of the story of the murders as the police will allow me to tell.*"

And finally, since she had someone she wanted to talk to, she took a walk on the beach. Fortunately, she was dressed for it in her beach-worthy sandals and shorts. Since the surf was up, only a small crowd populated the swimming and snorkeling beach; she set off in the opposite direction. Soon, she was near the end of the hotel property and could see Shipwreck Rock looming a short distance ahead. Though it was a perfect sunny day in the tropics, Louise shuddered as she recalled what happened last night on the precipice.

As she passed a tall pile of rocks, a man's voice called out. "So I see you're still among the living."

It was Bobby Rankin. She could hardly see him lying in a shady crevice between the rocks, his body propped on one elbow. Wearing only tattered tan shorts and a hat that years ago was white, he looked as if he might be an encrustation attached to the ancient rubble. She slowly approached him.

"It's all due to you, Bobby," said Louise. "I found out that the reason I'm among the living is because you have sharp eyes. That's why I came out to find you and thank you."

His face broke into a semblance of a smile. She felt free to come closer.

He patted the sand beside him. "Come into my den. Sit down. Make yourself at home. Now that the murders are solved, you ought to relax."

She laughed as she eased down next to him. "I marvel, Bobby, at how fast you get the latest news." Looking up at the twelve-foot-high monoliths on either side of them, she said, "Is this one of your favorite spots?"

"I gotta say it is." He cocked his head toward the rough, black walls with their myriad pockmarks. "Actually, I have a few things stashed in here where folks can't find 'em." He uncurled from his recumbent position and sat up. His face was drawn and sad. "I was here last night, Louise. That's why I saw you being dragged off."

"Thank you," she said. "I can never thank you enough." She couldn't help feeling pity as she looked at him. A wreck of a man, she thought, with bloodshot eyes, brown curly hair going every which way under that disreputable hat, bare bronzed shoulders held in an attitude of dejection.

He slanted a look at her. "You were worth saving. Though I guess I'd have done it for any good-for-nothing son-of-a-bitch, because I always have believed in the ultimate goodness of people. I'm excluding, of course, the gal who killed Matt Flynn and Dr. Bouting." He shook his head. "People like her have no regard for anyone but themselves. Selfish people kill others, one way or the other— they cause some of us to want to drop out altogether."

Louise knew this vague remark was as close as Bobby would ever come to telling her what happened to him twenty years ago, before he came to Hawaii.

He picked up a small shell and scraped it idly

through the damp sand, all his concentration on this meaningless activity. Sliding another glance at Louise, he said, "Didn't it give you pause to think someone was tryin' to kill you?"

"Yes, it did."

"Gave me a turn, too," said Bobby. He stared out into the waves. "It got me thinking about what I was doing here. Did I tell you I've been here for twenty years and three downturns in the stock market?"

"You mentioned you once were a broker but you didn't mention the downturns in the market. Are you beginning to rethink your lifestyle?"

Frowning, as if the idea were repellent to him, he said, "Yeah, I've been thinking about it since I woke up awhile ago." He leaned closer to her and held out the thumb and forefinger of one hand, pressing them so close together that they nearly touched. "Louise," he said in a husky voice, "that's how close you came to dying last night." His tortured eyes sought hers. "That's because I was stoned out of my gourd. The only reason I saw you was because I had to get up to pee. I struggled out of my little cubbyhole and there the three of you were, trotting down the path, with you draggin' your feet. I went back in here and thought about it for a while, trying to sort it all out. When the search party came by, I knew I'd seen what I just *imagined* I'd seen."

"Oh, Bobby," she said. She reached out and put a hand on his arm. "I'm eternally grateful to you. But let's say you hadn't figured it out and they had pitched me in the ocean—it wouldn't have been your fault."

He groaned. "Just the same, I can't help thinking about it. It makes me want to go straight, or at least a little straighter than I'm livin' right now. Maybe do a little more for people than I've been doin'. I'm thinking I might take up my buddies' offer."

"What did they offer you?"

"Part ownership of that surf shop on the beach where you probably rented your snorkel equipment. I've made a lot of friends since I landed here and I give my closest friends advice on investing. You know, 'get into techs, my friends,' and then, 'get the hell *out* of techs, my friends' . . . They got out in time: they've done real well with my advice. Now they want to show me their gratitude."

"That sounds perfect for you. It won't involve too much change." Louise realized she was slipping into a familiar role—the caring mother validating her child. Ironically, Bobby was older than she was, but he seemed to need validation.

He nodded. "Yeah, I know the surf shop business; it isn't that hard. And I have a business head. I didn't leave *that* behind when I came here from the mainland." With a sigh of regret he added, "I could even move into a house, I suppose, though that's a pretty radical step."

"Maybe one step at a time. Take over the job and then see if it suits you to, uh . . ."

"To come in from the beach, like the spy who came in from the cold? Yeah, maybe I'll do that." An ironic, soft laugh. "Unlike Alec Leamas, I hope no one shoots me when I climb over the wall." His gaze returned to the ocean, as if it had all the answers for him.

Louise stole a glance at her watch. "I have to get going, Bobby." She stood up and brushed sand off her bare legs, then came out of Bobby's cubbyhole in the rocks. He scrambled to his feet and followed her, his eyes squinting as he walked into the sunlight.

"I'd like to stay in touch," she said. "Can I write you at the surf shop?"

He smiled down at her, a real smile this time. "Sure. Pretty soon I'll have an e-mail address, like six billion other people on the planet. I'll drop you a line." He reached out a big, rough hand and clasped hers. "You take care, Louise, you hear? And stay out of trouble, now."

On the way to see John in the hospital, she, Marty, and Steffi stopped first in Lihue at Hamura's Saimin Stand for a bite of lunch. It was one of the restaurants that Matthew Flynn had recommended; just as Flynn had predicted, the food was delicious—and also cheap.

When they reached the hospital, John had just wakened from a nap. The three of them sat around his bed, happy to see his dark-lashed eyes wide open. "So you've heard my story," he said, in a weak voice.

Marty said, "Just the bare bones, John. Are you strong enough to give us the whole skinny?"

"Some of it, Marty." He turned to Louise and explained. "It was on the plane that I decided Anne Lansing had something to do with Matthew Flynn's death."

"Yes," she told her cohost, "so we heard."

"Dr. Bouting was so agitated—he only whispered to Chris Bailey, but I could hear it as I stood there. It was stuff like, 'I know she did it.' Then Chris whispered that she *wouldn't* do it. Then he said, 'I know she did it, because she loved him.' Didn't use her name, but who else would he be mumbling about? Fortunately for her, Anne got out of her seat with a pill in her hand and as soon as the old man saw her coming, he clammed up. So when we got to the Big Island, I decided to stick with Anne. But then, after awhile . . ." His partially bandaged face flushed with embarrassment.

Louise said, "She co-opted you?"

"Yeah, I quit suspecting her. I think Bouting quit suspecting her, too."

"Don't feel bad," Louise said. "She co-opted me, too."

Steffi Corbin chimed in, in the injured voice of someone who had been double-crossed. "Anne did that to all of us. She especially tried to cultivate me. I thought she was such a sweet girl. Now I'm worried about what she'll do with that baby she's carrying."

John looked blankly at Steffi. "Baby? She's pregnant?"

Marty leaned toward John and patted him on the hand that wasn't bandaged. "Just tell us your story, buddy."

"By the time we got down to the volcano action," he said, "I'd pretty much lost all my suspicions and I was just enjoying her company. Why should I be suspicious, when old Bouting was treating her like he usually did, you know, like a beloved daughter? Right at the outset—you must have seen it, too—the old man wanted to be by himself, so he told Chris to get lost. I went off with Anne up toward the vent, but she shook me. A little later, I caught sight of her following Bouting. She shooed off one of those Kauai cops who was hovering around, probably telling him that she'd keep an eye on the old gentleman. So I followed the both of them."

"Good man," said Marty.

"They got to a lonely spot in the middle. Not much action was going on, the hot lava just crackling its way down the hill toward the ocean. You may not know it, but Bouting *really* got into that volcano stuff—you should have seen him sitting there in the snack bar watching the videos of volcanists standing on the edges of the orange flows. So maybe it didn't take much for Anne to coax the old fellow inside the torches. Once in there, though, she throws his cane on the ground, then hurries him over—probably said something about a closer look—and gives him this gigantic shove. It lands him right into the lava. I shouted at her and, God, she came at me like a wild tiger. She shoved me toward the heat, but I fought her and she ran away, half choking to death. I got down and tried to pull Dr. Bouting out of that awful stuff. And then . . ." His wide eyes began to tear up.

Louise said, "You don't have to tell us any more, John."

Blinking away the tears from his eyes, he said, "No, I want to finish. I grabbed his hand and a big gust of smoke laid me low, literally. I could hardly breathe or get up, much less pull him away from that fire. It was so hot . . ."

Louise bowed her head. She'd had no idea of her cohost's true character. "Oh, John, you're a hero, trying to save someone you hardly knew." Impulsively, she leaned over and hugged him.

He grinned. "I like that hug. I think you really meant it. I didn't plan to be a hero, you know. And look where it's got me—my future in television may be affected. I may be scarred for life, despite what a plastic surgeon can do. I think it'll be okay with Linda, though. She likes used dogs and little animals, so a scarred fiancé probably won't creep her out."

"I'm sure of that."

"Another thing, too, Louise," he persisted, "I'm givin' up detecting. I don't think I'm suited for it."

"I'm not sure about that, John. You did pretty well. Next time, just don't talk about it so much." She remembered Tom Schoonover's warnings. "And there's also a certain, um, self-restraint that one needs if one is detecting. Maybe we both need to learn it."

"You mean, so as not to end up in the hospital."

"Yes," said Louise. "A little less hubris, a little more forethought. And don't worry about your future in TV. With those scars, you'll look handsomer than ever on camera."

A GARDENING ESSAY

TROPICAL PLANTS ARE VERY HOT

Tropical plants have been a hot topic among gardening aficionados for a decade now. And we must ask ourselves: In an era of periodic drought when practical experts drum in the message that we should plant regional and xeriscape plants, why do we still love tropicals?

It's a fact that there is a place inside all of us—a gene, perhaps—that causes us to love jungles. That's why so many of us leave snowy climes to take vacations in places like Hawaii, Costa Rica, and South and Central America; they are top tourist destinations, as any travel agency will tell you.

Perhaps this exposure to lavish plants under the ideal condition of being on vacation is why we like to bring the jungle home to our backyard gardens. The dramatic architecture of the plants with their huge leaves and serpentine branches and the vibrant color and form of the flowers please our eye and pique our imaginations. We think to ourselves, "Why settle for asters and roses when I can lift the garden out of anonymity with a few wild purchases?"

Ironically, when we go tropical, we're using plants like taro—elephant ear, it's called—cordyline and banana that were not admired for their beauty, but used as food mainstays to keep early residents of the Pacific islands from starving to death. Taro, cordyline, and banana and all the gorgeous horticultural goodies of Hawaii can now be found in your local nursery: gingers, bromeliads, orchids, birds-of-paradise, strappy-looking phormiums from the color black to yellow-and-green stripe, fluffy ferns, and stalwart, vertical bamboos.

In fact, there's a treasure trove of lush, warm-weather plants there for the buying. They've been bred and bred again and come these days with stripes, speckles, and spots, black leaves and maroon leaves. Their flowers appear in brilliant primary and secondary colors. If you go tropical, forget pastels, or at least use them sparingly.

Interestingly enough, nursery owners the country over have recently been advised that there's also a treasure trove of profit from selling tropicals. Many of these plants end up on the compost pile by the end of the season; that means that the gardener will come back the following spring and buy more.

The reality is that a tropical garden is not an easy thing to winter over. Lots of weary gardeners decide in the fall to discard these tender plants instead of taking the trouble to save them. Consider the banana, for instance, which was one foot tall when you bought it in the spring for $15. By September, you may have a ten-foot-high plant on your hands, with a huge root. You can ball it up in burlap and put it in the basement, but it isn't that easy and these roots have been known to turn to mush over the winter season.

Hard work also is involved in saving your cannas, dahlias (if you can be persuaded to think, as some people do, that they're tropical), elephant ear, and caladium. All these roots must be dug and carefully preserved in peat moss, some with different levels of dampness in the mix. For instance, keep the elephant ear on the dry side, but not too dry.

For some clever gardeners, the work is less. They bring the majority of these delicate beauties— taro and phormium, bird of paradise, cyperus and ginger plants—inside and use them as houseplants. They root cuttings of their begonias and coleus for a supply of new plants for the next season. Of course, there are some varieties that don't like this treatment. The datura, or Angel's Trumpet, for instance, prefers hanging out in a dry, cool basement during winter.

If the gardener has room, there is one challenging plant, the agave, that is an architectural wonder. This century plant is only hardy to zone nine. But a new five-foot variety might make the effort of over-wintering well worth it. Called *Agave vilmoriniana*, it has a personality of its own, with its curling, twisted, gray-green leaves reminiscent of an octopus.

Once spring comes, these delicate specimens are kicked out of the house. They will love the out-of-doors, undergoing a period of readjustment and then growing robustly until early fall when they can resume their identity as houseplants.

And then there are the smartest gardeners of all. They read up on plants and build their basic tropical-flavored garden from "doppelganger" plants. These are plants that look tropical but aren't tropical at all, but rather hardy down to zone four or five. There are quite a few of such plants: winter-hardy bamboo, with its great vertical look and delicate leaves; yucca, with strong, sword-shaped leaves; hosta, whose smooth leaves come in many colors, from blue to chartreuse and even green and white stripes; ferns, both big and small; crocosmia, which has graceful, long-lasting hot-colored stems of flowers in red, orange, or yellow; fat-blossomed hibiscus; round, leather-leaved bergenia; and red-hot-poker plant with its fiery blossoms. Some gardeners even view the flared-cup daylily as a tropical lookalike. But nothing frail about them: they are so sturdy that they might well outlive the gardener.

Locate these clever plants near other hardy and huge-leafed plants such as *Crambe maritima*, leaves three feet wide, and *Gunnera manicata*, with its eight-foot-wide leaves, and you immediately attain the tropical look that you want. The *crambe*, or sea kale, is incredibly dependable and each June rewards the gardener with clouds of small white flowers on stems hovering above massive leaves. Be sure to include some plants that lots of people don't realize come in hardy brands: the guava and the cactus. These two varieties have a definite tropical flavor.

Any combination of these plants can form the backbone of your tropical paradise. For more height, you might include a fat-leaved catalpa tree, which has dramatic leaves, flowers, and seedpods—how can you get more tropical than that? Ginkgo, Japanese maple and katsura trees, all with interestingly-shaped leaves, are other good choices for this garden.

When spring comes, the rest is easy. The hardy plants outdoors will be leafing out. You only need to retrieve the banana, phormiums, cordylines, taro, and the nonhardy bulbs and put them out to complete the scene. Many gardeners keep these tender plants permanently in pots.

Not all plants in this tropical milieu will be huge, for the understory must be taken care of. Chartreuse euphorbia goes well in the foreground, as do some shorter grasses. A plant or two of frilly white baby's breath can be a refreshing relief from the more intense colors.

To add the ultimate touch, combine the various "stories" or levels of plants by interplanting exotic annual vines. Two ipomoeas are easy to grow and would be particularly attractive in a tropical theme. One is the moonflower with huge white blossoms, *Ipomoea alba*, and the other, *Ipomoea lobata*, or Spanish flag. Flowers of the Spanish flag are a range of red, orange, yellow, and ivory on long, curved stems; they look enticing twined among blossoms of like or contrasting colors. The mandevilla is another spectacular vine. Mandevillas have large, funnel-shaped flowers of pink, rose, red, or white and will eagerly grow upward among the tree ferns and bamboos, to unite the garden "stories."

Any person who has visited the tropics will observe one thing: Tropical landscapes are crowded with tiers of plants. When you try to replicate this look in your own backyard, you must do the same thing—closely group the plants together to achieve a luxurious jungle atmosphere. You can make the job easier by borrowing a trick from professional landscapers. They insert free-standing potfuls of plants into a garden to fill bare spots. A water container filled with lotus plants or a pot of brilliant blue agapanthus would be a perfect choice.

Most gardners work on a budget (although some

Ann Ripley

don't and even go to the trouble and expense to import rented palm trees for their summer gardens). With a modest amount of money, you can work the same magic as the pros by cleverly populating your garden with "doppelganger" plants that will over-winter. Then, when spring planting season comes, you only need to buy a few fast-growing tender plants to create a tropical Eden.